# Euterra Genesis

## A NOVEL

Mark A. Burch

PUBLISHED BY Mark A. Burch

Library and Archives Canada Cataloging in Publication

Burch, Mark A., author
*Euterra Genesis* / Mark A. Burch

Issued in print and electronic formats.

Design and Layout by Tracey O'Neil, simplelifedesigns.ca

ISBN 978-0-9784528-7-2
eBook ISBN 978-0-9784528-8-

# WHAT READERS ARE SAYING ABOUT
## *EUTERRA GENESIS*

"Very few writers have the ability to broach various genres with skill, depth, and grace - but Mark A. Burch is one of them. After spending decades writing books of astute philosophy, education, and social criticism on the themes of voluntary simplicity, mindfulness, and consumerism, he is now exploring these necessary themes in literary form. His efforts are a resounding success. Burch's new novel, *Euterra Genesis*, is a book for our time: poetic, unsettling, but inspiring - and quite possibly prophetic. Read it and be enriched."

— **Dr. Samuel Alexander,** *Ex. Director,*
*The Simplicity Institute, Melbourne, Australia*

*Euterra Genesis* by Mark A. Burch offers a vision of how a small group of stranded individuals finds a way to reach each other amidst the challenges our society faces. As relatively isolated individuals surrounded by others unwilling to discuss climate change or the larger dysfunctions that fuel it, they have no way to clarify what troubles them, what is really wrong in the world, and what to do about it. This revelation is facilitated by their coming together as a reflective community. Here they can explore the problem as a large group of fellow travellers. They can deal with their emotions and imagine alternatives. In this community, they discover what they can contribute in response to the challenges ahead. Sociologically, what is interesting about Burch's book is that the first to arrive in Badger Coulee decide to actively seek out others who are in the same situation as they are. They develop a process to gather up these individuals and help them become part of a collective project that values them as individuals. They each discover a way to make their best contribution. Each of them is uplifted by their mutual validation, affirmation, commitment to a common cause, and celebration of their unique contribution to their common future. And so they are no longer alone, suffocating, and stranded. They are working hard to extricate themselves from a cultural dead end and to create a healthier alternative to consumer society.

— **Dr. Rodney Kueneman,** *(ret.)*
*Sociologist / Permaculturalist*

*Euterra Genesis* is a brilliant prequel to *Euterra Rising: The Last Utopia*, and both books belong on every book club's 'must read' list. Mark A. Burch offers a compelling look at the challenges facing our world and creates captivating characters that speak to the heart of every person who dreams of a better, more wholesome life.

— **Maria Kruszewski,**
*Writer, Educator,*
*Blogger @SimpleMoodlings*

An important feature of the story that not only presents an alternative to mainstream living, but that ultimately provides an imperative for abandoning the mainstream (i.e., the Ruination), is that is doesn't rely on boogeymen, conspiracies, or happenstance. It places culpability for the destruction of contemporary global society squarely in the hands of unbridled selfishness and blindness and the inability to conceive of an alternative. The boogeymen, conspiracies and happenstance are merely stressors on a system that has become irreparably brittle.

—**James Frey**
*Writer, consultant*

*Also by*
*Mark A. Burch*

# Euterra Rising:
## THE LAST UTOPIA

*Euterra Rising* is the story of a 23rd century culture rising from the ashes of the 21st century Ruination of consumer culture and the Great Forgetting that followed loss of the Internet. This is the story of the Euterran civilization from its emergence amidst crisis to the continuing challenges it must overcome as it navigates a future without fossil fuels or a stable climate. Euterra also faces threats from remnant groups such as the Brotherhood who still cling to the values of the past and who pursue them with ruthless desperation. When the Brotherhood discovers Euterra, two worldviews, two different value systems, and two societies collide.

For my brother Cary—who lent me his faith when mine was fading.

# AUTHOR'S FOREWORD

*"We who must die demand a miracle."*—*W. H. Auden*

*Euterra Genesis* is Beamer Farris's story. I haven't seen him yet, but I know he's out there somewhere. He probably wouldn't be comfortable in most social gatherings. At this writing, he's still too young.

I'm Mark Burch, the author of Beamer Farris's book, but not of his story. Neither Beamer nor I know who authored his story—or more accurately—authors it as I write this. But somewhere he exists. I'm sure of it. Somewhere he is growing into the awareness of who he is—what his story is—and eventually the manifestation of his story in history.

Beamer is not a big fan of social media—so you won't find him by searching on Google or LinkedIn. He will be someone you have to meet in person because his person is how he will touch you. So if you look for him on social media, you will be looking in the wrong place.

But, you might protest, if he has no social media presence, how do I know he exists? Doesn't everything that really exists have a presence somewhere on the Internet?

Well, you see, I'm not absolutely sure that he exists. But I'm pretty sure. He probably exists because we do—because we're all members of the human species who are alive now because of people like Beamer. So maybe, in writing his book, I'm not writing a novel, but rather a biography—or a memoir—or a prophecy.

I think you will probably agree that if we look at the broad sweep of human history, we have a disconcerting tendency to get ourselves into blind alleys. We're in one of them right now. The way we lived that got us into this blind alley is completely useless to get us out. So, here we are—stuck in this blind alley—just like in the movies, but with climate change, and failing governments, and consumerism clogging our landfills and oceans and arteries, and with capitalism in over-drive to a meltdown that will make 2008 look like a trailer. And none of us knows a way out—except for maybe Beamer Farris.

Beamer Farris is not a miracle, but in hindsight he will seem like one. We are all here now because over and over again we get ourselves into blind alleys and then along comes someone with a crack in themselves—or as Leonard

Cohen observed: "There's a crack in everything. That's how the light gets in." In that light we see who we are. We see our predicament and somehow we change. We become a new invention and a new story becomes possible. We find a way out of the alley—not because Beamer Farris leads us into a carefully planned alt-world—but because he is willing to be broken open. And then the light comes through. You see, it's never strictly because of people like Beamer Farris that we find the crack in the wall of our condition, but because of the light they kindle in the rest of us. So I invite you to meet Beamer Farris. He will arrive soon, but in the meantime, *Euterra Genesis* is his book and it is right here in your hands.

Mark A. Burch
2020

# CHAPTER 1

*All that arises does so from the ruination of something else.*

— FENTON LARRABEE, FUTURIST.

IN NOVEMBER OF THE YEAR 2026 C.E., it was nine months before the Ruination began tearing the world apart. Beamer Farris walked beneath the unblinking gaze of security cameras, through the bomb-proof glass doors of the Ministry of Environment, and stepped down into the sodden mush of a December evening. The damp air was redolent of vehicle exhaust and wood smoke. Overhead, almost touchable, there drifted the amber pall of smoke from forest fires that should have been out for weeks, but were still burning in the western mountains. Beamer sensed in that overhanging shadow something hidden, massive and irresistible. It was like a plough wind gathering itself, invisibly distant, biding its time, until it could shriek over the landscape laying down everything in a single direction. The evening draped itself over Beamer's shoulders grey as a mourning coat. He stepped onto the sidewalk and briefly felt like he was falling into the dark—or maybe flying—but if flying, then flying blind.

The Ministry of Environment where Beamer worked was an Orwellian formation of concrete masses and plate glass. It appeared to have been pushed by tectonic forces straight up from the bedrock. There was nothing about it that hinted at its mission in the world—no tree nor pond nor living thing except for the ever-present pigeons and small rodents diving for cover in the cracks of its massive foundation. Beamer imagined its designers might have been trolls more accustomed to delving in damp caves, or sheltering beneath low bridges, not architects by that name. As welcoming as a cement factory, its mass of concrete and glass had probably won architectural awards in its day—maybe in the 1980s or '90s when people tolerated such waste of energy and materials. Regardless, it had that timeless, grey ugliness that people create again and again even though they eventually come to deplore it. The architectural style even had a name—"Brutalist"—a term that could scarcely be more apt. Given its function, one might have hoped for something green-er. But concrete testified to permanence, or stability, or power, or maybe just stubbornness—all those conservative values that endured despite their con-tradictions. It was a grey impervious wall that kept the dogs out—only just. Beamer turned his parka hood up against the damp miasma and set out west along the slushy sidewalk to begin his forty-five minute walk to the apartment he shared with Vesper Lorenz.

The streets were slowly gathering traffic punctuated by horn honking and tire whining as people tried to maneuver around each other's vehicles with fogged windshields on slippery streets. In fairness, even for the diligent, it was hard to be prepared these days. One year winter didn't seem to come at all. The next year it roared in and settled down on the city like an ice giant. Earth was busy finding its new happy place unfazed by the discomfort of human beings.

The snow had continued on and off all day until there was a consider-able depth of it covering the sidewalks. Traffic was churning it into deep ash-en-looking slush. With sunset coming early this time of year, street lights were already winking on. Despite the up-tick in traffic late in the day, the muted ambience of his walk was even deeper now. Only the wail of emergency ve-hicles continued their lament despite the muffling snow. He strode steadily, the alternating movement of his arms and legs a soundless mantra that car-ried him down the street. His thoughts moved between the conversations of the day and consciousness of the moment as traffic signals, other pedestrians, passing vehicles and the incessant sound of pre-holiday advertising captured and then released his attention. He walked past a store with large display windows full of holiday attractions decked in glitter and blinking lights. A film from the spray of passing traffic had settled on the windows blurring the displays behind a grimy scrim. A holiday carol struggled through a speaker pointed toward the sidewalk. It sounded a quarter tone flat, or as if it wearied of its own gaiety. In the official season of joy and peace, he felt neither. But how could it be different? The few people who shared the sidewalk with him kept their faces down and eyes averted, both ears plugged with ear buds, and each person unconsciously keeping the distance from others dictated by fore-thought of self-defence—especially the women.

But Beamer didn't give himself permission to entertain such feelings for long. Today the lights were on, the crapper flushed, the 5G worked, so all should be right with the world. For now. And here he was: Caucasian; unam-biguously male; university degree that still smelled new; some student debt but a mostly unused line of credit and a new job with the government. Such employment still offered enviable perks and relative security. He was doing well enough for a twenty-five-year old. He should feel privileged like everyone said he was. So why did he feel like he was on his way to an execution?

He continued walking for several more blocks until he came to Burins Park. The sitting benches were heaped with snow. The walking paths were pristine. Not many people used public parks anymore, especially in the winter when it was too cold to sleep outdoors. Though he walked by this park every day, it seemed now that he was seeing it from a subtly different perspective. As he passed, he glanced into an oval-shaped clearing surrounded on three sides with blue spruces whose needled skirts drooped down nearly reaching the ground. The other side was bordered with ruddy-barked dogwood and ashen-looking lilac bushes, now bared to the cold. At one end of the clearing was an ornate lamp post and a sodium vapour light that gave the whole space a warm glow. The golden hue of the lamp in that protected place summoned childhood memories from the Narnia tales. Beamer kept to his pace but at the sight of the park he felt a tug of hesitation, a catch in his breath, that he was speeding past something that should give him pause, but he barely noticed and continued on his way.

He made it another few blocks. Up ahead was McMaster Bridge, an odd structure that he crossed every day on his walk to and from work. It was odd, partly because of its age, but also because it carried two narrow lanes of vehicle traffic, one railroad line, and on both sides of these, pedestrian walkways. It resembled a house added too over generations. The whole structure was a jumbled latticework of iron bars, rivets and rust. For a hundred metres it spanned a ravine gouged from the landscape by the Bison River which flowed slowly beneath a layer of ice clear as glass. From across the ravine Beamer could see a freight train approaching from the other side. It lumbered along only slightly faster than a walking pace, pulling a lengthy train of black tanker cars nearly invisible in the gathering darkness.

Beamer came to the end of the sidewalk and stepped out onto the pedestrian walkway that was part of the bridge span. He glanced absently down into the ravine noticing the reflected light from street lights cast onto the ice below. He had walked a dozen paces when there arose an ear-piercing shriek that Beamer at first thought might be squeaky wheels on the freight train. But the shrieking was accompanied by loud cracking sounds, deep moans of the bending of iron girders, followed by a cascade of concrete chunks falling into the ravine. When this began, the train was about halfway across the gully. But now it tipped sideways at an improbable angle. The trestle itself was bending toward the river and pulling away from the automobile bridge deck taking sizeable pieces of concrete with it. The train was falling in slow motion toward the river and taking the pedestrian bridge down as well. For what seemed like a long time, Beamer stared, frozen in place by the spectacle he was witnessing. But as the train tipped sideways, the walking bridge ripped in half and bent downward with a shudder that left Beamer standing on a slippery decline.

Awakening to his peril, he turned back toward the bridge pier that anchored the walkway to the lip of the ravine and scrambled toward the ravine bank. He had only just made contact with the sidewalk again when there was a belch of flame that ballooned into the sky and a loud roar that rumbled between the buildings of the city. Beamer was blown flat on his face by the explosion and felt a wall of heat pressing down on him from behind and above. Slowly he rolled to one side, hazarding a glance upward at the fire ball that was rising into the night sky.

Suddenly, very strong hands grabbed his parka hood from behind and pulled him violently away from the ravine. He was dragged along the ground, one coat sleeve snagging on some sharp protrusion from the pavement and ripped open bleeding eiderdown. As the space between his body and the bridge widened, whoever was pulling him away from the wreck slowed down and finally stopped. The man now moved around his body and came into view. "Eh, mate, you okay?" his rescuer gazed at him with concern.

"I think so," said Beamer, staggering to his feet. "Yes," he said, "I'm good. Thanks for hauling my ass out of harm's way."

"No worries mate," the man said. "Anybody else out there?"

"I don't think so," said Beamer.

The man smiled. "Right then. Carry on. Crikey! Some dinkum mess they'll have there." He chuckled and turned to watch the fire that rolled upward into the sky.

As Beamer stood transfixed by the flames, his rescuer disappeared into the gloom and smoke. Moments later there began a siren's lament each voice of which found its part in the registers of misery. He kept stepping slowly both sideways and backward, trying to get away but also captivated by the spectacle. A block farther south and he could see a glittering confusion of amber, red and blue lights, flashing sharply in the gathering darkness. At first the lights looked like a holiday display, but they were emergency vehicles. All were crowding at the near end of the bridge. Another bunch of lights was gathering on the other side of the river. A hellish inferno burned in the space yawning between where there once was a string of street lights and a ribbon of concrete spanning the ravine. The heat from the billowing flames beat against Beamer's face and chest as he stood watching. Arching down into the dark was the surreal looking freight train. Somehow the cars had stayed coupled together but the first few cars had plunged down into the ravine. The diesel engine was crumpled like a beer can in the bottom of the gorge. Just behind it was a ruptured tanker car the contents of which were erupting in wave after wave of orange fire. Behind it a string of still coupled tanker cars was hanging improbably into the abyss. Many of them appeared to be carrying oil or chemicals. The fact that the cars had stayed connected, together with the graceful curve they followed toward the river, made the whole scene look like a freeze-frame from a movie trailer. At any moment the action might resume and the train continue its plunge forward and downward into the snowy darkness. The trailing cars dangled there like unexploded firecrackers on a string, each waiting its turn to shake the city.

As Beamer watched, a police road block was being installed as the first layer of lights guarding the derailment. Police had set up their barricades at the first cross street intersecting the one Beamer walked along. They had lighted batons that they used to direct traffic away from the scene but masses of gawkers congregated just outside the road blocks. Soon the crowd voiced shouts of excitement and worried moans of apprehension. If this was a terrorist act, someone said, then a second bomb should go off shortly. But none did. Beamer pushed ahead for a better look until one of the police shouted at him.

"Step back! This area is restricted," he bellowed, though he looked just as bewildered as the thrill seekers.

"This is my way home," Beamer said as if his defence of daily habit could somehow restore the bridge.

"You can't cross here," the cop citing the obvious. "The bridge is half down and the train is hazardous product. Now move along."

Presently fire trucks started to arrive and their crews disembarked and commenced looking for hydrants and pulling hoses from their truck. They seemed to be searching around for the customary equipment for extinguishing fires and some approach to the fire itself, which was more or less confined within the river course but unreachable on that account. It couldn't be left to burn itself out because dense black clouds of toxic smoke could invade the city with any shift in the wind. The collapsed structure offered no sure purchase that would make it possible to fight the fire from above. So there it was—a necklace of flame curving gracefully toward the ice-covered river below—still ablaze in its oily fury.

The next bridge was two kilometres farther to the south. Beamer turned in that direction. But not before gawking more at the train wreck. He could clearly see model numbers on some of the cars, cars that were almost always used to transport tar sands diluted bitumen—'dilbit' to insiders. It was toxic and explosive. If any tank cars had ruptured, once dilbit hit the cold water it would solidify, sink and then was likely to go sliding under the river ice on its way downstream, or simply lodge as tarry blobs in the river bed. It would be impossible to contain or clean up until spring, if then. Each car carried 120,000 litres of dilbit. Despite the darkness and the dazzle of the flashing lights, Beamer thought he could count at least a half dozen tankers hanging precariously from the shattered tracks above. Reaching them so far out in the river channel with any sort of crane appeared impossible. As it happened, a search light winked on from the opposite bank illuminating the wreck. In this fresh light he could clearly see that dilbit was haemorrhaging into the water. Not quite an arterial spurt, but a venous ooze for sure. It was like a scene from a movie: distant, unreal, extraordinary and therefore scarcely believable. Things like this didn't happen in real life, Beamer thought. Except that they did. More often than ever.

Beamer turned south, resuming his walk home. Then, unaccountably, his body started shaking and his mind was flooded with anxiety so dark and so painful, he was paralyzed by it. He gasped to catch his breath and felt sweat drenching his body. Thus dampened and gasping, he continued shaking. He finally tried to steady his breathing and the attack slowly subsided. His own body felt alien to him, but he set one foot in front of the other and headed off again resuming his walk to his apartment.

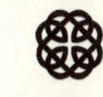

# CHAPTER 2

*You think you are an individual, unique in all the world.*
*But sit quietly and pay attention. Are you not instead a copy*
*of all you see? Becoming aware of this is liberation from it.*

— FROM AN ANCIENT PODCAST, AUTHOR UNKNOWN

IT WAS VERY LATE, or perhaps very early. Tatum Barnes hovered, god-like, over her work table, time-blind in the delicate task of placing a morsel of sphagnum moss in the miniature landscape she was making. In her mid-twenties, her strong body held in isometric tension over her work, her short, dark hair whorled elf-like around her head. When she worked at home she wore a sweatsuit but went barefoot to keep her feet tough for the hiking season she already anticipated with pleasure. She had wireless earbuds wedged into her ears with a podcast playing from her laptop.

"…when we think of our current predicament."

The voice was a mature baritone, almost like listening to one's grandfather reading a story.

"The relationships seem so obvious. We are riven with insatiable desires, hence consumer culture; hence environmental overshoot; hence our predicament: A culture trying to get ever more out of a limited planet. Clearly the problem seems to be in human nature, in our insatiable desires. …"

Tatum's fingers worked deftly turning stones and chips of plaster or tile this way and that until they fit her vision. She brushed white glue on a papier-mâché substrate to bind a finely powdered coating of green dyed sawdust which did nicely for lawn grass. The very thought of lawn grass seemed like a violation of the sacredness of the diversity of life—and yet lawn grass is what many of her clients insisted on. It didn't matter to them that every square metre of it was hungry for water, fertilizer, cosmetic chemicals, lawn mower fuel, and the precious claim on their own time to "keep the yard" while in the end it failed to produce one single morsel of anything eatable by human beings. Earlier that day she had poured Plaster of Paris into moulds which, once set, provided her with miniature slabs of concrete, curbs and patio blocks. Twigs became tree trunks and sculpted bits of moss became diminutive bushes and shrubs. While in her work, time stopped, except for the voice that filled that dimensionless space in her mind.

> "... except perhaps this isn't entirely true. What might it mean for us if desire wasn't in our heads at all? What if desire was not an eternally restless volcano of appetites that bubbles away regardless of where we live, or how we live, or in whose company we live? What if desire is socially constructed and might be socially reconstructed? ..."

Her work surface, a dining table recruited for the purpose, dominated her apartment living room, which resembled a tropical herbarium more than a room for tea and genteel conversation. Even though she lived in it half the year, there was something jerry-rigged, about it. It was more like a tinker's workshop than a space given much attention to decor or even to comfort. Her furnishings were minimal—several dining room chairs festooned with pieces of clothing recently washed but never folded, or maybe on their way to being washed. There were several bookshelves along one wall but they held as many plant pots as books. Ensconced in vegetation on one shelf was a framed picture of her wearing shorts, hiking boots, a t-shirt and utility vest, and a straw hat, frayed at the edges and set at a rakish angle. She stood on a rocky outcrop. Beside her was a young man wearing similar gear, his gaze direct but with a goofy smile, hair curly and dark, his body taught, wiry. Perhaps they were lovers.

The photo frame was tucked amidst a crowd of tropical plants that filled all the space on her window sills, over the tops of her bookcases, and trailed off to join more potted plants of considerable size—dragon trees, elephant-eared philodendrons, a hibiscus sending forth its single celebratory blossom and spider plants that trailed randomly like striped botanical predators. Festooned through all this vegetation was a braid of wires leading to pea-sized silver disks attached to each plant. These cables joined up in a central buss that Tatum had jacked into her laptop. All of this was another of her passions—botanical sentience. Once the sensors were connected to her laptop, each generated its own tracing on the screen. Together they looked like a multicoloured skein of yarns meandering over the screen in real time, or maybe an EEG tracing forty streams of consciousness.

Tatum had taken this study another step. She programmed sound audio samples unique to each plant so that as they responded to different influences—lack of moisture, changes in the light or temperature—all could be heard as well as seen on the laptop screen. The peperomia was a crumhorn; the Mugo pine was a flute; each plant with its own voice. By now Tatum could feed that botanical symphony through her earbuds and she would sometimes spend hours listening to the changing chorus of those vegetative voices. And she soon learned that they responded to much more than a mere lack of water or too little light. Intuitive though it was, Tatum could sense meaning in the sounds and images she let flow over her. The plants not only "talked" to each other, they sensed her emotions, her intentions, and sometimes registered changes whose causes were a mystery.

Tatum's kitchen evidenced the leavings of both take-out and homemade cuisine, with several wine bottles about, all of them empty. Bunches of herbs harvested from among large containers close to her windows were trussed up with twine and masking taped to a valence around her kitchen doorway. Most obvious, however, was a drafting board for design work and a litter of materials useful in creating scale model landscapes, among them pails of stones, sand, sphagnum moss and twigs. It had been the fourth day in a row that she'd been giving meticulous attention to this particular model. Clients ready to invest six figures in landscaping expected attention to detail, especially when Tatum's commission was twenty-five percent. Only occasionally did she glance out from her third floor window overlooking Burins Park to notice the coming and going of the snow storm that had lasted all day.

> "...that we are in many respects social creatures and are constantly making social comparisons, especially unconscious comparisons. Neuroscience shows that we are wired by evolution to imitate the behaviour we see in others. When others behave as if they desire something, we imitate the desirability of that thing until we desire it ourselves. This is the source of our suffering. So modelling and imitating desire is a source of desire and the new practice we develop should take this into account..."

Tatum pressed three more small stones into her diorama. Being a landscape architect was a little like being God, she thought. She fashioned worlds from what was at hand. And when spring came again, she would work on a much larger scale, for she was a permaculturalist as well as a landscape architect—a designer of self-replicating, self-maintaining, self-repairing communities of life that fed human beings as a fringe benefit. She stood up straight to survey her work, inhaling deeply the vegetative aroma of her living space. Even in her youth, leaning over the landscape model was a strain. She turned to a yoga mat always open on the floor and did the twelve steps of the Sun Salutation to loosen her Achilles tendons, hips and spine.

In this lacuna, her phone pinged through her ear pieces and she felt herself surfacing from the flow of her work and from the pleasant stretching sensation of the yoga. She picked up her cell and pressed the thumbprint sensor to unlock the phone. The "messages" icon showed new texts, one of them flagged for priority review. Tatum laid the phone aside. It would probably be another background screening for a potential new member of Badger Coulee—another of Tatum's hats. There were twenty-three "Finders" now who identified and approached people who might move to the Coulee. She was one of them. Her job was landscape design; her opus was permaculture; her passion was talking with plants. And between these worlds she drifted like a spirit, invisible, finding and retrieving…

"…Wherever you are, look around. If you're indoors, go find a window and look out. See the others there."

Tatum moved slowly toward the large window in her living room and stood there. She reached out absently, touching the key on her laptop that turned on the audio feed from her plants. It was already getting dark. The slate sky that emptied its load of snow during the day remained stubbornly invisible over the city reflecting back the dark mustard hue of the street lights. Pedestrians flowed past her gaze as they walked along in a mesmerizing tableau of mutual avoidance. But some distance below and across the street, she could see someone looking into Burins Park.

"You think you are an individual, unique in all the world. But sit quietly and pay attention. Are you not instead a copy of all you see? Becoming aware of this is liberation from it."

The figure across the street came to an open space in the park, now covered in a blanket of fresh snow. It looked like a man, hesitating, then moving on. Tatum noticed his plain black parka, his hiker's pack, his stature and demeanour. These things she registered consciously but their significance to her was unconscious. Then swelling from her earbuds came a subtle wave of sound, indescribable, compelling.

*That's funny*, she thought, her gaze lingering on him. And disturbing. She reached out her hand and placed it against the window just where he stood in the pane. He walked meditatively back toward the park entrance, paused, glanced up, and then walked on.

# CHAPTER 3

*In times of transition, those who were successful in the old
world are marginalized in the new, their energies moving
in retrograde toward ever-increasing disorientation. The
young, however, may have a sense of energy surging forward
with no clear goal, hence manifesting as anxiety or the
spontaneous eruption of unconscious contents into their waking
awareness. This cannot fail also to affect their relationships.*

— RUPERT PHILMORE,
THE PSYCHODYNAMICS OF CULTURAL DISINTEGRATION.

ALLOWING FOR HIS side trip and detour, Beamer arrived back at his apartment an hour and a half later than usual. Vesper was already back from work. She had swapped her office clothes for some leggings and a bulky sweatshirt and was curled up on the sofa eating from a box of phad Thai takeout. A television hanging on the wall jabbered celebrity gossip.

"Where were you?" she asked. Not waiting for him to answer: "I know it was my night to cook, but I didn't feel like it. So I got us some take-out. I put yours in the oven."

Beamer pulled off his coat and dropped his boots in a boot tray by the door. His coat reeked of oil, smoke and rust. "I was delayed," he said, voice flat.

"Delayed?" said Vesper, finding the tone just between query and echo.

Beamer decided to respond to the query part. "Yes. The weather was slowing everything down. Slower traffic. Slippery sidewalks. And the McMaster Bridge fell down taking a train with it. You know. That sort of thing." Beamer felt himself starting to shudder again—hoping for something—a word of concern perhaps? *Trauma is so private*, he thought.

"Yes. I drove home in it," said Vesper, still transfixed by the television. "There were line-ups at all the grocery stores, like the holidays, only crazier," she added. The part about the train and the bridge apparently disappeared into a special oubliette she kept in her mind for such news. Normalcy reined, spare no cost.

Beamer felt an interrogation coming. And Vesper, for her part, could also sense something about Beamer, something she had felt before. It was like an iceberg. Sometimes it rode higher in the water and sometimes lower, but it was always there until it rolled over, silent and cold, revealing another of its faces, or perhaps an old face remade by its time under the water—but the same ice.

"You had a bad day at work." Now her tone mingled guess and accusation, as if he might be the author of his own misfortune. Beamer almost always felt on his back foot with her, never quite at ease, never quite safe. So many things she said were like an ink blot test. They could mean anything, or nothing, and usually always more than one thing. What mattered was not the figure itself, but what the viewer said about it. It left Beamer feeling vulnerable, sort of like he was wearing a tuxedo with no trousers. Lately he'd decided it was a specifically feminine form of power. Sometimes he suspected that Vesper stayed with him not because of what they had in common—mostly sex and the financial break that came from sharing the rent—but because of what she thought was his potential. She was very protective of his potential. She didn't want to scare away that potential, at the same time that she thought of herself as instrumental in changing him so as to realize more of his potential. Maybe, he thought, she was more attracted to what she imagined he might become than by the person he already was. So he said nothing. He went into the kitchen to fetch his supper from the oven and returned to flop down at the opposite end of the sofa from her, pretending interest in what she was watching.

The television prattled on about some movie star who was giving half of his personal fortune to fight a resurgent Ebola-variant that had already reduced Africa's population by half in just a year. This was followed by video of disgruntled looking people lining up at food stores because of some sort of supply crisis that was spreading across the country. Then the station cut to a series of commercials about body bronzers, hair removal devices, and a clinically proven remedy for burning more belly fat. Apparently viewers could sustain this juxtaposition of news and advertising without danger of mental whiplash. Beamer felt himself drifting numbly into the slipstream of its contradictions, half hoping that Vesper would too.

"We interrupt this program for some breaking news," said the television announcer. "There has been a major train derailment and partial collapse of the McMaster Street Bridge. Authorities said…"

"You know it's starting to creep me out when you do that," Vesper said. Was it her comment about the "that" that he did, or seeing the coverage about the bridge collapse that snapped Beamer out of the anesthesia of the television and into a surge of anxiety?

"Do what?" he asked innocently—ignoring the breaking news—and trying to surf over the wave of panic that was rising up in him.

"When you do that disappearing act of yours. Then I'm thinking you're going off to build one of those crazy mandalas of yours."

"What's a mandala?" Beamer asked, almost naive. They had been around and around this one many times. She did the impossible: combining concern with accusation with judgement.

"I saw one on the Crystal Christ website when I was shopping for moisturizers. It reminded me of those things you make sometimes."

"It's not an act," he said, hoping somehow to skip around whatever Vesper had seen on some website, already sounding defensive even to himself. His anxiety added to the strained tone in his voice. His throat felt dry.

"Well what would you call them then?"

He waited, feigning a search for excuses that would also perhaps stoke Vesper's insecurities enough to kick the conversation onto a different track. He wondered briefly if doing this might be a form of sadism, then decided against it because it gave him no pleasure. His agenda was purely defensive. She was probably worried that her most valued future asset might melt down before her eyes, descending into mute catatonia, a prospect she wanted desperately to hold at bay.

"It creeps me out when you sort of go offline like that. Like you don't want to talk with me. Like you're gone somewhere else," she pressed on doggedly. "You've done this before," she reminded him. "Usually when you've had a bad day."

Beamer shrugged. It was true. "Call it whatever you want," he said blandly. "Sometimes I just have to draw back a bit and refocus. It makes me feel better. I don't know why."

"It still creeps me out, Beamer."

"Well I'm sorry," he said. But he wasn't. "It's not really about you. I don't know why it upsets you."

"That's just it," taking an injured tone. "It does upset me, because, well, it's just so weird, and I care about you."

*That's half true*, Beamer thought, but said nothing. Then finally: "No worries," he said lightly. "Some people drink. Some smoke. I go on retreat for a while. It could be worse."

"Well, do you want to talk about what got you feeling this way?" She sounded genuinely concerned, which always disarmed him.

"Thanks Vesper, but there's really not a lot to say. I've just been thinking that had I been only a few seconds faster on my walk, I could be at the bottom of that ravine with a six hundred tonne locomotive on my chest dripping dilbit in my face…is all." He looked back at the television, and spoke to it rather than to Vesper—or to himself. "What the fuck are we coming to here?"

She looked back at him with the slightest pout. Was she really that hurt or was this just a good opportunity to chalk up the tiniest quantum of guilt for being who he was—guilt that could be added to a growing ball of guilt redeemable later for much larger prizes?

A small clutter of mail was in the middle of the couch, all of it already opened. Vesper pushed it in his direction with her toe. "We got a notice today from Energy-One. They've set up a new billing system. Two different classes of customers, I guess. If you're an Elite Class customer your electricity is guaranteed, but at a higher price than now. Preferred Class, you still pay more, but not as much as Elite Class, and your power can be interrupted at any time without notice. I think it'll cost us another hundred a month to go Elite Class. Our taxes are also going up, and the garbage service, and the special urban zone maintenance levy. We probably need to redo our budget then. That's it—for today," she said ominously, returning her attention to the television. Beamer felt chastised, like she was dragging him away from his trauma and back into the "real" world of bills and taxes and budgets. Adult stuff. Why was that?

*News in Brief* ran ticker-tape fashion across the TV screen under the talking head of a grave looking announcer. "…Agriculture and Food Minister today announced that consumers should brace for more hikes in food prices, basic utilities, and water rates as drought enters its ninth year across the western Prairies and the Pacific coast. In other news, Biff-Biff Ren-Roo-Koo insisted today that new lyrics to her cover of the classic *Summertime*, were not a comment on the government's mishandling of climate change. In sports…"

Vesper was looking at the TV screen but her eyes were glazed, hinting inward distraction. Beamer got up from the sofa and went to the kitchen again to get a beer from the fridge. "Want one?" he called from the kitchen.

"No thanks," Vesper replied. When he returned, she used the remote to turn off the TV. The silence in the room felt uncomfortably deep. "So, how was your day?" she asked.

By now, tired of parsing Vesper's questions for their various nuances, parsing Vesper's feelings, parsing Vesper's hidden agendas, Beamer just took her question at face value. Come what may, it was easier to tell his story as it came to him instead of how he guessed she might want to hear it. Regular sex could only get you so far.

"Well," he said, "the day was the usual, you might say. I went to a meeting. I listened to a lot of things that didn't make sense to me and then, thank God, it was time to leave for the day. And then I tried to walk home but a bridge fell down right in front of me, just like that, and a freight train was leaking carcinogens into the river and burning right there. And I nearly burned up, but a nice Aussie guy hauled my ass away from the ravine. So I had to go round-about to get back home and that took some time, given the general confusion and all. And now I'm having a beer with you." Beamer gave a whimsical, despairing smile and then took a big swallow from the bottle he'd been clamping between his thighs.

Vesper regarded him silently for a moment. He could tell she was making a decision, but he couldn't guess what. Presently, she got up and disappeared into their bedroom emerging again moments later with a clothes hanger that had a dark blue pin-striped suit on it—a three piece suit—with a white dress shirt inside and a necktie with riotous patterns of iridescent aqua, sapphire, turmaline, and navy—a cravat Beamer knew enough to recognize as a power tie. He guessed she thought he needed to be more powerful or something. But in relation to whom, and powerful how, he wondered?

"I went shopping on my lunch hour," she said, "and I picked this up for you. I think you'd look good in it. It might up your game a little...at work... you know?"

Beamer felt something harden inside him even as he also recoiled. Her gesture was, in a way, as disarmingly generous as it was off-base. He loved that about her—what she shared with all those who sincerely believe that a kiss and a new bit of clothing can make it better. For Vesper, shopping made it better. All that was needed to shift the balance from madness to sanity at work was a new suit. But she sincerely believed it and Beamer was as loathe to demolish her sincere belief as he would have been loathe to demolish a child's belief in superheroes. Both would evaporate in due course and neither required his help.

"I hope I got your size right," Vesper said.

Beamer nodded. "I'm sure you did. Thank you." Then he tried to imagine what dressing better than his boss might do for his career.

An aside, "Do you smell something burning?" Vesper asked.

"My parka," Beamer replied.

"Oh," said Vesper.

# CHAPTER 4

*Calamity finds its source in denial.*

— BERTIE BREVIS, COMEDIAN

BEAMER'S OFFICE WAS ON THE THIRD FLOOR of the Ministry of Environment building which was one sign of his status in the Ministry. Higher status office holders got offices literally higher in the building, as if avoiding the ground was a prerequisite for career advancement. Size also mattered. According to protocol, Beamer's office was three metres by three metres square. No windows. No plants. No personal artwork or family photos on the walls. In fact, nothing on the walls. Government-issue grey steel desk, grey office chair, one additional chair for a visiting colleague or supervisor but no table for meetings or to spread out work. Meeting tables were only found higher in the building, and meetings were only called by others. Beamer attended meetings; he didn't call them. Two grey steel lateral file drawers in a laminate-topped credenza. Efficient. Economical. Spartan Revival—toughened from birth, focused on duty, ready to fall on your sword at the pleasure of the Minister. No visible sign of luxury, or even of comfort, that might upset voters or cue the press or the Opposition to a waste of taxpayers' dollars. While he was not allowed to have tropical plants, Beamer kept a small stoneware bonsai dish on his desk filled with variously coloured river stones. So far as he knew, there was no policy against bonsai dishes or river stones. Once he'd passed his probationary period, he'd already decided, he would try a cactus. He wondered if a cactus would register with his colleagues as the metaphor he intended it to be.

He logged on to his government-issue computer terminal which consisted of three generation obsolete hardware running five generation obsolete software, kludgey, but adequate to the obsolete tasks it performed. A scheduling notice popped onto his screen about a meeting that was called for the morning by Bartley Coombs, the Assistant Deputy Minister. It was flagged in red font, so, urgent. Time: 10:30 AM. Location: Room 7VR22. Topic: Confidential / Urgent.

Beamer entered the meeting room, noting with relief that he wasn't the last to arrive, but almost. Half a dozen people sat around a longish table with Coombs at the head. Behind him was a white board still showing ghostly after-images from previous meetings—many straight lines and dotted lines connecting boxes and circles, a few arrows here and some bullets there.

Bartley Coombs was balding, middle-aged, doughy if not yet obese, and stared like a basilisk in wire-rimmed glasses. His dress shirt and tie threatened strangulation beneath a glen plaid sport coat that probably couldn't be buttoned.

Beside Coombs and to his right was Cecil 'Packer' Patterson (Finance), lean as Coombs was plump, with eyes that darted about compulsively. Beamer found him especially difficult to talk to as he was so averse to eye contact that even in face-to-face conversation he looked at his shoes, or someone else's shoes, or the condition of ventilators, crown mouldings, or tiny defects in the drywall—anything except another person's eyes. Trust was an interpersonal challenge for Patterson. Among the occasional mercies that life offers, Beamer considered it one that he didn't have to work too closely with him. He speculated that Patterson might be on the spectrum somewhere for adult autism. But what of it. His position in Finance made him a bean counter at heart and if autism made that more pleasant for him, then onward.

To Patterson's right loomed Lucy Sunderland. She was a bright woman who was too loud and too aggressive. Her girth was matched only by her ambition. She bounced impatiently and vocally against any number of perceived or real glass ceilings like an untethered dirigible still trapped in its hangar. Her instincts were political rather than environmental. She never concealed the fact that she thought of her present job in Environment (Policy Analyst and Press Secretary) as a stepping stone to greater, though as yet undefined, professional goals. Beamer could picture her hiring the services of professional gentlemen. Since her expertise was in public relations not environmental science, Beamer wondered whether she fully appreciated what an inauspicious launch pad she had picked to begin her meteoric ascent through the civil service.

To Coombs's left was 'Frankie' Angeleno (Executive Secretary to the Minister). Her real name was Francine but for some reason she'd accepted a masculinized and too familiar nickname. She too was middle-aged (Beamer being the youngest of the group), brilliant, understated, courteous to a fault though not obsequious, and probably largely the reason that Coombs was sitting at the head of the table. When anyone called her Frankie Angeleno, she might have been taken for a Mafiosa, completely contrary to her actual temperament. She had decided long ago that her approach to career advancement was to advance someone else's career and then hope to be carried along in their slipstream, a choice that often made Frankie sad. Her work made Coombs look smarter than he was, a boon that he seldom acknowledged and scarcely deserved.

Beside Frankie was Brian Cooper (Hydrologist), an academic by temperament if not by vocation, quiet, introverted, sometimes withdrawn, but in spite of that had avoided paranoia and often had worthwhile things to say. He managed to garner a certain tacit respect from all present that manifested as his being excused from the jocular rituals that normally oiled relationships among bureaucrats. He seldom spoke, but when he did, others listened. At all other times, Cooper kept his own counsel from a measured social distance.

With all these others already seated, Beamer wound up at the far end of the table in non-verbal opposition to Coombs—an awkward coincidence. Others were coming, he hoped, which would give him the double opportunity of appearing gracious by relinquishing his seat to someone more senior while also moving out of Coombs' direct line of sight. But before he could do a mental roll call of who else might be coming, Coombs started the meeting and Beamer stayed put.

"So," Coombs sighed wearily even as he cast a penetrating glance around the table, "we have a problem. You've heard about the McMaster Bridge, I assume." All heads nodded. "Well, the damn train is still burning and we need to position the Minister on the right side of this."

"How is it our problem?" Lucy Sunderland snorted. "Shouldn't it be Emergency Measures handling it?"

Coombs shrugged. "They are—I guess. But people see all that smoke and the bridge melting in the fire at the bottom of the ravine and they see it as an environmental problem for some reason. So that makes it our problem. Maybe we can duck this one if the media don't dig too deep. No one looks at these things very closely anyway, especially for the environment. There's no one left in the media who has a grip on the issues. They don't know the difference between an organism and an orgasm. So they'll stick to questions about the economic cost—how many jobs lost, cost to replace the rolling stock and the bridge, et cetera. We just need enough generalities to give the Minister some talking points if he's asked. You know—the usual. 'We take these incidents seriously. The situation is being monitored. Environment is working with its partners in government and industry to coordinate our response. No threat to the public. Updates as we get them from the scene.' That should do. Lucy, can you stitch something together for the next news cycle?"

"Sure thing," Sunderland replied, taking a few notes as she spoke.

"It might not be quite that easy," Brian Cooper interjected.

"What's not easy?" Coombs asked.

Cooper shrugged, and then looked up from a doodle he had been scrawling. "Well," he said, "what's leaking and burning out there is dilbit. The solvents used to liquify the stuff are toxic, especially if they are burning off rather than just leaking. If there's no threat to the public at this point, it's only because of the way the wind is blowing. I don't know if EMO has an evac plan for the surrounding area. But if they haven't done it, we should be on their asses to make sure they do. Just in case."

Coombs looked pained. Reality always annoyed him. "Okay. Well, Lucy, can you also ping the EMO for a situation report? I don't want to bother the Minister with this stuff unless there's really something going on."

"There really is something going on," Beamer interrupted. All faces turned in his direction but almost immediately returned to Coombs. The new hire couldn't possibly have anything of significance to add.

"Yes Farris?" Coombs acknowledged him anyway.

"This is really Cooper's area," said Beamer, "but the dilbit that isn't burning is leaking into ice water. That makes it congeal and this stuff is so heavy that without the diluent it will sink. So it's probably slipping under the ice right now and being slowly pushed down stream until it snags somewhere. The river provides drinking water for half a dozen municipalities, to say nothing of other species living in the riparian zone. The carcinogens in the dilbit will be released into the water—not as fast as if they burned—but released for sure."

"The solution to pollution is dilution!" Patterson guffawed.

Beamer gave him as withering a look as he dared. "That was from the 1960s, wasn't it? My parents weren't even born yet. Seriously though, this stuff won't just wash away."

Frankie glanced around the table, then returned her gaze to the notes she was taking, always the assiduous archivist.

"So what would you recommend, Farris?" Coombs didn't fail to patronize, not even taking his own question seriously. Beamer took in all the faces around the table. Clearly their expectations of him were low, but by now they were casting for anything, even something from the new hire, or perhaps looking for a diversion.

Beamer chose to ignore Coombs's tone. "Having the EMO manage the spill on the ground is really the only option we have now, isn't it? I'm just suggesting that that being the case, we don't just wash our hands and let this drift off without another thought. The news cycle will move on, but we shouldn't. That gunk will still be in the river."

"What sage advice from the guy on probation," Sunderland resisted a sneer but came close.

"Okay," Coombs soothed. "We're all on the same side here."

Beamer wasn't sure. If the group had a centre of gravity, Beamer thought, it would be leaning in the direction of complacency—doing nothing, as long as the press didn't find out and the Minister didn't have to answer for anything. Somehow, this was so different from the work he imagined he would be doing after completing a degree in environmental science. That exercise by itself took the idealism and energy of his university days and dragged them through the fire walk of bad news that was the inconvenient truth of environmental awareness. The dynamic young defender of planet Earth and all her children was, after just four months of his probationary period, already slipping toward apathy and burnout. Deeper down though, Beamer could sense a smouldering rage and disillusionment. The effort needed to keep a lid on it brought him reliably to dread his predicament and what he could imagine of the future. He didn't know which way to turn and yet turn some way he must.

"Anything else, Farris?" Coombs probed. Beamer thought he was being more than fair and secretly wished he had some brilliant brainstorm that would outmatch the situation. But he didn't. "Not really," he admitted.

Meanwhile, Patterson had been absently doodling in his portfolio. Without looking up from his reverie, "They'll call a hearing, or maybe a town hall, about the bridge, if not about the spill as well. They'll either want to know what happened or at least have a voice in whatever comes next."

"Who, 'they'?" Sunderland sounded impatient and bored.

"Someone," said Patterson. "Probably the city. Or they could do it at our call, if we're discrete enough and make it look like the idea came from city hall. Environmental groups may also demand something from the city, or from us. No matter what we say, they'll demand greater transparency, more information, the usual drill."

Coombs gave a sigh. "Well, okay. Ears to the ground people. If there is some kind of a hearing process or a town hall, Environment should be there, but not centre stage if we can avoid it. That's it for now." Everyone packed up their tablets and notes and drifted out of the meeting room. Coombs, however, was hanging back from the group, occupying himself with erasing the few notes he had made on the whiteboard.

As Beamer was getting ready to leave the room, Coombs spoke up: "You know," he said carefully, "I was just thinking that at this point you might really be of help to us doing a bit of research—identify some key issues coming down the pipe, you know? Look down the road for us. Give us the perspective of youth maybe. Look into the forecasts, the projections. You know? See if you can get a bead on what's happening out there that we should be preparing people for, you know what I mean?"

Beamer inspected Coombs's face. He could auger omens when he saw them. He nodded his assent without saying anything.

"How long have you been with us, Farris?" Coombs asked casually, like it was just friendly curiosity.

"Four months," said Beamer, remembering that his probationary period was six months.

"Ah, I see," nodded Coombs. Did he look relieved? Beamer couldn't tell. "Well, I think some research would be a good way for you to go for now. Could you pull together a briefing paper for us in say, two weeks?"

"Of course."

"Great," said Coombs, his voice trailing off, already distancing himself from his own suggestion. "Great." He smiled and nodded. Then, as if remembering why they had all been meeting: "And also, if anything else comes up around this derailment thing, maybe you could drop in to the hearings or the town hall or whatever they call it, and just be our eyes and ears there, okay? Make no statements. Take no positions. You wouldn't even be an official representative but just an interested citizen who happens to work for Environment. Know what I mean?"

Beamer nodded again.

"Fine," said Coombs. "Okay. Good talk. Carry on then." He headed to the door.

Beamer went back to his office, checked messages, of which there were none, and then made his way to the ministry research library. It was battleship grey and dim as a crypt, half the lights having been removed to save money. The stacks were packed with all manner of consultation papers, policy documents, labour market studies, economic analyses, official reports and projections. A great deal of ink had been spilled to fill this room, Beamer thought, and yet, what he was looking for (what was he looking for?) wasn't there. Maddening. For the rest of the day he browsed the stacks aimlessly, reading bits and pieces with only the dimmest intuition as to what he was after. The very vagueness of his assignment stoked his paranoia because he could imagine it being used as a pretext for dismissal. He kept constant vigil on the wall clock that would announce his moment of liberation from this place, this day. Four months. What would it be like after forty years? Did anyone have forty years?

# CHAPTER 5

*It is only human nature to want to know the future.*
*Centuries ago, we turned to chicken entrails for this*
*purpose. Today we use economists. The predictive*
*accuracy of the two methods is roughly equal.*

— FENTON LARRABEE, FUTURIST

AFTER THE MEETING AT THE MINISTRY, Beamer retired to the archives building to pursue his research assignment. For the first couple of days he simply wrestled with getting a grip on what the assignment actually was. The focus of the work kept slipping and sliding about in his mind, like some slimy thing he was trying to pull up from under bog water. At one point he even thought that Coombs had given him an impossible assignment to set him up for probationary dismissal. As compelling as paranoia could be, however, Beamer couldn't imagine Coombs being that cunning. More plausible, he thought, would be Coombs' desire simply to give him something to do that would take Beamer out of sight and out of mind. He had to admit, he didn't feel that loved in the halls of the Ministry.

Presently, Beamer stepped back from his efforts to deliver on Coombs' shapeless demand. It could be that Coombs himself didn't know what he wanted. Here Beamer's past experience with vague assignments came into play. Lacking intellectual clarity, his fallback was intuition. Instead of trying to read everything in the archives about social and economic forecasting, or about the youth perspective on any particular issue, he relaxed his grip on the assignment and started to think of the archive as a sort of very large Ouija board. He let himself cast about with no particular agenda in search of those moments of resonance when a humming in his head told him that whatever it was he had found would eventually find its place in a larger, more significant whole.

So for days, he pressed on this way—casually scanning, selecting, saving, discarding—he worked like a sculptor adding clay here, sheering it off there, but all the while in search of that hidden inner form that he felt increasingly certain was there. Then it was as if he was an old school film developer peering down into a pan of chemicals while an image, a pattern, manifested before his eyes.

Here was a paper about chaos theory—the branch of mathematics concerned with disorder. It happened that you could start a pendulum swinging and it would swing back and forth in the same plane. Push the pendulum a little harder and at first it just swung back and forth faster. But push the pendulum hard enough—that is, add enough energy—and suddenly it would tip into a state of chaotic motion. If swinging slowly, the pendulum obeyed one set of mathematical laws; if swinging swiftly, however, a different set of laws applied.

Here was an article about glacial ice. Under ordinary conditions glacial ice is lost to seasonal melting and replenished by seasonal snow falls in a rough balance. Add a bit of extra heat to this process and at some point more ice melts than is replenished, exposing more bare ground and dust-darkened layers of ice above. The glacier is then set upon a course leading to total collapse; it was only a matter of time.

And here was a paper about the ratio of household income to debt. Most people needed to incur debt in order to purchase a house or a car. But these debts were secured by the assets they were incurred to acquire and over long terms with stable repayment rules. Indulge in consumer debt, however, the sort that comes with credit cards whose interest rates can change on a whim and compound over time and a point will be reached when the cost of servicing one's debts exceeds one's income—bankruptcy.

And here a piece about predator-prey relationships in nature. An abundance of rabbits and ground squirrels offers good eating to foxes and coyotes. Such conditions favour reproductive success. But the birth of too many coyotes virtually assures over-hunting of prey species and at last the collapse of fox and coyote populations.

Beamer kept discovering more and more examples of what amounted to trends that reached tipping points that resulted in unpredictable and sometimes unimaginable consequences—like population crashes.

Beamer steeped himself in such stories until he could sense the appearance in his mind of something new. His research had gradually drawn him toward the study of trends. It also had to do with tipping points. But there was some other missing something that he couldn't yet identify. Experience had taught Beamer that when arriving at such an impasse the best thing to do was to do nothing and simply wait for the deep brain to do its work.

After ten days of work Beamer had accumulated information on dozens of trends. Some were social; some were economic; others were environmental; still others were political or spiritual. On the tenth day, however, one word came to mind: Time. At first he didn't understand what it meant. Then his mind cleared. All trends were time-bound. They had beginnings, middles and ends. All trends also had a time course, a sort of arc through time, and some trends had tipping points—not all—but some. It was the difference between a trend in Tickle-me Elmo sales that sloped upwards for a while and then slowly declined, burning itself out in the swamp of commercial success, as compared to a nuclear arms race culminating in global catastrophe that everyone could see coming but that no one could predict.

Beamer went back to the beginning of his research to find trends that also had tipping points. Not all tipping points were important, he realized, nor were all trends. But some trends could be historical turning points, especially when the trend was rapidly increasing in strength. So Beamer constructed a timeline—a kind of horizontal calendar on which he could map trends and tipping points. He simply took his best shot at which trends would be important to the future and which not. And then it appeared: He discovered a moment in time about eighteen months in the future, when a number of important trends would reach tipping points together. This coincidence more or less assured that the tipping points would interact somehow and produce highly unpredictable effects. The swinging pendulum, if pushed hard enough, would break into chaotic motion around some new strange attractor that would give shape to the energy within it. But there was no way to foresee what exactly would trigger the convergence of tipping points.

Every trend was based on statistics. Every trend, therefore, had a certain probability of occurring, but also an error term—the likelihood that the trend might not appear as predicted. In the case of Beamer's timeline of tipping points, every point was actually a blurry band of probability—a bell curve of catastrophe that was only more or less certain to occur at a particular time. Beamer started doodling up a grid of numbers that represented not predictions, but their error terms, and the interactions of those errors, which could compound, like a loan shark's interest on a debt. He transferred his little grid to a spreadsheet and continued to add data, his heart pounding harder each time he ran the numbers.

If there was a consistent thread that linked together all of humanity's efforts to augur future events, or even plan for business as usual, it was in what they left out so as to create the delusion of normalcy. Since the taken-for-granted assumptions of each trend forecast were different, the invisible interactions of their errors were a composite and much more massive cultural blind spot. Every trend had a blind spot and the sum of all blind spots was a black hole large enough to swallow everything. The future,

Beamer realized, would be shaped within that dark shadow, not in the light of what people could see, but in the dark of what they took for granted. Even more disturbing was discovering that collapsing this delusion didn't require a "Big Thing" like a nuclear war or global pandemic. It could just as easily happen because of much smaller blind spots interacting just so—like the unpredictable actions of a single lunatic in just the right place at just the right time. The future, Beamer concluded, bites you from your blind side, like a wolf—or like a train falling off a bridge.

Beamer saved his file and closed his laptop. A tremor of shaking passed through his body like an electric current. The energies which only moments before had been focused in thought were now quaking through his body as raw anxiety. He steadied himself as he turned toward the exit, his only desire to leave the archive.

# CHAPTER 6

*Democracy is the worst form of government,*
*except for all the others.*

— WINSTON S. CHURCHILL

BEAMER SLIPPED THROUGH the door of Meeting Room 3D of the City Administration Building trying to be as inconspicuous as possible while at the same time trying not to look as if he was trying to be inconspicuous. He found a seat near the rear of the room which was furnished with several long tables arranged in an open rectangle the yonder side of which was arrayed with padded swivel chairs and microphones. More swivel chairs were arranged along two more sides of the rectangle but without microphones—presumably reserved for those who toiled in the civic interest but who should remain voiceless. At the near end of the rectangle was a single table and chair with a microphone, presumably reserved for whoever might address the people with both chairs and microphones—the hearing conveners. Coffee, tea and water were available on a side table. The room's decor of wood paneling, full-length draperies covering a wall of windows and carpeted floor made it relatively comfortable without pretending to luxury. An additional two dozen chairs had been lined up in rows where Beamer sat for those who had come to voice their opinions or just to listen.

In due course, people started drifting into the room. Most of them looked like bureaucrats who nervously checked sound systems and digital projectors. Some were the general public clutching their speaking notes or balancing laptops on their knees. Then came a line of seven people who filed into the head table chairs. All wore suits of some sort and all appeared official. A silver-haired woman sat down in the chair at the middle of the line-up. Leaning into her mic she said, "Alright, friends, let's get under way." The head table crowd nestled down into their chairs like so many brood hens roosting for the night.

There was some bustling in the room as everyone found their chairs, then the silver-haired woman in the centre seat said: "I'm Ramona Shepherd,

Assistant Deputy of Planning for the city and I'll be moderating our discussion. Beside me is…" and then she rattled off the names and official positions of the other head table people. "This is the first of several such meetings we will be having across the city to review the matter of the McMaster Bridge collapse and how the city should approach its repair or replacement. We welcome all your comments provided normal public decorum is observed. Today's speakers have been scheduled on a first-come basis among those who requested speaking time. Shall we begin?" There was a rustle in the room but no one objected to getting started.

Beamer observed that the city government had moved forward on the matter of repairing the McMaster Bridge with unusual promptness. It carried both rail and heavy vehicle traffic across the Bison River which now had to detour several kilometres round about, increasing traffic on those routes, adding to delivery delays and amping up driver frustration. The attitude of city bureaucrats was usually sullen and lethargic, but they were under pressure to get on with some sort of action. For their own part, the bureaucrats wanted time to negotiate cost-sharing agreements with higher orders of government, a process that involved its own obscure alchemy because, while the bridge was a city asset, it had collapsed into a river that was technically under provincial jurisdiction. The dilbit clean-up bill was also still in dispute as resolving it required provincial, federal, corporate and insurance company participation—a gruelling prospect at best. And, of course, none of these gears was about to turn without community consultation. Meanwhile the bridge still lay in the river and the tanker cars oozed dilbit.

"Very well then," Shepherd acknowledged. "Mister Joseph Spotted Bird, speaking for the Coalition of Regional Chiefs. Please take a seat."

A man with braided greying hair and wearing blue jeans and a buckskin vest decorated with beadwork rose from the audience and moved to the speaker's mic carrying an eagle feather. He represented a dozen Indigenous bands wanting to serve notice that the bridge was a colonial artifact that had been erected on sacred land without consultation. Since no formal treaty was in place respecting this particular bit of land, a consultation process was essential, as part of a new treaty negotiation, that would recognize and enshrine the rights of Indigenous people to the land. No repair or reconstruction of the bridge should occur until this process could be launched, together with all the necessary ceremonial observances. Should this demand not be honoured, Mister Spotted Bird couldn't guarantee that younger members of their communities might not take more direct action on their own behalf.

Unaccountably, Beamer felt himself carried out of himself. *A locomotive was rolling slowly toward him, its single lighted eye fixing him from across a river. It made no sound but it was angry, threatening. Perhaps it was a transformer about to change itself into something else and to mete out revenge. Any moment it should stand up in a myriad of hinged panels rearranging themselves into a form more suited to its task. But then the bridge upon which it rolled forward began to scream and bend and above its single shining eye the faces of two men, screaming...*

Beamer felt nauseous and sweaty. His heart pounded so hard he thought others must be hearing it. But the meeting went on and no one noticed.

Next came a representative from the Women's Safety and Security Society who insisted that the old bridge had never been a structure which was fully accessible to people with disabilities, nor had it provided amenities that would make it a safe place for women. So the Society insisted that any reconstruction of the bridge include special lighting, security cameras, and emergency alarm stations, plus level grades for wheelchair and infant stroller access and pedestrian foot traffic. In addition, Howard McMaster for whom the bridge was named, was a privileged white male and the time had come to more consciously embrace diversity by renaming the bridge in honour of a disabled woman of colour. The Society would submit a list of suitable naming suggestions to the recording secretary for the hearings.

Another brief was tabled together with an oral presentation by Clive of the Farby family, freeman-on-the-land, who argued that he had not freely entered into any sort of contract or agreement with the city to obtain his personal approval for the project which might, in the city's judgement, justify taxing him for its construction. Since the city, to Mr. Farby's way of thinking, had no legitimate taxation authority at all, he was serving notice ahead of time that he would not comply with any taxation demands. He also expressed his willingness to die, if necessary, in defence of freedom.

*The single lighted eye glared into view from across the river, but this time leaped forward to the middle of the bridge amidst the screaming and shrieking of tearing metal. Then it plunged down and down into shadow only to disappear in a cloud of flame. A great paw seemed to reach up from the fiery darkness and slam Beamer to the ground.*

Beamer shook his head to dislodge the vision, if that's what it was. Was this tableau grabbing him where he lived because of what it literally appeared to be, or did it symbolize something else entirely? He was sweating even more profusely now and found it hard to catch his breath. But again, no one seemed to notice, or if they noticed, they ignored what they saw.

Next came The River Keepers, Inc., who tabled a brief seeking assurances from the city and province that repair of the old bridge or construction of a new one would not further damage the riverine and riparian ecosystems, and that the polluters in this case bear the full cost of infrastructure repairs and environmental restoration, though they were not clear on just who they thought was responsible. In addition to guarantees of restoration of the river and a thorough clean-up of the escaped dilbit, The River Keepers suggested that the city, or perhaps the province, require that all transportation companies moving hazardous products through the city, whether by rail or truck, file restoration bonds obligating them to reimburse the community four times the cost of any future spills or mishaps.

The District Health and Wellness Promotion Association slipped out of their active wear and into business casual to press their concern over the health risks to people of the spilled dilbit and demanded to know what plans the city, or the province, or both, had in place to assure a thorough clean-up and recovery operation. They also expressed alarm at the potential of impacts to downstream communities who used the river as their source of drinking water and wondered how long the city planned to monitor water quality.

The Chamber of Commerce, for its part, really didn't give a damn whether the bridge was repaired or rebuilt, nor what it might look like once finished, but only that the work get under way immediately as money was being lost every day the bridge laid in ruins, and that the work be awarded to local contractors, only through a transparent and fair tendering process—of course. This would be the best way, they said, of creating local employment opportunities from a disaster and of avoiding lawsuits which were being prepared by some, not to be publicly named, Chamber members who wanted compensation from the municipal authority for loss of business due to the missing bridge.

*The flaming paw kept reappearing and slamming Beamer to the ground and no sooner had he fallen on his face and rolled over to avoid the searing heat the scene jumped back to the moment when the locomotive started its dive into the gorge. And again he was beaten to the ground by the fury of the explosion. To his imagination, his silhouette appeared to be charred into the bridge deck like a victim of Hiroshima.*

The Historical Preservation Society, on the other hand, cared a great deal what the bridge looked like. They reminded the city bureaucrats that the bridge had a heritage site designation. They went on at some length haranguing the panel about the signal role played by the bridge in the history of the city, its many period design features, its portrayal in local histories, so on and so forth, concluding with the firm demand that the bridge not only be repaired, but that this opportunity be taken to fully restore it with period accuracy to its original glory.

To his now dizzying mind, the testimony that Beamer thought trumped them all came from a parade of security agency officials including the city police (all wearing body armour), the provincial police (also armoured), the Federal Domestic Terrorism Agency, the RCMP, the Forensics Unit, the Environmental Protection Enforcement Bureau, numerous consultants and a phalanx of lawyers all of whom insisted that the site not be touched at all until their investigations were complete. This could take weeks, if not months, it being winter, which made their work slower and harder. Had the collapse been an act of God? Had it resulted from some form of negligence on the part of the rail company? Had the cars been overloaded somehow? Was it vandalism by local youth or anarchists? Was there a connection to Islamic inspired radicals? Had this been the work of home-grown terrorists (eyes cast askance at Mr. Farby)? Had there been some failure of due diligence or maintenance by the city? In short, no repair work should be started until they could figure out who to blame.

For Beamer, the sheer tedium of this paranoid recitation was calming. It was so predictable that it successfully soothed the surges of panic that had been washing over him, like cookies that his grandmother used to make, or the drone of the colour commentary for the hockey games his father used to watch.

Before long Beamer imagined that this review might go on for days, requiring from municipal officials the wisdom of sages, the patience of saints, and the political instincts of Pericles, even to define a "solution space" for the issue, much less to implement it. While a solution was being sought, time would be passing with no repairs to the bridge. And this was only one of dozens of such exercises convened to review municipal issues, projects and plans. Bureaucratic timidity, political correctness and pandering to commercial interests mingled with the bizarre claims of individuals who insisted on advancing their own pet theories rather than seeking workable solutions. There was also no shortage of people who took irrational or uninformed positions, suspected conspiracies, and treated each other and municipal officials with cynicism or open contempt. All of this presented the appearance of an ungovernable mob that gridlocked public institutions. Democracy was a good enough idea, Beamer thought, but it didn't work.

After three hours of listening to hearings and trying to endure his anxiety on top of a full day at the Ministry, Beamer felt fatigued and despairing. He quietly moved toward the meeting room door and went outside. The night air was damp and cold. A scattering of the brightest stars struggled through the haze of city lights and high altitude smoke. He set off toward his apartment, inhaling and exhaling deeply, like someone on life support.

# CHAPTER 7

*Make a beginning. Begin with what you have.*
*Bring its co-evolving nature under the loving*
*gaze of your deepest wisdom. But begin.*

— ONOKI TASIMOTO, ROSHI

TATUM BARNES MANEUVERED the cube van through the suburban street leading to her Finder candidates. The van was a clumsy vehicle to drive through the snow clogged streets, but it belonged to the Badger Coulee community and had to serve multiple purposes. When she wasn't using it to make deliveries to and from the Coulee, it was her ride on other errands and this trip was a Coulee concern.

Twenty-three seventy-eight Fernwood Drive was a ranch-style house with accent brick facia halfway up the walls and finished above with horizontal siding. A broad porch fronted the house with railings and carriage light accents. Its size and decorative features fit seamlessly with its neighbours—modest, unpretentious, and on that account, almost invisible. Tatum pulled the van into the driveway and shut off the engine. She thumbed her cell phone screen to call up notes for these candidates. John Hofsted (29) and Clovis Amyotte (31); John an elevator service mechanic employed by the Otis Elevator Company; Clovis a Bachelor of Nursing floor nurse at the Sunrise Regional Hospital. Two children, Brody (8) and Cate (6). A phone number and an email contact and that was it. Tatum had talked with them on the phone following up a suggestion from someone already at Badger Coulee, but they had not met in person. She thumbed her phone off and jumped down from the cab of the van and then made her way to the front door.

She looked around for a doorbell but before she could find it, the door opened and a woman stood in the threshold. "Tatum Barnes?" she said. She was of medium height and build with wavy dark hair just starting to show streaks of grey. Her manner was cordial but not effusive. She had the persona of many medical professionals of long experience—caring but no-nonsense.

"And you must be Clovis Amyotte," said Tatum. Clovis stepped back to let Tatum step in. She doffed her coat as John Hofsted entered the room from the kitchen and the two children came racing through the narrow hallway, ostensibly chasing each other, but secretly wanting a glimpse of the visitor.

"Downstairs hooligans!" John's deep baritone voice rumbling after the children even as they were already leaving the adults to their conversation. He was a big man with ropy forearms, solid shoulders, and large sinewy hands that, while clean, were work callused. "I'm John Hofsted," introducing himself to Tatum and extending his hand to shake hers. "I've got some fresh coffee on if we can repair to the kitchen."

"I never refuse coffee," said Tatum as she followed her hosts to a dining nook adjacent to the kitchen. John busied himself assembling the coffee, sugar and cream. Once the coffee was served, Tatum spoke first.

"So, I'm Tatum Barnes," she said, "and one of my pastimes is to act as a Finder for Badger Coulee—a sort of head-hunter, if you will. I'm not here to recruit you or to sell you anything, but to answer your questions about the Coulee, as you asked me to during our first phone call. I got your names from Jasper Beckett as folks who might be interested in what we're doing at the Coulee. Jasper's a mutual acquaintance, I guess."

Clovis nodded. "Yes. We've known Jasper since our university days."

"Which of your university days?"

"Both of us," said John.

Tatum shook her head. "There I go, making assumptions, eh? I thought you're a mechanic and Clovis is a nurse."

"I am and she is. First I got a degree in mechanical engineering, then a journeyman mechanic's ticket, because it turned out I liked getting my hands greasy better than designing stuff on CAD/CAM. Clovis and I met in a pub and one thing sort of led to another, as they say, and you see the hooligans. I think we met Jasper in the same pub."

"So, what would you like to know?" Tatum opened.

John and Clovis glanced at each other, then John said: "Tell us more about Badger Coulee."

Tatum nodded, collecting her thoughts. "Where to start?" she said. "Well, Badger Coulee is a ghost town—or it was a ghost town before we moved in. Turns out there are lots of little villages around that are aging or dead. So we picked one about a hundred kilometres south of the city for our community. Once upon a time the village had a few hundred people huddled around a grain elevator, a hockey arena and a church. As agriculture went from family farms to corporate farms, places like Badger Coulee emptied out. So there it was, with some streets, water mains and hydro hook-ups, but almost no people left, and a very affordable for sale sign in the yard. Perfect for what we had in mind."

"Some people would call Badger Coulee an 'intentional community,'"Tatum continued, "and it is intentional, for sure. I don't think anyone has come to the Coulee by accident. Some would call it a commune and others probably a cult. But it isn't any of those things. We're not a religion. We are a community. But you might call the heart of what we are doing a work of cultural co-evolution."

"Sounds pretty out there," John said.

Tatum nodded. "We're out there all right. But then they say there are a hundred thousand people ready to colonize Mars with no hope of ever returning to Earth. If we didn't have the Coulee, most of us would probably sign up for Mars. Seriously though, one of the things we have in common is that we think life in consumer culture under capitalism is doomed, plain and simple. We want a better alternative. We believe we can create one, although time is running short here."

"You have children at the Coulee?" Clovis interrupted.

"Oh yes," said Tatum. "We have more children than adults. It's a lively place."

John's expression became more serious. "So how did you guys get started?"

"You know, we don't know," said Tatum. "There's this guy at the Coulee named Fisher. We're not even sure that's his real name; but it's what he goes by. Fisher is pretty old now and is kind of in and out of a wheelchair. But a few years ago—maybe more than a couple, again nobody knows for sure—Fisher rolled into the village. We don't know where he came from or how long he'd been there when some of the rest of us showed up. But it turned out that everybody who was one of the first residents of the Coulee knew Fisher from before the Coulee. Now everybody talks about feeling some kind of attraction to the person of Fisher. He has a way of drawing people to himself. But he has no interest at all in running the place or being mayor or something. He's set up a little museum because his hobby is collecting old bits of machinery and tools, especially from before 1900. None of us is quite sure why he's such a collector. He's just there. He attracts us. We come. Somehow it's happening just like that. Nobody at the Coulee right now could tell you when they first met Fisher. He's like one of those friends you can't remember when you first met. You just know that you feel better after spending time with him."

"Woo, woo," said Clovis, raising an eyebrow in John's direction.

"Yes,"Tatum agreed. "A little bit."

"Do you live there?" Clovis pursued.

"About half the year," said Tatum. "By day I'm a mild mannered landscape architect and I earn my lentils by doing design commissions here in the city. But in spring, summer and fall, I try to spend as much time as possible at the Coulee. I'm also a permaculture designer. I help plan and plant the gardens at the Coulee. In the winter, I hole up in an apartment and do my landscape designs for paying clients."

"That's how you pay the rent? By doing landscape designs?" asked John.

Tatum sighed. "It's complicated right now. I make way more money than I need to pay the rent. Technically, all the money I make goes to the Coulee, and the Coulee pays my rent. The community is in a sort of transitional place right now—running two economies at once. One economy is internal to the Coulee members. It's a cashless material economy that provides everything to everyone equitably—a commonwealth of goods, we call it. It'll be the commonwealth that supports everyone when things in consumer culture come unzipped. But Badger Coulee exists right now like a little bubble floating within the moneyed economy of consumer culture. We had to create a sort of legal barricade, like a membrane between us and the world of money. We set up a co-operative community enterprise. It presents the face of a legal corporation for financial purposes to the outside world. But corporations are no longer part of the internal Badger Coulee culture. Within the co-op bubble is our community, operating on entirely different principles. We think of it as a useful lie. Outsiders think we care about money and need it for everything like everyone else does. But we just see the co-op as an expedient to keep the rest of the world out of our hair while we build an economy without money."

"But if we wanted to join the Coulee, I suppose we'd have to sign over all our assets to you right?" said Clovis, her tone suspicious.

"Not at all!" Tatum said. "That would be nice, but that's not how we do it. We have all grown up in a culture where money and financial gain are the main goals in life. A divorce from money may or may not be in the cards for you, but even if it is, it's something we do gradually. We're dealing with the full force of greed and fear here lady!" Clovis smiled at Tatum's barb. "You have to believe, in your bones," Tatum continued, "that the Coulee can and will care for you and your children, without money, before you can really let go of it—only when you really want, in your bones, to be freed from the delusion of it, is it time to let it go."

"So how does this work, exactly?" Clovis asked, her tone now openly cynical. "Let's get real. Who pays for lunch?"

"You and I aren't at that place yet in our conversation," Tatum said. "But if we were, this is sort of how it would go. You would decide to move to the Coulee. You would keep your credit cards and bank accounts and antique spoon collections and gazingus pins just as they are. You would get interest on your savings. You would pay your taxes. But within the Coulee, your work is for the community. The currency within the community is the currency of belonging, not money. While we are a community without money, we are not without work. Lunch must be prepared, and it isn't free, as I'm sure you understand. But we think the price of lunch at the Coulee is much more humane and consistent with a good life than what consumer culture charges. The community takes care of you and you take care of it. We practice a very strong form of simple living, but not without its pleasures. In any case, you join the community but your money doesn't."

"From the perspective of *outside* the Coulee," Tatum continued, "you're an investor in a co-operative social enterprise set up as an experiment in cultural co-evolution. Everyone sixteen years old or older has one vote in all matters pertaining to the co-op. One person, one vote—although we're exploring doing away with voting as well—but that's another story. If you decided to join the Coulee, you would deposit at least one tenth of your assets in the co-op which invests the money in the mainstream economy—as is the usual practice—but more like a foundation than a business. The difference here is that your investment provides the capital for the co-op, but any earnings over and above that capital belongs to the Coulee. That money is used to purchase tools and materials that help the Coulee become materially self-sufficient. As far as investing assets is concerned, everyone contributes the one tenth of their monetary assets and however much more they're comfortable with—some more, others less. While earnings on those investments belong to the co-op, the principle is still yours. If you decided to leave the Coulee, at that point, your principle would be refunded to you, but not the interest it earned. Joining the Coulee means giving up interest on some or all of your assets, but not the principle, which would be returned to you if you left. So there is what financial people call an "opportunity cost" in joining the Coulee. If you decided to live with us permanently, then we'd have another conversation about what you want to do with your money. You might want to keep some or all of it outside the Coulee for good—although that's not a decision we would recommend. All these arrangements are temporary. We expect that the global financial system will collapse within a decade or so, and perhaps very much sooner. When that happens, the bubble won't matter. Money will no longer be useful or perceived to hold value. What will matter is the material economy we managed to build together, within the bubble. So the real question here for the four of you is this: Do you want to try to ride out a global financial collapse on your own, or with a community? The collapse is coming either way." Tatum regarded them evenly. "That's how it works," she said.

They were silent for a moment then John got up to make more coffee. When he rejoined the women, Tatum said: "You've left out the most important question."

"Have we?" John replied. "And what would that be?"

Tatum regarded them both silently for just a moment, then said: "Well, we've talked about how Badger Coulee deals with your financial anxieties. But you haven't asked me why Badger Coulee exists at all. You see, life at the Coulee is only partly about how we do what we do, but much more about why we do what we do."

"Okay," said Clovis. "I'll bite. Why do you do what you're doing?"

"Badger Coulee exists," said Tatum, "because those of us living there—co-evolving there— share a similar perspective on the good life. We are not like-minded. We have a variety of views on a variety of issues. But we do agree that consumer culture is doomed. Its understanding of the good life is mistaken. It's marginalizing most of its members and it's killing nature. Maybe it's a delusion that grew up from the envy of kings and oligarchs. But wherever it came from, it is spiritually, socially and ecologically toxic. It's a suicidal lie."

"So you think you have the truth?" Clovis challenged.

"Maybe we do, and maybe we don't. Time will tell," said Tatum. "But at the Coulee, for starters, we see ourselves as co-evolving with nature and with each other. We don't aim to be masters exercising dominion over everything else. We also agree that the goal of our community should be the well-being of all of us individually and collectively. We aim to understand well-being directly, in all its richness and complexity, and not only as it pertains to human beings, but to all life. We disagree with the idea that amassing material wealth, and wealth seeking, is the best way to a good life. In fact, we think they are producing inequality and suffering."

"And you have this figured out—how to attain well-being without money?" Clovis pressed.

"No," said Tatum. "All we know for sure are two things: Consumer culture is not leading to a good life for most people or for nature, and second, we want to be part of a culture that is trying to figure out what actually does make for a good life. We don't have all the answers. But we are building a common project that is trying to find the answers. Badger Coulee is not a utopia; it's a work in progress. The requirements of this work are disciplining our way of life."

Clovis looked doubtful. "I can't get twenty floor nurses to agree on their shifts for the week and here you think you can invent a new culture. Sounds impossible."

Tatum shrugged. "Maybe it is," she admitted. "The likelihood of our success is difficult to guess at this point. One thing is for sure though: Our present way of life is not working. It's killing some of us directly and all of us indirectly and the burden we place on nature cannot be sustained. The Coulee may be a mistake; continuing the status quo is surely a mistake. Place your bets where you will, but no one gets a pass from the game."

# CHAPTER 8

*We peer through the pinhole of consciousness and think
we see reality. In fact, consciousness is a bubble floating
on a much vaster ocean, something that arises from the
ocean itself, which has its own mysteries and deep currents
churning and flowing through ancient hidden chasms. Some
things we can influence. Other things we can only witness.
The beginning of wisdom is knowing the difference.*

— RUPERT PHILMORE,
*THE PSYCHODYNAMICS OF CULTURAL DISINTEGRATION.*

LEAVING THE TOWN HALL MEETING, Beamer stepped into the street, the
cold air splashing against his face like a surf. But it did little to shake him
out of the fugue state that settled around him like a season of winter. This
had happened to him before—the feeling of displacement, like being from a
different time, a different place, marooned where he was by accident or mis-
adventure, wandering around trying to get his bearings, his sense of which
way was home. The anxiety which only moments before he felt stabbing at
the pit of his stomach was now slowly replaced with numbness, an emotional
anaesthesia, yet not devoid of purpose. His errand was clear in his mind even
though his feelings were not.

He walked on, turned a corner and went two more blocks coming to a sec-
ond-hand clothing store called Re-Pressed Memories. He entered the store.
The lights in the place cast a greenish-blue light through the interior that lent to
the place a miasma of decay. He went to one of the clearance tables and started
pawing through the drifts of musty-smelling clothing. Among the tables piled
with the cast-offs of the affluent, many other people milled about, poking listlessly at the goods on offer. Probably most were searching for one more affordable layer they could apply between themselves and the deepening winter. Some
faces were lined and gaunt; others obese and flushed. These anonymous shuffled
around him like hungry ghosts wandering a Bardo, searching and speechless, but

seldom touching. They bore no resemblance to the thinning throng of holiday shoppers chattering away in the mostly empty malls and upscale boutiques—the denizens of consumer culture who could still afford to shop for entertainment, even if all the dials were warning of a slow-down. No. On this side of town, shopping was the pleasureless task of stretching too little money over too much need. And this side of town was getting bigger every day.

Beamer, however, knew exactly what he was after. He went to the men's clothing section and found a pair of carpenter's trousers, a plaid shirt, a threadbare winter coat, some boots worn at the heels but still serviceable, a scarf, some gloves and a tuque. All the colours were drab, but colour was irrelevant to his purpose. He brought all these things to the checkout where he was parted from twenty-seven dollars and change for the lot. A clerk stuffed his purchases into a large bag and he went back into the street.

He walked on, clutching the bundle of clothing to his chest, until he came to Burins Park. Here he turned and entered the park, walking directly to the open space he had passed so many times before. The sense of being a distant witness to his own actions was still with him. The thought drifted through his mind that in this moment he was probably capable of anything—or nothing. He closed his eyes, trying to find some still point within, some place to pitch his tent. There was none. Instead, he felt a rising impulse to move, like the wave in a tidal bore. He opened his eyes and stepped into the fresh snow that blanketed the park lawn. He began to trudge forward through the snow, angling always a bit to the left, describing a path through the snow that made a large circle. Having completed his first circle, he stepped sideways to start another course within the first one. He kept trudging through the snow until he had outlined seven pathways enclosing what now was a circle about three metres in diameter at the centre of the space.

Here he waited for a few moments, still clutching the bundle of clothing. Then, in the centre circle, he carefully laid out the items in the bag. The tuque he placed at the north point of the circle, the gloves where they would belong relative to someone's body, then the jacket with the shirt, arms stuffed into the jacket sleeves, and laid open like a sacrificial victim had been flayed up the mid-section. The trousers he positioned carefully below the coat and finally the boots, open to the sky at the top, as if someone had jumped out of their clothes into the sky. Beamer then stepped carefully from one circle to the next and then turned to view what he'd made. He stood for some minutes just gazing into the centre of the circle and its array of discarded clothes. He had no idea what it was. But he smiled. He felt calm, in the present moment, in this place, and no longer bearing an enigma.

He turned around and started walking out of the park. On his way, he saw an apartment block just across the street. In the eerie light of the winter evening it looked like an enormous modernist sculpture of rectangles some of which were lighted and some dark, a tableau of light and darkness with no third dimension. It registered with him only subliminally that in one of the rectangles there appeared the silhouette of someone watching him from above.

From her fifth floor window overlooking Burins Park, Tatum Barnes could see the construction in the snow standing out in high contrast from the amber light of the lamp post. She saw a man sometimes walking with a purpose, sometimes pausing, then resuming his pace-making, then perhaps playing in the snow as he threw himself down in strangely contorted positions, then at last inspecting his composition and walking away. And through her earbuds Tatum could hear her plants—singing.

# CHAPTER 9

*Nearly everyone loves in some way or other. Some love things.*
*Others love themselves. Some even love others. Many can*
*give love at least sometimes, and sometimes we can genuinely*
*accept love. But to be love itself—that's something entirely*
*different. When someone is love, you never forget them.*

— OSIO SMITH, *TRANSCENDANCE*

THE NEXT DAY, Beamer found himself again walking away from the Ministry of Environment Building and in the direction of Burins Park. Most of the sidewalks had been cleared of the snow from a few days before, but this had been mostly pushed into gutters to await removal by snow ploughs—a rarer occurrence these days as cities struggled to maintain even basic services. Here and there people clambered over the snow banks to get to their parked cars. Walking was slow, but vehicle traffic was even slower.

Beamer's attraction to the park was a strange thing. He wasn't even sure himself why he felt drawn there; just an inchoate tingle of curiosity, yet not even that clear. He had no notion about why he wanted to visit the park again, no plan, no agenda, and certainly not to make another mandala. It was like a fugue state, or tracking a hunch.

When he got to the clearing in the trees, he saw that the clothing he'd left in the snow was gone—either retrieved by a conscientious parks worker or more likely appropriated by someone who needed more clothing and couldn't afford even the second hand store. Oddly, he thought, the clothing had been removed, but the form of the mandala lay undisturbed in the snow. It was as if the randomly passing strangers sensed something about it, akin to the feeling one has when in the presence of art, and not just an act of exhibitionism. It was a pale version of reverence, or perhaps appreciation. He lingered a moment looking at the clearing in the ochre blush of the street lamps. Then a voice came from behind him.

"Returning to the scene of the crime?" A woman's voice, droll, amused. He turned to see her sitting on a bench. Her face was plain but pleasant, a lock of dark hair drooping from under her parka hood half covered her forehead. Her feet were placed carefully side-by-side flat on the snow, her knees together in dark ski pants, and she was wearing a logan green parka trimmed with coyote fur. Her only concessions to fashion were scarlet mittens on her hands which were placed palms down on her lap, and a matching muffler draped, not tied, around her neck. She must have been sitting there the whole time, maybe a considerable time.

"Crime?" he replied.

"I saw you do it, you know—from up there." She gestured with her thumb back over her shoulder toward the apartment building across the street. It was the same window in which the silhouetted form had appeared. Now it surfaced from Beamer's memory, like frost feathers growing on a window pane.

"Do what?" Beamer challenged, feigning naïveté.

A sly smile pulled at the corners of her mouth as if to say, *you want to play? Then we can play.* "You came to the park yesterday, in the dark, after the snow storm, with a bundle of clothes. You stepped into this clearing and started making tracks in the snow and then you laid out the clothes as if—" she paused, inspecting his face closely for a moment, he sensing it not as judgement or evaluation, but as the tiniest pulse—of what?—of *intensity.* "—as if," she resumed, "some guy just left his clothes there in the snow and went sailing off naked into the sky."

"Quite an image," said Beamer. "Sounds cold."

That smile again, but this time with a slightly raised eyebrow. "Mmm. Exhibitionistic, wouldn't you say? Or maybe erotic."

"I doubt it," Beamer dismissed. "Do I know you?"

"I'm Tatum," she said. "Now you know me."

"Just like that?"

"Just like that. Why would you do something like that—with the clothes and all?"

"I don't know."

"Hmm," she mused. "I think you do know. At least you know some bits of it."

"What do I know?"

"Well, you may know that some Christian sects believe in something they call the 'rapture'—a moment just before the end of the world when God's elect are whisked away right out of their clothes to their heavenly reward while the rest of the world burns in the Last Judgement. Your composition there reminded me of that."

"That's what my girlfriend says. She says it creeps her out. But I'm not a Christian—I don't think. So it can't be that." He was talking with her—telling her things—as if he trusted her.

"Ah," she said. "Nevertheless, there must be something there for you." She continued to regard him intently from the one-down position of being seated on the bench. "Or maybe it's like that song, *We Gotta Get Out of This Place*... You know the one?" her expression more serious.

"Yes," Beamer said, "The Animals—1965. Maybe that's it. So are you a connoisseur of performance art or golden oldies music?"

"Is that what it was? Performance art?" She laughed. "Really? I thought it was more serious than that. You didn't just toss some clothes in a pile and be done with it. From up there," she cocked her head again in the direction of her apartment, "what you made looks like a mandala. It has four gates and four paths in the four cardinal directions. There's usually a central figure of some sort, but yours has fled the coop by leaping into the sky—or maybe being pulled. The central bit with the clothes is a square, representing humanity. The outer form is a circle, which usually stands for infinity, eternal return, the sacred principle—whatever you want to call it. People who know about these things say that mandalas appear in moments of personal or cultural crisis and symbolize the human predicament within the sacred compass. The Swiss depth psychologist Carl Jung thought that the appearance of mandalas in people's dreams were omens of some sort of major transformation—or calamity. But you seem to be dreaming while you're awake."

"Wow," said Beamer. "And here I thought I was just making performance art."

"Okay," she conceded, raising her mittened hands. "But an artist is not what you are, are you. And that's not what you did here, is it." They were statements, not questions.

"Tatum who?" Beamer deflected.

"I told you my name, so why don't you tell me yours?"

"My name's Beamer."

"Beamer? That's a rare name."

"Most people say it's just an odd name. Neither of my parents was a Trekkie. 'Beam me up, Scotty', or anything like that. But my mother named me after Lewis Carroll's poem, Jabberwocky. 'Hast thou slain the Jabberwocky? / Come to my arms my beamish boy!'"

Tatum shrugged and smiled with amusement. "There's no accounting sometimes for what people call their kids. Is that what the mandala is then, a doorway into Wonderland?"

"Maybe. So what's the rest of your name?" Beamer pressed.

"My name is Tatum Barnes."

"And you watched me making rapture mandalas from your perch up there," Beamer cocked his head, "and you're sure I know more about why I'm doing it than I'm willing to admit."

Tatum nodded slowly as she parsed what he said, then finally, "Yes. I guess you could say that. I have feelings for things like that." They regarded each other in a moment of silence and then Tatum spoke: "So that's what you call it? A rapture mandala?"

Beamer glanced away from her face and back to the now empty clearing in the park, covered only with tracked and rutted snow. "That's what my girl-friend calls them," said Beamer. "But she doesn't really know what a mandala is. Neither did I until tonight—at least not as much as you just told me."

"But that's not what you would call it?"

Beamer looked back at her. "I don't know what to call it." He paused, then, "It never occurred to me that I needed to call it anything."

"Perhaps not," said Tatum. "And yet, there it is. Is this the first one of these that you've made?"

Beamer sighed as if weary or resigned. "No. There've been others."

"Okay. So here we are. It's the middle of the night in the middle of December approaching the darkest time of the year. Your errand must be seri-ous or you wouldn't bother spending money and getting cold and wet making your mandala. You bring clothes to a public park and arrange them in a de-liberate display—something you've done before. But you're not a performance artist, or a Christian, or obviously crazy. You call these things mandalas but you didn't seem to really know what that word means. You're not a vandal or a nut bar, so this obviously has meaning for you. What do you make of it?"

Beamer continued looking at her with growing embarrassment as she spoke. Her insightfulness was disturbing. "Wait," he said, raising his hand to silence her. "Why are you so interested in this?"

Tatum looked away from him, casting her gaze back toward the clearing, trying to mute some of Beamer's stress by appearing casual, though it was late for that. "I get feelings about people. Plus, I have some friends who chime in on these sorts of questions sometimes," she said.

Beamer snorted. "And you're getting a feeling about me?"

Ignoring his dismissal, she said, "Well, yes."

"Why me? And what sort of feeling?"

Tatum's voice grew less firm. "It's hard to describe…"

In the moment Beamer's uneasiness and suspicion overshadowed his curi-osity. How had he wandered so far into something so personal with a virtual stranger? Maybe it was precisely because she was a stranger that he could go there. Now he felt vulnerable, exposed. He said nothing but his body language was unmistakable. He drew himself in and turned slightly aside, vigilant. Sensing that she had crossed Beamer's privacy boundaries, Tatum raised one shoulder and turned her head aside apologetically. "I'm sorry," she said. "I'm not handling this very well."

"I'll say," said Beamer, indignation rising but also feeling disarmed by her sudden embarrassment and awkwardness, feigned or not.

"I get these feelings about you because you do things like that," she nodded toward the clearing. "You know more than you understand. Some part of you wanted those clothes to be noticed by someone else. It was a message, not a prank. Maybe even a message from you to yourself. And it wasn't a message for me because you did your thing there in the park before you ever saw me. I've seen this sort of thing before. I know what you mean. And there are others who would know what you mean."

"So are you recruiting me for some cult or something?"

"Not recruiting," she replied, "inviting—maybe. And not a cult, but—something. We don't know what."

Beamer glared at her. He was both fascinated and disquieted by what she said. Her presumption annoyed him—that she thought she knew things about him after only ten minutes of conversation that he didn't know about himself. He also felt vulnerable. And yet he wasn't walking away, wasn't leaving. Why did their conversation have such a hold on him, like they were both suspended in time and space, and yet together? Perhaps because she was the first person ever to take his artefacts seriously? The thought made him even more uncomfortable. He wanted his madness in private.

"I'm sorry for how this has gone, I really am." She sounded sincere. "I hope we can talk some more, maybe tomorrow—or whenever."

"So you're going to give me your number now?" Beamer mocked.

"No. But I will be here if you want to talk more, here on this bench, around this time of day, for a few more days maybe."

"Look," said Beamer firmly, "I'm not sure I believe you are who you say you are or why we're having this conversation. Stay out of my head, understand?" His eyes smouldered, trying to hide the pang of reservation he felt.

"Of course," Tatum said softly. "As you wish." She stood up from the bench, clearly signalling an end to their conversation. She dropped her head, backing away from him, then turned and walked toward the street and the apartment building beyond. Then she stopped and turned back in his direction. "What's the rest of your name?" she called from her distance. Beamer made no reply.

Tatum walked out of the park leaving Beamer still gazing after her. She crossed the street and then stepped into the vestibule of her apartment building, buzzed herself in, and then dashed up the stairs to her suite. She opened her door to be met by the moist, loamy breath of the garden she tended in her rooms. She pulled off her parka and boots and hung up her mitts and muffler. Then she pulled off her ski pants to reveal leggings printed with leaf-like shapes. She opened her laptop and called the app that displayed the tracings from her plants. She spooled the recording back by an hour and then played it forward.

Normally, the tracings from the plants were long, smooth sine waves with occasional spikes or wrinkles when something of interest to them was happening—or about to happen. They could tell if she was planning to prune them, or if they were thirsty and Tatum watered them. Water was like a drug for them, sending their tracings into jagged mountains of celebration. If a plant could be said to have preferences, they seemed more interested in registering the intentions of others around them. Today, though, Tatum saw a pattern of tracings she had never seen before. The whole spectrum of tracings moved up the screen right around the time she had been sitting in the park. And instead of one or two plants registering a change, it was as if the whole group of them had raised their chorus together by a fifth. "Ha!" she said, and 'chortled in her joy.'

# CHAPTER 10

*In 1987, they said that 'sustainable development' was development that meets the needs of the present without compromising the ability of future generations to meet their own needs. Well, it's 2026. We've had two generations to get sustainable. Now you show me one goddam resource or species that's better off now than it was in 1987.*

— CALLER NO. 7 FROM *SERIOUS TALK WITH WILL PARSONS*

ANOTHER DAY and Beamer was again walking back toward his apartment. He sensed a gathering cloud of strangeness surrounding the figure of Tatum in his mind. Thoughts of her had gotten linked up with his homeward walks and passing Burins Park and mandalas—all becoming parts of a single sequence that would be re-enacted every day unless he wanted to take another route home. It was unusual these days for people to meet as they had, with no prior electronic handshake. Paranoia-fuelled anonymity was more the norm: people hiding behind layers of aliases, avatars and encryption at a time when miraculous communication technologies were supposed to bring everyone closer together. People shared the inter-subjective delusion of intimacy while privately they languished in their personal, sterile solitudes.

Who was Tatum Barnes? Assuming she was not the police (why the police?), or a stalker (exceedingly rare that a woman would stalk a man), the only remaining possibility was that Tatum was exactly who she said she was. And what was it that she said, exactly? That she watched people who were in the park from her window; that she was interested in Beamer because he made rapture mandalas in the snow; that she knew more about him than she was telling; that he knew more than he understood (whatever the hell that meant); that the raptures were messages, not just symptoms of derangement (how could she know?); she felt the same way as he did (whatever she thought that was) and that there were others who felt as they did; and she was inviting him to get involved in something for which she had no name—at least that she was willing to tell him.

The feeling that seeped into Beamer then was more dangerous than paranoia or anxiety, but he couldn't see the risk at the moment. What he felt was curiosity and, despite all his misgivings, the desire to talk with her again.

For one evening Tatum Barnes became The Mystery Woman in his imagination. By the time he reached his apartment, Vesper had already gone to bed. Her absence left Beamer free to pursue his curiosity which amounted to querying every search engine and social networking service he could think of for "Tatum Barnes"—in all the spelling variations he could imagine. At the end of it all, he had to conclude that either no such person existed or she had no online social contacts, professional or personal, that were accessible to a casual search. What was her profession anyway? He had no clue. Just one of many questions he now wished he'd asked when they were talking. But her wardrobe, mannerisms, and conversation all suggested an educated person and possibly a professional career of some description.

The next day he walked to work as usual—half hoping Tatum would see him and half hoping she wouldn't. On his homeward trek, he strode faster as he approached the park, at first not looking, not succumbing to the growing ambivalence he felt at the prospect of seeing her again. But in the very effort to do so, his ambivalence only grew more intense. There on the bench, facing toward the clearing and with her back turned to him was someone wearing a fur-trimmed parka with a scarlet muffler round her neck. Instead of being apprehensive about what Tatum might say if he talked with her again, he was more apprehensive about how he would feel if she gave up waiting for him. And without understanding any more about the question than he did about his impulse to make rapture mandalas, he knew that meeting her again would change everything. Could this be some part of knowing more than he understood?

He walked into the park with a confused mixture of feelings: apprehension for no apparent reason; determination pressing against invisible, perhaps wholly imaginary, resistance; courage absent any threat; persistence without clarity. The only thing that was clear was that he put one foot in front of the other until he stood behind the bench where Tatum Barnes was waiting for him. "Farris," he said. "My name is Beamer Farris."

"Please," she indicated the empty bench space beside her, "do sit." Despite the invitation to be at ease, her tone was cooler and more formal than the first time they met.

"Why are we here?" Beamer asked.

"Now that is the question, isn't it?" The way she said it opened a depth that wasn't part of Beamer's original intention. "Are we here," she mused, "to work, earn, produce, consume and then work some more, to the point of extinction? Are we here merely to sustain—more of this?" She cast her gaze vaguely toward the cityscape around them.

"I…" Beamer stammered.

"No more games," Tatum interrupted. "No more bobbing and weaving. Why did you come back here?" She fixed on him now, listening with her whole regard. She wasn't testing him, but she did sound pointedly intense.

"To see you," Beamer tried.

"Nonsense," she dismissed. "You said you have a girlfriend. You didn't come back here to see me."

"So why did I come?" Beamer wanted to hear her read his mind, especially the unconscious bits.

"Good question. Why *did* you come?" She wasn't helping.

"What do you want me to say?"

"Good god man! Surely you didn't come here to guess what I want you to say? This isn't about what I want."

Beamer felt stymied. Silence flowed in between them. Finally, "Why are we here?" she repeated, her tone softer, as if she was extracting a splinter.

Finally, "I came here because I make rapture mandalas in the snow." His voice definite enough that she accepted it, even though it was still mingled with some implicit wish to be right in her eyes, to pass her hidden test, whatever it might be. Why did he care?

"Continue."

"I came here because I know more than I understand—about the mandalas, I mean?"

She looked back at him, weighing what he said, without giving a sign as to what she thought. Then: "Beamer, do you think this is easy? Do you think what this is about is something you can just guess without effort—or that mere effort is enough? Do you think I know the answer for you? Do you think I even know it for myself?" Now there was something pleading in her tone as if she was standing by as he struggled to rouse from a coma, but in whose rousing she could have no other part than that of witness. They both sat there for some minutes looking at the clearing in the trees as the darkness settled into the place. Simply waiting together drew them closer. Presently, the sodium vapour light in the clearing gave a low hum, then flickered to life, slowly waxing in brightness.

"Light," he said.

Tatum looked at him, witnessing. "Continue."

"I came here looking for light," Beamer repeated. "I was just thinking about it here for the last couple minutes—that when I make one of those rapture things, I always feel like something dark is closing in on me, or growing in the air overhead, like a downpour—not just for me, but for everybody, all of us. And then I make one of those mandala things," his voice trailed off.

"And then?" Tatum prompted.

"And then, I don't know what to make of it. It's like an incomplete sentence, a dangling fragment, a grammatical error."

"I think you do know what to make of it. And I don't think it's an error."

Beamer sighed. "This is hard."

"Mmm, indeed," she nodded. "But consider this. Suppose you weren't making the mandala yourself, but you were like me, watching from that window up there across the street. What would you see?"

Beamer shrugged. "I'd see these tracks in the snow leading to a pile of clothes. It would look like some guy just jumped out of them."

"And what might that mean?"

"A wish to escape?"

"Maybe," Tatum said reflectively. "Is that all?"

"Maybe a hope?"

"Maybe."

"Maybe what else?" Beamer's impatience was palpable now.

Tatum looked more sympathetic, as if she guessed at something both more important and more difficult than she could express. "Maybe you're more grown up than that," she said. "Maybe the pile of clothes is not about wishing, or hoping, or anything comforting at all."

"What then?"

"Maybe it's a demand, or maybe a shot across your bow."

"Hell's bells!" Beamer exclaimed. "A demand for what? From whom?"

Tatum squirmed a little as she herself took in the strangeness of what she'd said. "Well, just think about it. You say you make these mandalas when you feel something dark coming—perhaps even menacing, no?" Beamer nodded tentatively. "And then pops into you the impulse to make this—this work—I don't know what to call it—opus, manifestation, thing. But it's not what most people do with snow. They make snow forts, or snowmen, or snow angels. They don't make depictions of raptures."

"So I'm worried about escaping something bad."

Tatum gave a little shrug, as if literally trying to wrap her whole body around some obscurity. "I'm guessing now," she said, "but I don't think you're worried exactly—though we all should be. Nor do I think you're trying to escape."

"So what am I?"

"You're dreaming—dreaming a nightmare. But you're waking up," she said matter-of-factly. "And you don't know what to make of it. But if Carl Jung was right, then that it should appear in the form of a mandala, no matter how crude, is damned important and doesn't just concern you."

They looked at each other, neither of them speaking. Beamer felt caught up in the simple truth of the moment. It couldn't be debated. It couldn't be avoided. It couldn't be argued or qualified or wished away. It was like his discovery of the tipping point coincidence. It was life slapping him in the face with something cold and wet and discomfiting, but also real and, as Tatum had said, demanding. A response was required. Not responding counted as a response.

Beamer cleared his throat. "So," he said, "what is it I'm waking up to?"

"What do you think?" Even now, Tatum was adamant.

"Why the guessing game?" Beamer groused.

"It's not a guessing game," she said—now more insistent. "Like I said, I can say whatever I like, but it's not coming from what you know as a fact of your experience. What can you say?"

He kept his peace for what seemed a very long time. He searched for words, trying to parse fact from speculation, knowledge from imagination, observation from projection. Impossible. Tatum sensed his paralysis. "Just say it," she urged.

"This," he began, this time casting his own gaze over the city, "all of this is passing away—or soon will. It's been scaring the hell out of me at work, you know? I shouldn't even be talking to you about it probably. But my boss gave me this assignment to review some trending stuff and try to come up with a 'youth perspective'—whatever that is—on environmental issues. But I started tracing these trends, especially ones with tipping points, where things go crazy on their own—like breaking into erratic oscillations or shifting away from a trend line and going after a strange attractor I can't see. Lots of people think about the trends, but not much about the tipping points. Capitalism likes nice smooth trends it can bank on, but not abrupt changes—for all their bullshit lines about 'disrupting'."

"And you think that's what the mandalas are about?" Tatum probed.

"I don't know," Beamer said with a sigh of weariness. "I don't know where the mandalas fit, if anywhere. But the thing that's really spooking me isn't the trends themselves, but when the tipping points are reached. I don't know what's going to happen; but I know when. I can almost see it, like one of those curtains of light they make with lasers at a rave or something. It's something that will literally happen, not a metaphor for some personal hang-up of mine, but something that will fall on all of us. The way we live can't continue. Everybody knows it. Nobody wants to believe it though. Some people think they can guess the game changer, but they can't. It's too complex, too deep. And there is no 'away' where you can go to avoid what will happen."

"The end of the world?" Tatum prompted.

"No," said Beamer with more certainty. "Like you said, that would be almost comforting if God reached down and saved some righteous people and blew up the rest and then handed us a shiny new planet all fixed up for our next round of self-indulgent excess. But no, I don't think it will be the end of the world. I think it will be the end of how we live in it, or maybe the end of us."

"And that's the darkness you feel coming?"

"I think so. Yes. Probably."

"Alarmist!" Tatum said, her voice changed as if she had become a different person. "What actual evidence makes you think that this way of life is threatened? We're the most powerful technological civilization in history. We have weapons. We have computers. We have the Internet and Google and Amazon and Facebook for god's sake. Look around you at the great city. Better yet, look at it from the air—all those sprawling suburbs, all that coloured quilt of farmland and light, those great tall buildings, the smoking chimneys, the bulging arteries of the super highways, the commerce that jams the rivers and the air routes and the oceans. We drill the seabed for oil. We split atoms for electricity. We splice genes like LEGO blocks and you can carry all human knowledge in the palm of your hand. All the land is our plantation where we harvest whatever we fancy, or whatever brings us profit. And think of the billions of people who get up every morning with one basic thought in their heads: How they can have just a little bit more—more food, more designer clothes, more holidays, more appliances, more toys, more lifetime. How could such a power simply stop?"

"I don't know," said Beamer. "But it will stop nine months from now with ninety-five percent certainty, nine months and eleven days with seventy percent certainty, nine months eleven days and twenty-one hours with fifty percent certainty. Because it all hangs by a thread hidden in denial. Google, Amazon, Facebook and all the rest, including the sum total of human knowledge you carry in your hand, all depend on the Internet, which in turn depends on steady electricity and a load of exotic materials some of which are in very short supply. All the rest, all of it, depends on cheap fossil fuels of one kind or another. On that account we have for a long time faced the dilemma of burning all of the fuels we can find and roasting ourselves in the bargain, or limiting our consumption to save the climate but at the cost of economic collapse. So far, we've opted to roast ourselves, or certainly our children. In any case, the prospect seems too far distant to worry about compared to the return on investment in the next quarter. Believe me; I've been researching this."

"On top of the economy," Beamer pressed, "there's us wasting the biosphere. The oceans are acidifying and littered with plastic scrap; the land is sterile and eroding; the water more polluted every day. Habitat is being destroyed and species lost as if an asteroid hit us. The invention of capitalism and consumerism is adding up to a mass extinction event for the only life we know. And there are precious few ways we can reverse the damage we've caused."

Tatum continued the contrary case. "But there are people far smarter and more powerful than us who are in control. They must have back-up plans."

"Well," said Beamer doubtfully, "there I would differ with you. I imagine some powerful people think they do have back-up plans, but I don't think they include us—people like you and me. And as to them being smarter or more prescient or altruistic than we are, I seriously doubt that. The people in charge of this train wreck are those who should be most pitied. Their feet are farthest off the ground. They're narcissistic psychopaths who are so totally tangled in the web of lies they've been spinning for the last three centuries they can't see their way out. Of all the people we might turn to, I would say that those responsible for creating this catastrophe would be the last people we should listen to about avoiding it. Their idea of power is money and violence, neither of which will be any use when things really unravel. At the moment, they seem to be powerful. But they soon won't be."

Tatum smiled at his intensity. "And?" she pressed.

"And," Beamer said, sighing, "we need to find a way out which is like people flying naked into a blizzard. What is *that*?"

"Exactly," said Tatum. "What *is* that?"

Again a silence grew. Beamer felt somehow lighter than before. Then: "You said there are others who also feel this way?"

"Yes there are," she confirmed. "But for now, maybe this is all we can do today. Way hasn't yet opened and way cannot be forced open. Before I say any more though, I need to know how much you believe what you just said. Do you really think this way of life can't keep on?"

"Yes, I do believe that," his voice carried more conviction now.

"And do you think the mandalas you make, the visions you have while making them, are true?"

"True for me," Beamer hedged.

"Stop that!"

"Stop what?"

"Stop that post-modern relativist bull shit!" She sounded fierce. "While the truth about which flavour of ice cream is the best may be different for different people, we're not talking about ice cream here. The truths that matter beyond the radius of my little world and your little world aren't like that. What's true is true, like gravity or electricity or love. It's not a matter of opinion, or popularity, or likes on Facebook, or the culture or time you live in. You know a thing to be true or not; it doesn't depend on likes. So is it true or not?"

Beamer looked flummoxed. "I don't know why this is such an issue for you."

"If what you say is true, then it's true for me as well as you. That makes it an issue for me," she said. "I need to know that you believe as a *transpersonal* truth that our way of life, this culture, is doomed. Otherwise, nothing else I might say about the other people who understand how you feel will make any sense."

"I'm sorry. I really am," Beamer said, almost pleading. "But I don't know what you're driving at."

Tatum sighed, but it didn't relieve the intensity in her tone. "Okay. Let me put it this way. For the last half century there have been a lot of groups who were disillusioned by the mainstream culture. Some of them struck off to form intentional communities of their own—communities that supposedly offered alternatives to the mainstream. Nearly all of them disappeared. Do you know why?"

"There must be a thousand reasons."

"No," said Tatum firmly. "There are only two reasons. One is that some of these experiments grew up from the vision of a single charismatic leader. When the leader died or moved on, the group fell apart, because it wasn't their *collective* vision that held things together. It was just the force of the founder's personality. The other reason is that deep down, many of those communities thought of themselves as 'experiments'—a kind of aristocratic hobby they could fiddle with in their spare time, or because of their idealism, or curiosity, or sometimes their indigence. They were like people browsing what they thought of as a cultural salad bar picking at this and that, but who knew they weren't *really* starving yet. And that meant that if the going got tough, they could always bail out and return to the still existing mainstream culture, despite the fact that it still had no future. They could always run back to mother culture. Their critical analysis may have been right, but it wasn't compelling, even to them."

"And so?" Beamer prompted.

"And so, if what you believe about our predicament is true, if your mandala is a true opening, a true manifestation of what this moment in history demands, there is no possible exit. Any alternative to it that we can imagine or create cannot be a mere experiment because anything we could return to will be gone. We'd have to get along with each other and make something that would last. That's why exactly how we jump out of these clothes we're wearing is so important. It must be based on truth, not idealism, altruism or one charismatic or autocratic individual. And whether or not you can accept it about yourself right now, you know something about what it is we have to jump into."

"How do you know that?"

"Because it's in the mandala," Tatum said with finality.

Beamer was quiet for a moment, as he felt an abyss opening under his feet. She really believed this. He really believed it. Suddenly, the whole prospect of his future, and the future of the society he lived in, shimmered and began to melt away. A shiver passed over him which was more than a draft of winter. Then: "You mean I would be sentenced to life."

Tatum looked startled, and then at last she smiled—the first time he'd seen her smile during their conversation—though it was a smile of relief rather than of mirth. She really was wound pretty tight, he thought. Then she nodded as she spoke. "You wouldn't be going to prison if that's what you mean. But yes," she confirmed, "this is a serious matter, because you know the alternative is extinction, both personal and collective. You know it as a truth as unyielding as gravity. Maybe you're wrong. Maybe we all are. If so, we're a pack of lunatics who need to change our meds. But if we're right, the price of not acting on this knowledge would be the ultimate one."

Beamer smiled back. "I think I would prefer to live."

"You would be amazed how few people do," Tatum said dryly.

"So, now what?"

"Now you have some decisions to make."

# CHAPTER 11

*The onset of a transition not only renders our own
behaviour opaque to ourselves, but socially, we appear
opaque to others. One symptom of this change is increasingly
strident calls for transparency. People call for transparency
when they feel blind. The old reality is breaking down
before their eyes, taking the visualization of their social
space with it. None of this is under anyone's control.*

— RUPERT PHILMORE,
*THE PSYCHODYNAMICS OF CULTURAL DISINTEGRATION.*

ARRIVING AT HIS APARTMENT, Beamer felt exhausted, like he was dragging anchor into port. Finishing his research, trudging through the snow, his emotionally exhausting conversation with Tatum had all left him weary and getting home much later than usual—something that frosted Vesper. She was nothing if not punctual.

Once he got in the door and doffed his coat and boots, Vesper was gazing back at him over the back of the sofa. The video screen was off which meant that Vesper wanted to talk. Her expression was a complicated mélange of dread, tearfulness, and anger all held precariously in check by a steely self-control and practiced communication skills. Beamer wondered how people could do that. His own mind was floundering in new waves of self-doubt about his own sanity, a sense of urgency living in the part of him that believed his own truth, and the problem solving bits that were just trying to find the right words—the honest words, the tactful words, the caring words, the words that kept doors open even as they were swinging closed—those right words.

"So," Vesper's voice was steady, like a sprinter waiting in the blocks, "is there some other woman?"

At first, Beamer couldn't read whether she was joking or meant her question to be taken seriously while asking it *sotto voce*. The conversation was going to be awkward, but he rolled his eyes and shrugged obliquely. "Of course not," he said, already feeling guilty for nothing. "I had a helluva day, worked late, and stopped in the park on the way home to try to clear my head. I'm sorry if I missed supper."

Vesper shook her head slowly, almost accusing. "You stopped in the park..." Was it a question? An accusation? And if an accusation, then on what grounds other than getting home late? Or the fact that most people didn't use parks in the winter. He wasn't a child with a curfew after all. "Beamer," she went on, "talk with me."

"I made a mandala," he said matter of factly, though he knew the reaction he would get. There was no point in jiving around. Having testified in his own prosecution he stepped sideways into the kitchen, skipping leftovers and reaching straight for a beer. Vesper waited silently until Beamer came into the living room.

"That's what you're doing now?" Vesper asked, her voice hard edged. "Making mandalas? It's just something I found on a stupid website!"

Beamer, somewhere between explanation and self-defence, shrugged in frustration. "The name doesn't matter. It's just a word. Call it whatever you want."

"I don't want to call it anything," Vesper said. "I want to understand it. You've done this before—once on a beach, another time on a golf course fairway and now twice in the snow. What's going on Beamer? It looks crazy you know."

"Yes," Beamer admitted, now sounding distant. "Yes, but I don't think I care."

"You don't *care*?" She sounded incredulous.

"It's just something that happens to me, like breathing or waking up in the morning. I just feel this head of steam building up inside, and then if I can make a mandala, I feel better. It's not hurting anybody." He looked back at her for some moments, letting a silence settle between them, even as she appeared as if through a telescope turned backwards. He hoped that she would recognize this shot over his bow as a provocation, a distraction. "This isn't about an 'other woman' situation and you know it." The truth of it helped him feel calmer.

Vesper looked away, shaking her head, although she believed him—which was even more troubling in a way. Another woman she could understand. She knew how she would handle another woman. But this, whatever it was, was another thing altogether... "So please, tell me again what this is really about."

Beamer took a breath—trying to parse whether Vesper had enough emotional distance on her forebodings to hear what he wanted to say. Nothing for it but to plunge in. "I'm not in bed with anyone but you," he said firmly, while in the same instant realizing that who he might be in bed with probably mattered less to Vesper than his emotional loyalty to her. Had that been compromised by a conversation as innocent as he had with Tatum? "But that's not what this is about," he continued. "I've told you before, I think this way of life we have is going to hell in a handcart and going pretty fast."

"A lot of people say that, but the sun still comes up, and the birds still sing, and shit still stinks."

"Yes, but the sun is warming us up and there are fewer birds and more shit than ever. Vesper, have you heard me over the last few months? I've got this government job that everybody is supposed to want and it's like chewing ashes all day long. It's so unreal it'll kill me in a year if I stay."

"So you want a different job?"

"It's more than that."

"What, more than that?"

"Something's coming, Vesper. I can feel it. I can almost smell it. It's right there in front of us—waiting in the next moment—the slightest shift away. It makes my skin crackle, like I'm being tasered. Everything we take for granted is changing, shifting underground, out of sight but moving everything. We need to change—somehow—or pass away. I want to be part of the change. I don't even know how. That's maybe why I keep making mandalas. Maybe I hope they'll show me something I don't understand now. Maybe they're some kind of doorway or something." His voice trailed off.

"Beamer!" Vesper's voice was genuinely pleading now, like his last words had touched something raw. "What can I do with that? *What can I do?* I *like* my job. I make good money. I like the people I work with. I like this apartment. I can shop for things and get things for people. *I like my life, Beamer!* What do you want me to do? Just walk away from it and go—where? Do you even know where? God, Beamer! Why would I do that?"

He looked at her with sympathy, not even sure himself that he was making the right choice. "You might do it because you want to stay with me," he tried. "Or, you might do it because you know that the future will not simply be a rerun of the past only more so. We're heading off the map here. Something is coming our way, Vesper. And either we take some hand in trying to shape it, if we can, or it will just happen to us whether we want it to or not. We're living in some speeded up delusion of the past. It can't last. It won't last. Did you hear me about the train blowing up and nearly killing me? And that's pouring oil into a river that a lot of people use for drinking water? Did you hear about the riots downtown because of food shortages in the stores? Did you hear about those things? The things that keep happening more and more often? And they're getting bigger all the time. And you think this way of life has a future?" This was grass they'd mowed many times before, enough times that Beamer always knew where it would end. He would be the Casandra, the negative pole to everything bright and shiny, the worst-case planner. He saw their future together through the lens of an impending event that would change everything. She saw impending events through the lens of their relationship and never the two could meet—though in her less guarded moments, Vesper would admit that larger-than-personal current events were starting to scare her too.

Vesper's face was streaked with angry tears. He could see her now, looking away, squaring her shoulders, her back straightening. "No," she said firmly. "I can't go there. No matter what happens, I don't want to go there. I won't go there. I *won't* even go for you. If I did, I'd only be going because of you, not because I really believed in it for myself. How is that fair? How could that be fair, Beamer? It all sounds crazy—paranoid. You sound crazy Beamer. You're barking mad, you know." She said it softly, with affection and condescension, as if he was a six-toed cat, and loveable on that account alone. There was also a tone of leave-taking in her voice, and of regret. It was true, she thought he was a bit mad—perhaps a lot mad. But she had never felt threatened in any way other than the strangeness of him sometimes. It was both off-putting and attractive, but only in a way.

Beamer's concerns—his *many* concerns—had been a subtext in their relationship from the beginning. He gave Vesper books about sustainable communities which she skimmed without reading. He dragged her off to lectures about climate change, and workshops on simple living, and panel discussions about food security, and gave her articles about pesticides and dying bees and melting glaciers and corrupt governments. He urged her to watch current affairs programs rather than sit-coms, to picket, to march, to write letters. He tried to be a mentor, an *agent provocateur*, a fellow explorer. But nothing about the hail of sparks he set alight caught fire in Vesper. In his way he had been as invested in changing Vesper as she was invested in changing him. But their daily experience always wound up leaving them on opposite sides of the table.

Their conversation was at an end. Vesper approached him tentatively, gently. They embraced without saying anything more, then holding hands went off to their bedroom. They made love slowly, attentively. This had always worked for them, always brought them back together across whatever distance had been separating them. This time, however, it was lovemaking that remembered its past, but couldn't imagine its future. They could both feel it. Their last kiss would be their final kiss.

# CHAPTER 12

*All cultures grow up around a myth—a creative fiction about
the nature of things. The myth is inter-subjective, meaning
that it is both shared among the members of the group,
the "inter" part, and carried in the brains of individuals,
the "subjective" part. This is the group's identity. When
the myth no longer interprets the experience of daily life,
then conditions are ripe for the collapse of the culture.*

— RUPERT PHILMORE,
*THE PSYCHODYNAMICS OF CULTURAL DISINTEGRATION.*

BEAMER AND HIS COLLEAGUES had all assembled again in the Environment
Ministry conference room. Bartley Coombs assumed his usual head table position flanked by Frankie Angeleno, Cecile Patterson, Lucy Sunderland and
Brian Cooper in places they had already staked out for themselves over the
course of many past meetings. Beamer's place somehow shifted around, as if he
was a migrant worker with no fixed address. Coombs was going on with various
items on his agenda which Beamer scarcely heard. He was nervous. He knew
Coombs would soon be fixing him with his blank stare, expecting a report on
his assigned task—presumably the task he had started working on before being
reassigned to the bridge failure hearings. Beamer hoped he could conceal the
fatigue and despair he felt for the whole exercise. And three, two, one…

"So—Farris," Coombs said, turning in his direction. "What have you got
for us?"

"What was he *supposed* to get for us?" Lucy Sunderland butted in. Her expression was that of a person who suddenly detected an offensive odour.

For an instant, Coombs looked annoyed, even with Sunderland, but managed a quick lateral pass to Beamer: "What were you after there Farris?"

"You asked me to do research on trends that might shape policies and regula-
tions we recommend to the Minister in the future. You told me I should bring a
youthful perspective to the question, although I couldn't find much on that really."

"I see," said Coombs. "So what did *you* find—over the last three weeks—if you don't mind telling us?"

"Well," Beamer said, a little lamely, "I spent part of that time in the bridge collapse hearings as you asked me to, but as to the original assignment, I can say that nearly all of our modelling is based on statistical projections each of which has its own sampling error and error of measurement. For interacting factors, the error margins also interact, effectively expanding the margins each time a new factor is added. So, the more factors, the more uncertainty. The more the model resembles the real world, the less its predictive value."

"So you're saying you came up with nothing," said Brian Cooper, half question and half declaration.

"Not exactly nothing," Beamer replied, a little defensive, "but probably not what you want to hear."

"What is it we don't want to hear?" Coombs again.

Beamer shifted a bit uneasily in his chair. "All of these models and projections are context-bound. By that I mean they all assume no fundamental changes in our society or our values. They assume the status quo."

"And?" Sunderland pressed.

"Well," said Beamer, "if you insist on the status quo, expect the unexpected." He looked around the table and every face was blank. "Let me give you an example."

"Please do," Coombs said testily.

"Surely you've noticed the food supply crisis over the last two weeks."

"How could you not?" Patterson this time. "It was like a developing country around here. Thank God they got it straightened out."

"But it wasn't," said Beamer. "And it isn't."

"Wasn't and isn't what?" Patterson pursued.

"It wasn't really a food supply crisis and it isn't straightened out," said Beamer.

"Okay," Coombs conceded, growing impatient. "So what was it and why isn't it fixed—and what does it have to do with Environment?"

"This mess started on the commodity trading floors, not in the supermarkets or on the farms," said Beamer. "And there was no real shortage of anything, just a perceived shortage fed by a bogus positive feedback loop. The crisis was at one level, imaginary, but at another level, it was real."

"Hells bells boy," Cooper chimed in, "You should write horoscopes. What the hell are you talking about?"

Beamer leaned back in his chair. "Okay," he said. "This is what went down. There are boys in red suspenders, as they say, on Wall Street and Bloor Street and Fleet Street and Beijing Financial Street who think they are in the boiler room of the capitalist dreadnought. The world they think they run was made by people who actually work for a living. But it doesn't stop them gambling with those other people's money. Occasionally they make mistakes. But their mistakes differ from the garden variety mistakes made by ordinary mortals mostly in their scale. The adrenaline junkies in the boiler room make really big mistakes."

"About seventeen days ago," Beamer continued, "some trader somewhere in the boiler room ticked a box labelled 'buy' when, had he been less under the influence of cocaine, he should have ticked 'sell.' The buy/sell order concerned five hundred thousand barrels of diesel fuel, a substance the boiler room boys refer to as a fungible commodity. Fungible commodities are goods that can be swapped for money, or other commodities of similar value, or can become the targets of speculators, every possibility taking its little vampire nip out of the value chain as fungible commodities flowed by on their screens. Since the business of fiddling with commodities can be both erotic and lucrative, it also has a hypnotic-like power to separate traders from the reality of the goods they trade."

"Every surprising catastrophe (and most catastrophes are surprising) also includes a coincidence of factors which might not usually occur together, but in such cases as catastrophes, suddenly they do. In the case of the diesel fuel, the buy order coincided with a pre-existing market trend toward scarcity of fuel and the buy order became the proverbial straw breaking the mule's back. The mistaken purchase of half a million barrels of diesel produced a dent in the supply levels for that fuel, at first locally, then regionally, and finally nationally. Already marginal supply levels appeared to computerized trading systems to be at a critical, and therefore potentially a profitable, shortage—a tipping point. Ever vigilant for feeding opportunities, traders issued more 'buy' orders to try to lock up supplies of fuel which, under conditions of market scarcity, were likely to increase in price. This snowballed through the market producing what appeared to be a catastrophic fuel shortage which, in the globally connected markets of the modern world, sloshed back and forth to some considerable degree before being damped out for other reasons."

"Nevertheless," Beamer continued, "when word got around that there was likely a diesel shortage spreading along the eastern seaboard of North America, buy orders continued to pop up as users of the fuel, mostly trucking companies and corporate farms, tried to lock up their supplies as hedges against real shortages and increasing prices. This in turn created what is called a positive feedback loop: rumours of shortages created actual shortages which then fed back as news of real shortages which further stoked rumours, and increasing prices at the core of the storm, et cetera, et cetera. Anxiety about prices soon became conflated with anxiety about actual supplies of fuel, although no real supply shortage existed."

"So you're saying this whole fubar situation was imaginary?" Lucy Sunderland sounded incredulous.

"The problem with your question," Beamer said with more respect than he felt, "is that it conflates 'imaginary' with 'unreal.' Even though it was a fact in the physical world that there was no fuel shortage, the belief that there was a fuel shortage—imaginary though it might have been—is still a fact, but of a different order. That we are constantly at risk of mixing up physical and psychological facts is half of what I have to say to you today. It's a problem I don't see a solution for."

"Anyway," Beamer continued, "it was in this situation that we discovered the meaning of 'just-in-time' production. Ever since globalized free trade became the status quo in the 1980s and '90s, both raw materials and finished goods moved around the world in a far-flung network of trade that depends on information technologies to run the communications side of the global trade network. Fossil-fuelled transportation actually moves stuff around. The move away from maintaining large inventories of goods in warehouses and toward a system where goods aren't supplied, or sometimes even manufactured, until there is an order for them—the 'just-in-time' meaning of the system— turned out to offer corporations another source of profits by reducing storage, insurance, and other costs. But this advantage for corporations came at the cost of making the whole system incredibly brittle, though invisibly so. Most of us have no inkling that such a system even exists, or how precarious is our way of life. Fuel shortages, imagined or real, can go through this system like an enema."

"So a few days ago, a buy order became a rumour, which became a trading opportunity, which created an imaginary shortage, which created real shortages in all sorts of things in addition to fuel, which first triggered line-ups and then riots, which destabilized governments. Shipping companies, worried that their rigs might become stranded all over the country because of fuel shortages, decided to park them in their depots for a few days while things got sorted out. This included trucks that shipped food, medical supplies, and all manner of goods to retail outlets. What most of us probably noticed was a lull in heavy truck traffic through the city. But after only two days, you must have noticed that the produce, meat and dairy sections of the grocery stores looked pretty picked over. By day three, perishables were gone, there was more grumbling in the check-out lines, more complaining, more grousing, and then near panic as shoppers cleared shelves of just about anything that was edible. Restaurants closed all over the city and hotels and convention centres were finding it hard to feed their guests. Major sporting events were postponed for lack of concession supplies. Doctors warned of critical shortages of medications. Car dealerships and repair shops not only faced shortages of parts, there were emerging shortages of new cars themselves. Just-in-time supply management assured that in most communities the population was about five days away from starvation, their usual sense of food security a complete delusion, but the whole arrangement was immensely profitable for corporations."

"Within four days there were demonstrations in six Canadian provinces and nine American states that threatened to destabilize their local governments. For their parts, governments passed emergency legislation ordering truckers back to work and a mostly useless inquiry into the causes of the food panic. It's obvious that the causes are structural, that is, they are built right into the particular status quo we've made for ourselves. After another two days, things returned to 'normal.' The news cycle moved on to other scandals. Nothing to see here folks. Move along." Beamer tossed his pen onto the table top in a gesture of finality.

The room was quiet for a moment, then Coombs retrieved his sense of control. "So what does this have to do with us here in Environment? I'm still not seeing the connection, Farris."

Beamer shrugged. "This is just an example. We live within a very complicated machine which I'm saying is more complicated and inter-connected than most of us appreciate most of the time. And there are ghosts in the machine, Mr. Coombs. Something like this food crisis—which wasn't a food crisis at all, but a system function crisis—will happen again. Looking backward, we can start to see the development of trends and tipping points which made the systems crash inevitable. But looking forward, the trends and the tipping points are a lot harder to see. Whatever part of the machine the ghosts visit will fail. And it may be a failure that isn't as easy to recover from as this last one was. Everything is vulnerable to these faults: our tendency to conflate reality with imagination and trends and tipping points we tend only to see in a rear-view mirror. The Ministry of Environment is not immune to these, but the trends and tipping points will appear in the ecosystem in addition to the economy. We manage the environment the same way we manage the economy. They cannot fail to mirror each other. This is a catastrophe waiting to happen and we could be addressing it from an environmental perspective as well as any other. We're mistaking our mission every day. We shouldn't be here just resupplying the toilet paper in our public campgrounds. We should be making the case that tipping points in the environment can crash the economy just as well as a tipping point in finance can."

Coombs slapped his meaty hands on the meeting room table. "You've given us a lot to think about, Farris." Though it seemed clear that neither Coombs nor anyone else was inclined to do that. "I think it's time for a break. I'm open to any ideas anyone has about how to follow up on this report, if at all. Have a think over lunch." The room emptied quickly except for Coombs and Beamer. Coombs looked at a loss. His hands were still palms down on the table top and now he spread his stubby fingers as wide as they would go, raised his eyebrows, and then, "You've got to give us something more than this, Farris. I don't see where you're heading or what use you thought this yarn would be to us. I'm trying to take you seriously here and I'm hoping this wasn't some kind of intellectual stunt or something. What are we supposed to do with this?"

Beamer looked back at his supervisor, his expression mirroring Coombs' own look of perplexity. The comment that what he said might be a stunt offended him but he felt it rolling off. There was a much larger ball of dread he felt considering the fact that he now thought he could predict tipping point coincidences. This was a familiar feeling, but now it evoked the image of Tatum and the park and the disturbance of the snow. He felt himself standing at the edge of something dark and abysmal. All of this mattered desperately. Finally, "I don't know what you should do," Beamer said, as he imagined his future in the civil service circling a drain. And he didn't care.

A couple of days later, Beamer stood outside Bartley Coombs' office door feeling remarkably tranquil as he held a number ten business envelope in his left hand. He thought that when it came to it, he would be anxious, but the exact opposite turned out to be the case. With every step, beginning with the very smallest ones of packing his duffle and back pack, handing his apartment keys to Vesper along with enough money to pay out his share of what remained of their lease, he in fact felt more grounded and calm. Vesper was upset but stoic. Beamer expressed his concern for her well-being without being sentimental or melodramatic. She accepted his expressions with poise and resignation. It was about as good a parting as one could hope for. Both were aware that their paths in life were diverging, perhaps had been diverging from the earliest days of their relationship. But Beamer was leaving without rancour and Vesper, he hoped, was letting him go without rancour. Now, standing outside Coombs' office, he was about to take another step. He could hear Coombs in animated discussion with someone on the phone. Beamer waited until the conversation seemed to be over, and then he waited a while longer to avoid appearing as though he had been lurking outside the door. He knocked lightly.

"Come!" Coombs shouted. Beamer pushed the door open with the urgency that mirrored Coombs' command and took a couple of steps to stand in front of his desk. Coombs looked up, his expression flushed red with the residue of annoyance from the phone call. But he also looked blankly at Beamer as if unable to recognize him. Then: "Farris! What can I do for you?"

Beamer proffered the sealed business envelope. "I'd like to resign, sir." The calmness of his tone threw Coombs' state of agitation into higher relief. "Immediately," Beamer added.

Coombs stared back at him blankly for a moment, then said, "Well, alright." As he imagined this moment, Beamer thought of Coombs forcefully urging him to reconsider his decision; or to remember how coveted was a position in the civil service, the benefits, the perks; or how much his colleagues depended on his insightful contributions to their shared task of protecting the environment, et cetera, et cetera. But in a moment all these were revealed as the rankest self-flattery. Coombs even looked relieved of some burden. "Alright," he repeated. "Is that your letter?" he asked, nodding in the direction of the proffered envelope.

"Yes," Beamer confirmed, then rummaged inside his back pack to withdraw a computer flash drive. "And I've brought this stuff which is from the research I was doing, in case someone else will be picking it up," and laid the flash drive on Coombs' desk.

Coombs nodded and then looked up at Beamer. "So, did you win the lottery or what?"

Beamer shook his head. "That would be nice, but no cigar."

"So what are you going to do now?"

Beamer chuckled hollowly. "As usual," he said, "you're asking the wrong question."

"The wrong question?"

"Yes. The right question is about what you should do now."

Coombs shook his head in puzzlement again. "I don't get what you're driving at Farris."

"You're in a position of power here. You have the Minister's ear if you want it. You should be setting off alarms everywhere. You must know that our present way of life can't continue as it is—not just the part that concerns the unravelling environment—but the whole thing. We're all captive on this runaway train," Beamer paused while a shiver of memory and anxiety flashed over his skin. "We can't sustain what we've built. You need to use all the influence you have, with whomever you have it, to start finding exits from this situation, not defending it to cover the Minister's ass. Look at the research on the flash drive. You'll see that I've identified a major tipping point intersection about nine months from now. At least a dozen important trends will peak and interact then. Maybe some of them can be stopped before then. You should be alerting people. The house our children have to live in is on fire, Mr. Coombs, and we need better from ourselves than just buying some sandwiches and having another meeting."

While Beamer spoke, Coombs' expression shape-shifted first one way and then another, finally settling into weariness and resignation with just a hint of stubborn anger. His eyes were cold and penetrating. "Do you think I'm an imbecile Farris? What you say may or may not be true…"

"You know it's true," Beamer butted in.

"…*but* even if I had air tight evidence that it *was* true, how far do you think that would go? There's uncertainty around every issue you've alerted me too and no damn reason to turn society inside out based on a theory—not even a theory. What you're giving me is a hunch. People's pensions are at risk, their investment portfolios, their mortgages. No Farris. I'm not about to flush my career down the crapper because of something a junior analyst dreamed up for a meeting in the nick of time."

Beamer nodded, his face grave. "Okay," he said. "Then this is the score. Something is going to happen. I don't know what, but it will. It's *the* thing, or things, that start the ball rolling. There may be violence or there may not. But if there is any interruption to the power grid, people on life-supporting machinery will be at risk on the very first day. In ten hours, most cell phone batteries need recharging. Depending on what the "something" is, people may be in shock, frightened, panicky."

"By day two," Beamer continued, "if the something happens in winter, people will begin to die from hypothermia. If in summer, they will suffer eat stress. Basic services like water, sewer and fuel supplies may be interrupted. The incubation period for influenza is two days and an increase in cases is to be expected if sanitation cannot be maintained. By day three, emergency back-up power to hospitals, jails, water and sewage plants will fail. Perishable foods will be gone from store shelves. Cholera incubates in three days."

"By day four or so, grocery stores will be empty and people may be fighting over whatever food and medicine is left. Diabetics will die in large numbers as their insulin supplies disappear. A black market will appear to supply emergency provisions for those who can afford them, but the entire system will be brittle and unstable."

"Lacking clean water, most people die of dehydration in five days or so. Most stocks of frozen foods will be spoiling and the Internet will probably collapse as its emergency back-up batteries are drained. Everything that depends on the Internet will also collapse—which is to say, just about everything."

"After about seven days, the forty percent of the general population who live with a life-threatening disability will die as medical supplies, drugs and skilled healthcare workers are exhausted. Also around seven days, pro-social coping behaviours that arise early in an emergency situation begin to fade out as well. Police forces and first responders will be the best armed gangs in town and most police will want to protect their families rather than risk their lives to help strangers. The same behaviour is to be expected from anyone with a badge and some kevlar."

"After ten days, the eight percent of the population with Type-II diabetes will likely succumb, dysentery will have incubated, and vigilante groups may have formed to impose some measure of order on the community. Legitimate governments will suffer elite panic and slowly dissolve in the acid of acute emergency."

"Note that these things are likely to happen within the space of just ten days. After thirty days most people over sixty-five, twenty percent of the population, will succumb to a variety of afflictions depending on the weather and exposure risks to a variety of diseases and malnutrition. Most people die of starvation within two months. In three months gasoline and diesel fuels spoil thus bringing to a halt anything that runs on a fossil fuel, including the vehicles and machines needed to recover from whatever the "something" was. If transport and production systems cannot be restarted, seed stocks spoil within two years, cell phones fail by design after three years, and things get worse from there. It's all just waiting to happen. All we need is the "something" and I'm telling you it will be here in nine months."

Both men stood glaring at each other across a desk which seemed as wide as the broad Sahara. Coombs, seemingly unfazed by what Beamer had just said, was the first to speak. "So," Coombs sighed, as what Beamer had just said made no discernible impression at all, "what are you going to do now?"

Beamer smiled to himself, then "I'm going to help some people build a bridge."

"Huh," Coombs mused, "how about that. I didn't know you had experience in the building trades, Farris."

"I don't," Beamer said. "None of us do. Good luck to you Mr. Coombs."

"And to you too, Farris." Coombs sounded relieved and dismissive. "Do drop in to HR on your way out. They will have forms they want you to sign."

"No doubt," Beamer said over his shoulder as he turned and walked out of Coombs' office, every step feeling lighter than the last.

# CHAPTER 13

*The task of deep transformation is often portrayed as a hero's quest. This sometimes involves literal movement through space or time, but it seems always to include walking among ghosts.*

— QUINTON FARRINGTON, *THE ARCHEOLOGY OF DREAMS*

"SO DOES THIS PLACE we're going to have a name?" Beamer asked. It felt like they had been on the road forever, but in reality, only about three hours. They'd driven to the end of a highway, turned onto another highway and driven to the end of that, then turned onto a gravel road over which their van had been slewing and rattling for three quarters of an hour. The first leg of their journey had taken them south past great expanses of open farmland, at this season covered in grain stubble and eddies of snow swirling through the decrepit looking frames of irrigation sprinklers. To a transient observer, the land looked much as it had for the last hundred and fifty years when farming was first started in the area. But with the aid of measurement and historical perspective, it was obvious that the topsoil was becoming shallower and the snow pack thinner every year. The land was, in fact, in drought and its fertility depleted to the point where meaningful yields could be got only with chemicals and irrigation. The rapidly changing climate was in fact tipping the balance in the long struggle between prairie and boreal forest in favour of the prairie. Their route took them east out of farming country and into aspen-spruce parkland, a more rolling land contour sprinkled with small ice-covered sloughs, glades of aspen trees and in summer, meadows of prairie fescues, purple vetches salted with buttercups, bluebells and black-eyed Susans. The area was better suited to grazing animals and haying than to large scale grain production. Eventually, the land came to be peppered with white spruce trees, balsam fir, tamarack and paper birch as the parkland gave way to the most distal fringes of the great boreal forest that went eastward to girdle the planet. The forest was the child of a mini-ice age 13,000 years ago called the Younger Dryas that lasted for about 1,200 years. The Younger Dryas was itself the off-spring of what some said was an interruption of the Atlantic Meridional Overturning Circulation—the Gulf Stream—that helped keep eastern North America warm after the Laurentide glaciation. Others thought it was the result of a cometary bombardment over the Great Lakes that dimmed the sun for years. When the smoke cleared, the story went, most North American Pleistocene megafauna (big animals) were extinct and the world resumed its slow post-glacial warming. Back then, nature orchestrated her own climate changes without human meddling. Shallow, sandy soils, high acidity, and other factors favoured forests which now were robed in snow deeper than any found on the flats to the west. Trees had a way of watering themselves if only there were enough of them.

The van Tatum was driving was stuffed with boxes, bags, and plastic tubs full of all manner of supplies, tools and notably, a dozen new solar panels. Any trip from the city to the country doubled as a delivery run. There was barely enough room to squeeze in Beamer's backpack and duffle bag, with Beamer himself cradling a large tub of salt between his feet in the front passenger seat.

"It's called Badger Coulee," Tatum replied, not taking her eyes off the road.

"Badger Coulee?" Beamer echoed. "Odd."

Tatum shrugged. "Yes. It was one of those things where we just adopted the existing name because nobody else came up with anything better. Keeping the old name also meant that nothing changed for the locals, and therefore drew no special attention to us. When you live in places where nothing much changes very quickly, any change is noticed immediately and gets to be a topic of coffee shop chatter—something we would prefer to avoid. Badger Coulee seemed good enough. So I guess you could call us Badger Couleans."

The van rattled along for a time, then Beamer asked: "Do you live at Badger Coulee then?"

"Ha! I'm not sure where I live. As you can see, in addition to other things, I'm a sort of transporter, so I'm on the road a lot. I live part-time at the Coulee and part in the city. Story of my life. Whenever one of us is coming from the city, we bring a truckload of whatever people need. My part at the Coulee varies with the season. In the winter, I spend quite a lot of time in the city doing research—finding people like you, working through social networks, personal contacts, public record research, that sort of thing. Then I figure some way to meet them, have a few conversations, and if things are agreeable, I invite them to visit the Coulee. It's a slow process, but so far it's been working for us. There are a score of other people scouting the same way. They call us Finders."

"And the rest of the year?"

Tatum shrugged. "Well, the rest of the year I divide my time between the Coulee and doing landscape architecture in the city. It's commissions from that that keeps body and soul together for the time being. I live very simply. So the commissions I make on a handful of contracts in the spring and summer are more than enough to keep me through the winter. My real passion is permaculture—which I do at the Coulee, but I slid sideways into it through landscape architecture. Odd passage, actually. Most people get to permaculture through fringy agriculture programs or environmental studies stuff."

"Sounds right up my alley," said Beamer doubtfully.

"Might be. Who knows? You'll have plenty of time to find out before fall if you stick around with us. There are lots of other things going on besides gardening. Some of my best friends are plants."

"Sometimes the way you say things sounds like there's more to say but you're not going to say it." Beamer watched for Tatum's reaction but there was practically none.

The scattered patches of conifers now massed ahead of them as a dark wall of vegetation that in this season took on a grey-green cast. The sun was lowering in the west and casting all the snow in a lemony-golden light. Tatum slowed down and turned off the gravel road back onto a paved one. It was as if she was approaching the Coulee round about rather than directly on the paved road.

"Welcome to Badger Coulee," she said. "Occupying a ghost town that used to be about four hundred people. Date of founding unknown. Business opportunities zero. Unemployment rate crowding ninety-five percent this time of year. Housing stock mostly fixer-uppers. Key attractions are solitude, ready access to nature and a big Quonset we no longer use for a hockey rink. It was the biggest building in town, so we called it the Barn."

"How on earth do you survive with ninety-five percent unemployment?"

"Social enterprise," said Tatum cryptically. "It takes some explaining."

"Ghost town?" said Beamer.

"Well," Tatum qualified, "we haven't seen any actual ghosts yet. But places like this are all over the prairies. In the 1950s when farming really started to mechanize here, the economics of it made larger single crop farms a better bet than the smaller mixed farms of the past. So bigger farms ate up smaller farms, and then eventually even the bigger farms were swallowed by corporations and non-resident land holding companies. Believe it or not, a lot of Europeans view land ownership as a form of security, even if they don't live on the land they own. So around here, the land may be owned by somebody in Germany, say, but rented out to a local farmer who actually farms it to pay his rent and take a cut as a share cropper. What this did was to empty the rural areas of people, since far fewer people were needed to manage the larger more automated farms. When we found this place there were only a dozen families struggling to survive here mostly by commuting to a larger centre to work a job until they could sell out. The rural municipality was flat broke and pretty much anybody with a pulse could be a reeve. So we made a few offers on some properties and 'Bob's your uncle' we owned a town—or at least part of it. Gradually more of us filtered in, squatted the vacant houses that were still livable until we could secure title and went from there. Now almost all the people in the village are Coulee people."

They drove past a number of small houses that might have been of 1940s or '50s vintage and all in varying states of disrepair, though some showed signs of recent efforts to renovate or maintain them. Some had over-sized garages that had probably been used to shelter extra vehicles or small home businesses like farm machinery maintenance, welding, construction trades or the like. They came to a small scattering of commercial and institutional buildings all of which appeared to be miniature versions of their big city counterparts—a rural munic-ipality office that shared a roof with a post office, a coffee shop combined with a gas station both now abandoned, a sturdy looking brick and concrete building that housed a water pumping and purification plant, a scattering of small service and outbuildings one of which apparently housed the works for a cell tower, an electricity transformer station, and a few others of uncertain use. One could tour the town centre of the place in one sweeping glance. Definitely the most promi-nent building in the hamlet was the aging Quonset. Its galvanized hull stood as a sizeable rebuke to the village that was slowly disintegrating around it. Beside the Quonset was a small equipment garage.

Tatum drove the van directly into the garage and killed the engine. "Welcome to the eighteenth century," she said dryly.

"Shangri-La!" Beamer quipped, feigning excitement.

"Well, sort of," said Tatum. "It's beautiful here, especially in the summer, as I hope you'll appreciate. But Shangri-La was both hidden and enchanted, and we're neither."

"So this isn't your hide-out against the coming apocalypse?"

"If only," Tatum smiled ruefully. "While I think we agree that the apocalypse is coming, we haven't figured a way yet to escape from it. I think the Buddhists have the idea when they call their most sacred doctrines 'self-secret.' They don't have to be kept secret because they're hidden in plain sight. The reason is that a person has to be ready for a teaching in order to get its meaning. Someone who isn't ready can listen to the teaching all day long and still not get it. The Coulee is like that. People come here all the time, just dropping in, or maybe looking for things to steal, or for barn siding for their rec room feature walls, or neighbours stopping in for this or that or because they're curious. We fix them tea and give them a cinnamon bun. But what most of them see here is a bunch of third generation hippies mucking about in the sand and the trees and the mosquitoes. What we're really up to remains hidden not because we deliberately hide it, but because they don't stay long enough to understand it, or if they ask us, we just tell them the truth—which they don't understand either."

"The only exception has been a group of Quakers," Tatum said.

"Quakers?"

Tatum nodded. "It started out with just one of them wandering into the Coulee one day. But instead of passing through, he stayed, and talked, but mostly listened. Then he disappeared for a few days, and then came back with two other friends, or Friends, as they call themselves. Now there are about fifteen adults and half a dozen children. They have a lot of Meetings and sometimes say things about the Light, and keeping silence, and looking for way opening—whatever that means."

"Weird," said Beamer.

"Actually, they're quite nice," Tatum defended. "They're definitely eccentric, but good hearted. A lot of us are more eccentric than they are, so we get along."

"So it's easy," Tatum continued. "If visitors *do* get what we're talking about, they usually want to stay, which we welcome. But most of them never come back and never bother us. Our life here neither interests nor threatens them, which is just how we like it. Cultural co-evolution isn't a coffee shop topic around here. But in the end, it's not a very good hide-out if things really go south on us. So we think of ourselves as a community in migration—although we don't know where we're going yet."

"Nine months," Beamer reminded.

"Yes," said Tatum. "You've done the math and we have nine months and for some reason I trust your math. And I trust you. Now we just need to figure out where to go."

They cracked the doors of the van and got out of the vehicle. A number of men approached the van, one of whom embraced Tatum in welcome while the others opened the rear doors and started unloading the cargo.

"Beamer Farris, meet Jasper Beckett," Tatum introduced the man she hugged. "Jasper, meet Beamer. Beamer's a new pledge."

Jasper extending a meaty hand which Beamer clasped in response. "Watch her," Jasper grinned, "she's a Permie and Permies are all Earth motherly and mysterious."

"You've been known to pull a hoe," Tatum retorted. "Could you let the House know we're here? I brought cargo, and I'm taking Beamer to find his room, the Board, and our lovely composting toilets. And, oh, there's two hundred more kilos of plaster of Paris for Changming in the van. It only comes in twenty kilo boxes, so watch your backs. He must eat that stuff or something."

"Consider it done," Jasper saluted and strode away toward a door in the shed.

"Grab your gear and follow, please," said Tatum.

They left the shed and tramped along a well-packed snow path leading to the Barn. The building itself was perhaps twenty metres wide and over a hundred long, and despite the name they had given it, probably never actually served as a barn. More likely it had been a community arena, or perhaps a farm machinery dealership. It appeared that dormers had recently been set into its sides, probably to lighten the space inside. Beamer noticed that most of the south side of the structure was covered in PV panels. This also happened to be the side of the building that faced away from the street, thus leaving the impression with passers-by that there was really nothing to see here.

As they approached the door, Beamer noticed a small, framed sign. It read: "Know this: Everything is on its way somewhere else. Have your ticket ready."

"Cute," Beamer quipped.

"Don't say that around Corbin Galen" she said. "I'm sure you'll meet him sooner or later. He's dead serious about those things. He puts signs all over the Coulee and changes them every few days. They're supposed to be reminders to all of us to practise mindfulness—even those of us who are still learning it. They actually sort of work—people kind of like reading them, like your horoscope or a thought for the day. And they sure beat 'Stay off the Grass'."

"Well," said Beamer, "'Have your ticket ready' makes you kind of pause."

"That's his whole point," said Tatum. "This way."

The inside of the Barn was completely different from the corrugated galvanized greyness of its exterior. They first came into a spacious anteroom with many pegs for hanging coats and sitting benches for donning and doffing boots. The anteroom opened into a lengthy passageway down the centre of the building and about half its length, the passage having been timber framed with timbers that looked like they had been laminated from pieces of dimensional building lumber salvaged from demolitions. The passage itself was lined with doors on both sides, some open, and some closed. Tatum led Beamer along the passage without making any side stops until it opened into a single, large room at the far end of the building. In the farthest wall of this room was an open fireplace made of field stone, and several smaller wood stove heaters at the perimeter of the room. The space was furnished with long picnic tables, lots of folding chairs and additional folding tables.

Tatum swept her hand dramatically around the space. "This," she said with mock grandiosity, "is the Board Room. It's called the Board Room because it contains the board—our dining hall. It's also our meeting room, multi-purpose room, and party palace all in one. Members of the Coulee who don't have their own houses meet here for most meals. A lot of us meet up at the Barn entrance for a run around the village every day at five. It's about a seven kilometre run, pretty fast, but you'll finish in time for breakfast. Breakfast from six to seven. Lunch around noon. Supper at six. We're mostly vegetarian here. Eat what's being served or fix yourself a peanut butter and jelly sandwich—as my gran used to say. We have some killer jams and jellies here though, if it comes to that. There's meditation practice every day in the Lighthouse—an old one room schoolhouse we've fixed up about fifty metres that way. All are welcome they say, or not, as you wish. The Lighthouse is also a yoga and martial arts dojo taught by Corbin Galen. Lessons are free. Times are posted outside. The whole place is also crawling with kids most of whom are home-schooled, although we do use the school house part-time where they attend some classes together. Now, please follow," she said.

They turned left out of the passageway to see a timber framed staircase against the near wall of the Board Room that took them up to a mezzanine. A balcony proper crossed the space with views of the Board Room below, and another, narrower passageway led back along the way they had come, but one level higher. This hall too was lined with doorways, and outside one of these Tatum brought Beamer to a stop.

"This will be your room for a while. You might think of the Barn as a combination community centre and half-way house. You're welcome to stay here until we find another place for you. There are about twenty other people living in this building right now. Midway down the hall on both sides are washrooms, toilets and showers. Everything is unisex, so cover up if you're twitchy about that sort of thing. Most people here aren't. Do join us for breakfast in the morning. I'll find you and get you to your entry interview."

"Entry interview?" Beamer looked surprised.

Tatum's expression was grave. "Yes. There are twenty questions. You're not allowed to know what they are beforehand. You have to get them all right or we kill you."

Beamer gazed at her blankly. Then she laughed. "Just get some sleep," she said, pushing the door open, then turning on her heel, she left.

As Tatum disappeared down the hallway, Beamer stepped into his new quarters. They were definitely Spartan but also to his liking. The ceiling of the room curved down from overhead, but its concave shape was relieved by dormer windows set into the steel that offered a pleasant view of the forest beyond the yard. The few furnishings all looked hand-built, plain, sturdy, practical. There was a twin bed, a pile of fresh bedding and linens, a chair, a small writing desk under the dormer window, a closet with built-in drawers in a wall shared with the next room. LEDs were both on the desk and over the door. On the desk lay an attractively bound book and a pen lay beside it. Beamer picked up the book and opened it. On the first page was an inscription in cursive writing: "You will need this book to make sense of what is about to happen." Then he rifled through the pages and all were blank—so a journal. The inscription reminded him of the sign left by Corbin Galen. Beamer felt himself smiling. For a moment, a thought passed through his mind: The inside of the Barn couldn't be guessed from its outside. What was this? Camouflage? Metaphor? Happenstance?

Beamer closed the door and dropped his duffle and backpack on the floor. He stood still for some minutes smelling and listening to this new place. It smelled of oiled spruce, and fresh air, and a hint of wood smoke. It was strangely quiet. What was missing, he wondered? Then it came to him: The city was like a bagpipe. Its drone notes were the steady roar of engines of every kind—cars, ventilators, railroad engines, chillers, compressors, the whole calliope of industrial life. And over these, more or less constant, were the chanter notes of sirens wailing hither and yon. If you lived with them long enough you habituated to these sounds and they became inaudible, unconscious, even as their steady keening trickled their messages of desperate suffering and violence deep into your mind. Here they were gone and in their place the steady beat in Beamer's ears of their memory—something that would take days to fade. He flopped down on the bed and just laid still listening until finally he slept.

# CHAPTER 14

*It has more than once been the case that the creation*
*of something new depended on the remembrance and*
*reshaping of something ancient. We think our histories tell*
*us everything, but treasures can be found in middens.*

— RUPERT PHILMORE,
*THE PSYCHODYNAMICS OF CULTURAL DISINTEGRATION.*

WHEN BEAMER HEARD the light tap at his door, he was already awake—
had been awake for some time, making notes in his journal. He'd awakened
early, first to the mild surprise of disorientation that comes with being in a
new place, but which resolved to memories of the previous day's road trip,
their arrival at the Barn, and Tatum's brief tour of the place. "Come in," he
said to the tap.

Tatum pushed open the door and stuck her head in. "Hope I didn't wake
you," she teased.

"No worries," Beamer replied. "I've been up for a while."

"The Board is laid," Tatum said. "We should eat. Then after that I'm taking
you to meet Fisher. I have to get back to the city this morning on another
errand so you'll be on your own."

"Thought I was having my intake interview this morning—the one with
the death penalty," he smiled, appreciating his own wit.

"Ah, that," Tatum nodded. "Yes, of course. Fisher will take care of that."

"What part?"

"This way," Tatum said, cocking her head toward the hallway.

They walked along the hall and then down the staircase into the Board
Room. Moveable Japanese-style paper and wood partitions had been slid
sideways along the back wall to reveal a cafeteria-like food service that offered
several options for breakfast. The dishes were church basement standard and
the people serving moved placidly from task to task chatting with each other
and anyone who stopped. There were about a dozen people already seated and

eating, one of whom Beamer recognized as Jasper Beckett, but the rest were all new faces. Most were talking animatedly considering the early hour. Beamer and Tatum made their meal selections and headed for a table.

"Where do I pay?" Beamer asked.

Tatum sat down. "You don't," she said. "At least not with money. It's our little experiment with a community of goods, but without the Gulag. You will have to work at something though or you won't eat around here for very long. We're hospitable, but not that hospitable. Don't worry about it. We'll find you something to do. You'll need to check in with Rudy at the House. Rudy looks after our administrative details and the House is a sort of office. He'll find you a work assignment and get you squared away with other details."

"What's a community of goods?" Beamer asked.

"The much older alternative to private property," Tatum said. "As I said back in the city, if there's anything we all have in common, it's the idea that the status quo can't last, and maybe even shouldn't last. We know we need to make something different, but a lot of us think that 'something different' will wind up being stuff we invent combined with stuff we remember—things that have served people well for a very long time plus some of our own bright ideas. It turns out that the longest lasting communities people have ever invented have been monasteries."

"Monasteries!" Beamer blurted. "Does that mean I have to be celibate to stay here?"

Tatum smiled, catching his glance. "Let's hope not. If so, I'm already out the door! We're not setting up any sort of religious community and we're not asking everyone to pledge allegiance to some creed or other. But what we are doing is trolling history for things that have worked for people, generation after generation, and in changing circumstances. Community of goods, or some similar practice, has been part of monastic life for millennia and across many different traditions and cultures. It was probably also the practice for the tens of thousands of years when we were hunter-gatherers. So part of our experiment here is to see if we can lift the community of goods out of its historical entanglement with religion and adopt its practice among ourselves for different reasons, as part of the culture we're creating."

"So your life here is modelled on a monastery?" Beamer pursued.

"Well, yes," Tatum said, "but that's a bit of an over-simplification. The recipe we've come up with so far—and subject to change as we go along—is: Take one monastery, fully developed from the high Middle Ages, subtract patriarchy, subtract religion, subtract (mostly) hierarchy, subtract naive obedience, and subtract celibacy. What is left are the monastic traditions of simplicity and stability of commitment—sticking with each other in good times and bad— plus the unique contributions arising from our historical situation, namely:

commitment to equity, plus commitment to Practice, plus a change in the purpose of the community. That would be a shift from a workshop for holiness in the monastic tradition to the project of advancing human well-being in symbiosis with nature. Laurel Fey and her group are working on the well-being piece, Corbin Galen, the Quakers, and the insight meditation group are working on the Practice pieces, the Permies are working on the symbiosis with the ecosphere piece, and more.

"No private property," Beamer mused. "Sounds communist."

"What if it is?" Tatum replied. "We're open to looking at communism too, for that matter—even though today it's a scare word that throws people off track before a conversation can even get started. But probably there would be consensus that we should leave out the bits having to do with militarism and authoritarianism and bloody revolutions. We're hoping we can create this way of life based on free and informed consent, and sheer attraction to what we're doing."

"I hope so."

"What we're doing is, apart from goods that are for personal use like your toothbrush or underwear, promoting the value that all the goods of the community belong to all the members of the community. So we might say that nearly everything we have and use is public property, or community property, or even a commonwealth. We use the social enterprises to build the commonwealth at the Coulee, at least until the basis for the social enterprises falls apart. For centuries, when people became monks, they renounced their right to own property. Renouncing material possessions was thought to free you to focus on spiritual work instead. But in joining a religious community they came into possession of all the goods of that community. So it's a paradox: none of us owns anything, but all of us own everything. We've added a more modern bit as well—that everything we all own is also owned and lent to us by the Earth and by future generations. So our aim here is to switch out the language of ownership by people for another language of symbiosis and trusteeship with the Earth. And we're trying to express this in a daily round of activities sort of like the monastic hours."

"You mean like Lauds or Compline—that sort of thing," Beamer interjected.

"Yes, sort of. In monasteries certain prayers and rituals structure time over the course of the whole day and throughout the year. The hours gave monastic life a certain shape which was also grounded in nature, the seasons, planting and harvesting, that sort of thing. Here at the Coulee what we've done is adopted the idea of following a certain practice of living which is structured in time just like the monastic hours used to be. The culture that is passing away tried to abolish time by using technology to run everything 24/7 as they called it, back when we used the old calendar, and to shield people from any sensory experience of the changing seasons and shifting daylight. At the Coulee we're recovering the more ancient understanding of ourselves as part of what is happening day in and day out, with the turning of the seasons, not setting ourselves above or apart from them."

"What if I said my personal property should include a Lexus?" Beamer challenged.

Tatum raised an eyebrow. "I suppose that would be okay as long as everybody gets to use it," she grinned. "If you were a musician you might have the use of a grand piano and no one would complain—even if it cost two Lexuses. The main issue with private property as we see it is not who gets to use something, but under what conditions can someone deprive someone else of the use of it? We don't want a community that systematically deprives people of things they need."

"We also want to keep an eye on scale," Tatum continued. "Today, people are deliriously out of touch with the idea of sufficiency. So their craving for private property grows to truly obscene proportions. This has been especially the case with corporations—those completely artificial persons created by lawyers rather than natural parents. We think there is something very dangerous and deluded about artificial people who can change the material welfare of countless real people and other beings. Nor do we think it's seemly for multi-billionaires to alter square kilometres of habitat, dam rivers, or consume huge quantities of resources in pursuit of personal whims, or just because they can afford it. We don't recognize any inherent right of a human being to become wealthy at the expense of others."

"So you tell people how much they can own?"

"No," said Tatum. "What we're trying to do is find out the amount of material possessions that is most conducive to well-being. The scale question is not about whether to own things or not. We know we need things to have a good life. But everyone here is a refugee from a society that had no idea how much was enough for a good life. That led to mindless accumulation for its own sake, and many people who were decidedly unwell."

"It sounds all warm and fuzzy," Beamer said skeptically, "but why do it?"

"There are a lot of reasons, but a big one is that over eighty-five percent of law is about quarrels over private property, or settling quarrels, or trying to avoid quarrels through contracts, or getting property from others, or protecting one's own property from others who want it, or want to steal it because they don't have any, or who want to vandalize it to act out their anger, and on and on. If we can learn to look out for each other instead of only ourselves, we could probably eliminate all those laws, all that litigation, all that negative energy and waste and conflict—to say nothing of disappearing a bunch of lawyers. We could also focus attention more on where it belongs—on how we're taking care of each other rather than who gets to keep the toaster."

"Idealistic," Beamer dismissed.

"Maybe. But the alternative is the status quo. Pick your horse and place your bets. People in monasteries have been living in communities of goods for at least three thousand years, when they have good enough reasons for doing so. Can we learn to live differently, if there are good enough reasons for doing so—like avoiding extinction maybe?"

"And supposing all this works," said Beamer, "who gets to be Holy Father Abbot?"

Tatum smiled and shook her head. "You'll get it after you've lived here for a while, but in addition to swapping private property for a commonwealth, we're also swapping out patriarchy, hierarchy, and titles of authority. We see leadership as something a group creates that doesn't reside permanently in any one person. Instead, leadership, and the authority that it confers, moves around in the group depending on what we need to decide. So we don't have an abbot, or else you could say that all of us are abbots from time to time, depending."

"Sounds like a recipe for endless meetings," said Beamer.

"Honestly," Tatum replied, "it can seem that way sometimes. But we're all trying to learn new tricks here, and that takes time. We do have a lot of meetings. But probably all of us hope that in time this creative process will settle down and we'll need fewer meetings."

Beamer nodded without further comment, accepting her explanation for the time being. "You said there were many people here but I only see a few dozen. Where is everybody else?"

"Most of the people eating here are staying in the Barn for now. We use this food service for the people staying in-house and when we get together for meetings, which is practically every night, although anyone can drop in here for a change if they want. But most people eat in one or another of the houses we've re-occupied in the village."

"And they're all occupied?"

"No," said Tatum, "not by a stretch. In its heyday this village may have had upwards of four hundred people. When we started moving in three years ago, practically all the houses were empty. Quite a few of the older ones had been demolished. So we did a survey of the buildings on hand, picked the best ones for immediate occupancy, and then we made a schedule for tearing down the others and recycling their materials to add rooms to the better houses. So we're in the process of reducing the number of houses while increasing the size of the ones we keep. It's more efficient for services and keeping our footprint small."

They finished eating without further conversation and Tatum rose. "Okay," she said, "I'll drop you off at Fisher's and then I have to get going back to the city. This way please," she motioned.

# CHAPTER 15

*"How am I to learn what I need to know?" I asked.*
*"Have you ever been fishing?"*
*"Yes, as a child."*
*"Describe how you learned to fish," the Companion said.*
*"I was quite young," I recalled, "maybe five years old. My father*
*rented an old wooden rowboat for a quarter which we took*
*out on a lake and then anchored some distance off shore. He*
*gave me the same tiny fishing rod that had belonged to him as*
*a child, and to his father before him. It was a brown rod stuck*
*in a wooden handle with a little metal bracket on the side for*
*wrapping up the line. He told me the rod's name was 'Corky'.*
*He baited my hook for me because I was afraid to touch the*
*worms. A couple of metres from the hook, he attached to the*
*line a float made of cork and then tossed the whole rig over*
*the gunwale. 'Now sit very still,' he told me, 'because if you*
*thump around in the boat, it will scare away the fish. Watch*
*the bobber. If it goes down in the water, pull up on the rod and*
*hook your fish. Watch closely. Be very still. Watch closely.'"*
*"That's it?" my Companion asked.*
*"That's it."*
*"Sit still; be quiet; keep watch."*
*"Yes."*
*"That is very good instruction," he said.*

— OSIO SMITH, *TRANSCENDANCE*

TATUM LED BEAMER AWAY from the Barn along a short, snow packed path to one of the streets that doubled as a sidewalk, sidewalks being a luxury of urban living probably never afforded to the original residents of Badger Coulee. They walked a short distance until they came to a house so small it likely had only one or two rooms. Smoke issued from a slender tin chimney protruding from its shingled roof. On the door was another framed announcement: "Don't just do something—stand there!" Tatum stepped up to the door, tapped on it perfunctorily, and then let herself in with Beamer in tow.

"Morning Fisher," she greeted cheerfully. "This is Beamer Farris. Beamer, meet Fisher."

The house was more spacious inside than it appeared from the outside, but was still barely more than an anchorhold. There was a central room with a small table, a couple of chairs and a twin bed neatly made in one corner. Behind a minimal partition was a tiny kitchenette. A small wood burning stove hissed and popped quietly near the centre of the room, while all its remaining wall space was shelves jammed with books and papers. Another door was visible in the rear wall of the house.

Pushing his way forward in a wheelchair with his hand extended to Beamer was a lanky greying man in his late sixties. He wore Carhartt bibs and a frayed woollen shirt typical of farm workers. Beamer clasped his hand which was large, calloused, and felt like the hand of a very strong man deliberately being gentle. "I'm Fisher," he said.

"My pleasure," said Beamer. "Tatum tells me you plan to kill me."

Fisher glanced at Tatum with a 'why-did-you-tell-him-that?' expression on his face. "Must be you rubbed her the wrong way or something," he shrugged at Beamer while raising an eyebrow to Tatum.

Tatum dug in the pocket of her parka and retrieved two large muffins rolled in paper serviettes that she handed to Fisher. "Snagged these for you from the Barn," she said, "in case you're tired of your own cooking." Then she turned to Beamer: "I should be back from the city by supper. Want to join me?" Beamer nodded with a smile of pleasure. Tatum left the two of them and then disappeared into the snowy morning.

"Surprise victuals," Fisher enthused, "and enough for company besides. Tea?" He wheeled over to the table that stood just under his front window and set the muffins on small plates.

"Sure," Beamer accepted, concerned to be sociable, but also welcoming the warm brew on a cold morning.

Fisher turned to a kettle of water that had been warming on his stove, retrieved some loose tea from a cupboard, carefully rinsed a small tea pot with some of the steaming water, added the tea, and then slowly poured in more water. He raised the kettle he held high above the tea pot so that the water formed a little cataract in the pot, blending oxygen and water with the tea. On the table beside the tea pot were two cups carefully positioned in relation to the pot and to each other such that the whole assemblage conveyed a subtle symmetry, and in that symmetry a certain tranquillity. Fisher performed each step of the process without speaking and with close attention to what he was doing—what seemed to Beamer to be an extraordinary degree of attention. He realized then that he wasn't seeing a man making tea; it was a ceremony.

"So you're the mandala guy," Fisher's tone was casual.

Beamer startled—then, "So my reputation precedes me?"

Fisher tapped a small amount of sugar into his tea. "I guess you could put it that way. But I wouldn't mind it. So far as I know, there is no special type of discrimination that applies to mandala makers."

"I hope not," said Beamer. "I've burned all my bridges to come here."

"What do you make of them though?" Fisher asked.

Beamer shook his head. "I don't know. They are more about emotions than thoughts, I would say. And maybe they're connected somehow to the work I was doing for Environment."

"And how do you see them connected?" Fisher pursued.

"I was working on this trend analysis and tipping point stuff. The more I worked on it, the more agitated it made me feel, like I was digging into something really dark. But it didn't add up with the nature of the work itself, which was kind of boring, really. So naturally, I felt like I was going crazy."

"Until you noticed the convergence," Fisher interrupted. He glanced down into the tea pot long enough to conclude that the tea was steeped. He poured some into Beamer's cup and proffered it like a sacrifice.

Beamer looked startled again. Fisher somehow knew what he was going to say before be said it—as if this was well-trodden ground for him. "You call it the 'convergence'?" Beamer said.

Fisher took a sip of his tea. "What's interesting to me is that you discovered it on your own and that it manifested emotionally. Doing that requires some very fancy statistical tricks—or—some totally new way of seeing things. Statistics just involves doing sums. Even machines can do it. But your mandala was a *physical* expression of an *emotional* reaction requiring an *intuition* about what is happening to us—or about to happen. You're a rare bird Beamer Farris."

"You call it the convergence?" Beamer repeated.

"Yes," said Fisher. "We know it's coming; we're just not sure exactly when." Fisher fixed his gaze steadily on Beamer now. "But you know when, don't you." It was a statement not a question.

"I have a guess," Beamer admitted.

"You have more than a guess," said Fisher. "You've done the numbers haven't you?"

"Okay," said Beamer. "It is more than a guess. But it's a normal distribution of probabilities not a fixed date."

"When?" Fisher pressed.

Beamer sighed and gazed into his tea. He would have tried to read the leaves had there been any. "Nine months, more or less," he said.

Fisher topped up his tea without saying anything. He stirred the tea meditatively, seemingly ignoring Beamer's presence, lost for a time in his own thoughts. Then—

"What did you dream?" Fisher asked, his tone casual.

"Beg your pardon?" Beamer snapped to attention from watching the tea.

"Last night," said Fisher. "Tatum brought you in yesterday, did she not? So you would have had one over-night with us. What did you dream?"

"Nothing," Beamer replied. "I was out cold."

"What you mean to say is, you don't remember what you dreamed," Fisher said. "Pity. We all dream. Cats. Dogs. Elephants. Dolphins. Rats. Parrots. Whales probably. Humans. We all dream. Tonight, put forth effort to remember what you dream."

"Remember what I dream?"

"Mmm. It gives us something more to work with." Fisher sipped his tea meditatively. "You can date the convergence, which is helpful, but there must be more. You need to be paying attention on all channels Beamer Farris, and dreams are one of them."

"So I've flunked the first question already?"

"The first question?"

"Yes. Tatum said my entry interview would be twenty questions. I couldn't know what they were ahead of time. And I had to get all of them right." Beamer didn't believe this assertion himself, but he was curious what Fisher would say.

Fisher looked amused. "She's messing with you," he said. "Besides, what you dreamed isn't the first question."

"No?"

"No. The first question is: 'Why are you here?'"

Beamer sighed. "Apparently I'm here because I make mandalas in the snow, or in the sand, or on golf course fairways. But I don't know exactly what they are."

"Me either."

"You either what?"

"I don't know either."

Beamer glanced up to catch Fisher's eyes. "Tatum told you then—about the rapture things."

Fisher looked back at him without speaking, his eyes steady.

"She thinks they're maybe a demand of some kind," Beamer continued. "But we don't know what they're demanding."

Fisher let out a short grunt of laughter. "That's pretty much Badger Coulee in a nutshell, laddie. You're accepted."

"Huh?"

"Just about everybody in the Coulee is on the same page with that. Each of us in his or her own way feels like there's this demand, but none of us knows what is being demanded, or by whom. Maddening, isn't it." It was a statement not a question. It had a certain tone of camaraderie, as though Beamer was being inducted into the society of all those being maddened by their shared moment in history. But Fisher didn't truly appear maddened. On the contrary, he looked like a hound on a scent.

Beamer started feeling emotional but didn't know why. Frustration? "So what am I—what are we—supposed to do with this?"

Fisher leaned back in his chair, cradling his tea mug in his sizeable hands. "If I had the answer to that," he said, "I'm afraid I'd be a prophet. But I suggest you start by writing down your dreams."

Beamer looked incredulous, as if he was sipping tea with some kind of eccentric. "Really?" he said. "My dreams. Really?"

Fisher shrugged. "Well, it's either that or you could build a bunker someplace and collect guns and canned goods, or get stoned, or fuck yourself silly, or get a job trading derivatives, or any of the other things people do to avoid this." His voice was firm. "We're in a jam here and everybody knows it. Most people avoid thinking much about what they know, but don't want to know. The way forward, if there is one, is not at all clear. As loopy as it sounds, I'm just trying to do what nature does in situations like this. She looks around at what's available and tinkers up something with whatever she has at hand—from whatever is possible in the circumstances. And in the circumstances bunkers or derivatives or intoxication are simply not skillful means. In the case of human beings, she sometimes offers clues in dreams. We need all the clues we can get. So I'm serious here. Yes, really."

"Right," said Beamer, still skeptical, then repeated: "Write down my dreams."

"Yes. And in the meantime, wander around. Meet people. Figure out something to do that helps feed us and keep us warm, but don't neglect your mandalas. Make your mandalas if you feel the urge—or whatever else they want to turn into."

Beamer nodded without speaking, sensing that their conversation was over. "Thanks for the tea," he said.

"Any time."

Beamer got up to leave, but then turned back: "Is Fisher your real name?"

The other man smiled, then, "I don't know. What is a real name, anyway? My parents named me Jonathan Quinn. Never liked it much myself. Didn't seem to fit very well. And what part of us is it that senses the fit between our names and our persons? How weird is that? But since I've been here, people call me Fisher."

"And why's that?"

"I guess it's because I really like fishing. Do you ice fish?" his eyes twinkled for the first time in their conversation.

"It's probably somewhere on my bucket list," Beamer replied gamely.

"Outstanding! There's a great little lake about twenty clicks from here. Jasper Beckett tricked me up with skis on my chair and a battery-powered belt drive like a power toboggan. I can tear along with the best of 'em. We'll do it." Fisher winked, slapping the armrest of his wheelchair, relishing the thought.

# CHAPTER 16

*"I trust you only so far." The saying implies that trust has*
*a dimensional quality—that it might have a limit, a*
*horizon beyond which further trust is impossible. It also*
*suggests that the horizon may be movable. Fossil fuels made*
*possible very large institutions and nation-states which*
*in turn made possible the delusion of ever-expanding*
*trust horizons. But since this is all dependent on fossil*
*fuels, sooner or later this delusion will surely dissolve*
*in the awareness that we were mistaken all along.*

— RUPERT PHILMORE,
*THE PSYCHODYNAMICS OF CULTURAL DISINTEGRATION.*

BEAMER PASSED THROUGH the food line in the Board Room and then
to a table with no one else sitting at it. People were filtering into the room
and a roaring fire was set in the hearth until the place resembled in Beamer's
imagination a mead hall from the early Middle Ages. He also noticed for the
first time that the room had a somewhat raised stage in front of the fireplace
and on one side of it a peculiar structure he had never noticed before. It was a
chair raised on a sort of platform about a metre high with a narrow stairway
wrapped spiral staircase fashion around it. On top was a wooden panel work
that enclosed a chair and a lectern. It looked like an ambo, or pulpit, which
might have been salvaged from a church, except the speaker occupying it could
sit rather than stand.

Beamer's inspection of this curiosity was interrupted when he spotted
Tatum coming through the food line and craning to see who might be in the
room. When she spotted him she smiled, raising her eyebrows in question, to
which Beamer swept his arm dramatically toward an empty chair at his table,
bowing in mock chivalry. She grinned more broadly then and threaded her way
through the now rapidly filling tables on her way to his.

"Big night in the Barn," Beamer quipped as Tatum sat down with her food tray.

"I'll say," she replied. "I hope all these people had reservations."

"How was the run to the city?"

Tatum's smile faded. She shrugged in an effort to find words. "Mostly routine," she finally said, but her movements testified otherwise.

"Mostly?" Beamer tried.

"It's getting weirder and weirder is all," she said. "Hard to pin down. It's like a lot of people are more aggressive now. You can see it when they drive, how fast they go and how impatient they are. Or when they're standing in line for things; there's no eye contact, no chit-chat. It's like everyone is afraid of something but we don't know what it is, or we're afraid of each other but we don't know why. I guess we're all sort of expecting a mass shooter to jump out of the check-out line shouting 'I'm not gonna take it anymore!' and gunning people down." Tatum gave a lame smile.

"With reason," said Beamer.

"Yes, I know," said Tatum. "But things are different somehow. It's like in the past we could hold those anxieties at arm's length—whatever they were. Now they stand right beside us in the check-out line, on the streets, in meetings, at football matches. You know?"

Beamer nodded. "They should all learn to make mandalas. It would be a great relief."

"Be serious," Tatum scolded.

"I am," said Beamer. "It's all part of the trend lines I was looking at. As things come unzipped, we'll certainly feel it somehow. And all that energy will have to go someplace." Tatum poked at her food listlessly, clearly thinking about something else.

"Okay," said Beamer. "What is it?"

Tatum looked thoughtful. "I'm not sure," she said. "I want to think I didn't see what I saw."

Beamer raised an eyebrow, inviting her to speak.

"You know the ring highway that runs around the city? Well, at the exit ramp for the highway that comes out here, it looked to me like the police, or maybe it was the army—how do you tell them apart these days?—were setting up a check-point or something. They stopped me, Beamer, and wanted to know what I had in the van."

"And was that a problem?" Beamer asked. "Maybe they were trying to catch your mass shooter guy."

"No," said Tatum, "of course not. But..."

Beamer raised his eyebrow again.

"They had some really big guns. Like machine guns I think."

"Armies have big guns," Beamer tried to reassure her. "They were probably on their way somewhere else to one of those bases out west or something.

Tatum shook her head slowly. "I don't think so," she said.

"Why's that?"

"Because all the guns were pointed in toward the city," said Tatum. She looked at him, worried, then resumed poking tentatively at her vegetables. "But I made it in and out once again. They should give me hazard pay."

"I'll vote for that," chimed Beamer. Her story made him uneasy. Hoping to change the subject: "Do you get paid?"

"Only in veggies," Tatum rolled her eyes. "Remember we're a moneyless economy here. So they could offer me twenty percent over base pay, which is zero, and twenty percent of nothing is still nothing, so I'd be just as far ahead as I am now. So it's a good thing we're creating this community where I don't have to think about getting ahead of anybody."

Beamer chuckled. Sometimes zero could be like infinity, swallowing whatever you threw into it. But in that moment he awakened to something else; he liked Tatum. He realized he'd missed her over the course of the day. He wished that she'd been able to spend more time with him and show him more of Badger Coulee. Even her half-hearted smile pleased him and the way she laughed—and she seemed to be laughing more now than when they first met. He thought she had softened since then. His initial impression of her would always be enigmatic, demanding—demanding that he notice, that he think, that he connect the dots, and live consciously rather than dismissively. If things like mandalas were happening, he should notice and take them seriously. He found these qualities in her stimulating and challenging. But now she held his eyes more steadily, she smiled more, and she allowed some lightness to grow between them, even familiarity, as if they had been friends for a long time. And with that thought Beamer realized that what he felt for her was something old, perhaps even ancient. Puzzling.

"But luckily I didn't have to haul plaster this trip," Tatum went on. "The stuff weighs a tonne."

"Plaster?"

"Yes. It's for Ai Changming. He keeps sending us off for more and more of the stuff."

"Who is he?"

"Changming? Haven't you met him yet?" Beamer shook his head. "Oh you must!" Tatum effused. "He's an architect. He uses the plaster for making models of things he wants to build someday. He might even be here tonight," she glanced quickly around the room looking for him, but not seeing him, she gave up. Tatum and Beamer went on talking for a few minutes when the conversations all around them started trailing off toward silence. The children in the room, of whom there were many, quietened what they were doing, even as they continued to do it. Near the fireplace someone carrying a book mounted the raised chair and sat down.

Beamer leaned toward Tatum and whispered, "What's this?"

She nodded toward the platform. "It's what we do instead of television," she said. "It's story time."

The figure on stage sat down with an air of formality, though not of condescension, the gravity of his presence alone being enough to quiet the room and gain nearly everyone's attention.

"A reading from *Walden* by Henry David Thoreau," he announced, measuring every word with perfect diction. Though there was a microphone on the dais, he didn't use it, preferring instead to project every word over the heads of the seated crowd. It made his speech sound almost theatrical though not self-consciously dramatic. It struck Beamer that this sort of thing, where an adult reads out loud to other adults, almost never occurred in his experience. It was a practice preserved perhaps only in monasteries which themselves were viewed as anachronistic, rare, exotic. People now turned to machines to be their storytellers even as they continued to crave stories.

Tatum leaned back toward Beamer, a gesture that allowed him to catch the briefest hint of her in the air being warmed by the fire—a scent like a warm meadow. "We often have these sorts of readings over supper," she whispered. "Sometimes just for fun and sometimes think pieces or debates. Anyone who wants to can bring something and read it. There's no set curriculum."

The man on the dais started reading Thoreau's account of why he went to the forest to explore the limits of simplicity. He said he wanted to learn whether poverty, voluntarily accepted, should hold any fears for him, but most of all he hankered to encounter life more directly, less mediated by the technology and social conventions even of his own day. He wanted to suck out all the juice life might offer him, whether bitter or sweet, and not come to the end of his life never having tasted it. The words flowed over Beamer making him forget his surroundings. He heard a kindred spirit who was less desirous of simplicity for its own sake than of how it might serve as a skillful means to his own awakening and to gratitude.

A few minutes more and Beamer noticed Tatum looking at him. She had witnessed him absorbed in listening, as if she wasn't there. He felt naked in that moment, in her gaze, but she was smiling.

The reading lasted only about ten minutes, though it seemed longer. There was something extraordinary here. What he heard was nothing like the caffeine fuelled torrent of words so characteristic of most media. Whoever the reader was, he respected language. Words meant something, and that something had value, and to appreciate that value, he had to linger over words and let them sink down far enough to actually touch him. The reader closed the book and descended from the chair. Then, after a space of time, Beamer saw Fisher pushing his wheelchair up the sloping ramp that led to the platform in front of the fireplace. He positioned himself front and centre, but said nothing for what seemed like several minutes, letting the ideas from the first reading settle down in the gathering like a fall of fresh snow. He reached for the wireless mic and held it just below his chin.

"Thanks, Jeremy, for sharing Thoreau with us tonight," said Fisher, nodding to the reader who had just sat down at a table. He paused again to let the room refocus its attention.

"Has anybody ever heard of such a thing as a 'trust horizon'?" Most heads shook doubtfully. "Nor I, until just recently. But learning about it struck me as giving us another bit of understanding about what is driving the shit storm we all see coming."

"You can think of a trust horizon as something sensible, a physical reality. For example, most of us trust our neighbours and family members because we know them personally. We can see them physically and we can generally sense whether or not they are trustworthy. So they are within our trust horizon. We believe their promises to us and they believe our commitments to them. We might extend this trust horizon a bit farther to constables or city officials whom we can meet for face-to-face conversations even though we may not see them very often. We trust them to protect and manage the community to everyone's benefit. As communities get larger, however, our relationships with others upon whom we depend for important things get more distant. Since we don't know these people personally, we have to extend trust farther to sustain the legitimacy of the offices they hold in the public interest. While I may trust my neighbour to offer me an apple he has grown in his backyard, do I extend the same trust to someone I've never met in China or Florida, and who may not even be a real person, as is the case with corporations? Wherever is the limit of my trust that is my trust horizon. But if we perceive these trusted anonymous others to be behaving in ways that violate our trust, our trust horizons shrink back in the direction of people we know face-to-face, or at least locally."

"I think," Fisher said, "that when the history of this time is written, the withering of trust will have been a major issue. Trust is turning out to be a more fragile thing than most of us could ever guess. It's more slowly earned and more quickly lost than most other social virtues. Of course there's no shortage of wrongdoing both among public officials and the business elites. The steady drip of toxic frauds, conflicts of interest, blind incompetence and sighted greed all gradually pollute the waters of public trust to the point where the landscape of community life becomes parched of goodwill and therefore barren of creativity. A casualty in the process is any sense of a common good to which people might devote at least some of their energy. Society, of that name, disappears. All that's left in its place is a loose jumble of individuals pursuing their self-interest—enlightened though they may think it is—and of course whatever flatters their egos. This creates such a pall in the general atmosphere of communities that people assume the worst of their leaders rather than expecting the best. Corruption is no longer shocking, but more or less expected. The shame is not in the act but in getting caught. Grasping selfishness is rational according to the economics of our day. Such an airtight partition has been built between morality and making money that 'business ethics' has become an oxymoron."

Fisher rocked back and forth in his wheelchair as if he was telling a bedtime story to a grandchild. He paused again to gather his thoughts, then, "'Heaven is high, and the Emperor is far away.' It's an old Chinese proverb about accountability. As long as the public imagination can keep its tolerance of corruption at arm's length, far away where neither the gods nor the emperor will notice, then we can sustain the delusion that we aren't being affected by any of that which we despise. But the media, it turns out, have more intimate access to the collective psyche, a more toxic perspective of human nature, and command more immediate attention than any government or corporation."

"Mass media gorge on blood, violence, graphic suffering, and sentimentality. Its reports are tales of seemingly random, irrational violence, hidden threats, and people who suddenly and without warning harm others. Evil is lurking everywhere without any preceding conditions or historical context. The most prized and often repeated stories are those about the downcast, the victim, the marginalized or the simply bizarre. It's as if the media say to everyone they interview—'First, show us your wounds—in detail—in high def—and with feeling. Show us how you are everyman yet marginalized, sensitive yet misunderstood, worthy yet overlooked, the walking epitome of miscarried justice and abuse. Then if we have time, we may listen to whatever else you have to say.' For media purposes today, people are constituted by their wounds, not their victories over them. All public officials are assumed to be corrupt. Every act is assumed to arise from self-interest thus making every act of altruism newsworthy because in the worldview constructed by the media, it is incredible and rare. Everyone is assumed to be a soft target awaiting injury—physical, emotional, or both. Trauma is everywhere. Of course, in the interests of 'balanced reporting' this gloomy vista is now and then relieved with a good news story of generosity, honesty, or kindness—but for never as much screen time, nor as richly celebrated, nor as meticulously documented as the daily menu of horror. It can hardly be surprising then that after two generations of this sort of psychic bombardment the result should be a society of paranoid psychopaths and self-isolates barely capable of social relationships. It's not an altogether promising basis for the collaboration, trust and cooperative effort we need to survive."

"But the psychological affliction of society doesn't end there. After community is dissolved in the acid of distrust, cooperation devoured by competitive self-interest, evidence-based understanding overwhelmed by superstition, and society reduced to an aggregation of strangers, opportunity still exists to make a buck. Social media, itself an oxymoron, fills the void left by the disappearance of actual company, with an endless flood of diversions, entertainments and distractions custom tailored to each individual's tastes and interests, all delivered discretely and affordably to each person in the hermetically sealed privacy of what passes for a home. A world of information and entertainment is available at our fingertips even if the reality of life is a multitude of people living in solitary trances induced by the glowing screens we watch. It's a colonization and enclosure of attention unparalleled in human history. This, as much as any other failure of institutions, or of the economy, or of technology, is feeding the rivulet that leads to the creek that joins the river that's becoming a flood."

"So part of our challenge here in the Coulee is to re-weave the threads of trust, especially trust of each other. Trust is all we have that can hold a community together. Trust might just get us through."

Silence arched over the entire gathering, as if everyone was holding their breath, and then, like free divers breaking through the surface of the ocean, the room erupted in applause and then rumbled off in fifty different conversations at every table in the room. Fisher seemed totally to ignore it, as if it hadn't been him speaking. He simply turned off the mic and laid it down, wheeled himself toward the ramp, and then between the tables on his way to the samovar and cookies at the back.

Beamer gaped at Tatum. "What was that?" he exclaimed.

Tatum smiled at him. "That," she said, "was your rapture mandala—channeled by Fisher."

"Channeled?"

"In a manner of speaking."

"So am I in Jonestown or what?"

"Hopefully not. Badger Coulee isn't a religion and Fisher would be the first to say he's not a prophet. But we're still spiritual beings and Fisher can sometimes be prophetic. Do you know what I mean?"

"I don't think so."

Tatum reached for his forearm, as if to steady him. "It's the difference between identifying as something compared to just letting it flow through you from somewhere else. Fisher can be prophetic sometimes, as can others here. But that doesn't make him a prophet. It doesn't define him, if you get my drift. If he had to be a prophet all the time, it would probably drive him batty, as it has done for a lot of prophets in the past. Fisher himself is much more than his sometimes prophetic ramblings."

"Right," said Beamer blankly. He was starting to feel like someone trying to play racketball with his arms and legs in casts. Tatum sensed his discomfort. "Enough of this," she said. "Let's get some air." She grabbed his hand and pulled him up from his seat, heading toward the hallway that led to the anteroom. He followed without resistance.

Reaching the vestibule of the Barn, they pulled on their coats and boots and stepped outside. The air was bracing and fresh, reminiscent of winters from Beamer's childhood when the season seemed much colder. The sky was clear and crowded with stars. Orion was rising, Ursa Major spilled itself over head and Polaris glistened above them. An aurora borealis draped the northern sky with blushes of emerald and pale rose. They strolled for some time without speaking.

"I don't know much about you," said Beamer.

"I'm sorry?" Tatum replied.

"You told me a couple things but I don't really know much about you."

"I don't really know that much about you either," she replied, "only the stuff I thought I needed to decide whether to tell you about the Coulee, and most of that was intuition. But, fair enough. What do you want to know?"

"Ah," said Beamer, relaxing a little. "Twenty questions."

"And if I don't answer correctly you'll have to kill me?" They both smiled. "You know I live in the city, in that god-awful apartment building, and I live here when I'm not there. You know I do landscape architecture and permaculture, and that I drive a truck, and in the summer I design flower beds for rich people and in the winter I walk under the stars with you."

Beamer couldn't help smiling to himself. "That's a good start, I guess," he said.

"Question two," Tatum prompted. "Or does that last one count for three—where I live, what I do, and my present moment awareness?"

"I don't know if I'll let you off that easy."

"Next question then."

"Next question: What is your favourite memory from childhood?

Tatum pursed her lips for a moment, then, "It's not like there were a lot of them, but let me see. My uncle Felix probably. He was my maternal uncle. He took me on long hikes in the bush. He made me a flower press for the flowers and plants we gathered on our hikes—probably the beginning of my interest in all things botanical. By the time I was twelve every bit of wall space in my room was covered by framed specimens of dried plants and flowers. And I remember once in the winter we went walkabout through the snow and came to this spot that overlooked a half-frozen creek. In the bends where ice could form, the water was still moving, but under this roof of ice that gave it the most mesmerizing appearance. It turned out that he had been there the day before and dug a little pit in the river bank and built a fire in it and when it burned down, he buried a pot full of porridge with raisins in the embers and then covered it up with sphagnum moss. When we got there the next morning, he dug the pot up and it was full of steaming, tender porridge that he sprinkled with crushed maple sugar and cinnamon. We sat there watching the stream and eating all of that porridge." She smiled as she remembered.

"And what about your father?"

Tatum shrugged. "My father liked sports and wanted a boy." Her voice trailed off. "What about yours?"

Beamer glanced away, then down toward his feet. "My dad served three tours in Afghanistan and even though he came back, he never came back, if you know what I mean."

"I'm sorry," said Tatum. A silence grew between them, then, "My turn," she said. "What quality do you most admire in a person?"

"Hmm," Beamer mused. "A sense of adventure maybe."

"Such as?"

"Well, I like hiking too, but especially rock climbing. I'm not ready yet for El Capitan or anything like that. But I like rocks and how awake I feel when I'm climbing them. And there are some gnarly rocks around here—really gnarly ones. But for me, crawling over rocks is just my way of being open to new experiences. You have to pay attention to each new hold, each step, the shape of each crevice or overhang. That's what matters—being open and awake." He smiled for a moment, then, "Next question."

"Next question," Tatum agreed.

"What is it that you fear the most?"

After a moment of thought Tatum said: "Well, there aren't that many things that really scare me, but I think extinction would be it."

"Extinction?"

"Yes. I mean it's one thing to face your own mortality, right? We all have to die somehow, sooner or later. We have to come to terms with that. But I find it a lot harder to come to terms with extinction. I mean, I want to think that my life matters. I want to make some kind of contribution to something bigger than my own life, my own pleasure. I don't need to have kids or be some celebrity. But I do need to know that I've made that contribution. Extinction ends that. It ends everything—everything that people have achieved and made and experienced—from the beginning. It'd be like we never existed. Then why do anything, right? That scares me."

"But most of the species that have lived on Earth have all gone extinct," Beamer said. "Do you think ours can be an exception? Look at the mess we're making of things."

Tatum shook her head. "In the deep future, who knows?" she said. "I just damn well don't want it to happen on my watch." The firmness in her voice was reminiscent of their first conversation, or perhaps it was defiance. She paused a moment, took a breath, then, "My turn," she said, her voice softening again. "What quality do you most dislike in others?"

"Complacency," Beamer replied without hesitating, "and his minions, willful ignorance, entitlement, and denial."

"Wow," said Tatum, "that's quite a list."

Beamer shrugged. "I could write an essay about each one, but it wouldn't be very edifying—mostly ranting actually—and I'd have to include myself sometimes. Believe me. Now you. When in your life were you happiest?"

"When I was twenty."

"Come on!" Beamer protested. "That's not an answer."

"Well you asked *when*, and that's when." Beamer gave her a 'that's cheating' glance. She relented. "I was twenty and this guy, William, and I walked part of the TransCanada Trail together. It took us spring, summer and part of the fall to walk about four thousand kilometres of it. The whole thing is much longer of course, but that took me most of my twentieth year. It was just amazing in every way. It changed me. It was exhausting, and sometimes boring, and sometimes dangerous, and sometimes we met really interesting people."

"And were you in love with William?" Beamer couldn't conceal the edge in his question, even though he tried to make it sound casual.

Tatum stopped and caught Beamer's eyes. "Yes," she said. "I was. I would have walked to Antarctica and back with him if he wanted to go."

"Are you still in love with him?" Beamer pressed. Tatum sensed his special interest in this particular question.

"I can't be," she said, letting her eyes fall.

"Can't be?"

"William is dead. After we got back to B.C., he was out with some of his guy friends, just for a day hike into this fjord in the Coast Mountains. He fell. I wasn't hiking with him on that trip. They said he just slipped. Just slipped…" her voice trailed off, bewildered. "So you see, I can't be in love with him."

"Yes you can," Beamer said.

Tatum's voice was firm and she found his eyes again. "Look," she said, "I loved William and I miss William and part of me still mourns William. But William is dead. He wouldn't have wanted me to carry his gravestone around my neck for the rest of my life. I remember my time with him as the happiest part of my life so far, and that's what you asked me, right? But my life didn't stop when he died—though for a while I thought it had—and now the memory of him warms me, even though I know he's gone." Her eyes were clear, tearless, but also questioning. "I want my life to be full of memories that warm me," she said, "and my time with William was the first one. I hope it's not the last." She searched his face now and saw his worry drain away. Beamer reached his arm around her shoulders and pulled her against him. She bent her head against his chest. Then they started walking again.

"Enough questions now," said Beamer. "Let's head back to the Barn and see if they still have anything hot on tap."

"I can make us some mulled cider," Tatum offered. "But you have to come to my shack for it."

"Are you inviting me for a drink?"

"Just a wee dram," she teased. "I promise not to take advantage of you."

"Well shit," Beamer groused. "What do I have to do?"

Tatum jabbed him in the ribs with her elbow. "Just stow it sailor. Let's get the cider hot first."

# CHAPTER 17

*"See yourself," said my Companion. "You have*
*aspired to do good but you have often failed in the*
*performance. So what are you: The aspiration or the*
*performance? If the performance, then you are lost. If*
*the aspiration, then you are saved. What do you say?"*
*"Who can tell which is most true of me? I aspire truly, and*
*truly I fail. Both are true; neither is true," I replied.*
*"Precisely," my Companion answered. "You are both*
*your aspiration and your performance. You are neither*
*your aspiration nor your performance. You are only one*
*or the other if you are judged or judge yourself. Ceasing*
*to judge is the Great Liberation, in which case, you*
*are neither saved nor lost. You are simply free."*

— OSIO SMITH, *TRANSCENDANCE*

BEAMER TURNED A CORNER with snow crunching under foot and passed three small houses to come upon a largish Edwardian style house painted in a number of different trim colours and a modest use of decorative accents. This, he guessed, was the House Tatum had mentioned when they first arrived at the Coulee. Being the next largest structure in the village besides the Barn and the Lighthouse, it served as the administrative office for the Coulee. Beamer walked up the sidewalk to a flight of stairs leading to a wide porch and a decoratively carved front door flanked with leaded glass windows. Beamer found a doorbell button which he pressed and then waited. Presently, a lean, greying man arrived to open the door.

"Beamer Farris?" the man asked. His voice was soft and wizened, matching his face and features which showed either age, or hard wear and tear. Sixty-something, bespectacled, he welcomed Beamer with studied cordiality if not effusive warmth.

"Yes," said Beamer. "And you're Rudy?"

The man nodded and stepped aside to let Beamer enter: "Rudy Byrne," he completed, "but you're welcome to just call me Rudy. If I had a title, it would be Porter. But we have no titles in Badger Coulee, as you have no doubt already learned." He closed the door behind Beamer and led him through a small anteroom to what a century before would have been a parlour. Now it was serving as an office with the usual furnishings and equipment. While Rudy did have a desk, it had been shoved up against a wall allowing him to swivel around and face his visitors.

Once Beamer had doffed his coat and taken a chair, Rudy fixed him in a moment of silence, then, "So what brings you to Badger Coulee Beamer Farris?"

"Tatum Barnes brought me," Beamer replied. "I guess finding people to come to this place is one of the things she does. And she found me."

Rudy nodded: "She found me too."

"So how did that go?" Beamer asked. "I'm curious."

"You want to hear my story?" Incredulous.

"Sure. Why not?"

Rudy shook his head, bemused. "I was a piece of trash and she recycled me."

"Well that's cryptic," said Beamer.

"Probably," said Rudy. He paused, assembling this thoughts.

"Well, I grew up pretty much like everybody else," Rudy said. "Mom and dad ran a convenience store on the corner of Jaycee and Ingram, in the city. We lived in a suite above the store. They worked all the fucking time, ya know? Both were old stock Newfoundlanders. My grandad ran a cod boat out of Petty Harbour-Maddox Cove for years, but my dad saw no future in it, so he and my ma moved here just after they got married. Then I was born, and then my brother Jerry, and they bought this store and settled in. They believed in the dream, eh."

"The dream?"

"Sure. You know. Work hard. Save. Work some more. Then you can get all the shiny little things you're supposed to want and kick back when you're sixty-five and enjoy the life. Maybe even fifty-five if you play your cards right. But it didn't work that way for them—or for me. Which is funny, because I turned out being probably the most educated person in my family ever. But it didn't matter a damn bit. I finished high school with higher than average marks and even did a commerce degree to top it off. They feed you this bullshit line about how greed (they call it ambition, or aspiration, or rational self-interest—anything but actual greed) and the markets work together to give us the best of all possible lives. Competition will bring out your best. Take out the next guy before he takes you out. If people have disposable income, sell 'em something, even if they don't need it—maybe especially if they don't need it—because it makes them feel richer than their neighbours. I couldn't see the contradiction at the time—the idea that we were expected to trust the system but at the same time everybody was trying to play the system to beat out the next guy. Lunacy."

"So you went into business like your mom and dad?" Beamer asked.

"Sure," said Rudy. "Guess it was in my blood. But not the corner store business. My sights were higher. I felt like a young buck with a swinging dick and brass balls." He chuckled at the memory of his self-deception. "I was pumped on the piffle they push in commerce school, so I decided on real estate—not being an agent, but a speculator, you know? It seemed the shortest way to 'money for nothin.'" Beamer looked blank, and Rudy shook his head. "Anyway," he continued, "I got a little loan from my dad—just a few thousand—but enough to make a down payment on a little fourplex and mortgage the rest. The fourplex was already rented, so I had a little cash flow right off the bat. The cash flow was enough to service more debt, so I bought another fourplex. After nine or ten fourplexes I bought my first apartment block. Now you have to understand that I did this in about a year. It's not in the commerce school playbook that it's possible to spread too much sail. No way. Nothing stops you growing, see. No matter what happens, it's just a management problem you can always fix with some kind of work-around. It's barking pathological optimism is what it is, but it's like a drug and also like climbing this really tall ladder; once you're going up, it's not a good idea to look down again. And it worked—for a while. I learned that, you know. Almost anything can work for a while."

Beamer nodded. "And then—"

"Then I met this girl, Patsy," Rudy went on, not needing Beamer's prompt. He grinned in a way that only a sixty-something down on his luck guy can grin—an improbable blend of sheepish and hideous. "Yes, she was wonderful. She had a way of taking my mind off things, you know? For a while there the mortgages got paid and Patsy and I went on a tear. My credit rating was fantastic, so we enjoyed life on plastic and pretty soon we got married. Did you know," Rudy said as an aside, "that a high credit rating isn't something they give you for having a lot of money? Hell no. You get a high credit rating by servicing lots of debt. It actually encourages more debt. They don't give a shit how much dough you have squirreled away, only how well you make your payments. So as long as you service the debt, you're a fucking hero. There used to be a saying: If you owe the bank a thousand dollars, you have a problem. If you owe the bank a million dollars, the bank has a problem. So they're just as hooked in the system as the schmucks they push into debt."

"So I got more rental units, off-loaded some of the littler stuff and bought bigger buildings. These deals took more time to work out although there were fewer of them because there was more money in play. But the principle was the same. While all this was happening, Patsy got pregnant, which put some more pressure on me. It was all getting to her too because the bigger the deals I was cutting, the more time I was away from home. And there's always something going wrong with this shit, some tenants' association after your ass, or the tax guys, or the building inspectors, or somebody. But it all had to be alright, eh? We were getting ahead and that's what it's all about, eh?" Rudy's story now included more question marks, subtly pleading with Beamer to understand, to agree, perhaps to collaborate with him in constructing some rationale or finding some meaning in the shape of his former life. Beamer started to wonder if telling his story was a fair thing to ask from idle curiosity. But Rudy seemed to need to tell it.

"Anyway," Rudy continued, "a time came along there when everything hit the fan—I mean more than usual. I don't remember what happened first. But Patsy lost the baby. Then she really got into a funk. She started out our marriage happy to be a sort of kept woman, if you get my meaning. She probably could have been happy just taking care of a house and kids. So having a baby was a big deal for her. And it really was for me too—but for different reasons probably."

"At the same time this was happening somebody somewhere with shit for brains decided to jack up interest rates—not by a quarter point or something manageable, but like eleven percent over just one year. We had rent controls then, so I couldn't increase my rents that fast. So that put me in a cash squeeze right there. But the interest rate increase put the binders on a lot of other people as well. Businesses started going tits up over night because they couldn't afford to borrow money. Some of them employed people that rented suites from me. When they lost their jobs, they couldn't pay their rents. So my rent income was going down at the same time as my mortgage interest charges were going up. Even though they couldn't pay their rent, a lot of tenants refused to leave even if I started eviction proceedings. So I wound up with buildings full of people refusing to leave and mortgage charges going through the roof." Here Rudy paused and Beamer kept his peace as well. Their conversation was starting to resemble the moments just before a train derailment.

Rudy sighed deeply, then leaned back in his chair. "So," he said, "I lost it all. The banks foreclosed my mortgages and even after they took possession of my properties, I was still several million in the hole. Bankruptcy was next. Patsy was losing her mind and eventually took off with somebody else—good for her. Haven't seen her since." He paused. His eyes filled for a moment and he was incapable of speaking. Beamer made no attempt to continue the conversation; he just waited.

"After that," Rudy said, "nothing else happened in my life. Somehow, I got into booze and one wasted thing followed another wasted thing, and nothing else happened. Can you believe that?" He looked at Beamer, bewildered. Beamer nodded without comment.

"You know what still puzzles me?" Rudy continued; then without waiting for Beamer to answer, he said: "What really puzzles me is what the hell did I do wrong? I played by the rules. I believed in the dream. And now here I am, enjoying the fine company of people in this ghost town. And you know, I'm grateful for that, but I still wonder what I did wrong, how I did wrong by Patsy, and how I wound up here."

Beamer let the silence between them be as he pondered everything he'd heard. Then at last, he said, "I don't think you did anything wrong. It's not wrong to believe in something, to try to better yourself, provide for your family, and have some pleasures in life."

"Yes," Rudy sounded unconvinced. "But I still wonder how it comes to this— and not just for me. Some sort of this same thing happens to lots of people. Lots."

"It comes to this because the game is rigged," said Beamer with a touch of bitterness. "And the genius of the game is that those who lose out blame themselves. It's a perfectly evil thing."

Rudy looked bemused. Then, as if he couldn't hear what Beamer had just said, "You know what I regret most?" Rudy asked. Beamer shook his head without saying anything. "I regret that I didn't pay my dad back."

Beamer nodded sympathetically, but held his peace, then, "And Tatum found you."

"Yes," said Rudy. "Yes she did." He smiled, as if enjoying a private joke. "I panhandled her. Can you believe it?"

Beamer shrugged. "Okay…" he said.

"She gave me ten bucks. But then she wanted to talk with me. For ten bucks, I figured I owed her that. Later she said it was one of her 'intuition things'. We wound up standing there for three quarters of an hour and I told her the same story I just told you. And she believed me! That's something, you know. If you're on the street, everybody has a story but nobody believes you. But she believed me, which was fortunate, because I was telling the truth. And then she asked me if I was tired of being on the street? Can you believe that? Anyway, I said 'Hell yes!' and did she know a way out of it? Then she said she knew of some people who might need a guy with my background—not the loser part of it—but someone with knowledge of real estate. Something or other about buying a ghost town. And I did of course, plus some law, accounting and building code stuff when I was doing my commerce degree. Next thing you know we're rattling along this gravel road and I'm a founding member of Badger Coulee. And the next day, I'm the community administrator— but nobody calls me that because we don't have titles like that in the Coulee. And here I am with you. Bob's your uncle. Tatum Barnes saved my life."

Beamer nodded. "She probably saved mine too," he said. Both men sat quietly for a few moments.

"Well," Rudy roused himself, "I don't suppose you came here to listen to my adventures in real estate. Where was I? Ah yes: Things you need to know about living in Badger Coulee. What were you doing before Tatum fetched you out here?"

"I worked as a policy analyst for the Ministry of Environment," Beamer answered.

"A policy analyst," said Rudy flatly. "What did you actually do?"

"I read a lot of stuff. Thought about it. Reviewed policy documents for the government. Made up information packages, briefing notes, that sort of thing."

Rudy peered over his glasses. "That sort of thing. Got it. Well here at the Coulee you might say we're still in the strong-backs-are-appreciated phase of our development. You probably also heard by now that we're not a resort or rehab centre here. Everyone is expected to work at something, including children over the age of seven. No work, no eat. So I'm going to suggest that you team up with Jako Menpaa and help him with bucking up firewood and delivering it to households in the Coulee. He'll explain what's involved and what he needs you to do. While we do have a strong custom of no-work-no-eat, this isn't a Gulag. If you give the wood detail a try and the work really doesn't suit you, there are plenty of other things to do."

"That sounds fine," said Beamer gamely.

"Ha!" Rudy barked. "Don't say that until you've seen the wood pile. Now let me see." He spun around on his desk chair and consulted a sheet of notes on his desktop. "Ah yes," he resumed. "Accommodation. I assume they have you bunked in at the Barn for the time being but you'll need a more permanent billet if you plan to stay very long. It seems that someone named Tatum Barnes is already offering you a rug by her fireplace if you like. So is that agreeable?"

Beamer tried to resist a smile but felt a blush rushing from somewhere in his chest all the way up to his hairline. He cleared his throat but still croaked, "That'll be fine. Thanks."

Rudy spun around again on his chair to conceal his own grin. "So," he said, "what else do we have here? Ah yes: Practice. We have a chap here at the Coulee, Corbin Galen, who is teaching meditation and yoga and some new form of a martial art that he's dreaming up—literally, he says. People are finding it beneficial. It seems to be taking us closer to what we want to be. He offers group meditation training every morning and evening, private sessions for those who wish at other times. We strongly encourage you to take part in this practice—for at least a year. He meets us in the Lighthouse at 6:00 AM and 6:00 PM. Have you ever meditated before?"

"Not really," Beamer said, "but Fisher says I should work with my dreams. So learning meditation sounds—well—why not?"

"Outstanding," said Rudy. "That just leaves money. Do you have any?"

Beamer gave an incredulous giggle.

"That's what I thought," said Rudy. "I don't have any either. But it's still a good idea for you to understand money at the Coulee, just in case you come into some money someday. We don't use money inside the community because we're testing the idea that money is corrosive to well-being, which is what we're trying to grow here. No one is paid in money for anything they do. But we are all working to create a material economy, not a financial one, which meets our material needs directly, without using money. This is possible only if we all agree to live very simply and very closely connected to each other and to nature. We don't measure wealth in dollars. We measure it in soil fertility and wetland reserves, and species diversity and abundances. So there's no hope here of getting paid anything that you can carry back to the city and party with. You'll have to party here, with what we can produce."

Beamer nodded slowly. "Yes," he said. "Tatum told me a bit about a community of goods, a sort of commonwealth."

"Yes, that's involved," said Rudy. "But even before we settled the Coulee, we set up a cooperative social enterprise. Anyone could contribute. People with assets who want to join the Coulee can park them in the co-op until they decide if they want to stay with us. Earnings on its capital are used to develop the material economy of the Coulee. We think the global financial system will collapse pretty soon, and when it does it will take the co-op down with it. But by then, hopefully, we'll have enough physical assets that we won't need the co-op. If you had some money, I would be asking you if you want to park some of it in the co-op. Since you're a pauper, we'll skip that bit."

"Recent graduate, temporarily unemployed, if you please," Beamer quipped.

# CHAPTER 18

*"Would it simplify my life if I gave*
*away half my shoes?" I asked.*
*My Companion answered: "Not if you have only two*
*shoes. But if you have more than two shoes, you are still*
*doodling in the margins. It is better to plunge right in, not*
*fearing death. Only then does one discover one's heart."*

— OSIO SMITH, *TRANSCENDANCE*

TATUM BARNES'S COTTAGE was a low frame building of perhaps fifty square metres. It was embedded in a tangle of now yellow, brown and grey vegetation awaiting spring. By summer the house would be ensconced in a nest of hazelnut and lilac bushes, a stand of raspberry canes and a bit farther off, cherry and apple trees. Beamer could see the remains of a rhubarb plant against the foundation to one side of the front door, and any number of mysteries that might be imagined lurking under the snow.

Tatum had Beamer in tow as she pushed open the front door of the cottage and both of them stepped inside. A wood fire popped and hissed in the grates of a wood-burning stove. Large windows nearly filled the entire south wall of the building which featured a single room for sitting and a small kitchenette. The room was furnished with a pair of comfortable chairs, several book shelves, and as many plants as could be fit on the window sills of the south wall.

Tatum pulled off her boots and hung her parka on a peg in the wall and Beamer followed suit. "This'll be home," she said as they stepped into the room. "Sorry if it's a bit warm in here but it's better for the plants. I had to bring most of them out from the city because I was spending too much time away from them. They'd get dried out and lonely."

"Lonely," Beamer echoed as he pulled off his boots and hung up his coat. His tone was bemused.

"Hey," Tatum said, "love me, love my plants. Come this way." She paced through the room toward the back of the house where there were three doors, poking her finger into the soil of the plant pots as she went by. Two of the doors led to bedrooms and the third to a washroom. All were open to take advantage of the midday sun and heat from the wood stove. "This'll be your room," she said as she led Beamer into a simply furnished bedroom with a single bed, a bedside table and a chair. There was also a built-in clothes closet and dresser drawers. A braided throw rug covered the floor and a heavy look-ing quilt was on the bed. A single window offered a view of a back yard with rectangular shaped humps in the snow that hinted at raised beds under the surface.

Beamer pulled his duffle bag through the door of his bedroom. "Nice," he said, his tone combining genuine gratitude with the slightest hint of disappointment.

Tatum glanced at him, amused. "There's a double bed in my room," she said, "so don't fret. Besides, everyone needs a room of their own."

Beamer nodded with relief. "Virginia Woolf, wasn't it?"

"Bingo," she said. "Come meet my friends." Tatum stepped back into the living area, glanced briefly at the state of the wood stove, and then went to the south windows where her plants were turning their leaves toward the sun. Her laptop computer was open on one of the shelves and Tatum touched a key. The display lit up showing a number of coloured tracings that waved lazily up and down. "It's a dilemma, you know? If I leave them in the city and then I'm away for days at a time, they get annoyed with me and scream for water and complain about the short daylight. But then if I bring them out here, I have to make sure the wood stove is going pretty good most of the time or they would freeze off. I need a bigger window—and more thermal mass."

Beamer was captivated by the tracings scrolling on the laptop screen. "I admit," he said, "I suspected you might be a cat lady. But nothing this bizarre. What is all this?"

"Ever heard of botanical sentience?"

Beamer scoffed. "I doubt that most humans are sentient, let alone my broccoli."

"Well," Tatum sighed, "if you look, you'll see it right there." She nodded to-ward the laptop display. "We humans live in this narrow band of awareness—seeing 'visible' light—hearing 'audible' frequencies—feeling 'liminal' touch pres-sures. Our mistake is thinking that what we see and hear is all there is. Of course if we think about it even a minute, we realize this isn't so, but most of the time we wander around in a fog of our own making. Microscopes and telescopes and microphones and pressure sensors tell us more about what we're missing. We also miss things that happen very fast or very slowly. So an order of conscious-ness that moves very slowly can easily slip right by us because we're too busy attending to relatively speedier things. Or an order of consciousness that aris-es only collectively among many linked beings rather than discrete individuals might be something that our biases incline us to miss."

"Okay," Beamer said, "but give me an example."

"The Pando tree."

"The Pando tree?"

"Yes. It looks like a forest of trembling aspens that covers 46 hectares. But all the trees are linked. All of them are clones of a single aspen tree, arising from a single plant. Together they weigh 6,600 tonnes and have a root system that is estimated to be 80,000 years old. That's nearly as old as modern humans. And all their roots are connected. If such a creature was sentient, might it be reasonable to assume that it was conscious on a different time scale from us? And if that's true, then we would probably need to learn its language at the speed it speaks—sort of like the Ents in Middle Earth."

"And that's what you're doing here?" Beamer asked, continuing to be transfixed by the laptop display.

"In a very simple way," said Tatum. "If I had a real lab and a rich patron I'd have way more fun. But what you see here is just a bunch of galvanometers that measure the electrical resistance between electrodes I've stuck to the leaves of the plants. It's sort of like a lie detector for plants. The tracings you see on the laptop show those electrical changes in real time."

"And that means your plants are conscious?" Beamer's tone was still skeptical.

"No," Tatum admitted. "But it does show some interesting things. For example…" She keyed the laptop to display a time series of measurements over the last hour. The tracings meandered over the screen for forty-eight minutes, then spiked upwards noticeably. "Do you know what that is?" Tatum asked, pointing to the spikes in the tracings. Beamer seemed to be holding his breath.

"That," Tatum continued, "is when you walked into this room twelve minutes ago. Evidently, the plants find you interesting—or maybe, exciting. They don't react to everyone that way."

"No guff," said Beamer, sounding more amazed.

"No guff," Tatum echoed. "And if plants had voices, what do you think they would sound like?"

"You're kidding," said Beamer.

"Not kidding," she said, stabbing a few more keys on the laptop. A sound erupted from the computer that to Beamer resembled a symphony orchestra tuning up before a performance. All it needed was the concert master to step forward and play the "A".

"Holy crap!" said Beamer.

"Holy something or other," Tatum agreed. "Now I wonder if I hooked them together somehow, they could harmonize? Or would a leader emerge? And which plant would that be? And how does their being in communication with each other underground affect their voices? Or is an entirely different song being sung underground? And on and on."

Beamer nodded. "And I suppose you've already come up with a practical application for this stuff."

"Well," said Tatum, "you might say so. They have a way to go yet before recording their first EP. It will probably wind up being an acquired taste any way you look at it. But I think they may already be set to take on a practical job for the Coulee."

"Salad?" Beamer grinned. Instantly the audio from the plants shrieked into a higher register of chaos and wavering uncertainty.

"Don't do that!" Tatum scolded. "They feel your intentions. And they don't get humour or irony."

"Sorry," Beamer said sincerely. Tatum keyed off the audio channels.

"Maybe they could be sentries," she said.

# CHAPTER 19

*"Am I not great? Will I not stand forever? Who can say to me, 'come here' or 'stop there'? Have I no reason for my pride?"*

— FROM THE PLAY, *I, CITY.*

EARLY IN HIS FIRST week at Badger Coulee, Beamer found himself assigned to a wood cutting detail. Many members had wanted to get off-grid as soon as possible on their arrival in the community. But apart from direct solar gain, which none of the houses in the Coulee had been designed for, the lowest carbon and lowest tech alternative to fossil fuel was a wood burning stove. So the Coulee provisioned itself with wood it obtained under a cutting permit with the government allowing for selective cutting from a forest stand only a few kilometres away. Beamer was not involved in the tree felling itself, a dangerous operation that required specialized skills, but was on hand when the cut was delivered to Badger Coulee as two and a half metre long cut logs. These required a chainsaw to reduce them to stove lengths, and then splitting and stacking the wood to dry. After a short lesson, Beamer was given a chainsaw to buck up the wood, and later a single bit axe, a maul, and some splitting wedges. He was also given enough armour for both his shins and feet to deflect the odd wayward blow from an axe head or a stray stove length of wood. The Coulee owned a hydraulic splitter but they used it only for species that were more difficult to split.

The pile of wood that had been cut but not yet split was approximately the size of a house. Seeing the pile, Beamer doubted that any human being could work his way through it in a single lifetime. Fortunately, Jako Menpaa was his mentor for the job, the fourth generation descendant of Finnish settlers in the region from the 1930s. The man was perhaps only two years older than Beamer himself, but built on the body plan of a cave troll. He smiled constantly, laughed often, and very much knew his way around sharp things.

For his own part, Beamer had listened attentively to the chainsaw instructions and even managed to saw a few dozen logs before looking for a change of pace. He found one particularly large log section which he set on the ground as his anvil, and then selected another length of paper birch which he stood on end on the anvil. He then stepped back and took a swing smartly with his axe. It being fairly cold, the wood birch, and his swing semi-accurate, the log split with a handsome crack into approximately equal parts. He picked up one of these and split it again, trying not to look at the pile that loomed beside him.

Jako stood nearby leaning on his double bit axe, an anachronism seldom seen because so few people knew how to use one without beheading themselves. Jako grinned genially as he watched Beamer's pathetic attack on the pile.

"How'm I doing boss?" Beamer asked as he loosed another swing at a log.

Jako chuckled. "No bosses here," he said, "just friends. You're doing okay. Just don't take off the armour for a while yet. Sure looks tiring though."

The day was overcast and cold, but pleasant enough for outdoor work. Nevertheless Beamer was sweating profusely and breathing hard. "I'll feel it tonight," he admitted.

"Why don't you take a breather," Jako suggested. As Beamer sat down on his anvil stump, Jako climbed slowly to the top of the wood pile, easily a story and a half high. He let his axe head slip casually down to the wood he stood on as if he was hardly holding on to it. "Ya see," he said, "this work is hard enough already, so you need to just relax a bit, take it easy, and look into the wood you're hitting."

"I do look," Beamer protested.

"Well," said Jako, grinning down at him, "you sorta look. You look at the wood, but you're not looking into it. Like this…" Jako then began to swing his axe which, once going, never stopped. When Beamer hit a log with his axe, the axe blade usually buried itself in the log and sometimes had to be pounded through with the mall. In a worst case, he would have to add the splitting wedges as well. But Jako was swinging his axe in a motion like a figure eight, in a constant, smooth, rhythm and logs just seemed to fly apart in all directions. He moved over the pile like a spider picking its way along a sticky web, but with the axe always in flight shattering first this piece of wood and then that, and with a casual push of his toe, another piece rolled down the side of the pile to the ground. He was unhurried in his work, but split wood was falling to the ground faster than it would have been possible for only one person to pick it up and stack it. Jako could have kept three other people busy just stacking. His activity appeared effortless, although he was clearly being careful with each swing, careful where he placed his feet, and especially careful of just how he hit every piece of wood. Hardly had he completed one swing than his eyes were searching for his next target, or his feet were moving either to push a split log over the side of the pile, or else to tip up the next target to just the right angle for the hit. "Why don't you stack for a bit?" Jako called down from the now steadily descending summit.

"Sure thing," said Beamer as he stood up and started loading split wood onto a toboggan they would use to bring it to the village. This he filled in around five minutes, but went on stacking more wood under loose cover they had built for the purpose. Jako kept on working for another hour, reducing the pile by at least two metres before he stopped. Then he stepped carefully down the side of the pile, flushed with the pleasure he took in such work. He sat down, but while resting, immediately turned to honing his axe blades to make them razor sharp.

"Fun, eh?" he grinned.

"Fun," Beamer agreed, though with some reservation. He sighed, finally catching his breath. He gazed back at the remaining pile of cord wood and realized it would be enough for only a few days. "It's a hell of a pile of wood," he said.

Jako chuckled. "Yes. Real wake-up call. Too bad more people don't see more piles of wood like that."

"And why's that?" Beamer asked.

"Did you ever fly anywhere in an airplane?" Jako asked.

"Not lately," Beamer said. "But I have done."

"Well, you look out the window and you see all that crop land down there all laid out like a monstrous big bed quilt. Seems to go on forever. Or else you fly over cities with the big glass buildings and the highways snaking everywhere all jammed with traffic like a wildebeest migration or something. From up there, or from inside that city, it looks so solid and permanent. Looks like there's nothing fragile about it. Know what I mean?"

Beamer nodded. Then, as if quoting someone else: "Am I not great? Will I not stand forever? Who can say to me, 'come here' or 'stop there'? Have I no reason for my pride?"

Jako smiled and raised an eyebrow. "Holy shit," he said, "you're a poet."

Beamer shrugged. "Just a line from a play I saw once. Anyway, why should people see wood piles?"

Jako found a more comfortable position on the stump he was sitting on, then said, "Because there are no free lunches." Beamer looked puzzled. Jako swung his arm in the direction of the wood pile. "What is that?" he asked.

Beamer wondered if this was a trick question. "It's a pile of wood," he said flatly. "And what else?"

Beamer looked again at the pile for whatever it was he was missing, then finally gave up. "Okay, what else?"

"It's a pile of energy," said Jako. "The thing is, it's a visible pile of energy. That's one of the beauties of simple living like we do it here at the Coulee. Lots of stuff becomes visible that used to be invisible. You appreciate stuff more, and you also worry more. People today get their energy through wires or little underground pipes running right to their houses. And those wires and pipes are coming from dams that are far away or from gas and oil wells or from coal mines that are far underground. The whole caboodle is practically invisible."

"What's more," Jako went on, "is that we see these buildings and highways and houses and bridges and stuff and all we see is buildings and highways. We don't see the energy that went into making all the materials they are made of, or all the energy it takes to keep them running and repaired. And we certainly don't see how hard it is to get this energy. We don't see whether it came from right next door or a couple thousand kilometres away and a thousand metres deep. All of this is out of sight and out of mind, mostly because it's literally underground—in mines and gas wells and pipelines and factories far from where we live."

Jako's tone was now one of stunned amazement, as if this should be obvious to everyone. But it wasn't obvious, even to Beamer. "So what's wrong with it being invisible? Who wants to see a bunch of pipes and wires anyway?"

"For a couple of reasons," Jako replied. "For one thing, stuff that's invisible can get forgotten when it shouldn't be. Most of the buried pipes have been carrying fossil fuels that we use to run everything. Down side is that we've changed the climate and will have to live with it for a long time, if we can live at all. For another thing, if we stop using fossil fuels and switch to renewables, which we have to do to avoid more climate change, then all of our energy harvesting will have to move out of mines and pipelines and get rebuilt above ground as wind mills and solar panels. For yet another thing, renewables can only supply about ten percent of the energy we use now. That means that if we want to keep consumerism humming, we'll need ten times the energy infrastructure we have now—something to do with fossil being a limited supply but with an unlimited rate of drawdown compared to renewables that have an unlimited supply but a limited drawdown rate. And as more renewable infrastructure is built, it will be competing with food production for user rights to the surface of the Earth. Crunch!" Jako chuckled bitterly. "So, seeing the wood pile helps you understand energy supply and consumption a lot better than a skinny little wire coming into your house, or the gas main you don't see at all. It's even better if you have to split the wood yourself! It's enough to make you want a smaller house."

Beamer looked decidedly more sober now. "I get it," he said, partly to himself.

Jako nodded. "Yikes, for sure. And that isn't the half of it. As climate change rolls along, there's more and more storm damage to everything. Just one nasty hurricane can take out a whole state. As more of these happen, we wind up using our remaining energy and other resources to repair the storm damage. That means that humanity as a whole is no longer adding to its material wealth. We're spending huge resources just to put things back sort of like they were before the weather changed. We're actually worse off than we were last year, even though the economists tote all of this up as economic growth. It's fucking loco."

"So I guess we'll all have to live more simply?" Beamer said lamely.

"Indeed we will," Jako confirmed, "but probably not how you think."

"Well," Beamer pressed, "smaller houses, no cars, fewer holidays—wouldn't that help?"

Jako nodded meditatively. "Yes, a little bit. But what we're all missing when we don't look at the wood pile is the fact that our super quick drawdown of fossil fuels has made it possible for us to develop a really complex society. The power of cheap fossil fuels lets fewer and fewer people supply more and more consumers doing more specialized things. People who can spend all day doing accounting, or massage, or vascular surgery, or studying Medieval French poetry, or gender studies, is possible only because of cheap fossil fuels. In a world run on renewables, life will have to be more local, and society itself will become much simpler. That will have huge effects on our quality of life. We'll have to live more simply, and not by choice."

Jako grinned. "On the up-side, maybe we can hope for fewer wars." Jako took a deep breath and then fished a wad of paper from his pocket and flattened it out so he could read it. "Okay," he said. "We need to get two toboggan loads of wood to two thirty-seven First Street. That's Changming's place I think, and two loads would be about half a cord, enough for a week unless it gets colder. Maybe we'll have time to bring him a couple more before the end of the day. He burns quite a pile of sticks heating that machine shed of his. Can you drive a power toboggan?" Beamer nodded tentatively. He'd driven a snowmobile a few times but was hardly expert. But his route was flat and open and didn't require dodging trees or navigating rough terrain, so he figured he could manage it. "Okay then," said Jako, handing him the slip of paper with the address and a key to the machine, "Off you go". He waved Beamer off and resumed climbing the wood pile.

# CHAPTER 20

*After walking many days, we came upon a rotunda in the middle of
a forest, a building which was not built, but rather grew from the
naked rock. It stood upon an immense slab of Precambrian granite
and in the four directions were four thresholds, and in its domed
ceiling, a portal of glass that revealed the sky both day and night.
Entering from the south door, I stood in a portico that ringed the
inner wall of the Hall of Practice. Arrayed in circles were broad stone
benches where people were sitting in contemplation. Rising from the
centre of the room was a column of living stone, uncut and unadorned,
and upon it a solitary crystal sphere, luminous, colourless, pure.
The Hall was full of people, but not a multitude. It was also full of silence and
light. I realized as I looked around, that while all were capable of coming
here, it may be that few find this place, or few have the fortitude to stay.
"What is it?" I asked, pointing to the crystal sphere.
"It is the Great Thing," my Companion answered,
"and all have come here to contemplate it."
"But what is it?" I repeated.
"What do you think it is?" asked my Companion.
"I don't know."
"Then it is 'I Don't Know,'" he echoed. "Your Great
Thing is: 'I Don't Know.' Meditate upon that."
"But what is it to all these others?" I asked.
"Who can say? Only they know what it is for them, just as
only you know what it is for you. It is never the same thing for
everyone, except that we call it sacred and it is beautiful."*

— OSIO SMITH, *TRANSCENDANCE*


BEAMER MOUNTED THE SNOWMOBILE, started the engine, and made
his first attempt to engage the clutch and move forward, which killed the
engine. He imagined Jako atop the pile looking down at him, probably grin-

ning, and he waved his arm vaguely in that direction to signal, 'I've got this.' He restarted the engine and gave it more gas as the machine strained to pull its toboggan sled loaded with wood. In due course it started to pull forward and he was off. He drove down snow-covered streets, as in this season they had become more highways for power toboggans than for cars. After a couple of kilometres he came upon First Street, and drove along it looking at house numbers. Two thirty-seven turned out to be a modest bungalow which fronted a massive garage or machine shed behind it. Beamer let the snow machine idle in the drive while he went to the door of the bungalow and knocked a few times.

A slender black man, he guessed somewhat younger than himself, pulled open the door. Despite it being winter, he was wearing only a t-shirt, shorts, and flip-flops. A gust of warm air issued from the room behind him. Like Fisher's cottage, this house was modest, but a little more spacious.

"Mister Changming?" Beamer asked.

"Oh my gawd," the other replied, "do I look Chinese?" His eyes twinkled with mirth and naked curiosity. "But do come in," he invited, looking Beamer up and down. Then he called: "Honey! Look what Santa brought!"

"I brought fire wood," said Beamer. "Where do you want it to go?"

"My name's Kyle," he self-introduced, ignoring Beamer's question as to where to unload.

"Hi Kyle," Beamer said. "Where do you want the wood?"

Kyle turned aside to direct his voice more toward the rear of the house. "Honey, come meet the new wood man!" Then directly to Beamer, "He's always carving on his maquettes. Sometimes he's mixing plaster or something and can't hear who's at the door—or me for that matter."

A door opened in the opposite end of the room and another figure emerged covered nearly head to foot in plaster dust. He was wearing a coverall, a dust mask and eye goggles. He sported an enormous mane of black hair now frosted with dust, making him resemble a lion. He strode to the door, pulled down his dust mask and lifted the goggles up to his forehead revealing clearly Oriental features. He extended his hand to Beamer. "Changming," he said.

"So I guessed," Beamer replied, taking his hand, which was stronger than he might have expected, given his gracile build. "I already met Kyle."

"Has he hit on you yet?" Changming grinned from a naked patch of skin around his mouth that had benefitted from the protection of the dust mask. He spoke without an accent.

"Not exactly," said Beamer, "but then I'm not really wired for that. No judgement though."

"None taken," Changming said. "But Kyle trolls for cod fish all the time—shameless slut. Do you want some coffee?"

"Thanks, but I left the power toboggan running outside. I brought your fire wood. Where do you want it?"

"Well, thank you. Could you just pull it around behind the shed there and we'll help you unload." Beamer nodded and headed toward the door.

"Are you sure you don't want some coffee?" asked Kyle.

"Maybe another day," said Beamer. "I've got a lot more deliveries to make. Thanks though." He left the house, remounted the snow machine, and drove it to a garage door at the rear of the building. The machine shed was certainly large enough to store the wood inside. There was also a passage door beside the garage door which might prove to be the best place to unload.

Beamer had no sooner dismounted from the toboggan than the passage door opened and Changming appeared, now swaddled in a down parka, garb better suited to the weather, though not for heavy work. Beamer loaded his arms with wood and went through the door to find Kyle wearing a coat now and some work boots and pointing to where they wanted the wood pile to be laid. Beamer started the pile by laying the split wood he was carrying in alternating layers to form an anchor column for the wood that would follow, but when he looked up from the work he stood staring.

The machine shed was a cavernous space lighted from overhead by some sodium vapour lamps that gave the interior an amber glow. But what filled the room appeared more like a movie set. There were work tables, mixing tubs for plaster, a wide array of various tools, especially rasps of different sizes, saws, trowels, dremel tools, extension cords tangling on the floor all half buried under drifts of plaster dust. And everywhere there were whole sections of tree trunks still in their bark, and branched sections of upper limbs, pieces of limestone and granite and sandstone, rolls of chicken wire, light gauge rebar, and on and on. But from the chaos of tools and materials on the floor there rose the most magnificent looking model of part of a building interior. It was like nothing Beamer had ever seen before. The inspiration was gothic—like a scale model for a transept of a cathedral or castle—yet the columns and arches more closely resembled the branching trunks of trees that both followed the logic of gothic arches and columns but fused them playfully with the organic forms of a forest canopy. The maquette nearly filled the machine shed and was large enough even to walk into, but Beamer couldn't tell from the model what scale it was compared to its intended size. He felt Brobdingnagian within it, despite its already considerable size. Clearly, however, even this massive model was only part of Changming's vision. Dangling everywhere from the walls of the shed were huge sheets of butcher paper covered with sketches of bridges, balustrades, columned halls and forums, avenues and temple-like structures, all of them informed by the same design sensibility— things carved in stone that might have grown from it instead.

Changming appeared at Beamer's elbow. "You like it?" he asked.

"I...I..." Beamer stammered.

"He likes it," Kyle chimed in.

"What is this thing?" Beamer asked.

"It's the future I want," said Changming. "It's the future I see. But it's also the past."

"How is that possible?"

Changming shrugged off the question. "How could it be possible that somebody jumps out of their clothes into the sky?"

"So, you heard about that?"

"We're a close group here," Changming said, casting his eyes over the maquette rather than looking too directly at Beamer.

Beamer shook his head. "But a guy jumping out of his clothes is a dream. This is real, or it could be."

"Anything that's possible can become real—can manifest—given the right conditions," observed Changming.

"Who are you?" said Beamer. "I mean, I know who you are, but..."

"My parents emigrated here from Hong Kong two years before I was born. I was born here, so I have no memory of living in China, other than visits to see relatives. I grew up here, finished high school when I was thirteen. Then I studied architecture and engineering and got a double degree by the time I was sixteen. Then I spent a term in Cologne and the Sorbonne learning about gothic architecture. I love it! I absolutely love it! I don't think high gothic architecture has ever been surpassed for sheer grace and minimalism of form. Anyway, then I spent four months in a west coast rain forest. I just did one of those volunteer things where you can join an expedition and help with camp cooking and specimen collections and crap jobs like that. It gave me a chance to sketch a lot of nature forms, especially of forest canopies, flowers, bark patterns, rock formations, fossils, all that amazing stuff."

"And then I discovered Christopher Alexander's *Pattern Language*. Have you ever read it?"

"Can't say that I have," Beamer confessed.

"Pity. Well Alexander was this guy who rambled all over the world studying archeological digs and ancient buildings, some still in use today—like the cave city of Petra in Jordan, and the Pueblos in New Mexico, and Angkor Wat in Cambodia—as well as consulting with a slew of other people about the most ageless, most elegant, and most beautiful design solutions for meeting human needs. They identified two hundred and fifty-three basic patterns that were the architectural equivalent of Jung's archetypes, or Chomsky's transformational grammar..."

"Whoa!" Beamer protested. "You lost me at Angkor Wat."

"Sorry," Changming said, though he wasn't. "It's something essential, you know? Too many architects are self-absorbed little poofs. But the spaces we live in shape who we are and how we get along with each other. Buildings shouldn't be about the designer's ego. We used to be able to afford that but we can't anymore. Buildings should be about the people who live in them—spaces that make us feel pleasure and safety and connection—that remind us about the best in ourselves. That stuff absolutely blows my hair back." With that, Beamer couldn't help noticing again the huge mane of black hair streaked with plaster dust that encircled Changming's face. He did indeed resemble someone who had recently taken shelter from a gale, or perhaps was a distant relative of the cowardly lion in *The Wizard of Oz*. "What I mean," he resumed, "is that these three things, gothic architecture, the pattern language, and natural forms got mashed up in my head somehow and came out like this." He swept his hand in the direction of the model.

"And then he met me," Kyle interjected.

"And then I met Kyle," Changming echoed, smiling.

"So how did you get here?" Beamer asked.

Changming shrugged. "Sort of by process of rejection I guess."

"Rejection?"

"That's pretty much it," he confirmed. "I came back here with all these ideas but got this really weird reaction from other architects. Everybody raved about the designs at the same time as no one thought they were feasible. They just don't fit the sleek, cubist approach or the tortured twists and turns of new urbanist styles. Besides, nobody thought I could find the money to build something like this, or anyone who would want to underwrite it."

"So you found your way here."

"No," he said, "Tatum Barnes found me—pining away in a basement flat making little balsa wood models and using dental tools on plaster maquettes. The dust drove my landlady crazy. Anyway, Tatum was taken with the style I guess and asked me if I had any hope for the future. I asked her if she was crazy, you know? Then she brought me here. She introduced me to some really fine people. And then they gave me this great studio space, don't you think?"

"I do think," Beamer agreed. "And what do they want you to do?"

"They have no fucking clue," Kyle chimed sarcastically, then giggled.

Changming looked puzzled himself. "Fisher just tells me to 'keep dreaming'—but to 'dream out loud' he calls it. Something to do with Jung's 'active imagination' or some such. I don't think anybody here is sure where all this is going to wind up. But the Quakers are saying they see patterns similar to these in their Meetings. What do you make of that? I don't understand how they can see anything sitting in a circle with their eyes shut, can you?"

Beamer shrugged. "Well," he said, "I'm not a meditator and I sure don't know what they could mean, so I've got nothing there."

"Me too," agreed Kyle.

"Me too," said Changming. "So I guess the way is to keep dreaming, as Fisher says."

Beamer nodded without speaking, then, "That's what Fisher tells me too."

"To keep dreaming?"

"Well, sort of," Beamer said. "He told me to keep making mandalas and to remember my dreams."

"And are you?"

"Since I came to the Coulee, I've been remembering more of my dreams, but I haven't felt the urge to make a mandala lately. Maybe the rapture mandalas were just for me, just my way of telling myself to get out of the situation I was in."

"Our dreams are never just for ourselves," Kyle said gravely. "Maybe you could stop making your mandalas because you started remembering your dreams. Ever think of that?"

Beamer glanced at Kyle, brought up short by the sudden shift from joker to philosopher.

"Fisher's like Tatum," said Beamer. "Everything they say seems to have layers and they never tell me which layer they're coming from next..." Beamer let his voice trail off as he scanned the workshop once again. "Would you mind if I come back here later for a while?" he asked.

"Any time," Changming replied, "but why?"

"I don't know why," Beamer confessed. "I just like how I feel when I'm here. I'll bring more wood or something."

"It's not the price of admission you know. Lots of people come here and just sit. None of us knows why exactly."

"Except the Quakers," Kyle again.

Changming chuckled. "Yes. They say being here is like being in one of their Meetings over there at the Lighthouse. They don't say much more than that. You should pay them a visit sometime."

"Why?"

"I don't know," he said.

The three men found themselves standing in the plaster dust, silently nodding their affirmation without knowing what exactly they were affirming or why they were doing it together.

Beamer was the first to rouse himself in the moment. "I'll get some more wood," he said, turned on his heel and headed toward the door.

# CHAPTER 21

*When they ask you who you are, say to them:*
*I am radiance unnamable;*
*I am before form and in forms;*
*I am unborn and I never die;*
*I fill myself with myself even as I empty myself of myself.*
*I am what cannot be spoken, or heard, or known.*
*I am before time was and I will be when*
*time completes its golden circle.*
*I am always.*

— OSIO SMITH, *TRANSCENDANCE*

BEAMER FINISHED HIS JOURNAL entry. He was learning that any movement of his body on waking caused dream images to slip back into the shadows, like the bodies of fish disappearing into a depth of water. But today he managed to capture the highlights of his dream from the night before and wrote them down.

*26 January 2027 — Dreams—ah, dreams: No dreams—that I recall. Just an image. Does that qualify as a dream, I wonder? This large bird, I think maybe a raven, was flapping and flapping and throwing itself against the roof of this cage, like it was in a zoo, trying to get out. That's all. Just that bird trying to get out. Woke up feeling angry.*

Tatum had gone on another errand to the city—either Finder business or a pick-up and delivery run. So Beamer had slept in his own bed for the night. He pulled on some clothes and started nosing around in the kitchen for some sort of breakfast. Unsuccessful, he decided to go to the Barn for what he might find there. Then he heard a chime coming from some distance off. It was like hearing a wind chime from a hundred metres away, distant, yet clear. It sounded familiar, though he couldn't think what might account for that familiarity.

He stowed his journal in the desk drawer, grabbed his coat and left his room. He could still hear the chime coming from outside—regular, insistent.

Beamer walked briskly through the snow, but none too directly, toward a spot vaguely mid-way between the Barn and the chiming sound. Coming from the opposite direction was Jasper Beckett whom he accosted: "What is that?" Beamer asked.

"What is what?"

"That chiming sound?"

"Oh, yeah," said Jasper. "That's coming from the Lighthouse. The Friends are Meeting and that's their way of letting anybody else know who wants to join them. They generally start the Meeting about ten minutes after the chime stops."

"Thanks," said Beamer. Jasper continued on his way in the direction of the machine shed. For his part Beamer went toward the Lighthouse. Once he arrived, he found another of Corbin Galen's little signs: "No matter how attached you may be to your own opinions, think it possible that you might be mistaken."

If this was religion, he wanted no part of it. He had grown up in an agnostic household where religious observance had never been part of the daily round—or the weekly round for that matter. On that account, his rejection of religion had none of the vehemence of those who had suffered trauma from a religious institution or cleric, but rather the indifference of someone who had neither been much involved nor had any desire to be. But the Friends were another matter. They were an unknown quantity. He was drawn by curiosity and the spontaneous prompting he felt in the moment—rather like the attraction he felt to Tatum back when they lived in the city. He was also curious about how the Friends fit into what was happening at the Coulee.

He approached the school house they called the Lighthouse and ascended three steps to a double door, one side of which he pushed open, and stepped inside. He was met immediately by an old Aboriginal man. His face was deeply lined with a bulbous nose, leathery looking cheeks netted all over with wine-coloured rosacea, and long, straight, black hair streaked with grey. His face mapped suffering. Yet he smiled, nodding his welcome and then said: "Have you ever been to Meeting before?"

"No, I haven't," Beamer said.

The man smiled and nodded again. "I see," he said. "Well, welcome. This is how things go," and he handed Beamer a small folded slip of paper. "You're welcome to sit anywhere. All seats are first class."

"Thank you," he said, accepting the slip and casting his eyes around the room for a place to sit. About twenty chairs were arranged in a circle with the centre of the circle left empty. A dozen or so adults and a half dozen children were already seated or nestled on laps, some with eyes closed, others looking fixedly toward the centre of the circle. The younger children were fidgety but amazingly quiet for their age. A couple of adolescents were participating as adults but with the characteristic awkwardness of their age and stage. At one end of what had been a one-room school were piled the tumbling mats that Corbin Galen used on weekdays. In one corner was a cupboard stuffed with rolled up yoga mats, bolsters of different sizes, foam plastic blocks the size of bread loaves, two piles of meditation cushions, and a couple of dozen nylon straps that may have been recycled seat belts. Tall windows were on the east and west walls of the building. Between most of the window frames steel rings had been screwed into the walls—rings that, together with the seat belts, must have been more yoga gear. But today all this equipment had been neatly stowed in the cupboards or stacked at the north end of the room.

He found three empty seats side-by-side and sat down in the middle one. He continued to survey the space looking for some sign that it might be a church. But there was no altar or pulpit or pews or song books or any of the other paraphernalia he expected. It wasn't even clear if anyone in particular was leading the gathering. He folded his arms and placed the ankle of one leg on the opposite thigh and slouched a bit into his chair. After a few moments he felt that for some reason his posture was simply inappropriate in the circumstances. No one had looked at him, or said anything, or gestured in any way. But he could already feel something about the group that tolerated neither empty formality nor nonchalance. Now he just felt awkward. He wished someone would announce a greeting or recite a prayer or introduce the theme for today's sermon or sing a song or something besides this—quiet.

Grasping for purchase, he opened the folded slip of paper he was given more than half expecting it to be some tract, or perhaps a donation envelope. It would be a relief to have something to read—anything. It said:

Sit still.

Be quiet.

Pay attention.

Speak only if spoken to.

That was it. Beamer wondered if this was some sort of joke they played on newcomers, but no one was looking at him in particular, nor was anyone laughing. Could they be serious? *Speak if spoken to?* His uneasiness increased a notch until he noticed Tatum coming through the door. She glanced around the room and caught sight of him. The greeter at the door didn't offer her a slip of paper, so she must know the routine. Tatum moved quietly around the outside of the circle until she could sit in one of the empty chairs beside him. She noticed the paper still open in his hand and the perplexed look on his face. She leaned close to his ear and whispered: "Don't try to figure it out. Just do what it says." He nodded wordlessly and then tried to go with the flow. Tatum let her eyes drift closed and exhaled deeply, a gesture that seemed to make her settle even more into the chair. If she inhaled again, Beamer couldn't hear it. He continued to look around the room for clues, for signs, for rules about how he should behave. Nothing. But he felt his spine straightening, his feet coming together on the floor, his hands in his lap, palms resting downwards on his thighs, and finally, his eyes too slowly closed.

He sat for a long time this way during which nothing seemed to be happening. Then across the circle came a stir as a man stood up—someone he hadn't yet met from the Coulee community, but whose name he would later learn was Alex Brighton. He looked ancient—in his eighties or nineties. He rose without assistance or visible fragility, but his movement was nevertheless slow and deliberate, as if the mere act of standing required that he focus his attention to extend his limbs against the downward pull of age. His hair was straight, shoulder-length and entirely white. His features were angular but radiated a craggy gentleness. Oddly large and very thick glasses were perched precariously at the end of his nose threatening at any moment to fall off and giving him an owlish appearance.

"I have a care, friends," he said in a gravelly voice, "that there are fires burning all around us. Fires we can't put out. They can only burn themselves out. So we need to stand as we were taught. Stand in that cool place—that steady place of careful watching—mindful of what has been, what is now, and what is to come." Then he sat down again. His words were like tiny ripples on an otherwise motionless ocean of stillness. No one responded in any way and the words hovered for a moment in the empty space in the circle before they seemed to sink down into some ether that swaddled them again in quiet. Beamer looked at Tatum who continued to sit, unfazed. No one moved nor was anything else said for the remainder of the Meeting. Then, as by some unspoken signal, everyone stood up, joined hands briefly, and then started exchanging handshakes around the room. The children leaped from their chairs like coiled springs, chased each other around the adults until finally they went rushing out the doors like a gust of leaves blown down a trail. Tatum joined the general circulation while Beamer found his hand being shaken, his shoulder slapped as if congratulations were called for. Various others introduced themselves, and then one or two people at a time straggled out of the Meeting room until it was mostly empty.

Tatum looked at him, amused. "You survived your first Meeting," she smiled ruefully.

"I guess so," said Beamer, "though I'm not sure. What was that?"

"What was what?"

"What did that guy say?"

"What did you hear him say?" Tatum asked.

"I don't know—nothing, I guess," Beamer replied.

"Nothing?"

"Well," Beamer revised, "not nothing."

"Not nothing is something then, right?"

Beamer shook his head wanting to dismiss this bit of verbal dodge ball. "Sure. Not nothing is something. But I don't know what it was."

"Hmm," said Tatum. "So you heard something but you're not sure what. That's something my love. You just need to figure out what it was."

"There you go again," said Beamer.

"Go where?"

"You're doing that thing you did when we talked in the park."

"It's who I am," she said.

"I know, but…"

"Listen," she started. "I'm talking like I did in the park because what you heard is similar to what we were talking about in the park. So it deserves a similar conversation. You can ask me what that was, but it doesn't matter what I think he said. What matters right now is the meaning it had for you. Only you know that. And maybe it's nothing. Maybe there was nothing there for you, specifically, personally, this time. Sometimes Meeting is like that. There's nothing there but the silence, the stillness. For most of us, for some reason none of us understands very well, the stillness itself is often enough. But sometimes there's more—something appearing in the form of words that is for the whole group, or maybe just one person in the group. It's never the same twice in a row. There were two dozen people there and what he said may have meant something different to every one of them. What it may mean for us as a group is something that takes a lot longer to gel. You have to be patient."

"And let it digest," Beamer offered.

"Yes. Let it digest."

They left the Lighthouse and began an aimless stroll through the Coulee. The air was clear and cool but lacked the biting sting of bygone winters. Even though it was near noon, the winter sun had a golden quality as it cast the branching shadows of trees on the naked snow. To Beamer the shadows resembled the tangled networks of veins and arteries in some ancient skin.

"What are the Friends doing here?" Beamer asked.

"What are they doing here?" Tatum echoed.

"Yes. I mean they don't seem to fit with what all the rest of you—all the rest of us—are doing here."

"And what is it you think the rest of us are doing here?" Tatum's question was plain and open, with no tone of challenge.

Facetiously, "Making rapture mandalas?"

"That's pretty good," Tatum said. "Actually, it's very good. That's probably exactly what a Meeting is—a group rapture mandala. They'd love that."

"Now you're mocking me," said Beamer.

"Well, maybe a little," Tatum admitted. Then she slid her arm into the crook of his elbow so that they could walk closer together. "But what the Friends are doing here is bringing part of what we think we need if we hope to create a way of life that can survive into the deep future."

"So you think we need religion for that?"

"No," said Tatum, "but I do think we need spiritual insight. We need a practice of steady mindfulness different from anything we had in the past."

"Oh-oh," said Beamer. "Here comes the Kool-Aid."

"I don't think so," Tatum replied. "I don't think we need a new organized religion, especially like the ones of the past. But spirituality—a concern for the ultimate questions in life—is wired right in to human nature. You can't just make that stuff go away. We have proof of that from the French, Bolshevik, and Chinese Cultural Revolutions and from other secular creeds. Dogmatic responses to the ultimate questions in life are never sufficient for thoughtful people. So no creed is going to offer an adequate vessel for the human spiritual alchemy, even that of science as we practise it today."

"And yet you told me that Badger Coulee is modelled after a monastery," said Beamer.

Tatum nodded. "I did. But it's a lot easier to live in than to describe."

"I still don't get what any of this has to do with our going over the cliff of extinction," said Beamer.

Tatum shrugged. "Because what is taking us over the cliff is at root spiritual. It's the wrong answers we've been giving to the spiritual questions of what human life is about. What's a good life? How do we live a good life? How do we live in a way that strengthens the whole community of life? Every culture answers these questions somehow—one way or another. Ours has answered them in ways that guarantee our extinction."

"So what are the right answers to those questions?" Beamer asked. "Do you have them?"

Tatum fixed her eyes on the ground ahead of her feet as they walked along. "No," she said simply.

"So what is it again that we're doing here?" Beamer pressed.

Tatum shrugged again. "Maybe just trying to live together so we don't re-peat the mistakes of the past. Maybe just learning from history is enough. I don't know. But what I do know is this: To the question of how do we live a good life—the answer of material affluence has been the wrong answer. And to the question of how do we live a good life—the answer of ever-increasing profit and power has been the wrong answer. And to the question about how we can live to strengthen the whole community of life—the answer that we don't worry about the community of life at all because all of it can be replaced by stripping and consuming resources as fast as possible, has been the wrong answer. They're wrong because they violate every other human value worth mentioning. And these are basically spiritual questions—questions about values—not questions that we can find answers to in science, or economics, or politics, or technology for that matter. All these things go where we point them. To unfix the fix we've got ourselves into, we need a new direction for our science, economics and politics. What that is though, is something I can't claim to have the answer to. Probably Laurel Fey does. She's way smart."

"And so the Friends?" Beamer asked.

"The Friends..." Tatum mused. "I don't think the Friends are important because they're Friends. But maybe they're our spiritual ear to the ground when we need all our ears open, as Fisher's fond of saying. In times of darkness somebody needs to mind the light. Why not them?"

# CHAPTER 22

*"Consider a pool of water," my Companion said.*
*And it came into view; a still pool of crystal clear water, surrounded by a mossy*
*bank deep in the forest. The surface glistened with light, but not from any source*
*overhead. Its depths were limpid but fathomless darkness. He tossed a pebble into*
*the water and rings opened in the flawless surface, spreading wider and wider.*
*"A pebble tossed in water is a common figure illustrating how*
*our actions can have consequences that spread out affecting*
*others," he said. "But the simile is too simple."*
*"How so?" I asked.*
*He tossed another pebble into the pool which landed on the surface*
*but didn't sink. It bobbed on the glossy mirror of the water,*
*neither skipping nor disappearing beneath the surface.*
*"Our lives are more than a single pebble toss—a single act. Our actions*
*are like a pebble that bobs at the surface making wave after wave of causes*
*pass into time. The waves are the pressure of our intentions, the causal*
*effects of our state of consciousness. Sometimes the pebble jumps around*
*erratically making choppy little wavelets. Sometimes, it moves up and*
*down in a slow, measured rhythm sending out deep, smooth undulations*
*that have long periods and great strength. Everything we do sets in motion*
*a train of consequences, whether we agitate the water or smooth it.*
*"If the pebble were conscious," he continued, "it might be remembering*
*things, or imagining things that induced jerky, shallow spasms. Or, it may*
*have calmed its mind and focused its intentions into slow, deep waves. But*
*in either case, the reality of where the pebble is would be the same. It is held*
*in the surface of the water like an image in a mirror. It is captive there."*
*"But what if the pebble became very still?" I asked.*
*He smiled quietly and was silent before answering.*
*"Indeed," he said. "What if the pebble could rest on*
*the water in perfect stillness? What then?"*
*"It would sink through the surface and disappear?" I offered.*
*"No," he said. "Then it is the water that moves the pebble."*

— OSIO *SMITH, TRANSCENDANCE*

BEAMER ROSE WITH THE SUN which, it being only a few weeks after the Winter Solstice, was almost eight-thirty in the morning. Tatum had made another run to the city and was staying in her apartment there. So he decided to make his way to the Board Room where he acquired his breakfast which he took alone at a table near the main fireplace. This morning the room was sparsely populated with even those few present looking to be in an introverted mood. Some were reading books, browsing tablets, knitting or engrossed in other solitary pursuits. This suited Beamer. While he could tolerate and sometimes even enjoy the company of other people, he often also found it oppressive and stressful. Mercifully this morning no one approached him or even acknowledged him from a distance, leaving him undisturbed in the hermitage of his own company. Within that hermitage, however, he felt busy.

A lazy fire smouldered in the great hearth at the end of the Board Room which gave more smoke than heat. Presently someone from the kitchen came by, jabbed at the embers with a wrought iron poker tempting here and there a lick of flame. Then he carefully placed four sizeable logs on the bed of embers. In a minute or two they were on fire lending to the hall a comforting glow. For a time he watched the flames curl in their fluid incandescence around the fresh logs. The fire's hypnotic movement passed around the pool of busy turbulence that Beamer could feel within, calming and centring him, and finally settling toward resonance with his thoughts. He wasn't conscious of exactly what he was busy with—only that he had been inwardly busy, and that now, despite the persistence of that feeling, the fire somehow helped him drift above it and surveil it, like scouting an ambush. He remained for some time floating over that gyre.

*See Fisher now!* The thought burst in as if someone was standing beside him shouting the words. Beamer jerked, the placid twilight of a moment ago now flashing away in the glare of attention. Without further delay, he brought his dishes back to the cafeteria window and then headed out of the Barn toward Fisher's cottage. He wrapped lightly on the door only to hear from inside, "Come!"

Beamer stepped in to see Fisher with a mug of tea in his hand, lounging back in his wheelchair with his feet up in the direction of the wood stove. "Tea for you there on the counter if you like," Fisher said, indicating a steaming mug of tea in the kitchenette. Without thinking about exactly how Fisher might know to make tea for him in advance of his arrival, he simply crossed the room, retrieved the mug and mumbled his thanks. Sitting at what served as Fisher's dining table cum desk was a woman Beamer had not yet seen on any of his walks, but he did remember her from the story night in the Barn. She appeared Icelandic—medium height and slender build with hair so blonde it was nearly white. She looked close to his own age. Her eyes were glacier blue and fixed momentarily on him with curiosity. After sizing him up it appeared that her interest in him quickly abated. Scattered on the table in front of her were dozens of plastic cubes about four centimetres on a side, possibly from a child's building set. They were of many colours and could be locked together in various shapes. She was casually fitting them this way and that, but with no obvious plan for building anything that Beamer could recognize.

"This is Laurel Fey," Fisher announced. "Laurel, this is—who are you again?"

"Beamer. Beamer Farris."

"Ah! Right you are. The mandala guy. But then I suppose you would be right about what your name is, wouldn't you?" Without apology Fisher turned to Laurel and said, "Meet Beamer Farris."

"Hey," she said, without looking up.

"Any dreams?" asked Fisher.

Beamer glanced at him, then remembered their last conversation. "Uh, no," he said. "I don't think so. Well, maybe. A bit of one."

"Everything is made of bits," Fisher said. "Do tell."

Beamer shrugged. "Just an image, really. There was this raven. At least I think it was a raven. A big black bird. It was like trying to fly upwards into the sky, but there was this cage in the way. Like the raven was in a zoo or something and trying to get out, but its cage had a roof and it was flapping against the roof trying to get out. That's all."

"That's all," Laurel echoed, her voice flat, as if he was missing something obvious. She continued to play with the plastic cubes without looking at him.

"Did you ask it anything?" said Fisher.

"Ask it anything?"

"Yes. It was right there. It was in difficulty. Did you ask it how it got there? Or why it was in a cage? Or where it was trying to go? Or if it had something for you?" Fisher pressed.

"No."

"Ugh," said Laurel. "Missed opportunity. Put forth more effort next time."

"I beg your pardon?"

Fisher tagged off Laurel: "It wasn't just any bird you dreamed. It was a raven."

"Well sorry," Beamer said somewhat defensive now. "I didn't think birds could talk."

"In dreams they can," said Fisher.

"Ravens," Laurel butted in, still not looking up, "were sometimes thought to mediate between life and death. They fly between worlds. Sometimes creators, sometimes the bearers of bad news. The Greeks and Romans associated them with prophesy and as being messengers of the gods. In Icelandic legend, ravens guided our ships from the Faroe Islands to Iceland. Following his murder, it is said that the body of the Christian martyr Vincent of Saragossa was protected by ravens until his followers could retrieve it and bury it properly, whereupon his grave continued to be guarded by them. A raven warned Benedict of Nursia that his food was poisoned by jealous rivals, thus saving his life, and later they fed Benedict during his retreat in the caves of Subiaco in Italy. Aboriginal legends depict them both as creators and as tricksters. They also appear in the myths and legends of the Norse, the Germans, biblical sources and tales from India. Your raven might be a Thor or he might be a Loki. No telling until you chat with him. He was caged right there for your convenience. And," she said with emphasis, "they can be trained to talk." The corners of Laurel's mouth turned slightly up as if she was enjoying this.

"I see," Beamer said, cowed. "Next time I see a raven in a dream, I'll put forth more effort." He felt that both of them were playing him now—perhaps even testing him. "You know a lot about ravens."

Laurel shrugged. "I know a lot about a lot of things," she said, as if observing that the sky was often blue, or that water was wet. Her claim was all the more believable on that account.

"And humble too," Beamer needled.

"Humble too," she confirmed matter-of-factly.

After a pause, Beamer asked: "What's with the blocks?"

Laurel stopped fitting and unfitting the blocks, dropping her hands in her lap. "Yes," she said emphatically. "That's exactly it. What is it with these blocks? Maybe I shouldn't even be working with blocks. Maybe I should be using bubbles, but they're too fragile, don't you think? Or maybe I could try Plasticine. That would be earthy, but probably too pliable. Glass is too brittle. Steel rusts and it's really heavy. Cadmium might be nice, but probably too toxic. Cellulose burns. Cloth is too flimsy. Plutonium would be interesting but we know where that leads. What's a person to do?"

"She's messing with you," Fisher interrupted. But Laurel was looking steadily at Beamer without a trace of messing. Then she lifted her hands from her lap again to resume trying to fit the cubes—into what? "No," she said with finality. "The cubes will be fine. I just need to call them cells instead."

Beamer looked at Fisher, questioning. "What's with the blocks," Fisher explained, "is that she's trying to invent a new culture. You could think of it as her rapture mandala."

"A new culture," Beamer gaped.

"Mmm," said Fisher matter-of-factly, then shrugged. "It's what we need, wouldn't you say? Our choices right now seem to boil down to trying to sustain our rotten-to-the-core culture or else come up with something different. Either we go extinct clinging to our mistakes, or we learn from them. Laurel is trying to learn from them."

"A new culture, just like that?"

"Well, I admit—as they say—it's a dirty job but…"

"…somebody's got to do it," Beamer completed in unison. "I don't think of people just making up cultures."

Fisher looked more serious. "Who do you think makes them up then? God? The ancients? Aliens? What do you think you do all day with other people? Aren't we always and continually making up our culture? Reciting the same stories to each other, over and over until we almost believe them?"

"You want me to believe that a woman playing with plastic blocks is going to show us a way around the shit-storm that's coming?"

Fisher pushed back on his chair and pulled his legs down to the floor, then pulled his feet up to place them on the foot paddles of the chair. He leaned toward Beamer. "Sit down," he said. Beamer looked around. The only available chair was opposite where Laurel sat. He slid carefully into the empty chair, Laurel glancing up briefly, then back to her work.

"Of course Laurel Fey won't do this alone," Fisher continued. "Every culture is like a crystal garden made of layer upon layer of accretions over time— stories, art works, ideas, values. Maybe you remember as a kid, we used to pour hot water in a jar and then mix in salt until the water couldn't hold any more. Then we'd let it cool and finally drop in a single crystal of salt which caused all the dissolved salt to fall out of solution, growing piles of crystals in the bottom of the jar. Laurel isn't trying to design every crystal. What she's trying to find is the seed that others can form around and bring us to some other way of living than the one that's about to end us pretty damn soon."

"And she can do this?" Beamer asked, incredulous.

"Who knows?" Fisher said. "We've been talking about it a lot, ever since we got together out here at Badger Coulee. The most pressing question is not how to rescue consumer culture from its delusions; no one can do that anymore. What we're looking for is what comes next. There is no going back. We need a way out. We either go over the cliff with everyone else, or we find that handful of crystals, the seeds, that can shake everything into a different pattern that just maybe doesn't repeat the old mistakes."

"And you think she can find it?"

"Well, maybe she can and maybe she can't. Time will tell. Laurel is an archivist. That makes her a strange bird from the start."

"I can find it," Laurel said.

"An archivist. You mean like a librarian?" Beamer tried.

"Well, sort of. Librarians curate many sources of information. Archivists zero in on one particular person, or institution, or event and try to gather and preserve everything known about it. What blows Laurel's hair back is epistemic structures."

"And that's what she's trying to do with the plastic cubes? Create epist... Episte-what?"

"Epistemic structures," Fisher repeated. "The big patterns that help organize how we know stuff and who we think we are. That's what the cubes are for."

"Cells," Laurel corrected.

"Cells then. Laurel, what are you trying to do with the cells?" Fisher asked.

She stopped fitting the cubes and set down her most recent assembly, an odd structure made of several series of blocks pressed together to form chains or wall-like pieces with cross-connections to other such pieces. If it was a model for a building, it made utterly no sense at all, Beamer thought. In fact, it looked more like one of those models of a folded protein molecule he'd seen in the biochemistry labs at university. Laurel placed the structure on the table and regarded both men quietly.

"Did you take chemistry in school?" she asked. Both nodded. "Then do you remember the periodic table?"

"Please don't test me on it," said Beamer, "but wasn't it that big wall chart with all the chemical elements on it?"

"That's it," she confirmed. "*The Periodic Table of the Elements* is a stunning intellectual achievement. It summarizes and organizes a great deal of what we know about the chemical elements that make up all physical beings. It also tells us how these elements interact with each other. It could even predict the properties of missing elements before they were discovered. Not only that, but embedded in the table is knowledge about how to create compounds of those elements, and the table itself can serve as an organizing structure for a huge array of other knowledge not directly related to things like atomic numbers and weights and electro-negativities."

"Whoa!" said Beamer.

"Okay. Okay," Laurel soothed. "This isn't about electro-negativities. My point is that we have this brilliant structure in the periodic table which serves what so far have been the main goals of science: to understand nature and to predict and control natural forces for human benefit. Understanding nature is pretty straight-forward—though certainly not easy. We can show we understand nature when our descriptions of how it behaves match up well with how it does in fact behave. Prediction is also straightforward in that we can see a correspondence between how we say ahead of time nature will behave and how in fact it does behave later in time. Control of the forces of nature can be shown by making things that start, stop or re-direct those forces according to what we want them to do."

"But the tricky word is 'benefit'. Benefit is a value word. When science is used to benefit people, we can't stop there. We have to ask, what do we mean by benefit? To whose benefit? What consequences follow from trying to pro-cure benefits of this sort? And so on. The answers to those questions aren't found in science, or in any tool of science, including the periodic table."

"So the upshot being?" Beamer pressed.

"The upshot being that we're in the jam we're in because we got the science right but the benefit wrong. We have to fix that."

"How?"

"Ah, yes," she sighed. "How indeed. I suggest we use science to interrogate benefit." Her face lit up, then she started to giggle with excitement. She loved this chase. It didn't seem to fit with what she had just said, making her seem eccentric—just as playing with the cells did.

Beamer didn't get what she found so amusing. "Continue," he said.

"Suppose for a minute," Laurel began, "that we stop mixing up science with its technical gadgets, or even with its findings. Suppose instead that we just look at science as a very useful method for observing and making sense of the world. Suppose we admit that somewhere along the line, science got hijacked by capitalism into making stuff for a consumer culture. So 'benefit' came to mean continuous growth in material affluence and addiction to the profits that obsession with growth could make. This understanding of benefit has led us to where we are now—facing extinction—ironically caused by affluence. Any understanding of benefit that leads to extinction must be mistaken because extinction ends all possibility of benefit. What other species works so hard for its own extinction? Idiotic, isn't it. So we've got ourselves to this cultural dead end. Ha!" she said, chuckling bitterly. "Cultural...dead...end. Get it? Ha!" Then refocusing: "We have to interrogate the idea of benefit itself. We can use the tools of science to do it. We need to discover the real, non-suicidal meaning of benefit, or else use what we learn to create a different meaning of benefit."

"Interrogate benefit? What does that even mean?" Beamer challenged.

Laurel scrunched up her face as she tried to pull apart a pair of the plastic blocks that were stubbornly locked together. Finally they gave, and she said, "There! Those can't go that way. They have to go this way." Then she muscled them back together within the larger structure she was working on. "Ah, yes," she said, "benefit."

"Well, again suppose for a minute that current events are teaching us one big lesson about our relationship with nature—that if we want to live into deep time, we need to live as symbionts, inter-dependent partners with nature, rather than as masters and controllers. So this is our first great big master rule for living well—that whatever culture we create in the future must be symbiotic within nature, not parasitic, or toxic, or extractive. Whatever bright ideas we come up with for new widgets or pastimes, they must always promote symbiosis, or at the very least, not diminish it."

"Harmony with nature. Check," said Fisher. Laurel glanced at him as if he was messing up her sand painting but carried on.

"Okay," she said. "So now the interrogating benefit piece. Maybe 'benefit' is entirely the wrong word. It still has overtones of growth and accumulation because it's easy to think of benefit as something material like a pension payment or a fringe benefit—something that adds to your horde."

"I think what we should be concerned with is a good life—and always, of course, in symbiosis with nature. Accumulating material benefits may not always contribute to a good life. But what I'm suggesting is that it could be a good life that we are using science to increase, and not so much material benefits."

"I think, when things finally fall apart, there will be a lot of angst about technology. A lot of people will be scrambling to rebuild technologies of all sorts and the material benefits and comforts they temporarily provided. We've been totally entranced by our tools and now we can't imagine a civilized life without them, or even with fewer of them. But maybe this is the very thing we need to set a new course, strike off in a new direction. Maybe we need to conserve certain technologies, but not the whole circus, and certainly not ones that make technology the centre of attention. Maybe this new culture puts technology in its place, someplace farther back in the bus and not always driving the bus. Maybe in this new culture, technology is not the principal measure of success for our species—but works in service of things we value more. We don't need a gadget for everything."

"So, suppose we create something like a periodic table, but it's not a chart on a wall about chemical elements. It's a bunch of cells, like this thing I've been playing with. Suppose that every cell has something in it that we think is essential to a good life in symbiosis with nature. It might be something from a wisdom writing, or a particular piece of art, or some practice like yoga or long-distance running. It's not about predicting or controlling physical elements. It's about a sacred chemistry for well-being. The chemistry of love—if you will—but not of romantic love: Rather, it's love as eros, the creative principle of life and ever more life. The table would summarize what makes for a good life. But it also represents an ongoing search for new elements that might further increase well-being, and new compounds made from known elements that yield surprise results—emergents. Whenever we put something in a cell that we think may contribute to the good life, it becomes a hypothesis about well-being. We could then use scientific methods to test each hypothesis, and keep testing them over time, as we evolve as a species along with our planet."

"At the start," Laurel continued, "we would probably have a very large number of candidate hypotheses about how to create a good life. But when we start to apply scientific method to them, maybe we could winnow them down to some simple fundamentals. This is just what happened in the early days of the physical sciences. They faced a bewildering variety of natural phenomena and observations that eventually got sorted out by identifying the central organizing principles or natural 'laws' that made sense of them. Maybe we could do a similar thing with human wellness and ecological fit. Maybe we could create a story about the good life based on verifiable, repeatable laws of well-being that we could support with evidence and refine over time."

"But self-proclaimed experts on happiness are a dime a dozen," Beamer objected. "Just give your heart to Jesus. Or submit to Allah. Or give me your money. Or shop at Mega-Mart. Or go kill for the cause—whatever I say it is."

"I know," Laurel admitted. "So we put each of those in a cell of the table and start to interrogate them using the methods of science. I don't think we can start from a prejudiced position. All wild ideas, or passages from old books, or proclamations of demagogues are fair game as long as they claim to benefit rather than harm humanity or violate the principle of symbiosis. Science doesn't tell us what is worth doing. Its role is to tell us how much difference it makes to a good life to do one thing rather than doing another. What to practice is the process of on-going value choices, while scientific method can be used to detect and measure differences in their effects. My point is that we no longer take them at their word, nor on the authority of some historical personage, nor because of the bullying of powerful institutions—whether of religion or the state."

"But humanity is such a fractious lot," Beamer protested. "How do we get everyone on board with something like this?"

Laurel shrugged. "We don't. We can't. All we need are some people who will do it. Maybe not very many at all. Who knows? Besides, we have to stop the conceit that a cause or idea is made valid merely by how many people support it. If what all of us here at the Coulee think is going to happen actually does happen, then billions of us won't even be here to argue. I just think that there's been enough blood spilled because of what some goatherd said three thousand years ago, and their followers who want to defend it and preserve it forever unchanged and unquestioned, amen. I would rather be part of a society that pursues an open-ended search for a good life instead of pretending they already know what it is. And I prefer that we pay attention to our experience and learn from it, that we come from a fearless place where we can test the truths we profess. If they can't stand the test, then they aren't true, and I think we'd be better off abandoning them than feeding our children lies and delusions and calling it faith. I hope as we moved along with this project, we would discover some really strong principles that made it easier to test new ideas as they occur to us. Just imagine though: A whole society seeking neither material affluence nor power nor growth for its own sake, but a good life for everyone on a flourishing planet. To me that's worth doing. I could give my life to that."

"Okay," Beamer conceded. "But why the blocks?"

Laurel shrugged. "People understand things in different ways. Some like words. Others like music. Still others like sculptures. I'm trying to find a form here that communicates what I'm thinking. That way, we might have a physical object to talk about in addition to pretty airy ideas. That would include more people, I hope, and give us a better chance of identifying important elements we might have overlooked otherwise. I don't even know if it'll work, or if I can build the table in this form. I'm just trying here..."

"I'm still not sure I get what you're driving at," Beamer confessed.

Laurel sighed again, not with consternation, but more a sense of sharing a challenge with a fellow explorer. "Okay," she said. "Maybe think of it this way." She dragged a blue block to the centre of the table, ignoring for a moment the much more complicated structure she had been working on. "Let this block represent a cell we think is fundamental to overall well-being. This cell is sitting on the table—the first storey of something that could be much taller, but we don't know how tall yet. So setting it on the table means it's foundational to a lot of other things higher up. Let's suppose this cell represents *t'ai-yo*—that hybrid practice that Corbin Galen is working on that combines t'ai-chi and yoga into a new practice. But we don't just stuff all of t'ai-chi and yoga into the cell. For example, classical t'ai-chi-chuan consists of one hundred and eight movements, but several of them repeat. There are ten single whip movements in the set; seven brush knees, six cloud hands, and so on. So deleting or reducing the number of repeated movements simplifies the set without losing its unique beneficial elements—or at least we can use science to determine that. We also know of twenty-one hundred yoga asanas, but the vast majority of them are variations on a handful of fundamental postures. So when he's done, Corbin might emerge with a physical practice that consists of a hundred movements or so that creates in the practitioner all the benefits of both traditions. Then we can use science to test which practice regime—t'ai-chi alone, yoga alone, t'ai-chi and yoga in combination, in their full or simplified forms—produce the greatest benefits in well-being. Since this cell is foundational in the sense that we can't imagine any practice more fundamental to either of them, then *t'ai-yo* becomes the foundation upon which we might build other cells—for example *kin-hin*, walking meditation, or ballet."

"So you think this sort of idea can be applied across the board of human activities and beliefs?" Beamer asked.

"Well, we don't know yet. We're just getting started. But I see no reason to rule out say putting our practice of a community commons into a cell, probably another candidate for a foundation cell, and then explore the contribution it makes to well-being. The same for what Ai Changming is doing with architecture, and the permies with food production. All of it, all of what we can imagine, could find its place in this structure as long as it's symbiotic with nature. Once we get more proven candidate practices into the Table, it will be much easier to see what is foundational to what, to pick out errors and fix them, to understand why we learn our A, B, Cs, rather than C, B, As. And all of it needs to flow into some kind of practice—to be made real in our lives, not just something we profess to maintain an illusory group identity."

Beamer's glance returned to Fisher who was already looking at him from across the room. "So," said Fisher, "what do you think?"

"I'm not sure what to think," Beamer confessed. "I think I understand where she's trying to go with the idea. I'm just not sure how a sculpture can be the seed of a whole new culture."

"Neither am I," Laurel confessed. "But whatever it turns out being, it's got to be pretty."

# CHAPTER 23

*More often than not we look to experts for guidance in*
*times of confusion. But equally often we find renewal*
*appearing first in lives that have been broken.*

— RUPERT PHILMORE,
*THE PSYCHODYNAMICS OF CULTURAL DISINTEGRATION.*

BEAMER SHOWED UP at the woodlot at the appointed time only to find Jako
already stacking the last of a small pile of split logs under the loose cover shed
they used for temporary storage. They had at least ten chords under cover and
Jako said there was enough wood for now and they should both take a day off.
So Jako saddled up on the power toboggan, Beamer climbed on behind him
and they drove the short distance back to the Coulee. Beamer got off the machine close to the Barn and Jako continued on to the cottage he shared with
his wife Hilda and their four children.

Now with time on his hands, Beamer stood for a moment casting his gaze
around the Coulee when his eyes came to rest on the Lighthouse. Changming
had told him that the Lighthouse was used both as a school and a practice
centre for meditation. So he set off in the direction of the old school house
which even early in the morning had light coming from its generous windows.

He got to the front door of the building only to see another one of the
small, framed announcement boards that were everywhere in the Coulee. It
had been mounted considerably lower than eye level for an adult, so he had to
bend a bit forward to read it. This one said: "You are fortunate indeed to have
been born in human form. Therefore, apply yourself promptly and with diligence to that which furthers." Beamer stared at the notice. That he was born
in human form seemed obvious enough. But apply himself how, and to what?
And what was it, exactly, that 'furthers'? Furthers what?

He rapped on the door of the building and waited. No one came to the
door. So he pushed it ajar and stepped inside. This part of the building was a
single fairly large room with a hardwood floor, tall windows, some pendulous

light fixtures dangling from the ceiling and two ceiling fans that churned the air quietly from above. The floor was covered with zabutons arrayed in neat rows, about thirty in all. All of the mats were occupied by children who appeared to be as young as eight or nine and some as old as twelve, most dressed in sweat suits of various colours.

A man stood at the head of the group, forty-something, medium height, gangly and wan looking, dark dishevelled hair. His body looked as if he had been beaten up, or only recently survived a third round of chemotherapy. He was barefooted like all the children and wore a nondescript grey sweatsuit. And yet entirely apart from what his body looked like, he stood erect and moved with a quiet grace that forced Beamer to revise his first impression of someone who was a beating victim to that perhaps of a dancer on the edge of anorexia. So this must be Corbin Galen, Beamer guessed. When he noticed Beamer come in he motioned for him to stand at the back of the room and wait. Then he returned his attention to the class.

"Alright then—feet together—stand straight but relaxed—hands with palms together in front of your chest." Corbin's delivery of these instructions was also surprising to Beamer in as much as he expected from such a body a weaker voice, more wounded. Instead, Corbin voiced his instructions as if every word was weighty, pregnant with hidden significance, enticingly mysterious. The way he spoke left Beamer feeing like he wanted to hear more. What was deep or mysterious about "feet together"?

"Begin *surya namaskar*," Corbin said. "Hands together—reach back—bend forward—now palms on the floor." The children reached back, their youth making them supple as willow, then swept their arms overhead continuing into a forward bend, pressing their palms flat against the floor.

"Again," said Corbin. Not "good." Not "wrong." Just again. The children returned to a straight standing position and all brought their palms back together in front of their chests, and stood waiting until Corbin himself mirrored the pose, a gesture they followed carefully, then they all reached back together. Corbin looked around the group without comment. "Again," he said. They repeated this series of simple movements three more times before Corbin said, "*Ardha padmasana*." His voice combined a no-nonsense demand for respect and attention with unmistakable affection. At this, all of the children settled down on their mats in a cross-legged position.

Corbin's gaze drifted over their faces, then settled on one girl, perhaps ten years old. "Madeline," he said. "What were you thinking when you were reaching back over your head?"

"I was thinking how cold my feet are," she said, blushing.

Turning to a boy this time, "Pablo, how about you?"

"I was thinking about that squirrel chucking away outside the window."

Corbin looked around for another target. "And how about you Mbali?"

"I was jus' stretchin' my arms," she said, a tiny smile raising the corners of her mouth.

Corbin smiled. "Just so," he said. He picked up a small mallet he had at hand and struck the side of a large brass bowl that chimed melodically and continued to ring for quite some time. All the time the chime was audible, the children listened as it gradually faded away. Corbin placed his palms together in front of his chest, bowed slightly, and then all the children mirrored his gesture, rose and headed to the back of the room to retrieve their coats and boots. For a moment Beamer felt mobbed, but they more or less ignored him giving him little more than a furtive glance as they got ready to leave. Strikingly, there was no chattering or horseplay. They applied themselves silently and diligently to leaving the room. In a few moments, Beamer and the teacher were the only two people left.

"Corbin Galen," he introduced himself with the same shallow bow as he gave his departing students. Then he walked toward Beamer with a hand extended. "How may I help?"

"Beamer Farris." Beamer shook his hand, deceptively strong in the grip. He had to revise his appraisal of Galen once again after actually touching him. Maybe he wasn't a broken down bantam weight boxer, or a chemotherapy survivor, or even an anorexic dancer after all. Maybe, Beamer thought, he was an ultra-marathoner, one of those spindly runners that you might think could be bowled over by a light breeze who was nevertheless tough as jerky and spent his free afternoons dragging truck tires and cinder blocks around the neighbourhood.

"Ah!" said Corbin, "the mandala man." His glance was direct yet soft, and completely focused on Beamer's eyes.

"So rumours of my madness have preceded me even here," said Beamer, self-deprecatingly.

"Indeed they have," Corbin smiled.

Beamer shrugged. "Haven't made a mandala in weeks. Must be losing my edge."

"It's winter," Corbin said. "Some streams run leaner in winter."

Beamer looked around the room, then back at Corbin. "I guess so. Rudy said I should drop in some day—get to know you. How did you get here?"

"Like everybody else, I guess," Corbin said. "Somebody found me, brought me here, and here I am. It's a long story." Beamer noticed that Corbin's eyes were grey, the sort of greyness that comes from the darkening of one's lightness and the enlightenment of one's darkness—the unmistakable gaze of an old soul.

"I could listen to a long story," said Beamer.

"Hmm, would you like some tea?"

Tea, Beamer had come to appreciate, was the nearly universal social ritual at Badger Coulee. They weren't a dry town on principle, and from time to time, locally made beer, hard cider and sometimes mead were on offer at the Board Room. But tea was the universal lubricant for all sorts of conversations. Corbin led him out of the large room into an annex that was once office space, now converted to storage and a living space for Corbin, including a small table where Beamer sat down as Corbin busied himself preparing their tea. He went about it with the same ceremonial formality as Fisher did and presently their mugs were full and steaming and Corbin sat down.

"I got here through a drug rehab program," said Corbin, watching Beamer's reaction carefully.

Beamer raised an eyebrow with a conspiratorial smile. Should he take this seriously? "Huh," he said. "I got here by acting out my psychosis in a public park. Go figure."

"I definitely want to hear that story someday," said Corbin. "Actually I'm not having you on. I'll spare you the tedious details, but some childhood crap led to self-medication which became a habit. The splendid body you see today is the legacy from that chapter of my life—well, not just a chapter—more like a whole book, a horror story, really. Luckily I crashed but didn't burn completely. I was homeless, jobless, and clueless, but somehow got myself into rehab. I met this other guy in the program—Frito we called him because he seemed so close to being crisped—who was doing pretty well for himself. But I couldn't tell what it was in the program that was keeping him sober. We started talking, you know, and he asked me if I ever learned yoga? I told him I thought that was for twenty-something women. He laughed. Said I should come with him to a class and we could see if I was woman enough to stay for the whole thing."

"So I went, you know. I wasn't really that interested in taking on this guy's challenge so much as I was curious. So in we went and I'm expecting this little slip of a girl in a spandex leotard and with an aromatherapy nebulizer going in the corner someplace and chunks of bamboo wind chimes rattling away in an open window. Instead, I see this guy who looks like a cross between a bouncer and a sumo wrestler, except he's not the least bit larded up, if you know what I mean. A hundred and ten kilos of solid muscle, I would guess. He was just very big. You would think someone like that would lumber around, but he moved like a snake—a very big snake." Corbin smiled as he remembered.

"Frito said this was Sensei—the teacher," Corbin continued. "That was all I needed to know about him. And that man turned out to be the hardest ass I ever met. I mean he wasn't nasty or cruel or violent in any way, but once you were in his dojo as he called it, he was like a dog with a bone. He started me with simple moves into and out of yoga postures, the asanas. But he had twenty other people, both men and women, in the room as well and he was teaching all of us different things. I couldn't understand how he kept us all straight. Anyway, he'd teach me something and then leave me to practice on my own while he wandered off to torment somebody else. I'd get just to the point where I felt like slacking off and there he'd be, right behind me, saying "Pay attention!" or he'd teach me something new and then wander off again. Occasionally he would demonstrate an asana or a movement and it was mind-boggling to watch because never in the thousand years would you think a person the size of him could bend that way. But he did. We had classes every other day with open practices in between. After a couple of months, it felt like I was living in that dojo. I'd go out of there swearing never to come back. The stuff he was teaching was ridiculously hard. But the next day, when class time rolled around, I was back in the dojo waiting for Sensei. He never smiled. He never dumped on anybody—ever. He hardly ever spoke except for 'pay attention!' or 'again!' or 'do this.'" But after a couple of months all I wanted to do was please him—succeed for him—show him. Damn well show him!"

Corbin's voice caught audibly. It was still an emotional memory for him. "So after a few weeks the rehab program wrapped up. I guess that was how long it took for them to play all the tricks they knew, which wasn't very many. But Sensei kept going, like some gigantic energizer bunny, but not the least bit cuddly. As time passed, I found out yoga was only part of what he knew. He was accomplished in t'ai-chi, chi-gong, kung-fu, and some Taoist martial arts we don't even know the names of in the west. Around then I discovered two things: One was I wanted to learn it all. The other thing was that I lost all desire to use. Something about standing on my head maybe, or counting my breaths, or the dogged discipline of Sensei, just changed me inside. I started to spot toxic desires as they arose, recognize them as just another form of thought, and that somehow gave me the ability to change my mind. I realized that it wasn't as easy as just tapping the ruby slippers and flying home to Auntie Em, but the combination of everything—the yoga and the martial arts, the meditation and diet, the discipline and routine, the focus on something other than me—all of it added up. It all added up to make the difference."

"I stayed with Sensei for six years, doing nothing else except one form of practice or another, in class and out. I wanted to learn everything Sensei knew. But when I finally left him, I realized I had learned all I could learn from him. What else he still knew that I hadn't learned yet? That would be worlds and worlds..." Corbin's voice trailed off in search of words. Their silence grew until Beamer finally spoke.

"And then," he prompted.

"And then I opened my own dojo," Corbin said. "That's really mostly what you do with that stuff, you know. T'ai-chi doesn't make you richer or get you in the sack with anybody. It's a teaching that changes you as you practice. But what you do with practice is share it. It's self-rewarding. But it doesn't get you anywhere else except ever more right back here. So I started teaching, passing on the practice. I had to live like a monk, because that's what you do when you're a monk, but without the habit. People won't pay much to be sane; they would rather be rich than sane. So teaching this stuff, living as a Sensei for others, is always marginal these days. Maybe always has been. So you have this choice to practice the wisdom you have and accept that you will live like a monk—very simply, but not without compensations—or you can give up the practice, have more stuff, and die rich."

"And it was the 'die' part that turned you off," Beamer guessed.

"Pretty much, that's it."

"So now you have your dojo going, how did you get to Badger Coulee?"

"Ah, that," said Corbin. "Well, I'm minding my own business teaching yoga and stuff and along comes this woman named Elizabeth. So can I call her Betty? No. Elizabeth. How about Liz? No. Elizabeth. She signed up for the beginners class but I was suspicious right away because she really was a slip of a thing with a spandex leotard and a mat that was frayed all around the edges and sort of beaten down flat in the middle. Either she got her gear second hand or she really used it a lot. She had me stumped why she would take yoga from me and not another twenty-something in spandex just down the street. But she kept coming and I started to get the feeling that I was being observed, and maybe rated somehow, you know, while she mostly pretended to be learning stuff from me."

"Anyway, after a few weeks of pretending that *bhujangasana*, cobra pose, was a stretch for her, so to speak, the other shoe dropped. She started cornering me after class with questions about other stuff than *bhujangasana*. At first I flattered myself to think she might be stalking me. But look at me! Anyway, it was stuff like: Did I think sustainability was possible anymore? Did I think a change was coming? Did I think our way of life could last into deep time? What is deep time anyway? So this went on and on."

"Sounds familiar," Beamer interjected.

"Yes," Corbin said, hardly pausing to ask himself how "yes" might be a response to "sounds familiar". "Anyway," he continued, "she kept coming back and asking me these posers and I guess I must have come up with reasonable answers. So it turns out she's a person called a "Finder" and there's Finders all over the countryside fanning out from this place called Badger Coulee, a couple dozen of them, looking for people who pretty much get it that the long term prospects for humanity about equal those of a snow cone in July, and it's time to try something different. And she knows of this ghost town, do I want to come? So before I really knew what I was doing, I closed my dojo and then I'm having tea with Fisher and then I'm here—with a new dojo before the old one even cooled off. That's it."

"Sounds familiar," Beamer repeated.

"What part?" Corbin asked.

"Meeting a Finder," said Beamer. "Mine was Tatum Barnes."

"Ah, yes," Corbin said, nodding his head. "I know of her."

"And then meeting Fisher—supposedly for tea."

"Have you met Laurel Fey?"

Beamer nodded without comment.

"So, what did you think?"

"A bit of an odd bird," said Beamer.

Corbin nodded, raising an eyebrow. "Well, she is that," he agreed. "But do you understand what she's doing?"

Beamer shrugged and sighed. "Part of it, maybe. Fisher said she's trying to cook up a new culture—one that isn't suicidal like ours is. And she talks about that periodic table of hers."

"And what do you make of that?"

"I think of culture as something that takes a lot of people a long time to dream up. I've never met anyone who thought they could do it on their own."

Corbin gave a chuckle. "She doesn't think she can do it alone. But she does think she can find the starter piece that could make the whole thing go. Most cultures start that way. They grow up from only a handful of basic ideas and values. But they have to be powerful values—powerful enough to push the rest of the culture to manifest through the efforts of lots more people. I think that's what she's after."

"And what are you after?" Beamer asked.

Corbin glanced out the window and reflected for a moment, then, "I think I can help her fill in some blanks."

"How?"

"Well," Corbin said, "I think Laurel's trying to create the seed for this new culture—basically some answer to the question: 'Since we're all here together, what are we here for? What are we doing? And why should we do it?' The answer that our culture gives to those questions is: 'We're here to get rich. Everyone should be trying hard to get richer because that's how we get the best out of ourselves. And we should do this because it's how you have a good life—which seldom means morally good, but rather, pleasurable. At the end of the day, it should truly be said that a good time was had by all."

"But that isn't working, is it," said Beamer.

Corbin shook his head. "Decidedly not. We're pegging the meter for stress, illness, violence, conflict—fires burning everywhere and the lid just barely staying on. It's worse than rehab. Hardly any nudge and the whole thing will blow. Everybody knows it. But this only adds stress because there are no ready alternatives. So people just keep pedalling until they break or drop."

"And Laurel has an alternative?"

"Maybe," Corbin mused. "She's gone to the core of the matter, I think, and come back with something different. She says that the idea that getting rich always leads to well-being is a mistake. If that was true, then we should be vastly happier than our ancestors, which we aren't. So what she's offering instead is to make well-being the centre of our culture and move getting rich more to the margin. And to make it a question, not a dogma. Or you might say, while we're here together, we could be pursuing well-being rather than wealth. What well-being is, and how we come to experience it, is something we need to find out, not something we already know. We know we like pleasure, of course, but pleasure alone doesn't fill the bill. Not only that, but how to have a good life is not a static thing. It's something we discover and apply and revise and renew, over and over again."

Beamer nodded slowly. "And what you're doing is part of that?"

"I hope so," said Corbin. "I know that practices like meditation, yoga, t'ai-chi and others increase my well-being. On top of that, they don't cost anything really. There is no down-side from these practices for the environment or for other people. You don't even need to wear clothes. But what fascinates me and keeps me up at night is the hunch that these practices have a common core of some sort."

"A common core?"

"Yes. Many paths, same mountain, sort of thing. I want to know more about the mountain. That's what kept me going with Sensei so long. It was something he never talked about. Nobody ever talked about it. But you could still feel it there. There's thousands of yoga asanas, hundreds of meditation techniques, five or six different schools of t'ai-chi, more in chi-gong, more yet in the martial arts. But probably not all asanas are equally effective in contributing to well-being. Yoga is pretty static in practice while t'ai-chi and chi-gong are more dynamic. So could we come up with a practice that blends some parts of yoga with other parts of t'ai-chi or chi-gong so that the practice itself becomes more effective in promoting well-being? And could we add beauty to the mix so that practice is more like a dance than a series of static poses or katas—something that's beautiful in execution regardless of your body type? I don't know. But I can't stop thinking about it."

"And that's what you're working on here?"

"I think so," said Corbin. "When Laurel gets around to unveiling her periodic table, I want to reserve one cell of it for whatever we eventually call this thing I'm working on. The common threads in these things are that the body and mind are one thing; that practice is key, not just declarations of belief; that well-being is an indirect effect of practice, a surprise emergent of doing these other things; and that if we put forth effort, we can evolve from tradition. So I want Fey to reserve one of her cells for what I'm working on. I can already see how it would fit."

"And you think that's all we need—more yoga will save the world?" Beamer couldn't conceal his skepticism.

Corbin leaned back in his chair and first gave up a bark of laughter, then a gale, his eyes watering and face blooming red. "In my dreams!" he gasped. Then he took a deep breath and settled himself. "No," he said more seriously, "I don't think more yoga is all we need. But the problem with some of these practices historically is that they were thought of mostly as ways that individuals could attain enlightenment, or holiness, or union with God, or some such. Aiming only for personal benefit, they fell into another error—missing the fact that we are all related, linked up in many ways to each other and to the universe. The beauty of Laurel's table is that it might include what I'm working on, a physico-spiritual practice to cultivate well-being, without reducing every other aspect of life to that single practice. We are physico-spiritual beings, but also social beings, and ecological beings, and economic beings, and aesthetic beings. It all matters. It all counts. What Fey's trying to do is give a structure where all these things can fit together, work together, in right ordering. Then, someday, we might look at that Table and see how to live a better and better life, together, and with everything else on our planet here. It would be a start anyway—more than we have now, which is a disaster about to happen."

Beamer felt himself smiling. "So where do I sign up?" he asked.

"Sign up for what?"

"Beginner yoga classes."

Corbin chuckled again. "Any time you want. The schedule is on the door. But you have your own yoga to do."

"I do?" said Beamer, densely.

"Yes," Corbin confirmed. "Your mandalas."

"Ah, my mandalas."

"Yes," Corbin pressed. "If you are here, now, with us, there must be a reason. Every mandala represents a state of the entire universe at that moment—yours no less than any other."

Beamer looked at Corbin who was looking back at him gravely. "I'm not even sure my mandalas are real mandalas," Beamer said. "They aren't really circular or symmetrical or anything."

"Then," said Corbin, "the problem is with your definition of a mandala, not with what you made."

# CHAPTER 24

*Hope is no use in a real battle. In a real battle one
should cultivate courage. Every day meditate on death
by drowning, or in a horrible fire, or by falling from
great heights, or in combat with a thousand enemies.
In such straights, courage is useful; hope is not.*

— ONOKI TASIMOTO, ROSHI

ALL AROUND BADGER COULEE winter was slowly loosening its grip on the land. It was not yet warm, but neither was it cold as were the depths of January and February. Nearing the Vernal Equinox now, the daylight lasted noticeably longer and the land, which had braced itself against the cold, now sensibly relaxed and softened as break-up approached.

Beamer continued to work on the wood delivery detail. His log splitting technique had improved steadily, though he continued to wear armour on his lower legs and feet. In the process of making his deliveries, he had met nearly everyone living in the Coulee, or at least all who used wood for fuel.

On a couple of occasions he had also taken the power toboggan into the forest east of Badger Coulee. To the west of the village were more open expanses of aspen parkland that beckoned those with a need for speed. But it was the depths of the forest that attracted Beamer and the mysteries they concealed. Once in the forest, you couldn't see for twenty kilometres in every direction and he found this sense of enclosure consoling. In parts of the forest that had been 'managed' for fuel wood and pulp, there were roughly hewn logging roads and electric transmission rights of way that he could traverse with relative ease. But farther to the east there stood older growth forest—not having been logged for a century or more. Here he had to go slower, though occasionally the forest had been opened by fires or beetle-killed timber falls. In the spring, these areas would be crowded with the pinkish-purple spikes of fire weed, and where the soil was shallower close to bedrock, there would be profusion of wild blueberries, bear berries, wild raspberries and rose hips. Now, however, the snow had not yet cleared from the forest understory and not even in the open areas were there any signs of the profusion of flowers and plants that would crowd in during high summer.

There was considerable clutter of spruce branches and in lower areas alder thickets so dense he couldn't see through them much less traverse them. So he had to pick his way at low speed trying to avoid being slashed in the face by the undergrowth and ever mindful that he would eventually have to turn his machine around to head back. More than once he wished he'd worn snow-shoes instead but the extent of his survey would have been much smaller. One of the compensating pleasures of exploring a forest in the winter was that it was almost impossible to get lost. Unless a severe storm beset him, he could simply turn around and follow his own tracks back to where he came from.

About thirty kilometres east of the Coulee, Beamer met an impenetrable wall of forest growing on much more rugged terrain. This must be the border proper between the aspen parkland of the west and the high shield country to the east—boreal forest growing on rock formations a billion years old. The land felt haunted, calling him ever more urgently. But exploring it was a task that had to wait, and one that could never be done trying to thread a quarter tonne of snorting power toboggan through the understory.

Making his way back to the Coulee, Beamer found the weather still cold and damper than winter. So the prospect of a meal in the Barn was attractive indeed. He entered the cottage he shared with Tatum, stripped off the clothes he'd been wearing that were now redolent of sweat and balsam fir sap. Then he showered quickly and went back to his room to re-garb for supper. He pulled on some heavy work pants—general issue for the Coulee—a t-shirt with a wool sweater over, some wool socks and the fleece-lined moccasins he wore indoors. Then he headed for the Board Room already late for supper.

The Board Room was crowded but relatively quiet. As Beamer emerged from the food line, he noticed Laurel Fey standing on stage beside an object that looked like an abstract sculpture which Beamer guessed was the most recent version of her periodic table. She was holding forth animatedly, point-ing first to one part of the assemblage and then to another, naming cells, ex-plaining relationships. Beamer cast his glance around the room and discovered Tatum sitting with four other people at a table near the front of the room. He made his way to her and pulled a chair into an empty space at table while setting down his tray and a steaming mug of mulled cider. Tatum smiled when he sat down and squeezed his hand in silent greeting.

"Laurel going on about her table?" he whispered to her. Tatum nodded silently as she continued to listen closely.

Fey was just wrapping up her point as Beamer sat down. Fisher sat in his wheelchair to the left of the stage listening along with everyone else.

"...so that's how I think this might work for us," she said, stepping back from her construction. "We already have some of the parts now," she mused. "People here are already doing so many things that could be parts of a new way forward—Corbin Galen's experiments to combine yoga and t'ai-chi, Changming's work with design, the meditation training we're doing, and the permaculture. All of them are settling together toward this larger whole. I can feel it. I can almost see it."

She paused, then looking more directly at the crowd, she resumed: "But now we've seen some actual food shortages this winter—not because there is no food, but because we can't seem to get it to the people who need it. This used to happen mostly in southern countries. Now it's happening here. The same shortages are showing up with fuel and medicine and repair parts and even new products. It's happening everywhere and more or less at the same time. And none of the shortages are actual shortages, if you get my drift. I think it's more because the powers that be spent all this time since the 1980s setting up this global economy where just about everything is made far away and swapped for something else far away. We've lost control over the things we need. Greed is at a record high, and trust in politicians and order-keepers is at a record low. So any little twitch in the system—a crop failure, a labour strike, a change in the price of something, hackers, epidemics, terrorists, plain old vandalism—almost anything can short out the system and drop the lights. It hasn't really been a big problem for us at the Coulee yet because we've been here working toward self-sufficiency for the last three years. But everybody knows that can't last. We still have a long way to go on the self-reliance front. Our turn is coming, one way or another, sooner or later. So you could think of this periodic table idea as attracting us toward something we want and the storm gathering outside as pushing us, daring us, demanding of us, that we make something new."

A rugged-looking guy in coveralls piped up from the back of the room, "When do we start digging the bunker?"

Fey was unfazed. The question was predictable. "Really?" she replied. "You think we should build a bunker?"

"It beats dying," he retorted. "As I see it we really have only three choices: We build a bunker and hide, we run away somewhere, or we die. The time is certainly coming when other people will want what we have here. It won't matter to them what we tried to do here. I think your vision is beautiful. I would die protecting it. But doing yoga and keeping a permaculture garden are not going to protect us from being picked clean when things get really tough."

"We get that," a woman piped up from the middle of the room. "But a bunker? I don't think so. I'm with Laurel on this one because a bunker can only protect us so long—even if we did want to live behind a wall. Sooner or later we have to grow food. We need parts for our tools. We will need medicines.

And we'll need to breathe free air. Bunkers are at best temporary shelters. Then you have to come out and make a living somehow."

"Making a living is something we're getting better at every year," said the guy in the back. "The question will be keeping the living we make."

"So we go all Snaky-Yankee and arm up?" Fey challenged.

"I suppose," the man in back replied glumly.

"But look at us," Fey demanded. "Do we look like an army? Can you really see me blowing somebody's brains out?"

The guy shrugged helplessly. "Well," he said, "if you're about to get yours blown out, I guess we'd see then, wouldn't we."

Fey shook her head. "What you say is compelling but unpalatable."

"Guess you don't like my idea then, eh?" the man grinned as a ripple of laughter relieved the tension in the room.

"Right," Fey nodded. "Don't get me wrong," she said, "I like you fine. It's just the idea I find unpalatable."

"We all do," chimed in someone else, "but if not that, then what?"

Another man stood up. Beamer recognized him as the same person who had spoken during the Friends Meeting he attended a few weeks before. He stood where we was, silent, casting his eyes around the group. Silence seemed to hang around him like an aura that captivated everyone's attention with his mere presence. "Way hasn't opened yet," he said quietly. "When it does, we will know it. Before it does, we have to wait."

"Wait for what?" challenged the man from the back.

"Just wait," the old man said. "We'll know what we waited for after we wait for it."

"Well, you lost me there," said the other man. But a murmur spread through the group, inarticulate yet palpable, like a flock of birds in tight formation, turning in silent unison.

Fisher then pushed his wheelchair up the ramp to the dais in front of the fireplace. "It looks to me," he said, "like this bears more discussion, but maybe for later. Soon. But later."

No one replied directly to Fisher's suggestion but all appeared to agree as one by one they returned to their various table conversations. Laurel Fey set about disassembling her construct, this time in fairly sizeable sub-assemblies rather than tearing it all to pieces. Tatum turned to Beamer.

"You went walk-about this afternoon?" part question, part guess.

"More like drive-about," Beamer replied. "I took one of the power tobog-gans. I was just scouting hiking routes for summer. Needed some fresh air."

"Like you don't get enough of it splitting wood," Tatum needled.

Beamer rolled his eyes, then returned to finishing his meal. Tatum chatted with another woman at the table until she decided to go with some others who were drifting off, leaving Tatum and Beamer alone. Beamer was leaning back now sipping his mulled cider and enjoying the warmth radiating from the fireplace that, following his afternoon in the bush, was working its relaxing magic.

"Next question," Tatum opened.

"Aw, really?"

"You haven't told me all your secrets yet, have you?"

"Just about."

"Oh no!" said Tatum in mock horror. "The mystery is gone from you. What will become of us?"

Beamer sighed, feigning weariness. "Oh, alright. If you insist. Same rules though."

"Same rules," Tatum agreed. "Have you made any of your mandalas lately?"

"No," Beamer answered, "at least not physical ones."

"Not physical ones?"

"I just haven't," said Beamer. Then he smiled. "Everybody around here wears all the second- hand clothes—so I've got nothing to work with."

"Truly?" Tatum challenged, raising an eyebrow.

"Not truly," Beamer confessed. "I guess I haven't felt like making a mandala maybe because I'm dreaming them instead."

"Dreaming them?"

Beamer looked away from Tatum toward the pennants of flame that fluttered in the hearth, then looking back to Tatum: "Yes. Last night even. But it's gotten hooked up somehow to Fey's playing with her blocks—her cells, I mean. I had this dream last night where I couldn't see her, but I could hear her fiddling with those blocks, and I could feel her there. You know, how in dreams you can tell from the feeling of a person that they're in the dream, even if you can't see them exactly. I realized she wasn't just fiddling around, trying things at random. She knew what she was doing—not like we usually know things like phone numbers or birthdays—but this other kind of knowing that guides you when you yourself don't know where you're going. But then, when you get where you're going, you look back and you realize that you really did know it all along—somehow. You know what I mean?"

Tatum pondered for a moment. "Like having a baby."

"Like what?" said Beamer, trying to make the connection.

"Yes. Like having a baby. If you've never had one before, you may think you know what to expect from reading books and stuff, but that's not the way it is. Your body takes over and does its thing. Your body that has been evolving for three billion years through millions of species knows how to have babies, even if consciously you don't have a clue. So you either trust it and cooperate, or you go to the hospital."

"Interesting," said Beamer.

"What part?"

"Well the end of my dream was back in the park where we met that night, except you weren't there. It was just this person standing by that lamp post in all these shabby clothes, but he looked really young, I mean, not a child or anything, but young, like us. He didn't say anything. He just looked at me and then blasted out of his clothes like a shot—straight up. He went so fast, I couldn't even make out his form. He was just a streak—like somebody beaming up."

"And what do you make of that?"

Beamer shrugged. "I really don't know. But I don't feel the urge to make a mandala any time soon. And dreaming about Fey's cubes and this burning man in the park makes me think they're mashed up—connected. And I think whatever is coming our way is coming sooner rather than later." He returned his gaze from the fireplace to Tatum. "That's more than one question," he said.

"It was a multi-part, long-answer," she conceded. "Your turn."

Beamer looked back to the fire and let the vision of it carry him for a few moments. "If you could live in the future you dream about," Beamer asked, "what would that be like?" He looked back to her for her answer.

She sighed heavily: "I don't dare think about it."

"Really?"

Tatum shrugged and dropped her gaze. "Well, maybe I could dare. But it's easier not to. If I dare think about it, then it means I have hope, and if I have hope, then I can suffer if my hope is disappointed. It's easier to imagine an apocalypse that's a sure thing than it is to imagine a good life that's only a possibility."

"But isn't that our problem right now?" Beamer said. "If anything kills us, it probably won't be bad government or greedy corporations or some lunatic fringe. It'll be a failure of imagination."

"I think it's guilt," she said, her voice taking on the tautness of emotional control.

"Guilt?"

"Yes—good old Abrahamic guilt. Deep down we still have the moral sensibilities of camel drivers with family issues from 1,500 B.C. We expect a just world—not that people bring justice into the world—but that the world itself is a just place that will punish and reward people according to what we deserve. And when we look at what we do to the world, to each other, deep down, maybe we think we don't deserve a dream. We deserve a flood, a fire, a verdict with a sentence attached. Until we have that, the decks are too cluttered with our guilt to leave any room for hope, or dreams for that matter."

"And you believe that?"

"Hell no!" Tatum snapped. "But I *feel* it. My guts believe it. We were all raised in the same poisonous over-culture. We absorbed these feelings with our mothers' milk. Getting beyond them takes more than changing our opinions. It's a failure of imagination, to be sure. But we don't give ourselves permission to even have an imagination. I remember going to a street demonstration once about something or other, and there was this person wearing this t-shirt with the slogan: 'Consume. Obey. Be silent. Die.' I thought, that really sums it up. Nowhere in there does it say dream or hope."

They were silent for a moment as the fire hissed and popped in the hearth. Then Beamer turned to Tatum, his eyes wet and glistening. "You haven't answered my question," he whispered. "You are worthy. What would you dream?"

Tatum took his hand in both of hers and pressed the back of it against her cheek. Then she kissed it tenderly and let their hands rest in her lap. "I would dream," she said, but her voice caught in her throat. She began again, "I would dream," now she gritted her teeth against the sobs that wanted out, against the flood that had been dammed there for a long time. The flood she deserved.

Beamer squeezed her hands and pulled her gently to her feet. "Let's get out of this place," he said. She let him lead her by the hand through the mostly empty Board Room, out the door and back to Tatum's cottage. There he pulled her down on his bed, embraced her and pulled her close. She sobbed wordlessly—for a long time.

# CHAPTER 25

*Perhaps it is better to live more simply, in a more stable
and understandable society than to chase after affluence
in a society we neither control nor understand—unless
you are willing to trust all of this to an artificial
intelligence. We should at least have the choice.*

— FROM AN ANCIENT PODCAST, AUTHOR UNKNOWN.

BEAMER SAT IN CHANGMING'S workshop. He'd used the excuse, at least to himself, of bringing another load of firewood, even though the previous load had not yet been entirely consumed. In his own mind, he needed some practical reason to pay a visit. The plain desire to be in the workshop without knowing why threatened to unmoor him from the world of reasons, the world that still made a kind of sense to him. Yet, here he was—in truth, for other reasons.

He sat cross-legged within one of Changming's larger maquettes. It looked like a section from a gothic cathedral but also a forest grove. Four tree-like columns rose to define four corners, four directions, their limbs arching overhead in an increasingly detailed and complex tangle of branching forms. And yet they were not a random tangle. There was a certain untamed symmetry in their relationship, something wild, but symmetrical too. Or perhaps the brachiate forms were not tree branches at all, but arteries, or sinews and muscles instead. Or maybe it was a tangle of ivies, thickened with age, a building growing itself out of the ground offering its stony grapes to anyone who crept inside. The quality was exactly that of an untouched forest, or desert, or ocean beach, or mountain range: In the very absence of evidence of any conscious structure imposed by a human being, such scenes were nevertheless beautiful. Somehow Changming had captured this quality and fashioned these forms with no trace of ego—no self-conscious telltale of his own part in the process. As he sat in the maquette, Beamer cast his gaze around inside it and felt pleasure, shelter, the desire to linger and steep in the energies it was conjuring.

He was not alone. After he had settled himself, he noticed that there were others in the shop as well, faces familiar to him from the Friends group. They were sitting some way off, silent, eyes closed, as if listening intently for something, except for one—Alex Brighton, the man who spoke in the Meeting and again in the Board Room after Laurel Fey. He stood now at the side of a model balustrade, his gaze focused on the floor, swaying gently from side to side. As he stood there, he issued barely audible whispers of, "This way. This way." Maybe he was a prophet or maybe just daft, Beamer thought. But then mandalas were probably daft as well. In fact, the world seemed to be literally flooded with daftness.

"If you don't go find the Friends, sometimes they find you." Beamer startled. It was Changming standing just behind him, his voice lowered.

"They do?"

"Well not on purpose," he amended. "Things just have a way of working out."

"I hope so," said Beamer vaguely, not at all sure what it was that he hoped for. He nodded in the direction of Brighton standing at the balustrade. "Do you suppose he's off his rocker?"

"Perhaps," said Changming reflectively, then, "There is a story from ancient China, Taoist I think, maybe in the *Chuang-tzu*. It's about a hunchback named Su. To outward appearances Su suffered from a great many afflictions, from the description of him, probably a scoliosis spine and congenital dwarfism. These made him startling in appearance as well as disabled. The Chinese have a deep-seated cultural aversion to anyone with a physical abnormality. His fellow villagers viewed him with pity and revulsion. But when the Emperor's Imperial Guard came to the village to conscript young men for the army or for civil works, Su was exempted. He made a good living washing and tailoring and raising his own rice, enough to support a family of ten. And every year when the Emperor distributed grain and firewood to the crippled, Su received both. He lived long."

Beamer glanced up at Changming. "And the moral of the story is?"

"He lived long. That's it. Chinese stories don't have morals," he grinned.

"They don't?"

"No. Chinese stories are about reality, not morality. They just point out something about reality. They assume that a life based in reality will be a moral life. It's not our disobedience to a moral code that makes us miserable. It's denying reality that makes us miserable."

"And as for those who are off their rockers?"

Changming smiled. "As for those who may appear to be disabled in some way, what at first appears to be a deformity may in reality be something quite different."

"And you think the Friends are like that?"

Changming shrugged. "I don't know what the Friends are, or why they stick around with us. I do believe, however, that they are doing something within this group that we all need, something essential in as much as we wouldn't be the same without them. Maybe we wouldn't even be capable of achieving what we're trying to do here. I find it really mysterious actually, but it's consoling too."

"Like having eyes that see the invisible," Beamer said.

Changming nodded. "One thing's for sure," he said.

"And what's that?"

"If they don't see the invisible, they sure are looking hard for it."

After making three more wood deliveries, Beamer turned his power toboggan back toward the equipment shed. The snow was melting fast and it wouldn't be long before he would have to trade the toboggan for some other means of haulage, as long as people still needed wood. He parked the machine and then headed back to the Barn.

The Board Room was relatively empty and quiet. He managed to avail himself of the remains of a vegetarian casserole, some fresh bread and tea, while the day's fatigue flooded into his limbs. After eating, he went back to Tatum's cottage.

When he opened the door he found Tatum sitting at one end of her bed, her back against the wall and her legs extended to her desk chair, her ankles crossed casually, bare footed, her expression rakish. Beamer noticed that she had procured gifts—a pair of pillar candles standing side-by-side flickering in the lengthening shadows, two bottles of wine, a large tray of various dried fruits, smoked salmon, nuts, and some cheeses.

"Wow," said Beamer. "What's the occasion?"

Tatum smiled and pointed to the candles with her toe. "We have about that long," she said, "then I have to get back to the city. So take off your clothes."

"How long is that?" Beamer asked as he started pulling off his shirt.

"Not sure exactly," Tatum said. "All we can do is make the best of it. Now lie down here. Let's start with you face down. Hard working men need to relax sometimes."

"What about hard working women?"

"Never fear," said Tatum, "I'm looking forward to my turn."

Beamer did as he was told. He could hear Tatum behind him freeing herself from her clothes as well, whereupon she straddled him from behind and applied a warm oil to his back and shoulders, gliding her hands down toward his waist. Once he was well coated, she began pressing from his waist upward toward his neck, her hands firm and definite. Aside from the simple pleasure of her touch, Beamer could feel an energy that went far beyond skin-deep. It penetrated his muscles right to the bone, so patient, so deliberate were her movements.

"You must be a Reiki master," Beamer mumbled with his face against the mattress.

Tatum continued working on his back for a few moments, then, "Can't claim any special master thing," she said. "I just love you is all."

"I love you too," he mumbled back.

For the next hour, she applied herself with diligence and attention to every part of his body until she lifted her hands and said, "Okay, flip-a-roo."

Beamer rolled over obediently, though it felt like gravity had mysteriously increased making his body feel incredibly heavy. "Oh!" said Tatum in mock surprise. "What have we here?" Beamer smiled like an idiot but said nothing.

Later they had curled up together, Beamer with his back against the wall, Tatum leaning against him, their legs intertwined and the candle light flickering on their bodies. "You're not a bad Reiki master yourself," Tatum purred.

"Oh yeah," Beamer said lazily. "I studied under all the great masters—lifetimes ago." He paused, his attention captured now by the candle. "We're down three centimetres already."

"So does that mean our candle is half empty?"

"Mmm," said Beamer, "I think it's more than full."

They stayed curled together for some time, the boundaries of their bodies blurring and fading in the warmth of their contact until they revived and made love again. Afterwards, Tatum slid out of bed and asked, "White or red?"

Beamer was still cloud-hidden but managed, "White, please." Tatum poured their wine and brought the tray of snacks to the chair beside their bed. They sipped wine for a while and feasted on the victuals without speaking. Then Tatum curled again within the arc of Beamer's body, her gaze fixed on the pair of candles. Night had fallen outside and except for the atoll of light they occupied, everything else was swallowed by shadow. It was easy to feel as though this was all there was, this pool of light in an otherwise dark and featureless expanse, this pool of light and their bodies floating within it.

"Why wasn't this enough for us?" Tatum wondered aloud.

Beamer was silent for a long time, thinking, then, "Maybe we were just afraid, you know? And probably we still are."

"Afraid?"

"Sure. Human life is short and pretty fragile really. That scares us because we can't tolerate the idea of not-being. So we start hankering to pile up all sorts of stuff to protect ourselves and comfort and distract ourselves and try to convince ourselves that we will exist in some form forever. Scratch the greed and vicious competition of consumer culture and I think you'd find fear just underneath. Fear of losing what we have. Fear of never being able to get what we want. Fear of missing out, even when we're not sure what we're missing out on. Fear of being left behind, even though we don't know where we're going. Fear of not having enough, even when we don't know how much enough is. It makes us crazy."

"And do you think there's any other way to be?"

"Not everybody is crazy, you know. And that's a hopeful thing."

"How do you mean?"

"Well," said Beamer, "think of all the different cultures, both now and in the past. People are capable of being happy in a lot of different ways. We don't always soil our nest."

"Seems like we've done it now," Tatum's voice was resigned, sad.

"That's for sure," he agreed. "But even in our own culture, there are people who are living differently, more simply, and with more awareness. I'd be really fucking disappointed if we were all going over the cliff in the same runaway train."

"But that's just it," Tatum objected, "this train is taking both the sleeping and the woke on the same ride."

"Maybe not," said Beamer. "Look at what we're doing here. It's great. It's hopeful. It's something positive."

"Is it enough though?" Tatum asked. "And is it in time?" Beamer sensed how important it was to her to be convinced, to find some rational basis for hope.

Beamer shrugged. "I don't know if we can know that. We just have to keep going, keep focused on that crazy thing Laurel is building. Keep focused on each other. If things were really as dark as we fear, there could be no exceptions, you know?"

"What do you mean?"

Beamer let his hand slowly stroke Tatum's soft belly. "Well, just think of it. If we humans are as bad as we sometimes think, then how come there are people like Socrates, or Diogenes, or Henry Thoreau, or Gandhi, or Scott and Helen Nearing, or hundreds of others? They lived for different values and showed us a different way. If we are all so alike, where did these characters come from?"

"They're all spiritual prodigies," said Tatum, "mutants, maybe."

"But that's just what we need, isn't it? Mutants? Some off-the-beaten-track possibilities? Nobody's built us a road yet. We have to go cross country, don't you think?"

"Yes," Tatum agreed. "That's what we need. But these people have been around a long time and no one ever listened to them. What's different now?"

Beamer squeezed her closer. "Now, my love, is a teachable moment. Who was it? Samuel Johnson, who said: 'Nothing concentrates the mind like the prospect of being hanged in the morning.'"

Tatum chuckled dryly. "That's harsh," she said.

"I think it's hopeful though," said Beamer. "Besides, maybe we're teachable, you know."

"Like how?"

"I read about these experiments," Beamer sounded excited. "They brought this bunch of meditators together and had them concentrate on a single intention, to move the acidity of a water sample up one point. And they did it.

They could also change its temperature. In another experiment, they could change the behaviour of random number machines on the other side of the world—electronic devices, Tatum! In another experiment they studied the ice crystal patterns forming in water when meditators imagined different emotional states like love, or anger, and it changed the shape of the crystals. The studies have been replicated over and over. These are facts. We can do this. And these are physical objects that are being changed just by how we focus intention, not something mushy like how people respond to a questionnaire. And if we actually started believing in ourselves more, let ourselves believe in our possibilities as well as our mistakes, well, then…"

"Then what?"

"Then doing what we're doing here gives me hope, Tatum. Who knows what we might learn to do if we really concentrated our minds, as Johnson says, on what you're doing with permaculture, and Corbin Galen with his martial arts, and Changming, and Fey, and the Friends—and all the rest. Consumer culture has been growing for two centuries. Imagine what we might accomplish if we gave ourselves as long, but aimed in a different direction."

Tatum rolled over and buried her face in the curve of his neck, then slid slowly down his chest, inhaling deeply, filling herself with the smell of him, the warmth of him. Then she looked up at him. "Perhaps," she said. "Perhaps you're right. Perhaps we can. Perhaps."

They snacked a little more without speaking, then slipped off to sleep only to waken in the night and make love again. Their candles were burning down but still alight when they fell asleep in the early hours of the morning. Tatum was the first to awaken to the new day, curled within the crescent of warmth made by Beamer's body, his arm cast over her, holding on. As her eyes opened she saw the candles again, only one of them was still lit. Reflexively she pressed herself back into the curve of Beamer's body as if recoiling from something. But deeper still, she felt a warm ember within herself—the ember they had kindled in the night. And that was enough.

The next morning Tatum slipped out of bed without waking Beamer. She pulled some items of clothing from her closet then left her room gently pulling the door closed behind her. The fire had burned low in the wood stove and after pulling on her clothes, she added a couple of stove logs to the fire to take off the morning chill for Beamer. She grabbed a couple energy bars for the trip back to the city and then pulled on her winter boots. Her hand was on the door knob when her gaze fell on her open laptop. She paused, touched the space bar, and watched the screen flash awake. A shriek suddenly erupted from the computer until Tatum could mute the audio. She listened intently for a moment until she was sure that she hadn't wakened Beamer. Then she looked at the tracings coming from her plants. She had never seen such a pattern before—or rather, the lack of a pattern. The tracings from her plants were no longer the skein of lazy sine waves that braided themselves across the screen. Instead she saw a ragged tangle of saw-tooth wave forms laced together with sudden spikes and moments of flat-lining only to revive later to resume spiking and snarling with the other tracings. No wonder they shrieked when the audio was on. *That's funny*, she thought, even as she felt a shadow of apprehension draping itself around her. She logged off the computer and shut it completely down, hoping to hide this from Beamer. But why did hiding it disturb her? From what was she trying to protect him? Or herself? She closed the laptop, shaking her head as if to dislodge the whole train of thought and the memory of the discovery that led to it. She turned away from the laptop and stepped out into the early morning chill. The cube van awaited her parked in front of the machine shed. She made straight for the truck and left the Coulee just as the sun blushed the eastern horizon. *Red in the morning*— she thought.

# CHAPTER 26

*One should prepare always for that which is worse than one can imagine. For it is often difficult to distinguish the ending of a thing from the beginning of something worse.*

— ONOKI TASIMOTO, ROSHI

BEAMER, BEFOGGED WITH SLEEP, scrunched toward Tatum's side of the bed to find it empty and cold. She'd been gone two days already and would doubtless be away longer. He rolled over again trying to go back to sleep but his bladder got the better of him. He sat up, got his feet on the floor, and then ambled out of the bedroom naked in the direction of the washroom. A grey light filtered through windows at the end of the hallway—perhaps from the sun not fully risen, or possibly just overcast. Looking out the window, the Barn too seemed uncharacteristically quiet, even though it might be the early hour that accounted for it. But there was something about the light that drew Beamer closer to the window. He peered out upon what looked like a world made of glass.

April was called a "shoulder season" in the region of Badger Coulee, a quaint expression meaning anything could happen. Most of the snow had already melted leaving large areas waterlogged and puddled. As the day previous had warmed, water evaporated in an invisible cloud of humidity. By late afternoon and early evening, however, a shift in a lazy jet stream drew colder air from the Arctic toward regions farther south. It was more often the case now that such shifts in the jet stream were dragging the Arctic polar vortex farther south, sometimes locking it in place for weeks. In the dark of night the cold air met the pooled moisture from the day before and the moisture condensed on everything—relentlessly, silently, layer by layer. At first, ice crystals formed that made one of those fairyland scenes so coveted by photographers and greeting card designers. But soon the ice crystals became ice layers growing on everything like tree rings, including electricity transmission lines and poles.

Coincidentally, ice on the rivers was also breaking up under the power of the spring flood. Rising waters lifted massive ice sheets, cracking them like panes of glass, only to float along the current until they found a tight meander where the ice sheets could pile up in a jammed up tangle stories high. When the jam failed to clear itself, it became an ice dam, sending torrents of water up from the river course to flood all the surrounding land. Four different rivers converged in the city, two of them major. Every spring they threatened to transform what for millennia had been a trading and transportation nexus into a local emergency. Once there had been aspen groves and prairie grasslands. But since colonization by Europeans it had become a sprawling city with its streets and suburbs, its sky scrapers and stadiums, its markets and highways, and even boasted its own nuclear power station.

Now Beamer gawked at the scene outside the window, captivated both by its surreal beauty and an overtone of menace. *Catastrophes should be noisy*, Beamer thought. Downpours should come with ear splitting thunder. Tornados should roar like freight trains as they rumbled through the landscape or down the main street. Cloudbursts should be horizontal, like hurricanes barreling into a coast, tearing down signs, peeling off roofs, shattering glass and throwing the furniture around. These things should be properly biblical, like they were in the Sinai in 1,500 B.C., or in Hollywood, with lots of sirens and sub-woofers going. But the fact remained that sometimes catastrophe lurked quietly, just behind the curtain of denial.

As Beamer stood staring out the window he heard someone approaching from outside. It was Jasper Beckett. Beamer went to the door to let Jasper in, feeling the sudden blast of cold air shocking him more into wakefulness. "This is gonna be trouble," Jasper said.

"Have you heard any weather reports?"

Jasper shook his head ominously. "There's nothing on the radio," he said, "probably because there's no radio. Just dead air. No TV either. And no cell service, so no Internet. In fact, there's no electricity."

"So we're blacked out," said Beamer.

"Except for our PV arrays, but they're not working either. They're all covered with ice. Output is down to about ten percent barely trickle charging the batteries. I keep telling people we should get some windmills in here so we can hybrid the power system, but we haven't done it yet."

"Does anybody have a battery or hand crank radio?"

"I do," said Jasper. "That's what I've been using to find the weather report. But like I said, there doesn't seem to be any radio out there to listen to."

"Holy crap. And you tried all bands?"

"I've got AM and FM but no shortwave on this set," said Jasper.

Beamer weighed this news, feeling graver by the minute. His first thought was of Tatum. He hoped she hadn't gotten caught somewhere on the open highway while the ice was forming. And now there was no way of contacting her.

"Okay," said Beamer. "FM reaches only about a hundred kilometres. So if there's nothing on those bands that must mean the storm took stuff down for at least a hundred clicks in every direction. It worries me more though that there's no AM traffic. AM goes a lot farther than FM. Dead air on AM means the storm was really big—regional instead of local—or if not the storm, then the blackout."

"Blackouts happen out here," said Jasper. "They usually have things back up and running in a few hours. Lots of people have back-up gen sets for their milking machines and incubators and stuff."

"Do we?"

Jasper snorted. "The PV solar is supposed to be our back-up—at least the survival stuff we need to run. But we never thought there might be a storm that could cover up the panels like this. Snow cover you can brush off, but ice sticks."

"It's a learning curve." Beamer sounded resigned to chronic human unpreparedness. "But even if you had windmills, they would probably be off-line too. Batteries might help. But old lady nature is a patient girl. She frosts everything one ice crystal at a time until there are tens of thousands of tonnes of it all over everything. We're probably best off just to build a big fire in the Board Room and wait for spring I guess."

"Yes, well, maybe," said Jasper doubtfully. "The last weather report I did catch said something about a switch up in the jet stream with a possibility that an Arctic vortex might nest over us for a while—maybe quite a while. The temp outside the Barn is minus sixteen C—not likely to melt any time soon." Both gazed at the deceptively beautiful landscape a moment more, then Jasper said, "You know, maybe we should just do a walkabout to make sure everybody is okay. We could also drop in on Farley Clemens. He's got a ham radio and if he has back-up batteries, we might get some news that way."

"Sounds like a plan," Beamer agreed.

Jasper looked him up and down with a doubtful expression. "Maybe better put something on though," he suggested. Beamer shuddered a little as he realized he'd been standing at the window, naked all the while.

"Right on that," Beamer acknowledged as he headed off toward his room.

In a few minutes Beamer and Jasper were in the Barn vestibule suiting up for the cold weather. Jasper tossed Beamer what looked like two hands full of tangled up springs. "Bear claws," he said. "Helps to walk on really slippery ice." With some guidance Beamer managed to pull the devices over his boots giving them a covering of twisted wire that could bite into icy surfaces admirably.

What opened before them now was an eerily surreal world. It was both terrifying and tranquil. Cars and trucks that had been left outside stood enrobed in translucent layers of ice. It would take half a day to disinter a vehicle and then, where to drive it? All the tree branches were encased in ice and clacked together overhead sounding skeletal and menacing. When a branch failed, it failed suddenly and with no warming. They simply snapped off and plummeted to the ground, some weighing hundreds of kilos, then shattered into a thousand shards of icy twigs.

But what touched Beamer most deeply was the appearance of the trees and even the weeds and grasses from the previous year. Every tree and bush was bent down, as if grieving or oppressed by some invisible force that crushed the spirit as well as branch and twig. It was the exact image for how Beamer felt inwardly at the sight of it. All the world was weeping ice, crying from under its burden.

"Let's start on First Street," Jasper suggested, "and then work our way around every block."

Beamer nodded. "Onward then."

So they started walking, going house to house, stopping to see if all was well within, where necessary helping to chip open doors so that people could leave their houses if needed. On their fifth house there were clear signs that a roof collapse was in progress, creaking menacingly as they hurried to get a door open and retrieve the inhabitants whom they escorted back to the Barn for food and shelter. Then they returned to their survey of the village.

As Beamer and Jasper continued through the village, a couple of people emerged from their houses to join them on their patrol. Here and there they could see curls of wood smoke ascending from some houses suggesting their occupants were up and about. Many houses were so poorly insulated that once fires were laid in their stoves, the heat that leaked out would eventually thaw their icy encasements. Other houses were intact but with no signs of anyone astir. Beamer could readily imagine waking up in the morning, looking out the window, and then going back to bed, like a bear having second thoughts about leaving its den.

As they made their way toward the edge of the village, there came a loud creaking and snapping sound that combined the din of shattering ice and bending metal. Some way off in the midst of a stubble field, a power transmission tower was turning in slow motion, twisting slowly to one side as it finally collapsed in a tangled pile of metal. Then there came a series of thunderous bangs as one of the power lines snapped and divotted massive chunks of sod in a blinding shower of sparks. Presently the discharges stopped.

"Fuck me!" said Beamer. "That's harsh."

Jasper looked on, then raised his arm in the direction of the tower. There in the distance, tower after tower had collapsed until they were out of sight—at least a dozen of them. "This'll chap a few asses in Minnesota," Jasper quipped. Then they both started laughing—laughing louder than the quip warranted—but they continued laughing, until tears were freezing on their cheeks.

As their laughter faded to quiet chuckles, they continued to look at the fallen row of towers. "Yes," said Beamer, "but this can't be good, can it?"

"No it can't," Jasper agreed. "That's big electricity there and the line wasn't strung in a day. We probably better finish our rounds here and get back to the Barn and chip a few panels clean. I think we're going to need them."

So they turned back into the village when next they saw the angular remains of the cell phone pylon looking like a mashed up Eiffel Tower. Its back-up gen set had started when grid power was lost, but now it ran ineffectually trying to power an antenna that was a heap of ice-encased steel. Then both Jasper and Beamer felt a kind of abandonment and isolation unique to their generation. They had grown up with the sense of always being connected to others, no matter how contingent or illusory those connections actually were. Now they looked at each other without speaking, each aware of what the other must be feeling, the sinking loss of connection, like being dropped into an abyss of infinite departure. But in that same moment they were also able to recognize each other as Honourary Fellows of the Order of Failed Technology. And in place of their first feelings of isolation there came flooding back an awareness of each other.

Finally Beamer said, "Okay. Well. There goes Facebook." He glanced around. "Which way to Farley Clemens?" Jasper turned and set off with a will, and Beamer trailed behind.

They walked for a few minutes toward the edge of the village where Jasper and Beamer came upon a man holding a very long pole that he was using to delicately tap the ice from an extremely fragile looking antenna. Miraculously, it appeared undamaged, but would surely be so if any breath of wind came up. Little by little, he was making progress removing the ice when he saw Beamer and Jasper approaching. "Watch your step," he called in a sarcastic tone. "I haven't had time to sand the sidewalk."

"Farley Clemens?" Jasper called to him.

"Maybe," the guy replied. "Are you from the government here to help me or what?" He advanced on Jasper and shook Jasper's hand vigorously, then extended it to Beamer who returned the gesture.

"What news?" asked Jasper.

Farley laid down his de-icing pole and glanced up at the antenna one last time. Satisfied that it was as clean as may be, he turned to Jasper and Beamer. "Okay, come on in." The men headed through the front door of Farley's house. He obviously lived alone as the place showed no sign of anyone else's touch— or even of Farley's touch. It was rare to find anyone living alone in the Coulee, but Farley was the index case. What did clearly show proof of time and attention was a table against the back wall of the little cottage that was crowded with ham radio gear—not only sufficient to carry on broadcasts, but tools and parts enough to build radios themselves. Despite the general collapse of the grid all around them, a number of lights blinked quietly on instrument displays. Farley clearly had power.

"How'd you do this?" Jasper asked. "Even the Barn is off-line with the ice on the PV panels."

Farley chuckled. "I've got beaucoup batteries. But I also cleaned off my panels this morning. Service should be restored shortly. Please stand by." Farley closed a breaker and even more lights flashed to life. "Charging as we speak," Farley announced. He lowered himself into an over-stuffed swivel chair and pulled a microphone closer to his face. He pressed a button, then announced his call sign, released the button and waited. Static. He pressed another key on a display that activated a search function, seeking out anyone who was on the air. "News in a minute," he said, his attention fixed on the dials and lights. A laptop jacked into the maze of cables and boxes on the table was compiling a list of all active stations within range. A cluster of active stations were cluttered around the city.

"There you go," said Farley. "Everybody's chatting this morning." One by one, Farley clicked on the call signs, and one after another came the calls of distress. Ice damming all along the rivers was causing flooding into the city from multiple locations. In some places, ice was piled up in great sheets a metre thick and as big as tennis courts, then sliding loose and slamming into the walls of buildings as it went or gouging holes in dikes along the river banks. Behind these masses of ice were hundreds of thousands of horsepower from the force of the river water insisting on spring. There were calls from stranded vehicles, or at least the ones with citizen band radios, and other radio hobbyists passing along messages, issuing alerts, working in tandem with emergency services. Sometimes Farley could detect only half of a conversation. At no time could a coherent account be discerned from the bits and pieces of messages full of panic, urgency, and hopelessness. The ice, they all understood, would be gone in a week or two once the weather warmed. But high water would be with them for weeks. Sprinkled into all this radio traffic were references to the Energy-One nuclear station. Something about flood water having reached it. Something else about radiation entering the municipal water system. Something about scramming the reactors. What did "scram" mean anyway?

All three men had grown pale. "Okay," said Beamer. "I've heard enough. We can't do anything from here. The power is out everywhere. The roads are solid ice. We have to hope Tatum is staying put, and the other Finders too. Let's go back to the Barn and see about removing more of the ice on the PV panels. That should be something."

Jasper was nodding in agreement when Farley spoke up: "I can do something from here," he said, a little defensively. "My panels are clear. My batteries are charged. My set works. I can do something."

"Of course," Beamer said. "I didn't mean…"

"I can work relay for now and help out the city from here," said Farley, ignoring Beamer's apology. "In between calls, I'll try and put together a news report for you later this morning. Weather and sports will have to wait," he said wanly. Jasper and Beamer took their leave and made their way back to the Barn.

# CHAPTER 27

*It is often the case that waiting is the better course.*

— ONOKI TASIMOTO, ROSHI

TATUM BARNES AWAKENED realizing that she had rolled herself up tightly in her duvet while still asleep. For a moment she felt like she was camping, trussed up there in her private little cocoon of warmth. Her nose and cheeks were icy cold even as the rest of her curled in a tight ball under the covers. Gradually she awakened to darkness and silence, conditions that were rare in the city. She opened her eyes and saw in her bedroom window a still dark sky speckled with stars. Such sights were rare in a city awash in light pollution. She sat up in bed, still clutching the duvet around her body, swung her feet off the side of the bed and searched for her slippers which had mysteriously disappeared. She stood up, bare footed on the chilly floor, and looked out her bedroom window which had become partly frost-covered near the bottom of the pane. The city below was silent and dark. Nothing was moving. The trees in the park across the street were bending earthward under a glaze of ice that also covered every other surface she could see. But the ice itself appeared to be moving, spreading out amoeba-like, slowing flooding the street below. From somewhere out of sight, an ice jam was doing its thing on at least one of the city's rivers, silently, slowly, but inexorably filling the streets with water that would become ice if it stayed cold enough.

Tatum grabbed her cell phone. The time said 7:15 AM, still an hour before sunrise at this time of year. She activated the phoning application, tried calling both Fisher and Beamer, but a notice flashed on the phone that service was temporarily unavailable. She tried texting, checked email, checked her weather app, tried to activate Google, all without effect. For a moment she wondered, "*Is this it? The 'it' we've been expecting? The beginning of the end of*—it?" She felt a surge of anxiety at the thought but suppressed it in the practiced manner everyone had learned so as to keep the status quo humming.

"Shit. Shit. Shit." she muttered to herself as she shuffled into her living room. There was her mostly finished design maquette for the landscaping project, and all around the room, her plants. Now she imagined that they were crying out with cold stress.

She shuffled back into her bedroom, tossed the duvet on her bed and felt a cold shiver wash over her body. But she ransacked her bedroom assembling first some undies, then her long underwear, pants, heavy wool socks, a cotton undershirt followed by a flannel shirt followed by a wool turtleneck fisherman's sweater, whereupon she felt both warm and more capable of movement than when rolled up in a duvet.

Her poorly insulated apartment building was heated electrically, so she realized there would be no heat until power was restored. Obviously there was a blackout underway, and there had never been any building code requirements to design and position such buildings so as to take advantage of passive solar heat. So there was nothing for it but to hunker down and wait. But her plants couldn't hunker. What to do?

She went to the washroom, plugged the bathtub and sink, and then started drawing hot water. There was still water pressure and the hot water was still coming. As the tub and sink started to fill, Tatum brought her plants into the washroom and crowded them around the tub, on the vanity and on the floor. The steam and warmth from the hot water started to fill the room, making the climate more tropical than anything offered by the living room. Once the tub was brimming, Tatum shut off the water and closed the bathroom door. It would take a great deal of cold for a considerable time to freeze all the water in the bathtub, which Tatum thought would give her plants the best odds possible of survival under the circumstances. She then returned to the living room and looked again at the park across the street which reminded her of Beamer and the Coulee.

As she watched from above, the first rays of sunlight started to filter into the canyons of the city. She considered herself fortunate. While she wished she was at the Coulee, had she left the night before, she probably would have wound up off the road somewhere, coated with ice. The delivery van was loaded now and parked in the underground parkade beneath her building. It was safe enough there and could probably just wait until things thawed out and the streets were sanded. While the ice storm was daunting, weather like this seldom lasted very long this time of year. She consoled herself that priority would probably be given to restoring power to the city first—in the name of commerce and security, in that order, and all other things bright and profitable. She had no inkling of the damage to the grid that had occurred in the countryside. There was nothing for it but to hunker down and wait.

So Tatum went to her kitchen and did a survey of her resources. Hopefully the water would stay on, but rather than make an assumption she would later regret, she started drawing water into every available container in her kitchen.

In a few minutes she had about thirty litres of water, enough for two weeks if she used it only for drinking. She never really considered the apartment to be a home. Rather, it was a handy temporary campsite until the day when she could live full time at the Coulee. Now she browsed her cupboards and assembled enough energy bars, crackers, musli, raisins, and canned goods to last several days if she rationed herself. Tuna on crackers. Yum. So she made little piles of victuals for each day of her anticipated confinement, hoping that it wouldn't come to the point where she would have to leave her apartment in search of something to kill.

She checked her phone again to discover no bars. She realized that her phone battery itself was a limited resource. The charge level was at about seventy-five percent, but those things were always guesses, depending on how the phone was used. Texting would probably be okay, but best to avoid video calls or web browsing. She decided to shut the phone off completely to conserve the battery and fire it up twice a day to check for bars, texts, and other news.

Outside the sun was offering light splintered into a thousand blinding reflections from the ice that covered everything. About an hour after sunrise, Tatum heard a heavy diesel engine growling in the street below. It was a plow truck with its blade down scraping ineffectually at the glazed surface of the street, but leaving behind a fan of brine mixed with sand that would soon start to melt the ice and offer some measure of traction to all the cars that still couldn't move. Bur as the truck passed by unawares, a dark stain upon the pavement came spreading around the street corner from behind Tatum's building. The stain marked the silent advance of flood water.

Tatum retrieved her duvet from the bedroom, pulled her couch to a position where she could see outside, and plucked *The Left Hand of Darkness* by Ursula K. Le Guin from her bookshelf. If a flood was underway, there was nothing she could do about it. She rolled up again in her duvet and flopped on her couch where she could read while keeping an eye on the frozen city and the rising flood water outside. She'd been wanting to read Le Guin for a couple of years. It was a book William had given her. Now as she started reading it, it struck her as ironic that the story was set on a planet in a permanent state of glaciation.

As she scanned the book, another sound coming from far off broke the silence. It was some sort of siren—an ululation that went higher, then lower, then higher again, unlike any other siren she had ever heard. It sounded like it was coming from the west, although the city buildings made it difficult to guess its direction. *What lay west?* Tatum wondered. The Westgate Mall. Numerous low commercial buildings, some low income neighbourhoods, a rail switching and maintenance yard. And, oh yes: The Energy-One nuclear power station.

# CHAPTER 28

*I sat on my accustomed bench in a park sweeping around me like a quiet green sea.*
*The crab apple trees were in blossom, white and deep pink, and the arbour vitae*
*were putting forth fresh growth. Spruce bows were tipped with light green and*
*the canopy overhead was awash in the luminous transparency of new growth. It*
*being afternoon, the whole garden lay in stillness, though the life of the city moved*
*around it, a muddy grey torrent of flood water that parted to pass round the island*
*world I floated on, green and living, in a river of concrete and machines and glass.*
*Gazing once more around me, the whole expanse was an ocean lapping almost*
*motionless in air that held its breath. As far as I could see, all the way to the horizon,*
*bobbed the heads of people floundering in the water, eight billion I reckoned,*
*more or less, and most of them children. There was little sound, but clearly they*
*struggled, close to exhaustion, and as I watched, many went down, but there*
*always were more appearing, and always more than had passed from sight.*
*"Most can't swim," came a voice from beside me on the park bench. "They*
*do well just to tread water." A man sat there, ageless, bright-eyed.*
*"They look pathetic," I said.*
*"It is what it is," he said dispassionately.*
*"It still looks pathetic to me."*
*"You care then?" he asked.*
*"Of course I care," I replied. "Especially for the children."*
*"Caring is painful," he remarked, "and noble."*
*"I wish I could save them," I said.*
*"Each must save himself, but each can also help*
*others. You can help, but you can't save."*
*"Then I must help."*
*"Must you?" he asked.*
*"I want to help, then." I said.*
*"Why?"*
*"Because I feel myself drowning in every one of them."*
*"Ah!" he said. "That's a true reason. But helping will hurt you even more."*
*"So?"*
*"So," he said, "follow me."*

— OSIO SMITH, *TRANSCENDANCE*

TATUM BARNES HAD LEFT the Coulee to return to the city a day before the ice storm and blackout. Because of the thickness of the ice, it took another several days to melt most of it, leaving the Coulee free to make repairs and resume its routines. When the ice cleared from their solar panels, power was restored to all the houses and buildings that were off-grid, but this didn't replace grid power which several buildings still used, nor such utilities as cell phone service. Restoring these would take longer. With the reduced need for wood in the warmer weather, Beamer divided his time between less frequent wood deliveries, and assisting with the tool repair and replacement inventory work in preparation for the coming growing season. Tools beyond repair needed to be added to the next delivery list from the city, if and when that might be possible.

By the end of the day, Beamer headed off toward the Barn and a meal only to find it crowded with more people than he had ever seen there before. All the usual tables were full, more had been set out, and people stood around the edges of the room and leaned against the walls. Even the mezzanine was set with chairs and some people sat on the floor with their feet hanging over the edge. Beamer found some wraps that he could eat out of hand and an empty bit of wall space where he could stand and listen. Clearly, another confab of the Coulee was under way.

At centre stage was a man Beamer knew as Frank Vissar. He was tall and very thin, the stereotype of the lanky introvert, who nevertheless sported an enviable mane of thick, ebony hair, a strong jaw, and darting, hyper-vigilant eyes. *Perfect match for Laurel Fey*, Beamer thought, who by comparison seemed downright chill. When Beamer delivered his wood, Vissar had been conventionally courteous, but clearly appeared to have been interrupted in his mostly solitary pursuits as one of Badger Coulee's more talented computer wunderkinds. In the moment, however, Vissar seemed to be holding the attention of two hundred people, attesting to his versatility, if not his comfort in the situation.

"...so this is something I think we should be planning for and acting on right away," Vissar said. "We need to think hard about what happened the other night, and then get quickly past just thinking and start doing stuff."

Fisher was sitting in his wheelchair close to the dais and motioned toward Vissar to get his attention, then, "What do you suggest we do?"

Vissar rolled his eyes in a where-to-begin expression. "I'm not sure," he confessed with humility. "I can suggest things, but the implications of this are many and unclear. We're going to need all our heads together and even then..." his voice trailed off in uncertainty.

"Okay," Fisher reassured, "you don't have to be Nostradamus. But what can you say?"

Vissar took a deep breath. "So," he said, "the grid was down for sixty-seven hours. Even before the ice storm, it's been happening more often and lasting longer all the time. I don't think anybody planned for an ice storm that co-incided with a flood. But it's not all weather-related. The weather isn't help-ing because we've had another record warm winter and that means more ice storms instead of nice cold snow, and then more lines come down. But it also feels to me like the system is buckling somehow, then recovering, then buck-ling again. I need to research it and figure out why it's happening. But we just need to appreciate that what's happening to the grid might be a symptom, not the disease. There may be more things at play here than just an aging power grid, even though it manifests through the power grid."

"But for our purposes, might it be enough just to know that it is happening, regardless of why?" Fisher pressed.

Vissar's gaze darted to the ceiling and then back again to Fisher. "Yes," he admitted, "I guess so. Anyway, whenever the grid goes down, so does the Internet, and everything runs on the Internet these days—every fucking thing. When the grid wobbles, you don't see it right away with the Internet because the cell system has back-up gen sets, and phones have batteries that will last a few days, if the towers aren't knocked down. A lot of the ISPs have back-ups as well. And the Internet itself was designed to route packets around blockages or outages, so it's easy to think nothing is amiss until the whole thing crashes, and when it does, it really does. We wouldn't necessarily notice how far gone it is until the down time on the grid exceeds the battery life of the back-ups—or their fuel reserves if we're talking generators—in most cases twenty-four hours, or a few days at most for hospitals and stuff like that."

Laurel Fey had been sitting close to the fireplace as usual and was busily taking notes. "So what you're saying," she piped up, "is that the Internet could drop out any time."

Vissar nodded slowly. "Yes, more or less. And then anything that depends on the Internet, which these days is practically everything. And it would go out all at once. No flickering or brownouts. A lot depends on how long it's down and how much of it comes back. The longer it's down, the bigger the problem we have."

"So are you suggesting we buy more generators, or stock more fuel, or what?" asked Fisher.

"What I'm saying is that we stock more of everything," Vissar said flatly. "But that's impossible. So we need to have a conversation right quick about what's important to have back-ups for and what isn't. Storing more fuel for our own gen sets only makes sense if the global Internet is still working. If we're the only node with fuel, then there would be nobody else to talk to. So after a certain point, having fuel wouldn't matter a fig if nobody else has any."

"But it's just a blackout we're talking about," someone called from the middle of the group. "We've got wood heat, stored food, and land to grow more food."

"Maybe," Vissar said ominously. "But maybe it's more. I said, these days, everything hangs from the Internet. In the event that the Internet is down for a long time, say a week, we've already seen that there could be food riots just like we did during that phantom fuel shortage back last fall. If for any of several reasons it was down for two weeks, then we'd have even bigger problems. The economy would stall out, just as if there was a general strike or something. Automated buy and sell orders would flood financial markets. Most people in this country are only one pay cheque away from defaulting on their mortgages, and a couple of pay cheques away from bankruptcy. The financial system would tank. Deliveries of almost everything would slow to a trickle or stop. It would only be a matter of days before they declared martial law, which would prolong the economic interruption even more because it would slow everything down. It would be a mega-mess. I'd be out of my fucking job."

The room erupted in laughter as everyone visualized the tragic irony of a computer geek predicting his own obsolescence—a contingency that Vissar viewed with far less levity. It seemed funny partly because the crowd needed a laugh, but also because the prospect seemed so far-fetched. Computers were household appliances. The Internet was as taken for granted as gravity. Those who programmed and operated the Internet seemed as secure in their work as brain surgeons. How could anyone worry?

"That would certainly be a problem..." Fisher sounded reassuring, but Vissar interrupted him.

"It's worse than a problem," he said. "Much worse." He was shaking visibly and drops of perspiration appeared on his face.

"How is it worse?" Fisher asked.

"We'd lose our memory," Vissar said, his voice cracking. A wave of silence passed over the room every bit as profound as the Friends Meeting. "We've been using computers for almost seventy years now, and extensively for the last fifty years. Practically everything we know is in computers somewhere, or in the brains of living people who are super-specialists at what they do. If the sweater really unravels and we lose too many of those people, and the Internet to boot, we will lose most of the stored knowledge of humanity. We only have to interrupt cultural transmission for one generation and we're back in the Middle Ages; one more generation and we might as well be living in trees again. The whole society would become a demented babushka trying to take care of eight billion grandchildren. How likely is that?"

Vissar inhaled deeply and exhaled slowly before continuing. "So what I suggest is this: I suggest that we think of everything we don't want to forget, and then get it the hell off the Internet—and out of computers. We need to start with useful knowledge like how to grow and preserve food, how to make clothes, how to set broken bones and deliver babies—stuff like that. And not only that, we need to start imagining what the future will be like without this economy, without this government, without this technology, and sure as hell without fossil fuels. Then we need to figure out what would still work in such a world to provide us enough to eat, and dry places to sleep, and clothes to wear, and for fuck's sake, a little bit of pleasure. And we need to do it right damn quick." Vissar's words were biting, but everyone understood his emotions. It was not as if anyone at the Coulee had not already imagined some of this for themselves. But the recent blackouts had brought all of these forebodings to the surface and now lent to them a compelling urgency. The collapse and disappearance of 'normalcy'—however problematic it may have been—appeared imminent.

"Guess we need to get more printers," Fey muttered to herself.

"And," Vissar added, "while we're doing all of that, we need to find another place to huddle. Badger Coulee is great, but there's nothing here between us and trouble except a snow fence. We should be better hidden or better defended and preferably both. Either way, we should start packing." The room started buzzing from every direction. Then Fisher stood up.

"Okay," he said. "How about this." He pointed to one of the tables in the Board Room. "I'm calling this the permaculture table. And this," he pointed to another table, "is the energy table. And this one is for transportation, that one is for health, that one for childcare, and that one for shelter. If I missed anything, make another group for it. Otherwise, if you know stuff about any of these things, get yourself around the table that matches. After we shuffle around, every table identify a table leader. I don't care if you elect them or draft them or appoint them, but they need to hang out for all the discussion and then meet up with me around noon tomorrow in my shack. And bring your notes."

"You heard what Frank said," Fisher continued. "So around your tables start planning what we're going to do about food, transportation and all the rest in a future without the Internet or fossil fuels, or maybe even without government. All ideas are welcome. Leave your ego at home, and think practical."

Laurel Fey raised her hand. "We need a coordinator table. Somebody has to fit all these pieces together."

Fisher nodded. "Brainiac table on Laurel, right there. Oh, one other thing. You'll come up with lots of ideas but most of them will wind up on the floor. The reason for that is that whatever you come up with can't just recreate the jam we're already in. Whatever you come up with has to be a solution to our predicament, not another predicament. And we know quite a bit about what that solution space looks like. So an idea stays on the table only if it's symbiotic with nature, only if it will work on current sunlight, only if it doesn't increase substances extracted from the Earth's crust, only if it's non-toxic to the biosphere, only if it doesn't increase the stock of human-made artifacts, only if it equitably shares risks and benefits in our community, only if it's a solution we can develop and apply locally, with local labour and materials, only if it makes sense in the long term, only if it's low on energy intensity, and for the gardeners in the room, only if our production of food can demonstrate a positive energy return on investment. If your idea violates any of those conditions, it's off the table. All set? Then shuffle."

Everyone seated stood up all at once and the room suddenly looked like a kicked open ant hill. But surprisingly quickly, all the tables were populated. Somebody produced a pad of chart paper and notes started appearing on the blank pages.

Beamer watched all this feeling somewhat humiliated. He had just learned how to split wood—a skill he acquired only after joining the Coulee—and perhaps the only thing of practical use that could balance off his entire formal education. In a moment of blinding clarity he realized that if the cookie crumbled, ninety-nine percent of everything taught in schools of his generation wouldn't be worth a piss in the wind.

"Beamer!" it was Laurel Fey waving him to join her table even as she was starting feverishly to take notes from the discussion already under way.

"Me?" he said.

"Yes, you," she repeated. "You were a bureaucrat, right?"

"Of sorts. I was a policy analyst actually." Why did it feel like he was confessing a sin?

"So this is what you guys do, isn't it? Make plans? Do research? Coordinate things?"

"On a good day," said Beamer.

"Well," said Laurel, "help us make this a good day."

# CHAPTER 29

*We can understand cascading effects
as just one damned thing after another.*

— FENTON LARRABEE, FUTURIST

TATUM MANAGED TO DEPART the city late in the day toting twenty more PV panels that she added to a pile of new blankets, some plastic pipe for one of their rain water collection rigs, and most exciting, a hundred kilos of various garden seeds. She could already feel her green thumb itching, wanting to get into the tree nurseries and orchards they had planted at the Coulee and see how they had wintered over. Before long, the compost piles would be thawing out and in need of turning, and the hugel beds would be ready for planting and mulching. The bees would emerge and the peeper frogs would start their ancient chants in the sloughs. No matter how things went in the world of people, she thought, every spring nature was especially visible in going about her business. Her garden grew without us. It was a hopeful thing. Tatum thought of spring as a kind of second chance—another opportunity to live wisely and simply and in relationship rather than in opposition. Nature could be harsh and dangerous and utterly intolerant of stupidity, but there was also a quality of forgiveness in it as it busily healed and regenerated the damages done to it from the previous year. These second (or third, or fourth) chances were nothing merited by humanity. They were just the plain, impartial goodness that the world offered to all its children.

Despite the longer days following the equinox, it was already evening by the time Tatum headed out of the city. Just getting around had become a challenge. Even though the ice was mostly gone and the flood receded, there were more detours, some because of frozen water main breaks or frost damage to pavements that left them crumbling and treacherous. In other respects the city was taking on a decidedly developing country appearance—those places around the world where the wrecks of cars and trucks, the rubble of the last war, the debris from the last hurricane or typhoon, or just the middens of human beings were never taken away, out of sight, but rather simply scraped to one side to make room enough for life of some sort to continue. Human bodies may be removed from these piles, and anything that might still be usable, whether of one's own or of departed others. But in many places cities resembled ant hills with multitudes of people scurrying around on top of them never really going anywhere. And in the streets, people wandered, aimless. Like Port-Au-Prince—or Detroit.

So threading her way through the maze took time and the sun was setting when Tatum escaped the city, made it past the new "checkpoint" on the perimeter road, and started her drive through the countryside. Snow still filled the ditches and the sloughs were brimming with water. Crop land had mostly cleared of snow, though fields would be sodden and sure to swallow farm machinery whole for at least another month. But back at the Coulee, it would be time to start transplants by the thousands in readiness for planting in late May.

An hour and a half later, Tatum was still droning along the highway, slowed now and then by surface breaks in the pavement growing there like skin cancers under the force of the spring thaw. Often she had to slow down or swerve over the centre line to avoid these pot holes, but little by little, she made her way, if not good time.

Then something struck her as odd. A jacked up four-by-four truck followed her down the highway, not exactly tailgating, but following steadily nonetheless. Its headlights were high enough to pierce through the back of Tatum's van all the way to her rear view mirror, and glared as well from her side mirrors. She adjusted the over-dash mirror to bend the glare away, but the light coming from the side mirrors continued to be a distraction. *Why didn't people dim their lights if they were going to follow so close*, Tatum thought. When she banked into a curve, she noticed there was a second truck behind the first one, following closely.

Their convoy came to a long, straight stretch of highway and Tatum wished they would just both pass her and be on their way. She took her foot off the gas to encourage the trucks to pass. At that moment, another vehicle turned onto the highway just at the limit of her headlights. It looked large—not likely a grain truck at this time of year—but something. As she approached it, she saw a large flatbed tow truck lumbering onto the highway. Thinking she would have to pass a vehicle going so slowly, Tatum put on her turn signal to change lanes only to hear a blaring horn close beside her. In a matter of moments, the jacked up four-by-fours had positioned themselves one behind and one beside her while the tow truck ahead was slowing down. Her only choices were to slow down along with the other vehicles or to drive into the ditch, which at this season would be full of icy water and gumbo. So she slowed down and brought the van to a stop, surrounded by the other vehicles.

Tatum's heart was hammering in her chest though she didn't feel consciously afraid. It just all seemed very odd—these people stopping her on the highway like this, in the middle of the night, with a tow truck nonetheless. Maybe they thought she had a flat or something? Some part of her was pursuing a different line of thought. It was the hair-raising alert that she shared with all other mammals. This part caused her to reach in her pocket for her cell phone. She just managed to activate the phone with her finger print and punch in 911 before the driver side door was abruptly pulled open and a very large man wearing a balaclava and a dark cover-all grabbed her by the lapels of her parka and pulled her out of the driver's seat of the van. He said nothing at all. He was one of five men who had spilled out of the trucks and were already busy lowering the deck of the tow truck, turning off the engine of Tatum's van and dousing its lights.

Upon being dragged from the van, Tatum fell on her knees on the pavement only to be yanked up violently into a standing position again. The man who held her felt impossibly strong. "What the hell!" she shrieked at him, then tried to kick him in the groin. But he simply dragged her around the end of her van in the direction of the ditch. None of the men said anything, even to each other. They knew what they were doing. Each knew his part. All had practiced their parts many times before. They were cold. They were efficient. They didn't need to say anything.

Tatum's last gesture was to press the call button on her cell phone and just catch a glint in the eye slits of the balaclava. "Nothing personal, lady," he said.

# CHAPTER 30

*"What did I do to deserve this?" I asked.*
*"If by 'this' you mean your life, this present*
*event or moment in your life, you did nothing to*
*deserve it. You chose it. You volunteered."*
*"But why would I choose adversity?"*
*"Because adversity has something to teach you, or*
*because you have taken adversity on yourself to save*
*someone else from it. Which, do you suppose?"*
*"I don't know," I said.*
*"Yes you do," the Companion replied. "Look within. Do you*
*have the capacity to suffer for someone else, someone you've*
*never met, someone you don't even know who deserves your*
*sacrifice? Do you hear within you the 'Yes!' that is willing*
*to plunge into pain, knowing it can never be eternal, never*
*mortal? If you find that capacity within you, then you have*
*chosen your adversity for the sake of another. If you cannot find*
*such willingness within yourself, then the adversity is your*
*own, and you have chosen it for what it will teach you—to*
*bring you to the moment when you can choose it for another."*

— OSIO SMITH, *TRANSCENDANCE*

JASPER BECKETT WAS taller than a dwarf, shorter than a Viking, but in nearly every other respect resembled them both. His body was solid and strong, his sienna hair rolled into dreadlocks that reached nearly to the middle of his back. His face was adorned with a fulsome beard that he sometimes braided together with beads. His role at the Coulee was that of quartermaster, or less militaristically, their stores-man, or more in keeping with Badger Coulee's monastic inspiration, their cellarer. He'd been at Badger Coulee since its founding three years before and was childhood friends with Tatum Barnes who teased him by telling others that he already had his beard in kindergarten when they first met. Their friendship had always been platonic but fierce and lifelong. He was the bear circling her camp in the night, keeping worse things at bay. His was the steady blue eye that measured her romantic interests, not from jealousy, but from protectiveness. In her own mind Tatum never thought she needed much protection but indulged Jasper's need to feel protective of her—until she did need it, and he wasn't there.

So perhaps it was that sense of having failed her, of not having been there for her when she needed him, that fixed him in front of her cottage door, as if his boots had been pegged to the ground, rocking slowly from side to side, his knuckled right hand poised to knock on the door, but suspended there in mid-air, waiting. Waiting for someone to give him a shake and say: "Wake up, Beckett. You're dreaming Beckett. There's a truck to unload. Tatum's brought another load. Haul ass!" But he didn't wake up. He felt caught in a nightmare and he couldn't wake up. He should knock. Maybe that would wake him up.

Beamer had been working especially hard for the past couple of days. With Tatum in the city, it kept his mind off her to work till he dropped, exhausted, into his bed. If he had to sleep alone, he wanted to sleep soundly. But it was already mid-morning when he was dimly conscious of someone standing just outside his door. He roused himself, pulled on a pair of sweat pants, and went to the door.

Beamer pulled the door open to reveal a very large man with lots of red hair, his knuckled hand poised in readiness to knock on the door. His face was tear-streaked and his mouth part way open as if he'd been cut off mid-sentence by something unspeakable. Their eyes met and Beamer saw blue eyes already surrounded by blood-shot whites, welling tears that oozed over his eyelashes and trickled down, disappearing into the wilderness of his beard. And Beamer knew.

"Jasper?" asked Beamer, perplexed.

Jasper managed a raspy breath—enough for him to visibly stiffen and stand straighter. "Tatum's gone," he choked. Having gotten this much out, Jasper renewed his effort to stand straight, to somehow contain this, to not fall—to just not fall down.

"Gone where?" Beamer asked, his own voice starting to shake. *Fucking stupid! Dumb as a bag of hammers! You stupid—dumb—fuck! he thought. Fucking gone is what he said.*

Then the two of them just stood there looking into each other's eyes. Jasper's were still welling tears but Beamer's eyes were strangely dry. Ice, they say, flows like water, only very slowly. Something like ice started welling up in Beamer. It started low in his belly, then spread upward and downward until it filled his body, ice that capped a river the flow of which was slowing, slowing, and finally stopped, glacier-like.

"How?" Beamer could hear the quiver in his own voice.

Jasper shifted now from one foot to the other as if getting out the first two words had broken a crust that had held him captive at the door. Slowly he lowered his hand. "We think," he choked, "that she was murdered. They jacked her van. Took the whole thing and just left her. Somehow she got off a 911 call before she…before she…" Jasper took another deep breath, "before she passed. She left the line open and that's how the Horsemen found her."

"Where?"

"About fifty clicks north of here."

"No!" said Beamer, his voice edged by the effort to contain his emotions. "Where is she?" he asked.

"Oh, sorry," Jasper apologized. Now he looked like someone trying very hard to say the right thing, in spite of his own grief. "The Horsemen have her body—until they finish—you know—their investigation. They need to get hold of her family too."

"We're her family!" Beamer shrieked. The suspension of belief that had numbed him suddenly gave way and he started charging from one wall to another, bellowing incoherently. The most impossibly bitter compound of rage, sorrow, shock, and pain flooded every part of his body until he had to expel it somehow. Then he dived for the kitchen sink and vomited violently and without cease until Jasper was afraid Beamer himself might die from the sheer effort of it. He moved into the room where Beamer was gripping the edge of the kitchen counter heaving into the sink, and brought his arm under and around Beamer's belly which was now cramped and twitching. He held him, like a child who had sickened in the night, bent down and held him through one siege of retching after another until finally he stopped. He gently pulled Beamer through the cottage and onto his bed where he curled there, exhausted, gasping.

Jasper let Beamer go, but pulled his desk chair alongside the bed, sat down, and waited in silence.

For his part, Beamer felt himself drifting now in something motionless and cold. It was like a featureless sea under a featureless sky, bled dry of all colour. He was a monochrome being floating on a monochrome ocean of death. Had he the energy to form an intention, he would have intended to sink down, down in the darkness, just to be with her. If that's where she was… Was she there? Where was she? *Where was she?*

"…about fifty clicks north of here…"

Beamer's eyes fluttered open for a moment. *Was I so stupid at reading signs? he wondered. Why did I ever let her go?*

"Why did I ever let go," moaned Jasper, not caring whether Beamer heard him or not. "Ever since we were kids, I used to look out for her. She hated that, but I did it anyway. I should have gone to the city with her, rode shotgun for her."

"Me too," Beamer sighed, letting his eyes slide closed. "Thanks for coming by, Jasper," he said, the irony of the comment settling on him with its huge absurdity. He laid still now and Jasper sat beside him for a long time.

# CHAPTER 31

*There is a cruel paradox in human experience that
it is amidst the great currents of history, amidst the
impact of things over which we have no control, that
we must nevertheless do the work required of our
individual souls. This can be overwhelming.*

— RUPERT PHILMORE,
*THE PSYCHODYNAMICS OF CULTURAL DISINTEGRATION.*

THAT EVENING, AT JASPER'S URGING, both of them left Tatum's cottage
and went to the Board Room. Jasper pressed for them to eat something but
when it came to it they both just took mugs of tea and nothing more. For
Beamer the world had taken on an aspect of unpleasant surprise. He was surprised not to feel hungry. He was surprised that he asked for tea and not mulled
cider, because mulled cider reminded him of Tatum. He compulsively scanned
the gathering crowd—realized he was looking for her—and was surprised she
wasn't there. And a voice in his head kept reminding him: *But she's gone. She's
gone.* And he surprised himself in wanting to be close to Jasper, physically near
him, as if doing so made it possible for him to continue standing. Somehow
they had become companions of a special order of those who have both loved
someone who was untimely taken from them. He'd wept repeatedly throughout the day until coming to evening he was utterly spent. No more tears existed
anywhere, he was certain. And yet he hungered for them. It was like needing to
scream and having no mouth. In this he felt sere, stumbling numbly from one
moment to the next, none of them making much sense.

As they looked for a place to sit, Beamer noticed that a great many people
were assembling in the Board Room, more than he'd ever seen there before, even
for Laurel Fey's lecture. Many approached him to hug him, some of whom he
hardly knew, and could hardly believe would know how much Tatum meant to
him. But they kept coming, many of them solemn-eyed or weeping as well. But
interlaced with the grief was another emotion: fear. To Beamer it was a distant
and irrelevant feeling at the moment, but he sensed it nonetheless.

Once the room was full and people had settled down, Fisher appeared at the front of the room but this time allowed someone to help push his wheelchair up the dais and park him beside the ambo. He cradled a mic in his lap. He held no formal office in the Coulee; no one did. But he brought an elder presence wherever he went, and tonight especially, Coulee members appreciated that. Beamer also saw Laurel Fey in her customary place in the hall, her cheeks and eyes flushed from weeping, their redness set off by her pale skin and white hair. Farther back, Changming and Kyle sat together, their hands clenched in each other's grasp, as did many others. Then throat clearing sounds came from the dais.

"Friends," Fisher's voice croaked. He cleared his throat again and pressed on. "Friends, as I'm sure you all know by now, Tatum Barnes was killed last night on her way back from the city to the Coulee. The police tell us she was murdered, which makes this news especially cruel. I'm sorry to say I don't have many more details. Her death is under investigation by the police. The coroner has custody of her body until they can notify her family. Apart from that, they aren't saying anything about what they know. Only her body was found by the road, so we guess it's a carjacking and they had the equipment necessary to steal her whole vehicle, not just its contents. Anyway, that's really all we know right now."

"The Friends are planning a Meeting in celebration of her life next Thursday at noon in the Barn here so that everybody who wants to can come. Tatum often joined the Friends for their Meetings."

Fisher let the mic drop back into his lap, pausing in what he said. He appeared laboured with the task of finding the right words for the situation. The room remained still until he spoke again.

"I know how difficult this time is for all of us, how much we need stillness and privacy, and how much we want to share our feelings and support each other. But I'm concerned for all of us. I don't think it would be wise to delay this conversation, given what's already happened. With the loss of Tatum, I think we've crossed a Rubicon of some kind. Tatum's death was deliberate, and heartless. Those responsible were after what she was bringing here in that van. They probably didn't even know what she had in it; whatever she had, they wanted it. To me that means that things out there are getting sketchy enough that some people are now willing to kill simply to get stuff of whatever kind before that's no longer possible. Maybe they somehow knew what she was bringing back here and maybe they didn't. Maybe they were just planning to sell whatever they got, including the van, to get more money. God knows there are enough people on the edge these days. But I don't think we can assume that we're safe here, or safe in transit. This is something we have to discuss—right now."

A murmur stirred in the crowd as people turned to each other, their grief fading into the background while their fear moved into the foreground. Everyone knew what Fisher was driving at.

"I've thought a bit about this," he continued. "There are some things we should do right away. Then we need to talk about the longer term. We should start going everywhere in pairs, even in the Coulee, and especially at night, both driving and walking. No kids out running around on their own. We need to keep all the children in view of some adults, all the time. If you don't already have someone, pick a buddy before you leave this room tonight. Also have a back-up for your number one buddy in case you can't reach them. As many people as possible should be carrying their cell phones with half a dozen of us on speed-dial. If you don't have that app, install it right away."

"We also need to call in the Finders from the city. I think there were twenty-three of them at last count, including Tatum. Have them come home and bring along their joiners if they can make it quick."

"Next thing—there are only two roads into and out of this place. I think we should keep an eye on those roads. I don't mean getting all paranoid and setting up checkpoints and stuff. I mean just keeping an eye peeled for anything unusual. If you're agreeable, I think the people best situated to do that job are those whose houses are closest to the edge of the village, coming and going. You know who you are, but check in with me later tonight so we can make sure everybody understands their role."

"I think it's unlikely that these people will visit us by travelling overland on power toboggans or ATVs because they can't carry much loot. But it's not impossible. So those of you living anywhere near the perimeter of the village should keep your eyes open and heads on swivels. Call your speed dial list if you see anything that concerns you."

"Next thing—a couple days ago we had a meeting here and set up some planning groups for a move somewhere else and how to increase our self-reliance. Your groups are continuing to meet and everyone is coming up with really good ideas, some of them turning into plans. The group leaders are meeting together regularly to work on making the pieces fit as well as possible. I know we are already working hard on this and there's only so much we can do not knowing for sure where we might go. But in view of our recent loss, I think we need to double time all this work. Get the ideas written down. Refine them as much as you can with the time we have. Download and print whatever information might be helpful from the Internet. Start lists of stuff we need to make your plans happen. First try for things that we can do right now, right here, and anywhere we decide to go. I also think we should pick two or three teams of people to start scouting for a new place to live. Eyes wide open. All ideas welcome."

At that moment, a man stood up in the middle of the room. It was Alex Brighton, peering over the glasses that still perched precariously on his nose. He was always present, but seldom noticed, until he chose to be. He cast his gaze around the room and as he did so, without saying anything, he gathered all attention to himself. "Way is not yet open," he said matter-of-factly. "Wait." And then he sat down again. By now, most of those living at the Coulee had heard about his cryptic pronouncements, but they were mercifully short and while obscure to most of his listeners, the other Friends seemed to know what he was talking about. So Brighton was suggesting they wait. For what? For how long?

Then Laurel Fey stood up. Fisher nodded, ceding the floor. "Listening to all of this," she said, her voice full of urgency, "I know all this is terrible and scary. But I'm also really worried that we could lose sight of all the good reasons we had for coming to the Coulee and for staying here to build it. I'm not saying I want us to stay in this particular place. No. I agree with Fisher. That would probably be dangerous and it's already been tragic. But what I'm saying is, I don't want us to give in to fear and forget what we wanted to create here. Our shared project matters more than simply being safe. Tatum knew that, I'm sure, or she wouldn't have taken on some of the things she did. We owe it to her not to forget why we're here, what we're trying to make, what we believe in. What's happening now just makes it more urgent, that's all. That's all I have to say." She sat down heavily, a shallow scowl on her brow, as if she herself hadn't fully expressed her concerns, but didn't know what else to say.

Fisher nodded in Laurel's direction, acknowledging her words and her concern. He waited a moment for what she said to sink down into the group, then he picked up the mic again.

"So maybe our task here is quite simple, as Laurel Fey never tires of reminding me." Fisher smiled in Laurel's direction. "We're not here to figure out how to sustain the unsustainable culture of the past. We're here to create a new one. That's what Tatum was after; some way of acting out her love for living things, her simple way of living, and the community she found here with us. So you have to be the generation who is remembered for what it created, not who it killed. We need a name for what we want to build. Maybe it's a utopia. Or maybe, we could call it *Euterra*."

Suddenly, Jasper started slamming his massive hands together in a steady beat—clap...clap...clap! And one by one, then in twos and threes, then in scores, the rest of the assembly picked up the clapping. Jasper grinned at Laurel as he clapped and she looked back at him, at first wondering, but then smiling broadly. In this they began to remember the world as they understood it before Tatum's death; before this very personal shock fell so close to home. In the moment, they touched again the reassuring anchorage of their shared trust of each other and the shared project they had started, even as it was evolving from the darkness of potentiality toward the light of realization. And in that memory, they found a measure of strength.

For his part, Beamer sat and listened. Most of what was said seemed like it concerned other people on some far away alien planet. He stood beside himself, watching himself, abstracted and indifferent, even to the expression of so much sympathy from the others. None of this concerned him anymore—except for one thing. One phrase lodged in his mind like a thorn.

An apocryphal story says that in ancient Tibet, Buddhist monks drilled holes between their eyes so that pegs soaked in special herbs could be inserted into their brains. It was believed that this sort of treatment conferred a special level of spiritual attainment, if only one could endure the pain of the ritual.

For Beamer, the thorn between his eyes was the words, "We can't stay here." He had no idea what it meant and no idea why, out of all that was said that night and amidst the noisome fog of his grief, this alone stood out with clarity.

# CHAPTER 32

*The intention behind doing a thing is as important as doing the thing itself. Greed, guilt and fear are all unskillful reasons for doing something. Changing one's mind—now that's different.*

— ONOKI TASIMOTO, ROSHI

BEAMER STAYED IN THE BARN until the meeting dispersed in the early hours of the morning, although he retained little memory of what was said. Conversation, even about very important things, just swirled around his head and left his mind as soon as it arrived. It was all part of the general surreal quality that everything had taken on since Jasper's visit earlier in the day. And all of this mingled with a distant sense of urgency—that important things were happening and he should play a part; that he should get off dead stop and contribute somehow, somewhere, to address the threats to the Coulee. But no sooner had these thoughts formed than they dissolved again into the grey background of his grief leaving behind only a sense of guilt with no clear idea what it was he felt guilty about. As more people began leaving the Barn, Beamer too shuffled off toward the door that led to Tatum's cottage.

When he got back to his room he pushed open the door and saw in Tatum's room the two pillar candles standing side-by-side where he had left them since the last evening they spent together. He'd left them there as a warm reminder of their night together thinking they would be replaced with new ones eventually. Now they looked more like a memorial than a memento, and seeing them triggered another surge of sadness and emptiness. Can emptiness surge? Beamer wondered. *It feels like it can, so I guess it can*, he thought. But nothing followed from that except for Beamer collapsing on his bed, his consciousness dimming from the sheer exhaustion he felt. Then he slept.

When he awakened the next morning, it was already late. He felt well for a few moments, just as if nothing had happened the day before. His mind felt stuck in history while current events had moved on leaving him behind. When he caught up with himself, he remembered the shattering loss of the day before.

He got out of bed. Bright sunshine poured in the window of his bedroom, spring proclaiming itself in spate. Many trees around the Coulee were heavy with buds or in full blossom, adorning the village with leis of pink, white, fuchsia and yellow. He remembered Tatum's comment the first day she introduced him to Badger Coulee that it was a beautiful place, especially in the spring and summer, which she hoped he would see and appreciate. Now he was seeing it but through a grey scrim and far away. The light filled his eyes but was powerless to lift his heart.

He left his room and Tatum's cottage and walked to the Barn vestibule. There he donned boots and grabbed his sweater that hung there on a peg. As he turned to leave by the front door, he noticed that the message in the little frame on the door had been changed: "Pain is unavoidable. Suffering is optional." The thought flitted through his mind that someday he hoped to be enlightened enough to disentangle the two.

He stepped out of the Barn into a warm ocean of flower scented air. His intention was just to amble about, which felt consoling. Simple movement summoned life back into his limbs which otherwise would have festered in motionlessness. But almost immediately he headed toward Changming's workshop. He didn't bother going to the front door but went instead to the rear door which he knew was always left unlocked.

Beamer entered the workshop to find it only partially lighted. The studio always looked chaotic to Beamer, but today it looked chaotic in a peculiar way. He saw Changming standing motionless before an open crate, his head bowed, and tools in both hands. "You know," he said, not looking up, "I never know how to pack this stuff." Then he looked up at Beamer, his cheeks tear streaked, eyes bewildered. His normally immaculately groomed if flamboyant hair was now an unruly mop.

"Me either," said Beamer. "Can I help you pack?"

Changming sighed. "Sure," he said. "Thanks. We just need to pack in case we know where we're going." He dropped a rasp he was holding into the crate and started to sob. "I guess we should always live with our bags packed, eh Beamer?"

Beamer picked up a giant spatula that Changming used for mixing batches of plaster. "Does this go in here," he asked, standing over the only open crate in the room.

Changming nodded. "Sure. Why not."

"It's good you can cry," Beamer said. "I can't anymore—at least for today. Maybe tomorrow."

Changming nodded again. "You know, I was thinking how lucky it is that the speed of light is what it is and that other stars and planets are so fucking far away."

"Really," said Beamer.

"Yes," said Changming. "Because that means that totally fucked up humanity probably can't infect the rest of the universe with our fucked upness. Do you ever think of that, Beamer?" Changming's voice caught in his throat.

"May I just sit down?" Beamer asked.

"Anywhere you like. Every place is filthy."

"That thought's sort of comforting."

"What? That every place is filthy?"

"No," said Beamer. "The part about the speed of light and other planets. That part."

"How did we ever come to this?" Changming asked, his voice distant.

Beamer sighed. "The fuck if I know."

"So, what are you going to do?"

"Well," said Beamer, "I'm going to help you finish packing. Then I may go walkabout or something."

Changming dropped another tool clattering into the crate. "Oh, I'm practically done," he said, standing amidst the copious clutter of his workshop.

"What are you going to do?" Beamer asked, as if they both stood before the smoking crater of a nuclear blast thinking: Okay. What now?

Changming shrugged and then looked at Beamer. "I thought I'd make Tatum a stone."

"A stone?"

"Yes. For her grave—or something." He reached toward his workbench to retrieve a pebble of granite, too heavy to lift with just one hand, but small enough that it could be cradled in one's arms. It was smooth as river stone. "I thought she would like it if it was small and simple and natural looking, you know?" He had already used a chalk to mark out her name and some dates beneath it. "But I didn't know what was her birth date or middle name, or even if she had a middle name, you know, because some people don't have middle names or if they do sometimes they don't use them, or if they have a hyphenated last name then it gets to be too long if you add the middle name with it, you know, and"—he started sobbing again, rocking the stone back and forth in his arms like a swaddled infant—"I didn't know what words to put on."

Both of them stood in silence for a moment while Changming rocked the stone. Beamer stepped closer to Changming, reached out to embrace him while he still held Tatum's stone between them. Beamer released him, then said: "Put 'loved.' She'd like that."

"I'll be back soon," said Beamer as he turned toward the door of the workshop. "Hang in there."

"Sure. I will do that," said Changming.

Beamer left the workshop and headed back toward the Barn.

# CHAPTER 33

*We cannot work at grieving. Healing happens for*
*us when we let the Grief-worker within go its way.*
*Even in its chaos, it is lawful. And in the process we*
*may discover something completely unexpected.*

— ANDERS CABOT, *THE FOUR AGES OF CHANGE*

FOR THE NEXT SEVERAL DAYS Beamer tried to pick up the threads of his life at the Coulee but it was as if he wandered about in a daze. Occasionally, and unpredictably, the fog of grief parted and he was overwhelmed by tears. The first couple of times this happened it caught him by surprise and to his embarrassment, although whoever he happened to be with at such moments was usually respectful and sympathetic. Then he began to see these storms coming, like the summer clouds that could pile up over the prairie dragging draperies of rain behind them. He could feel them rising in him. With each renewal of his capacity for weeping, he wept. Then dry eyed and empty once more, he returned to daze-walking.

During this ordeal, however, Beamer discovered something: At its most extreme, when his tears were unstoppable and the depth of his pain seemed bottomless there was, as it were, another self standing behind, or sometimes beside him, witnessing his suffering. This other self watched with compassion but was unmoved by what it witnessed. That figure of himself stood still, resolute, peaceful and unafraid. So at times there were two Beamers, or Beamer and his Companion, who endured Tatum's passing together, one of them nearly destroyed by it, the other the compassionate witness offering its silent assurance that he would not be destroyed. This reality—for it was an inner reality for him—wasn't something he had the energy to question or to analyze or to doubt. It was just steadily there for him and all he could muster at the moment was gratitude.

Some days later, as they promised, the Friends convened a Meeting to celebrate Tatum's life. Her body was still in the custody of the coroner and would be interred later when it was released. She had been a regular attender at the Lighthouse gatherings, which was her spiritual community. But for this gathering, the Friends had secured the Board Room to accommodate everyone who might attend. Chairs had been arranged in concentric circles with an unadorned table and a single candle at its centre. When Beamer entered he looked around for a seat and noticed one next to Jasper, whom he joined. Everyone from the Coulee that Beamer knew and others as acquaintances made their way into the circle, together with several others who Beamer assumed might be some of Tatum's family. Presently a woman stood up and offered a brief introduction to the Friends understanding of Meeting and the customs respecting remembrance of the dead. Then she said: "A Meeting in memory and celebration of Tatum Barnes," and sat down.

There was a considerable period of silence before anyone stood up to speak, and when they did, it was not a prepared eulogy, but a simple memoir of how Tatum had touched that person's life. And on it went, for over two hours, one speaker after another, each telling some personal story about their history with Tatum, releasing their stories into the collective consciousness gathered in the room, gathered to remember her. When it seemed that the last person had spoken, again the silence lengthened.

To his utter surprise, Beamer felt words forming inside his mind: *Stand up!* He glanced around half expecting to find someone whispering in his ear. There was no one there, but the message was both urgent and sweet. So he stood up. He felt like an idiot. Most of those assembled continued in their silence, many with eyes closed, but a few noticed him stand. Having done this much, he wondered what he should say, but all his thoughts seemed just to be getting in his way. At last he took a breath and said, "I loved her." A few heads nodded but most remained motionless, steady, because of course, they had all loved her.

As the assembly was dispersing, Changming made his way through the crowd toward Beamer. The two embraced for a moment. Then Changming held Beamer by both shoulders at arm's length and looked firmly in his eyes. "I will make her a stone," he vowed, nodding once decisively. Beamer returned the nod as Changming tightened his grip on his shoulders in farewell, then released him and headed toward the door.

It was only a few more days later and Beamer stood outside Fisher's cabin. He rapped lightly on the door. "Come!" called Fisher.

Beamer stepped inside. Fisher was holding up his tea pot. "Tea?"

"Yes, thanks," Beamer replied.

The two were silent while Fisher prepared the tea, then, "So, how are you doing?" Fisher asked.

Beamer sighed and looked out the window at the far end of Fisher's table. He didn't say anything for some moments, gathering his thoughts, which were remarkably few. "Kind of hard to describe it," Beamer confessed. "Most days, my head feels like it's floating about a metre over my body, watching myself go by." He shook his head and glanced out the window again. "I can't get her out of my mind."

"Huh," said Fisher, but gently, "you'll never get her out of your mind, son. I would bet that you don't really want to. But you will have to find a way to live with her there."

Beamer nodded without comment, then, "Fisher, I've got to go walkabout. I've got to leave the Coulee for a while...try to get clear again. I'll come back. I promise. I'm planning to anyway. But right now I just need to walkabout."

"Are you sure that's a wise idea, so soon..." Fisher's voice trailed off.

"I don't know," Beamer admitted. "But right now, when I'm here, all I can see is her, you know? Somehow, as we fell in love, I shrank and we grew—if that makes any sense—and we were inseparable from this place, from this community. Right now I'm feeling like I've not only lost Tatum, but most of myself too, and my sense of this community. If I come back here to live, I want it to be because I feel something for everyone else here, not just Tatum. And I need to know it's me really feeling it, not some mash up of Tatum and me together. I just need time and distance to get this stuff sorted out, you know?"

Fisher nodded reflectively. "Yes," he said, "I think that's pretty clear—pretty solid. Do you want to go alone?"

"Yes," Beamer said firmly.

"I see. Well..." Fisher seemed lost in thought.

"'Well' what?"

Fisher set his tea mug on the table, dropped his hands into his lap. "Beamer, these things happen to people. It's called life. It's about all most of us can handle even on our good days. You need to do this work, that's true. It's necessary and healthy. I just hope you keep something else in mind."

"What's that?" Beamer asked.

"Things are winding up here, Beamer. What happened to Tatum is, I'm afraid, only the first taste of something much nastier and bigger that's still on its way to us. You have to do your work, for the sake of your own soul, but you have to do it somehow in the middle of this predicament we're in. Just watch your back, will you Beamer?"

He nodded, extending his hand toward Fisher. "Thanks for all the tea," he said, managing a mirthless smile as they shook hands.

"I'll pass the word," Fisher offered.

"Back as soon as I can," Beamer said as he headed out the door.

His tea remained untasted.

# CHAPTER 34

*Some things can only be resolved by walking.*

— OSIO SMITH, *TRANSCENDANCE*

IT WAS LATE MAY when he set out. The ice had left the sloughs and rivers by mid-April. The trees that set their leaves early were washing tender shades of green into the tangled branches of aspen, birch and alder like a developing photograph. Day by day the green pushed back the more somber hues of winter, a greening that even penetrated Beamer as he walked.

When he stepped out of the cottage under the load of as much hiking gear as he thought he might need, he turned this way and that, like a compass seeking north. And as if following a compass, north beckoned him. So he set out that way, trudging under the weight of his pack and his grief. After walking for three hours he was a mere fifteen kilometres north of Badger Coulee. He doffed his pack and sat down at the roadside for a break. Badger Coulee was not on a main road to anywhere—which was one reason it was picked for the purpose. But its isolation also meant that very little traffic passed on this road, most of it routing around to the west of the village and back toward the city. So it was luck that found a local farmer on his way north to the highway, who stopped to offer Beamer a ride, which he accepted. They exchanged few words, which suited Beamer just fine, and in another hour their road met the highway.

"Heading into the city?" the farmer asked.

"Thanks," said Beamer, pulling on the door handle to open the door, "but I think I'm going the other way."

"Fair enough," the farmer replied, mercifully not asking for more details.

Beamer retrieved his backpack from the cargo box of the truck, which then turned west into the flow of traffic heading to the city while he stood on the shoulder looking east. There was still a considerable stretch of cultivated land to the east before he would meet the bearded wall of the boreal forest, but he could feel it there, calling him, nonetheless. So he turned eastward and started trudging along.

It was not his intention to hitch-hike, especially given recent events, but the fact remained that he was a long way from anywhere in particular, and while the days of May were often warm, the nights could be decidedly cool. He trekked along, not thinking much about the weather, just letting one vehicle after another whiz past him on the highway, inhaling deeply the fragrant spring air. Sometimes there wafted up the musky scent of last year's vegetation rotting in the ditches, or a breeze carried over a newly tilled field, earthy and warm. But whenever the breeze shifted out of the east, he could detect the faintest rumour of balsam firs, their heady, aromatic essence lending a tingling quality to the air. This aroma called forth a feeling from which he'd been estranged now for weeks; he felt a subtle lift in his spirit. Not yet happiness, even by a stretch. But it was a lilt of feeling that reminded him of moments in his life when he could breathe, when his heart was beating instead of silent, and when his thoughts about life included a future.

Another truck pulled alongside him with a crew cab and two men wearing quilted winter coveralls and company issued baseball caps with the logo GCC on the forehead. The truck was outfitted with ladders, hot-rods—long, insulated pikes used for handling live high voltage wires—loose rolls of cable, and an assortment of other tools that looked relevant to electrical trades. The guy on the passenger side lowered the window and said, "Heading east?"

Beamer nodded.

"How far you going?"

Beamer shrugged. "As far as I can I guess."

"Want a lift?"

He hesitated, but again decided to trust this pair. "Thanks," Beamer said. He wrestled his backpack behind the front seats and squeezed himself in on the passenger side. They were called crew cabs, but the crew needed very short legs, Beamer thought.

"Sing out where you want to get out," the driver said. "I'm Wally and this is Sean." Beamer reached between the front bucket seats to shake their hands. "Beamer Farris," he introduced. A country-western station crooned in the background as they picked up speed heading down the highway.

Beamer realized that he had been several hours without human conversation and already he craved it—perhaps another sign of spring? "So were you guys around for the big blackout?" he asked.

Wally cast a glance at Beamer in the rear view mirror as he drove. "Nope," said Wally. "Guess we dodged a bullet. We come from farther out west and we didn't get the ice."

"It was quite a thing," said Beamer. "Lots of ice. Don't think I've ever seen that much ice. Sort of pretty, but quite a mess."

"Mess ain't the half of it," Sean chimed in.

"Zip it!" Wally said, his voice tense.

"Awe, what the fuck," Sean replied. "I'm just makin' conversation. He's just a hitchhiker for fuck sake."

Beamer heard the tension between the two, wondered what he might have said already that wound their springs. Hoping to deflect the conversation away from whatever land mine he had nearly touched off, and remembering the appearance of their truck when they stopped for him, Beamer said: "So are you guys coming through to help with fixing all the downed lines?"

"Yes," Wally confirmed, "that's it." He sounded relieved for some reason.

"Well, sort of," Sean chimed in again. "We work for General Contracting and Construction. We were hired to help with the nuke repairs."

"Nuke repairs?" asked Beamer.

"Yes. The ice storm weren't the half of it. Somebody tried to blow the Energy-One nuke there just west of the city."

"Will you fuckin' zip it, I said." Wally glanced again at Beamer, this time looking decidedly nervous. Beamer tried to sound casual, as if he might be more interested in how the pre-season baseball line-up was going, but these two knew something.

"It doesn't fuckin' matter," Sean said. "It's gonna be all over the news by tomorrow anyway."

"Blow Energy-One?" Beamer repeated, trying to keep his voice light, unconcerned. Just making conversation.

Sean turned part way around in his seat so he could see Beamer as he spoke. "No shit," he said, as if this was the latest bit of news confirming his favourite conspiracy theory. "The ice storm was pretty localized really, but somebody used it as an opportunity."

Wally looked annoyed. "Will you stuff your screwball theories on who's doing what to who?"

"There was ice damage, for sure," Sean kept on, his voice sounding like he was taking Beamer into his special confidence. "But it didn't come anywhere near the nuke. There was somebody up there, goddammit, waiting for the right time to drop shit into the system."

"It wasn't shit they dropped in the system," Wally corrected. "It should've been you."

"Damn straight it wasn't shit," said Sean. "It was military grade C4."

"You wouldn't know military grade C4 if it bit you in the ass," scoffed Wally.

"Doesn't matter," said Sean. "Ice storm happened. Somebody blew a hole in the Energy-One nuke. The blackout spread farther and faster than anybody could account for just because of an ice storm in the southern prairies. Those lines go down and the grid compensates, eh. Relays start poppin' and computers start hoppin' shunting loads and spinning up turbines to fill the gaps, you know. But this time the whole midway went down—all the way to the Maritimes. The damn grid doesn't just do that all on its own. It needs help. Like there must have been people all over the country ready to pull something like this just waiting for their chance, see. Then along comes an ice storm and the ice jams in the rivers and the flooding in the city that gives them the perfect cover. Joe on the street doesn't have a fat clue about how the grid works, so if you tell him an ice storm out west caused a blackout in Quebec, he'll buy it. But that ain't what happened."

"You don't know what happened," Wally dismissed.

"Well then you tell me what did happen, smart ass," Sean retorted.

"You know we're not supposed to talk about this stuff—to anybody," Wally said.

"Oh fuck a duck," said Sean. "You know it don't matter a damn. It'll be old news by Wednesday and everybody'll buy the ice storm story."

"And why shouldn't they?" said Wally. "It's probably true—or true enough."

"Because the story ain't over yet," said Sean, his voice dropping from defensive to conspiratorial again.

"What do you mean?" Beamer asked.

"Because this wasn't the real deal."

"Oh, my blessed Aunt Margaret!" Wally growled.

"It was a practice run," Sean asserted, "A test. Had it been an actual alert, we would have been really fucked."

"Because the Internet would fail?" Beamer put in, recalling Frank Vissar's warnings.

Sean shook his head. "Naw," he said. "The hydro grid doesn't depend on the Internet. The Internet depends on the grid. The grid has its own network. They don't control the grid using the same wires you watch your porn on. The engineers are at least that smart. But I could still take the grid down with a box of dynamite and a dozen hobby drones."

"He has these spells," Wally said apologetically. He glanced at Beamer, trying to guess if he was buying this latest dismissal. For his part, Beamer was growing more and more curious but trying hard not to show it. The best way to stoke the fire, he thought, would be to deny it.

"Yes," Beamer said. "I don't buy much of that stuff."

"You fucking well should!" Sean sounded like he was charging up for another round. "Everybody worries about the transmission lines—that somebody will blow them up or something. It makes good television. But if a tower falls down, we can get it back up in a few days. But you have to look for the choke points in the system, see, and those are the converter stations, not the towers. They change the juice from high voltage DC coming from up north to low voltage AC we need for the city. There's only two of them that handle power for the whole city, one primary and one back-up. Take a dozen little drones, trick them out with a stick of dynamite each, load up your swarm software, and Bob's your uncle. It would be like cluster fucking the whole station."

Beamer raised an eyebrow. "Hmm," he said. "Don't they have spare transformers, just in case?"

Sean grinned broadly as if he felt positively euphoric at the prospect of disaster. "Nope," he said. "Too expensive. They make the transformers in Europe. Takes minimum six months to replace them."

Beamer himself was disturbed by the direction of the conversation. "Well," he said, "I hope nothing like that happens."

"Me too," Sean agreed, though Beamer wondered. "Thing is," Sean resumed, "it only takes one nerdy nut bar with some connections and a bit of cash to shut down the whole continent. You just need to buy lots of drones, preposition them all over the country near the converter stations, program them with the way points they need to hit, then launch them all with a phone call over the Internet. Then you've fucked the Internet using the Internet. How sweet is that? Ha!" He slapped his thighs in the sheer pleasure of his own supposed genius.

"Fuckin' hell," Wally growled as he pulled the truck onto the shoulder and stopped. "After that, I need to take a leak. Then I'm gonna report your ass."

Wally descended part way into the roadside ditch for a measure of privacy to relieve himself while Sean remained in the truck fidgeting. "He won't really report me," Sean said.

Presently Wally got back in the truck, rummaged in the console to retrieve a bag of beef jerky and then said to Beamer, "Hungry?" Beamer shook his head while Wally scooped up a fist full of the jerky chips and put the truck back on the road again. "Anybody mind if we listen to something else for a change?" Sean looked cowed, Beamer nodded, and Wally cranked up the country western station that had been the musical wall paper for Sean's end of days suspicions. They then drove down the highway for the next several hours no one saying anything. But for his own part, Beamer was captivated by what he'd heard.

Farmland and pasture disappeared behind them as they drove east. The landscape became more rolling, then broken by outcrops of granite, quartz and sandstone, all of it littered with spruce, balsam fir, pine, tamarack and alder. The shield loomed up in front of them and slowly swallowed them in the dense boreal forest, a band of forest that circled the northern hemisphere across North America, northern Europe, and finally Siberia. By late afternoon they were well into it.

At a nondescript crossroad Wally pulled the truck to the shoulder and stopped. He leaned back over the driver's seat and said: "You said you're heading east, but this is our turn-off going north. You want to stick with us, or bail out here?"

"Thanks guys," Beamer replied. "I think I'll bail here."

Wally raised an eyebrow. "You know, this is the middle of nowhere," he said. "Lions and tigers and bears, and all that."

Beamer nodded his thanks, trying a smile. "They've never bothered me before," he said. "Thanks again for the lift."

"No worries," said Wally. "Good luck wherever you're goin'."

Beamer extricated himself from the crew cab and pulled out his backpack. He waved off the truck which turned north on a highway and disappeared into the bush. Traffic on the highway was relatively light, but no one else offered him another ride. He felt very tired and decided that instead of pressing on, wherever "on" went, he would walk a bit more with an eye for an overnight camp site. All the land around appeared to be crown land or a timber lease area, so he guessed he could settle down for one night unmolested—except maybe for lions, tigers and bears—most probably bears.

After a short walk he came upon an open space in a glade of spruce trees that was only about fifty metres from a stream in spate. The floor of the glade was richly paved with old spruce needles that made a spongey, soft mattress. Beamer had brought a small pop-tent which he erected in a single, skilled gesture. After laying out a groundsheet and positioning the tent on it, he spiked down the perimeter of the tent and then deployed its storm sheet, though he didn't see any sign of rain. He fetched some fresh water, built a tiny fire, but big enough to heat his supper. He treed his backpack to keep it from attracting bears and raccoons and settled down in his sleeping bag for the night.

Outside his tent a colony of peeper frogs rehearsed in the ditches and a lush breeze shushed through the spruce bows. As the darkness deepened, the sounds of things that move in the darkness came forth. Tiny feet scurried through the fallen spruce needles, now and then stopped to tear apart a fallen spruce cone checking for seeds. A brief sigh of some night bird coming to roost in the bows overhead, and now and then, the sound of something much larger, snuffling in search, sniffing in curiosity, and finally snorting in rejection. In this dark world, Beamer started to feel at home, even welcome. Most conversation was chemical, not visual or auditory. It was the wild democracy of the forest darkness—all comers welcome, no matter how you dressed.

Beamer laid in his sleeping bag listening intently, but not with apprehension. All these sounds were familiar to him from his past forays into the bush. But as he lay still, there came an unexpected warmth against his left side and on his shoulder. It was as if someone was laying against his side, warming it, in the dark. Beamer felt himself settle into it, wishing mutely that it would just dissolve him, absorb him, into its warmth. He drifted there for a while in that vague presence and then he slept.

He awakened shortly after sunrise. The night had been cool but not freezing. Nevertheless, he wanted most to be under way again. He retrieved his backpack from the tree he had hung it in overnight, rolled up his sleeping bag, struck his tent, shook the dew off the storm fly but discovered the ground cloth relatively dry situated as it had been on the dry spruce needle bed. Rather than light another fire to cook something, he fished in his pack for a couple of energy bars and in ten minutes was repacked and ready to set out.

He returned to the shoulder of the highway and resumed his march eastward. He had no real destination in mind—only the intuitive certainty that when the time came, he would know where to go, how far to go, when to stop. After all, his walkabout was not concerned to get him anywhere in particular. He had no elder to lead him, no song lines to follow. He had no destination, so far as he knew; only the expectation (hope?) that the walking itself could heal him. So he kept walking.

He walked an entire day without the offer of a ride, and though walking on the shoulder of the road was easy going compared to trail hiking or making way cross country, he still made only about twenty kilometres under the burden of his backpack. Again he found a suitable spot to camp overnight and resumed his march the next day.

He trekked for five more days this way, feeling stronger and thinner every day, until he came to the outskirts of a small town. This virtually assured he would get no rides, unless perhaps he deliberately waved his thumb. But the town offered him the chance to restock his food rations and wash some clothes. He had money enough as well to allow himself one night in a motel where he could shower, sleep in a bed and enjoy some free coffee in the morning.

Again, Beamer made his way to the highway and started walking east, but this time with the growing sense that he was actually heading somewhere in particular, not just anywhere. It was annoying, vague, insistent, obscure—like an ear worm—a song repeating itself in one's mind to the point of distraction.

A family stopped by the road driving an RV the size of a house on absurdly tiny wheels. They offered Beamer a ride which he refused, but simply because, once inside the vehicle, he didn't think he would be able to see out. It was important that he see out, that he not miss something by blindly passing it. So he thanked the vacationers for their offer and sent them on their way, reflecting on how much it seemed to take to make some people happy.

No sooner had the RV disappeared from view but another pickup pulled off the road and Beamer got in. This time his driver was a fifty-something woman named Edna who owned a small seasonal resort farther east. The truck ran heavy, apparently loaded with cargo of some sort which she had lashed down under a tarp. She chatted away incessantly only asking occasional questions of Beamer, but otherwise enjoying her own stories best, especially her jokes. 'Did he live in the area or was he just passing through? Looked like he was packed up for camping but wasn't it pretty cold still to enjoy it? She had lived in the area all her life. Good Finnish stock. Grandfather settled back in the 1930s, but it was impossible to make a living on the shield by farming. Just rocks and acid soil. Better to cut pulp or work in a mine. Gold everywhere, and nickel and copper and stuff. Maybe highland coos could survive, but her grandfather never tried them. Just went on pogey and bought moonshine instead, especially when he found out his fiancé back in Finland decided to take up with somebody else. Guess waiting for ten years for him to get the homestead built just wasn't her cup of Red Rose. Did he know much about Finland? Had he ever had a sauna? Now there was relaxation! Takes a while to get used to so many people naked, but eventually you do. It's more of a social occasion, really, than it is a bath. Anyway, all her family was in the area, or back in Finland, and she ran a fishing lodge and guide service about four hundred clicks up the road. Hauling stuff for the summer season coming up. Did he like fishing?' And on and on. For his part Beamer didn't mind. The days on the road, the physical exertion, the change of scenery and routine, the privacy and a certain measure of solitude even in the company of the people who were passing briefly through his life, all worked their emotional alchemy. He answered questions—briefly; but he answered them. He found himself smiling at jokes, if not laughing— outright laughter still felt disloyal to Tatum—but smiling was possible. And his thoughts shifted subtly from their old centre of gravity in memory toward an emerging centre in curiosity. Where was it he was supposed to go anyway?

For at least two hours they had been following the curving highway as it threaded its path between outcrops of rock, low mountains, and mesas of granite thrust up hundreds of metres from the pre-Cambrian shield. All of it was tree studded and sprinkled with small lakes and ponds crowded with honking waterfowl, red winged blackbirds, kingbirds, robins, hermit thrushes, harriers, and a multitude of chipping sparrows. Over them all swooped monstrous ravens and the occasional bald eagle. The landscape was dramatic and moving, though not as overwhelming as true mountains like the Rockies or the Cascades.

"Could you stop here, please?" Beamer asked.

"Here?" asked Edna. "You sick?"

"No," Beamer replied. "But could you stop? I need to get out here."

Edna looked at him sidelong and shook her head. "Okaaay," she said, not really thinking it was okay. She pulled over and Beamer got out, grabbed his backpack and looked off to the south.

"Loch Speare is over there, right?"

Edna nodded. "Yes, about eighty clicks, if that's what you mean by 'over there'."

"Great. Thanks."

"Great?" Edna snorted. "You mean to walk in there?" she said, nodding her head toward the wall of forest bordering the road and the rock-strewn, marsh-ridden landscape it concealed.

"I do mean to," said Beamer.

Edna shook her head doubtfully. She had lived all of her life in these parts and she knew only too well what could happen when city people started wandering around in the bush, even with their GPS.

"You got GPS?"

Beamer shook his head. "Don't need it this time," he said obscurely.

"Anybody else know where you are?" she pressed.

"Yes," Beamer lied. "Lots of people do." But he thought it a minor lie in the distribution of all possible lies. Everyone at the Coulee knew he'd gone walkabout, though admittedly they had no idea where or what exactly it meant to do so. "Yes," he reassured her. "I'm fine."

"Right," Edna said doubtfully. "Okay, then, it's chimo here I guess. Good luck."

"Thanks Edna." Beamer watched her resume driving down the road, once glancing up at her rear view mirror to catch a last sight of him. Then she kept driving.

For a moment the highway was empty of traffic. Beamer turned south to look at the barricade of forest that stood before him. Then he scrambled down into the drainage ditch and up the other side, clambering up on a curving, ancient boulder that resembled a giant turtle thrusting its carapace up from a depth of water. From somewhere high overhead he heard a croaking sound gargled together with caws and squeaks. A massive raven glided above him dragging its shadow over where he stood. He cinched his backpack up higher on his shoulders and hips and plunged into the trees.

# CHAPTER 35

*"Of leaders there are four kinds:*
*The first rules through popular acclaim and the*
*skillful manipulation of allies and enemies.*
*The second and better kind of leader captures the love of*
*the people who then follow him of their own accord.*
*The third and still better kind leads from behind by first*
*listening to the people and then making it appear that his*
*ideas are their ideas and he is merely their servant.*
*The fourth kind of leader, and the best, leads invisibly*
*from within so that everything he does seems to the*
*people to have first appeared in their own dreams."*

— *WRITINGS FROM THE TANG DYNASTY*

WHEN THE RUINATION STARTED in earnest, everyone saw it coming—and no one saw it coming. Everyone knew what caused it, and no one knew what caused it—what came first or what came next. Its more conscious victims might have likened it to spending time with a terminally ill relative whose organs were failing one by one. The less conscious people, like the relative on the gurney, simply suffered without knowing why. The collapse of everything that they expected made them angry. Trust horizons caved in on all sides and people were left with the neighbours they had, for better or worse. The everyday miracles of twenty-first century technology, the taken-for-granted miracles, stopped working one by one. Maybe it was the failure of the nuclear reactor just west of the city that caused grid collapse, or maybe the grid collapse in the face of really bad weather dragged the reactor along with it. And probably the reactor had nothing to do with it; probably it scrammed for its own reasons. Day by day people began to feel like an enormous weight had settled on them, slowly but inexorably crushing everything. The reactor scramming itself into an automatic shutdown, undoubtedly for technical reasons, didn't annoy people as much as running out of tooth brushes, telephones that didn't work, flat tires for which there was no repair, the last pill in the bottom of the bottle. Suddenly, everything was very visibly connected to everything else as all of it collapsed in a silent, slow-motion crash.

And this was not a predicament unique to the city. Maybe it started with the city, or maybe it started in some other city, or not in the city at all. The city was one thread in a tangled ball of threads that spanned the world. It was the dark side of globalization come home to roost. It was the payment due on all the deferred maintenance deficits, all the mortgages owing, all the artificially cheap gazingus pins that could be ordered up with a tap or a click. This great ball of delusion began to unravel across the whole world. No one knew why. Everyone knew why. As bigger things began to collapse—or more often, simply stop—everyone was surprised how suddenly it could happen.

The physical side of the Ruination, while catastrophic, was perhaps not as telling as its psychological aspect. In every disaster of recent memory, there was always help and hope coming from outside. There were always experts from outside, and food and water from outside, and experienced workers from outside who arrived in a few days to start setting things right—getting things back to normal—setting up tents and latrines. But in the Ruination, the outside disappeared—or became just another inside. Normal could no longer be found. Life now required constant innovation in very stressful situations. Life was becoming a Frankenstein's monster of work-arounds, jerry-rigs and kluges. Heads were being sewn onto elbows and kidneys transplanted with brains. Grown adults began to feel like abandoned toddlers as the familiar beliefs about all manner of things, and especially relationships, began to sag and give way. In a sense, the Ruination could be likened to a funeral that brings together a dysfunctional extended family, to remember the dead, surely, but also to bicker over the remains. The reassuring delusion of "outside" faded into story, then into legend and finally into myth. Outside was gone and with it, any hope of normal.

And then there was time. Before people had fretted about how much time they had, or how little, or when they needed to be somewhere for something, or how much they were making per hour. But now people learned a new meaning of time. When the power grid collapsed, many things stopped instantly—motors stopped running, alarms stopped keening, fans fell silent, chillers stopped chilling, pumps stopped pumping. People discovered that in one day frozen food will start to thaw. In two days diabetics are in shock and addicts are raving in their withdrawal. In three days or less, gasoline is gone. In four days, grocery stores are empty. In five days, lacking fresh water, people succumb to dehydration or water-borne diseases, and in six days they become very, very hungry. In a month, unless they were obese to begin with, people starved. The very young and the very old starved first. In two months so many people had died or killed each other that any hope of a social or economic return to normal was a delirious fantasy.

As the Ruination began to unfold, a tiny ecovillage called Badger Coulee was too far away, too eccentric, too small to matter to much of anyone. Viewed from outside, Badger Coulee enjoyed a measure of invisibility. On account of its isolation, it would be accounted as collateral damage in the struggle for survival among the larger fish in the pond. Viewed from the inside, the death of Tatum Barnes made glaringly obvious that invisibility and invulnerability were different things. Her death felt to Badger Coulee like a prophesy, a warning, a personal assault. It pressurized the psyche. These feelings led Coulee members into a twilight consciousness that fused angry grief with frantic preparation. They must leave the indefensible bald prairie location of Badger Coulee but to go where? They must secure the children and elders, but how? They must prepare, but prepare for what? They must act quickly and decisively, but on what plan?

The energies of Badger Coulee surged this way and that, to be sure, but not blindly and somehow avoided blowing up entirely. The committees Fisher had suggested, together with their implied tasks, provided a minimal structure to focus group activities. Unknowns would be set aside for the time being. The group was welded together by a certain self-confidence that come what may, solutions could be found as the need arose, if not in advance of that need.

In all this fray, and perhaps partly because of it, people carried on with their lives. Laurel Fey and Jasper Beckett found each other in what appeared from the outside to be a most improbable relationship, proof some thought of the old adage that opposites attract. Corbin Galen doubled and then redoubled his meetings for meditation practice that offered an inner anchorage in a swiftly tilting world. After packing all his tools, Changming continued sketching and designing and modelling on a smaller scale his visions of the future he wanted to build. And within and over it all was the silent but resonating presence of the Quakers. Somehow, what they were and how they conducted themselves spread a blanket of silence over the frenzy of the Coulee's preparations and anxieties. All things were possible in their company, especially that which seemed impossible. Against all the assertions of realism, Badger Coulee was feeling the first tingling, ravenous claims of its impossible future: To build a new culture upon the ruins of everything that had gone before. But first they would have to survive as a people.

When Beamer Farris returned to Badger Coulee, he had been away for over a month. Some thought he had returned to the city. Others thought he might have fallen victim as Tatum had to the desperate people doing desperate things to get what they thought would secure them, come what may.

Still others knew the attraction Beamer felt to wilderness. And others feared he might have harmed himself in his grief. No one recognized him when he walked back into the Coulee, making first for Fisher's house.

No one was more preoccupied with such thoughts than Fisher. As the days since Beamer's departure grew in number, Fisher began to appreciate more the depth of his wound. As more reports arrived at the Coulee about what a cauldron the world was becoming, Fisher's anxiety for Beamer grew. Not helping were the constant demands on his time to square circles, such as trying both to tighten Badger Coulee's security against totally unknown and unpredictable threats but also to manage the permaculture gardens for the season, while also drawing plans to move the community to an as yet unknown place. They were forces pulling in opposite directions for which he had no decision tree. One thing was unmistakable however: Everyone now understood that their life together was not an exercise or a drill. They were all in.

Then late one afternoon close to the summer solstice, Fisher heard a rap at his door. It had been a stressful day and he felt exhausted and irritable. "Come!" he snarled.

The door swung open revealing a man, thin as a wraith, bearded, his clothing ragged and soiled, one boot with the leather torn near the ankle. He was obviously young but tanned and weathered looking as a bristle cone pine. He dropped his backpack on the floor, little more than a metal frame with various wads of gear bungee corded together in a single massive lump.

"Beamer?" Fisher asked, incredulous.

The figure in the door gave an old smile. "Yes," he said, "I believe that's right. That was my name."

"Come in, come in!" said Fisher, grinning. "I thought you were raven bait by now. Sit down, sit down. I've got lemonade, tea, probably some rye, you know, the usual."

"Water would go well," said Beamer. "I've gotten kind of used to it." He sat down uneasily in one of Fisher's chairs as if he had consciously to position himself and prepare for the luxury of seated conversation. "Funny," he mused, "how after a few weeks of not having things like chairs, you get used to not having them. Then it feels odd to sit on one."

"No doubt," said Fisher as he pushed his wheelchair around the room to fetch a glass and fill it with water, handing it to Beamer. "So tell me," Fisher said. "Tell me…" His voice trailed off. Beamer looked at Fisher and Fisher looked back at Beamer. Beamer stood up, came closer to Fisher's wheelchair and reached down to embrace him. They held each other, not needing the customary back slapping that shields men from their friendship. Presently Beamer released him and returned to where he was sitting.

"So," said Fisher, "tell me what happened."

Beamer sighed deeply the sigh of weariness—not despair, not resignation—just exhaling the day's fatigue. "Well," he said, "it was lots of picking my way through the bush and wading through streams and squishing through the mud and climbing on rocks, which part we can skip for now because it's all pretty much the same. I've kind of been off-line, so I haven't heard much news. I assume things haven't gotten any better for us since I left."

"No," said Fisher, "they haven't—except maybe we're more packed than we were—all dressed up with no place to go, you might say."

Beamer cast his gaze around Fisher's little cottage, which looked much as it had before he left. "You don't look packed to me," he said.

Fisher shrugged. "Wherever it is the rest of you go, I'm staying here."

"Like hell," Beamer objected, immediately feeling that his objection was disrespectful. "The Coulee needs you."

"Well, that's very touching, but somebody has to stay here after you get going. There will be stragglers. All the Finders in the city are refusing to come in until the last minute, whenever that'll be, and we have the two teams still out looking for property elsewhere. And then there will be all the folk they're gathering up. Their first stop when they all come home to roost will probably be the Coulee here. Somebody has to keep a porch light on for them, keep the Barn warmed up, do the laundry, make cookies, that sort of thing, you know. And the best person for that job is me."

Beamer looked back at Fisher in desperation, but said nothing to contradict him. He seemed clearly to have made up his mind. "Discussion to be continued," Beamer said.

Fisher shook his head. "Not on this one," he said with a tone of finality.

"I found us a place," Beamer said, half hoping it would loosen Fisher's resolve.

Fisher jumped in his chair. "You did?"

"I think so," said Beamer. "It's harsh, but beautiful, and I think a lot safer than here. It will be hard living there, at least at first. It's also a long way from here—nine hundred clicks east or thereabouts, I would guess."

"Ah, well," said Fisher. "We could really do it."

"Yes, we could really do it, if the rest go for it."

"So," said Fisher, "do you think we're ready to climb this mountain?"

Beamer chuckled. "Ready or not, we must climb it."

"And you think that's amusing?"

Beamer shook his head: "Only because it really does involve a mountain."

*The End*

# ACKNOWLEDGEMENTS

QUOTATIONS THAT APPEAR at the beginning of chapters are works of fiction. Any resemblance of the title of a work or citation of a reference to an actual person or literary work is unintentional and coincidental.

I would like to thank the many people that assisted or supported me in one way or another during the writing and publication of this book. First, my spouse Charlotte for her steadfast support to, and affirmation of, my writing efforts and for proof-reading the manuscript. Also my thanks to Sig Laser, Samuel Alexander, Maria Kruszewski, Rodney Kueneman and James Frey, for their reviews of the manuscript, to Sharon Chisvin for her copy-editing services, and to Tracey O'Neil for her brilliant book design work. Finally, my thanks to McNally-Robinson Booksellers for hosting my book launch for this title and their steadfast support for local authors—even self-published ones.

Thanks to The Religious Society of Friends for a loosely paraphrased version of *Advices and Queries - 17* appearing on p. 184 of this book, From: Canadian Yearly Meeting of the Religious Society of Friends 2011, *Faith and Practice*, Ottawa, Ontario, Canada, p. 183.

www.ingramcontent.com/pod-product-compliance
Lightning Source LLC
Chambersburg PA
CBHW060355030726
47497CB00003B/720